Seed

Seed

Chronicles of Jeremy Nash
Book 2

Frank F. Fiore

WordCrafts Press

Seed
Copyright ©2013
Frank F. Fiore

ISBN: 978-1-962218-78-8

Cover concept and design by Mike Parker.

Published by WordCrafts Press
Cody, Wyoming 82414
www.wordcrafts.net

On the Great Day of Purification,
a mystery egg
—or seed—
will grow from the core of the earth
and destroy this world
and usher in a new one.

So prophesied the Hopi thousands of years ago...

Grand Canyon
Twenty-one Years Ago

The hot wind, funneling up through the narrow canyon walls, was suffused with something ancient and alive.

Despite the heat, eleven-year-old Jeremy Nash shivered with pleasure. He loved these research trips with his father, Austin Nash, who was Professor Emeritus of Native American History at the University of New Mexico. More than anything, Jeremy loved ditching the drudgery of the sixth grade to explore the world—despite increasing opposition by his mother.

The world, in this case, was the Grand Canyon. And since it was so far removed from anything young Jeremy had yet to see, the Grand Canyon could have been Mars. Now, as he stood looking across from the south rim of the canyon, between the Hopi House and the rustic historic El Tovar Hotel, Jeremy decided this was the most beautiful place on earth. He could not imagine anything being more astonishing or awe-inspiring.

Just the day before, at the dinner table, his father had announced that Jeremy would accompany him on a research trip the following day. One minute Jeremy was picking at his mashed potatoes and wondering how he was going to get out of doing homework, and the next he was preparing for a trek to one of the most wondrous places on earth. He was delighted beyond words.

Jeremy hadn't been able to sleep a wink all last night—and his homework was all but forgotten.

Now here he was, standing in the plaza of the great Hopi House. As the sun began to set down the canyon to the west,

Jeremy waited with his father for the sacred Kachina dance to begin. Although his father had introduced young Jeremy to many Native-American traditions, the rituals of the Kachina ceremonies were the boy's favorite. As explained by his father on the plane ride here, tonight's celebration would be the most special of all—The Blue Star Kachina ceremony.

Just the sound of it sent another shiver of excitement coursing through the young boy. His father had explained that there was an ancient Hopi Indian prophecy stating that when the Blue Star Kachina made its appearance in the heavens, the Fifth World would emerge.

The Blue Star Kachina ceremony—the rarest of all Kachina ceremonies—was in honor of this apocalyptic day, which the Hopi called the Day of Purification.

As his father had further explained: "This Day of Purification will come when the Blue Star Kachina dances in the plaza and removes his mask for all the world to see."

Granted, a lot of that didn't make sense to young Jeremy—but then again, a lot of Native American religious traditions were still a mystery to him. He loved hearing the stories. He hungered to understand such mysteries. To delve deeper into them. To explore them. He had his father to thank for that, he knew. His father had taught him at an early age to appreciate the wonders of the world and to respect all cultures. His father walked the walk, immersing himself in the Native American culture—even wearing a beautiful Navajo silver and turquoise watch band that his father promised would be his someday.

After the whirlwind preparation of the night before, Jeremy and his father had landed in Phoenix early that morning, rented a car, and driven out to the Grand Canyon. Jeremy was excited—perhaps a little too excited. His father had caught him hopping from leg to leg.

"The restroom, Jeremy, is inside the hotel," his father said easily, grinning. "You have just a few minutes before the ceremony begins. Now hurry."

Jeremy entered the rustic lobby of the El Tovar spanned by large, hewed timbers noticing the different animal heads lining the walls. A bison, a fourteen-point buck, even a mountain lion. He found the bathroom easily, and when he was finished and feeling decidedly more comfortable, he exited the restroom, climbed the stairs to the ground floor, and—heard the sound of angry shouting. Hands still wet, he paused in the hotel's empty lobby. The shouting was coming from upstairs. Most of the guests and staff were outside awaiting the beginning of the ceremony—a ceremony Jeremy himself desperately wanted to watch.

But the shouting piqued his interest.

As he walked towards the stairs, the exchange grew more heated, reaching him in bits and snatches. Try as he might, Jeremy just couldn't make out what was being said—or more like yelled.

He checked his trusted Star Wars watch. The dance would start any minute now. The dance, of course, was the whole reason he and his father were here.

There was more shouting from above.

Jeremy turned to the hotel's lobby door where his father was waiting. He took a step toward the exit.

And then something slammed against the floor.

Hard.

Without thought, Jeremy did what came naturally to him. He turned away from the door and headed for the rustic staircase.

Jeremy had read enough spy novels to know one should keep to the far edge of stairways and hallways. The stairway trick worked brilliantly, and he ascended with nary a creak.

Now, heart hammering as he moved slowly along the long hallway, the old adage wasn't holding up so well. Despite his best efforts, some of his footsteps still creaked.

And with each creak, the blood drained from his face.

Luckily, whoever was doing the shouting didn't seem to be

paying much attention to old floorboards. Way up ahead was an open door. From his angle within the hallway, Jeremy could see there were at least a couple of people inside.

He continued forward. A wayward floorboard groaned loudly, and Jeremy nearly turned tail and dashed away. But he continued forward.

Golden sunlight spilled through the room's open door and splashed across the hallway before him. As he approached, there was a lull in the arguing, and Jeremy had a sense that someone was pacing in the room.

He continued on, keeping to the walls, sensing he was no longer in the public section of the hotel. He had ventured into the actual living quarters of those who ran it.

"But I am the Pahana," shouted a young man suddenly. "I have the proof!"

Jeremy stopped at the sudden outburst. From his position in the hallway, he could just see inside the open door—an angle that afforded him a glimpse of a bed and a dresser. Someone was sitting stoically on the bed. And someone else, pacing anxiously, occasionally appeared and disappeared in the doorway.

Jeremy cautiously took another step.

As he did so, his view into the room expanded considerably, and now he could see a very old Native American man sitting on the bed. Jeremy recognized the man's traditional garb instantly. He was a Hopi Shaman.

"Lower your voice, my son," said the shaman quietly, his voice barely reaching Jeremy's ears. His gentle tone matched the dignified attire of a Hopi Shaman—a simple, red button-down shirt, a dark blue beaded vest, tufts of long white hair under a red and white bandana. The only hint of opulence was the traditional ornate squash blossom silver and turquoise necklace that hung from his leathery neck. "We do not want our guests—"

"I could give a damn about our guests." The young man appeared into view—and Jeremy received a bit of a shock.

The young man was, in fact, completely blond. So much so that Jeremy wondered if the man was an albino. The young man paused in front of the seated old man and pushed back his long locks of yellow hair, revealing what appeared to be steel blue eyes. "I have the missing piece, and you've seen it. Why do you continue to doubt the inevitable? I am the Pahana."

There was a sudden noise from beyond the hotel, and Jeremy knew the Blue Star Kachina ceremonies were about to begin. Even now, his father was probably worried or looking for him. Still, the young boy found himself glued to the spot, unable to tear his gaze away from the sight of the young blond man and the aged Hopi Shaman.

Missing piece?

The question raced through Jeremy's mind. He found himself inching closer to the open door as the old shaman spoke again, "As much as you would like to believe you are the promised one, my son, you are not."

Promised one?

Jeremy inched closer. He knew he shouldn't be here, eavesdropping on these two, but he couldn't help himself. There was something going on here—something mysterious—and he just had to know more.

Jeremy stopped next to a long, polished table covered with ornate pottery vases and fresh cut flowers.

The young man with the flowing blond hair paused in front of the door, his broad shoulders blocking Jeremy's view into the room. The young man slapped something down on the dresser top. A piece of paper, perhaps. "I have the translation."

Almost simultaneously, the young man seized a clay pot on an end table, raised it, and smashed it to the floor.

Two things immediately happened—almost in unison.

The Hopi Shaman stood up, aghast at what the young man had done, and Jeremy's fingertips, which had been absently touching the lip of one of the vases on the table next to him, tipped it over. One vase crashed into another, and they both hit the floor with a hellacious crash that nearly stopped his heart. Flowers and water dripped across the tabletop and onto the floor.

The young man in the doorway spun around, and as he did so, Jeremy was off and running—as fast as he possibly could.

As he flew down the stairs, taking them three at a time, stumbling once and nearly tumbling the rest of the way, he knew he was in some serious trouble. The look on that young man's face had been one of utter fury when he had made eye contact with Jeremy.

Running footsteps sounded on the floor above him.

Oh God!

Jeremy reached the landing and dashed across the hotel's empty lobby. Without looking back, he plunged recklessly through the doors and out into the hot evening. And there before him stood his father. Jeremy had never seen such a welcomed sight.

"Where the dickens have you been, boy?" asked his father, frowning. "The ceremony is about to—"

But he didn't get to finish. Jeremy hurled himself into his father's arms. The man grunted and stumbled back, throwing them both off balance.

"Hey, is everything okay?"

Even from outside, the boy could hear the sounds of heavy footsteps pounding through the hotel lobby. He took his father's hand and dragged him forward. "Yes! Sorry, dad. I just got distracted with some...art. Come on, let's hurry!"

His father, unaware of what was going on behind them, obliged by hurriedly leading the way back to the staging area.

As torches blazed around the dusty plaza, the ceremony began. As it did so, Jeremy anxiously looked back once over his shoulder and saw nothing, no young blond man and no elder shaman. Just as his heartbeat returned to normal, the first of the dancers appeared in front of the crowd.

The dancers wore elaborately carved masks and headdresses, many with long eagle feathers extending from the crown. Jeremy had seen Hopi masks in the past, but these were markedly different. Instead of a painted face, these masks bore only a single blue star. No eyes, no mouth—no indication that they could see through the mask. The effect was surreal and a little frightening, at least to the young boy. Each dancer carried a small bell in one hand and a fistful of arrows in the other.

Jeremy found himself marveling at the strange movements of the dancers. He knew they were telling a story—an ancient story—but his young brain couldn't wrap itself around the meaning. He knew from his father that the masked dancers were believed to embody the powerful spirits of earth, sky, and water.

Maybe they are telling the story of the world, he thought.

The dancers circled each other, and as the beating of the nearby drums grew in intensity, a strange, cold wind suddenly swept low over the ground. Jeremy shivered. Others in the crowd felt it too. Jeremy saw them look furtively around.

The dancers now rang their little bells—randomly, almost chaotically. The result was an unsettling, raucous cacophony. Just as the ringing reached a fevered pitch, the ground beneath Jeremy's feet began trembling.

The dancers briefly paused. The sounds of the bells stopped.

The rumbling grew in intensity, and Jeremy's first thought was that something was going to burst out of the ground. Or that a jet airplane was going to land in the middle of the Grand Canyon.

And then the trembling turned into all-out shaking. Someone in the audience screamed. Jeremy's father wrapped an arm around his boy's shoulders.

One of the Kachina dancers suddenly yanked off his Blue Star mask, screaming. He fell to a knee awkwardly, got to his feet and stumbled toward Jeremy and his father. The boy stepped back in horror as the Kachina dancer collapsed at his feet, blood pouring from his nose, ears, eyes, and mouth.

Jeremy's father knelt immediately next to the bleeding man and just as he did so, the violent shaking stopped. The young Hopi man, as far as Jeremy could tell, was dead.

Confused and horror-stricken, he looked over to the stage and saw that all the dancers were now down around the plaza. All bleeding and convulsing.

A moment later, they were all still.

Somewhere Over
the Southwestern United States
Present Day

This is shaping up to be one hell of a shitty day, thought Jeremy Nash, gripping the arm rests of his seat. The plane swooped and fell and did things he was sure no plane of this size was ever meant to do.

It wasn't enough that he'd spent the entire day being *interviewed* by the Israeli Defense Force about the terrorist incident in Jerusalem—a long story that Nash was writing a book about. Or that he had been awakened in Rome by a frantic phone call from his sister, Alyson—a phone call that rocked his world, a phone call that sent him scurrying off for a flight home. No, now he had to deal with this hellacious storm which was doing its best to drive the big 777 straight into the ground.

As the plane dipped again, sending Nash's stomach up into his throat, he glanced over at some of the other Business Class passengers who were clutching airsick bags. The elder couple sitting across the aisle held each other closely, their frightened faces a matching shade of green. Nash was sure he didn't look much different. He was also sure he shouldn't have had that second helping of sushi for dinner just a few hours earlier.

Think of something else. Get your mind off your stomach. And definitely get your mind off raw fish...

Despite himself, he nearly gagged at the thought.

So he took his mind off his stomach and put it onto his younger sister. In particular, her frantic phone call. What was it she had said? Their parents murdered? They didn't die years ago in a caving accident? Killed for something they discovered in the Hopi End of Times Predictions?

Ridiculous! No. Absurd!

In fact, after having just been awakened from a deep sleep, he entertained the possibility that he dreamt the whole crazy phone conversation with his sister.

Nash, who had been in Rome writing his next book, *A Taste of the Apocalypse*, had hoped to finish the manuscript and send it off to his publisher then he could work on a lecture in Berlin on crypto-history, a lecture he was completely unprepared to give. But with the phone call from his sister, everything was placed on hold.

As an expert debunker of conspiracy theories, myths, and legends, Nash was often asked to give such lectures. Hell, half his time seemed to be spent behind a podium, poking holes in everything from Elvis faking his death, Bigfoot, and UFOs to the various 9/11 conspiracies.

And the Hopi End of Times predictions from so called prophets citing everything from the Mayan Doomsday Calendar, various Native American visions, Biblical prophesies, and Nostradamus were no different.

Bunk. All bunk—

The big 777 suddenly dropped, a frightful feeling that sent Nash's stomach back up into his throat and caused his seatbelt to bite deeply across his lap. Nash stifled a groan. The older man sitting next to him looked calmly up from the voluminous report he was reading.

"Are you all right?" asked the man, looking over his reading glasses.

"Yeah, fine," mumbled Nash, marveling that there wasn't a sign of worry or concern on the man's face, as if the plane wasn't in the middle of some of the worst turbulence Nash had ever experienced.

The plane shuddered violently and slewed to the right. Nash dug his nails deep into the armrest with something close to a death-grip. When the plane steadied again, and Nash's heart rate returned to something close to normal, he looked over at the older man—who had, remarkably, gone back to reading his heavy tome.

"This type of flying weather doesn't bother you?" Nash asked, and just as the words left his mouth, a passenger behind him vomited profusely. Nash covered his own mouth, fighting back his gorge.

The gray-haired man smiled and patted his own stomach. "Cast iron. Grew it years ago as a storm chaser."

Nash nodded. "You were one of those crazy guys who flew into hurricanes."

"In my youth." Then almost to himself, "In my youth." He held out his hand. "Perhaps I should introduce myself. I'm Peter Somerton."

Nash shook it and noticed the Zuni silver watch band inlaid with turquoise and orange coral on his wrist. It reminded him of his father's. "Jeremy Nash," he said.

"Well, Mr. Nash. You don't seem too affected by the rough weather, either. Are you a pilot?"

Nash thought the old guy was being much too kind. After all, he was certain his face was anything but calm. Still, Somerton had been spot-on about one thing.

"Private pilot," said Nash.

"What do you fly?"

"A Cirrus SR Twenty."

"Good plane," Somerton remarked. "That's a do-it-yourselfer, right?"

Nash nodded. "But I bought this one already assembled."

The jet dropped again, and Nash's embattled stomach did a flip-flop. In all his days flying small private planes, he'd never been in weather like this. Nash privately wished they hadn't closed the flight service. A good stiff hit of Crown Royal would do him good about now.

Nash decided to continue the small talk—anything to take his mind off his stomach. "So, what's a storm chaser doing in Rome?"

"Geophysical and climate conference," Somerton said,

adjusting his tweed jacket that had bunched up above his faded blue jeans by the jostling of the plane. "We discussed the increase in geophysical activity and the effects of the current climate changes we are experiencing."

Nash unconsciously frowned when he heard the words *climate change*. Somerton noticed.

"You don't believe in climate change?"

"If you mean global warming caused by man," Nash answered, "No. I believe in what Mark Twain said."

"Climate is what we expect," Somerton said over his reading glasses. "Weather is what we get?"

"Exactly." Nash smiled. He just might like this man. "Is that what was discussed at the conference? Global warming?"

"That was not the real focus," Somerton replied, somewhat guarded. "We're more interested in the causes—or cause," Somerton emphasized the word *cause*, "of not only the increasing inclement weather around the world but its growing intensity coupled with the rise in geophysical activity of earthquakes and volcanic eruptions."

"So, what kind of climatologist are you?"

"I'm not," Somerton replied. "I was a member of the cultural committee."

"Cultural committee?"

"Yes. I was an indigenous culture representative."

Nash was about to ask more when the captain's voice came over the intercom. "Ladies and gentlemen, we're approaching Albuquerque International Airport. Estimated time of arrival is fifteen minutes. Please fasten your seatbelts and raise your trays to the upright position."

Nash nearly choked on laughter. He doubted anyone had had their trays down. And if so, whatever had been on the trays had by now soaked through the occupant's clothing.

Nash looked out the window to his right as they descended into what looked like a nasty thunderstorm. From his vantage point, which included most of the starboard wing, he could see nothing but churning gray clouds and flashes of lightning.

Not good.

And just as Nash was about to turn away, something caught his eye. A flare of something bright. Incredibly bright. Coming up fast from below.

Something completely unimaginable.

My God!

And then the plane was hit by something—hard. The whole thing shuddered and slewed to the right as a fire erupted just under the wing.

The right engine! Sweet Jesus!

Someone screamed. And then seemingly everyone was screaming.

This isn't happening, thought Nash. I'm dreaming.

The captain's voice suddenly came over the intercom: "Ladies and gentlemen," he said calmly. "I'm declaring an emergency. Please follow the instructions from your flight attendants."

A worried-looking female flight attendant in her twenties, who was standing at the bulkhead, picked up a microphone and spoke into it, her voice broadcasting ominously throughout the cabin. "Ladies and Gentleman," she began nervously, "you will need to assume crash positions."

And now there were wails and screams. One or two people stood up and looked around, panic on their faces. Nash was sure he looked no differently.

Good God!

The flight attendant continued, undeterred, "Please lean forward and place your head between your legs. If you have a pillow or soft jacket, place your head on that. The captain will tell you when it's safe to sit back up once we land."

Nash assumed the position and placed his head between his knees, face pressed into the small seat pillow he had been given. In that position, with his eyes closed, his ears seemed to

pick up every whimper and prayer, every *I love you* and *It's going to be okay.*

He heard it all, but mostly he heard his own blood pounding in his ears. He was also keenly aware that should he die now, there was no one to tell him that they loved him.

He was going to die alone, and somehow that made dying even worse.

The plane shuddered violently, followed immediately by more screams. A sudden updraft seemed to lift the plane and toss it about from side to side. Nash had an unsettling image of a kite on a string.

A kite in a storm.

A burning kite.

Sure that he was going to lose his lunch, Nash lifted his head to vomit to the side—and chanced a look out the window.

The engine fire was out. The fire suppression system had kicked in.

Oh, thank God!

Next to him, Somerton was singing. No, humming. Nash turned to the older man and saw something remarkable. The man was just sitting there, eyes closed pleasantly, a small grin on his face. More incredible, he seemed to be humming a tune that sounded vaguely like "As the Caissons Go Rolling Along."

The plane dropped again.

Nash gasped, and many around him screamed. Next to him, Somerton continued humming.

He's crazy.

Nash looked out the window again. The city lights of Albuquerque were coming up fast—rapidly filling the window from horizon to horizon.

Oh, God. Here it comes.

The big 777 swerved from side to side, jerking Nash violently. The whole craft seemed to groan and shudder as a steady stream of prayers and cries filled the cabin. Nash's own breathing was coming hard and fast. Next to him, his new companion continued humming steadily along. The tune was now the "Star Spangled Banner."

The jumbo jet shuddered so violently that Nash thought the wings had surely been ripped off. A quick glance out the right window showed that the wings were still very much in place, but the lights of Albuquerque were rapidly getting closer.

Too rapidly.

The captain made a final announcement. They were landing and to please maintain crash positions—and may God be with them all.

Nash wasn't a religious man. In fact, he'd spent much of his life debunking many religious claims, but he prayed now.

With all his heart.

He also once again assumed the crash position, and with his crazy neighbor humming insanely next to him, the next few minutes were the longest in Nash's life.

Although the entire cabin held their collective breath, Nash heard the flaps opening and the engine winding down—and he heard something else. An odd flapping sound.

The wing's been damaged.

He forced himself to calm down, until he realized it didn't really matter how calm he was. After all, he might be dead in the next few minutes—

Easy, boy.

Nash found himself thinking of his father, of their amazing trips together around the southwest. He found himself longing to be in his old man's company once more. He thought of his loving mom, and of her home baked chocolate chips cookies that were to die for.

Bad choice of words.

And then the 777 slammed hard into the tarmac. So hard that Nash would have been hurled over the seats had he not been strapped in. As it was, the breath was wrenched from his lungs,

and he found himself gasping as the airplane vibrated violently. Nash imagined a trail of plane parts strewn along the tarmac in their wake. Oxygen masks dropped from above, landing squarely on his bowed back. For now, he ignored it.

And then something amazing happened. So amazing that Nash nearly wept.

The plane quit grinding. In fact, the plane quit making any sort of noise at all...other than the plaintive whine of its turbines shutting down.

Someone clapped. And now everyone was clapping. People stood and hugged; tears were pouring down faces. Nash turned in stunned amazement to his seat mate and saw that the old man was looking at him, a twinkle in his blue eyes.

"We made it," said Nash.

"Any landing you can walk away from..." smiled Somerton as he calmly stood and opened the luggage compartment to retrieve his bag.

Albuquerque International Airport

Fire trucks and emergency vehicles swarmed the plane, and soon all passengers were exiting through the rear emergency doors. Nash, more relieved than he had ever been in his life to leave anything, grabbed his carry-on from the overhead compartment and followed Somerton down the center aisle.

Once outside and standing in the cool night air, after waving off the help of a paramedic, Nash felt like a new man. He wanted to see his sister more than anything. He wanted to hug her and tell her he loved her and that he was sorry for being the world's biggest jerk sometimes when they were growing up. More than anything he wanted a milkshake from McDonald's, his extremely rare guilty pleasure.

Somerton clapped him on the shoulder, wished him well, and set off into the night across the tarmac, whistling. As Nash watched the older man go, marveling, someone spoke up next to him.

The speaker was a very old man, and he was talking urgently to one of the paramedics. "I tell you, young man, I saw it rise from the desert. It was a missile."

The paramedic placated him, "Now, now...."

The old man grew angry. "I flew sorties in Korea, young man, and I know my surface to air missiles."

Surface to air missiles?

Nash recalled the light rising up from beneath them. The explosion. The plane taking a sudden turn for the worse.

Airport security suddenly appeared behind Nash and took

the arm of the old man, steering him away from the others toward a waiting black car. Nash noticed other such security personnel observing those who departed the craft. One caught Nash's eye and held it. A cold shiver rippled through Nash, and he instinctively looked away. As the rain came steadily down, he hurried across the tarmac with the others and kept his eyes down. As he did so, he heard the old man's voice again. *I know my surface to air missiles, young man.*

What the hell was going on?

After spending an hour or so being interviewed by airport security and investigators from the FAA, an exhausted Nash finally worked his way through the crowded airport, bags in hand.

As he did so, he passed a crowd of people staring up in open irritation and anger at the flight status board. He looked up and saw that half the international flights were delayed or canceled.

He wondered if any of this had to do with the explosion on his own plane. And, like a true conspiracy theory nut, he wondered if the explosion would even be reported in the news.

Downstairs, as he passed the ticket counters and heard heated arguments between the passengers and the airline personnel behind the counter, he stopped and asked what was going on.

A young man, standing in line and holding a faded green backpack with a University of New Mexico patch on it, answered: "No one knows. They had a problem with a plane coming in. Someone said it looked like it was on fire, but we're not getting any news. And they're saying something about commercial airlines unable to fly above the Arctic Circle, and so the polar route is closed. Navigation problems, they claim. Whatever the hell that means." He raised an eyebrow and frowned. "Just another lame excuse to screw the public."

Nash agreed. Then again, his opinion of commercial air flights wasn't exactly at an all-time high at the present moment.

A shuttle bus pulled up outside the terminal. Nash lifted the collar of his jacket over the back of his neck and braved the thunderstorm outside. Even though it was a short dash to the bus, Nash still got soaked in the driving rain. He hopped the bus, and in a few minutes he was at the general aviation terminal.

Inside, the service desk was empty. Instead, pilots and employees were gathered around a TV screen in the adjacent pilot's lounge. He headed over to the lounge and saw what the others were watching. Dead whales filled the TV screen. Hundreds of them.

In the background, a news announcer was saying: "...and the beachings are reported up and down the entire coast. Whales and porpoises line the sand from San Diego to Portland."

Image after image of beached sea mammals filled the screen, where scores of on-lookers watched and tried to help. Nash made sympathetic noises, but he really wasn't in the mood to get caught up in this. Why such creatures chose to beach themselves, he didn't know, and he suspected marine biologists probably would never know, either. It was certainly a damn shame—

And then he spotted an airport employee at the service desk. As he shouldered his bags, the announcer continued, "In other news, large numbers of Canadian geese have not flown south, and many are dying in the frigid weather up north..."

The world's going to hell in a hand basket, he thought and hurried over to the service desk.

"I need to rent a plane," he said. "A single engine with some horsepower. I'm flying to Roswell."

The young female employee looked at him as if he had lost his mind. She motioned out the nearby glass door. "In this weather?"

"Then let me rephrase that," he said. "When does the National Weather Service say conditions will clear up enough for IFR? I'm instrument qualified."

She shook her head. "It's a no-go, sorry. General aviation is grounded. Period."

Nash considered his options, then left the general aviation

building. Outside, he hailed an airport shuttle and headed back to the car rental terminals, silently cursing this shitty day.

And it's still not over....

Farmington, New Mexico

William Big Man waited impatiently in the dining area of the Holiday Inn Express in Farmington, New Mexico.

He's late, he thought.

Big Man pretended to read the free local newspaper while he kept an eye on the front door. He was aware that he—along with the other power plant interns working on the Navajo Reservation—would soon be setting out to work in a small caravan.

It was early morning and many of the workers were eating together. Most straight out of college, many of the interns had made it known that that they hoped to someday work for Arizona Public Service. Big Man—a short, stocky Hopi—could give a shit about working for APS. He, of course, had another use for the internship—one that he and his fellow Ecotopians had planned carefully for over these past several years.

Around him, the other interns were wrapping up breakfast—polishing off their coffees and juices and gathering their work supplies.

Big Man impatiently tapped his fingers on the armrest.

Where is he?

He casually checked his watch again. The caravans would be setting out in less than ten minutes.

Located inside his wrist, just beneath the watchband, was a small tattoo of a stylized goddess surrounded by the symbols for earth, wind, water, and fire—the identifying mark of a member of the Ecotopians. Big Man turned his wrist away, keeping the tattoo mostly hidden. Although few would understand its sacred meaning, he was uncomfortable with displaying it so openly. He had earned the tattoo and was proud to be a member. Others didn't need to know his business.

Simple as that.

Around him, his fellow interns broke into laughter. Big Man had no idea what they were laughing about, nor did he care. Having lived alone most of his adult life—both on the Hopi Reservation and off—Big Man had little need for the company of others. He knew the other interns looked at him strangely. After all, he had barely said two words to any of them since his internship began months ago.

And just as he looked up from the tattoo, he heard the unmistakable clicking sound of a metal tipped walking stick on the floor tiles behind him. He turned his head and saw a tall thin man carrying a briefcase in one hand and a hand-carved Hopi walking stick in the other enter the motel—a white man with long blond hair tied back in a distinctive Native-American style.

The white man's name was Hayden Mayer, and at the sight of him, Big Man breathed a sigh of relief. He also felt an odd chill course through him. He always felt that way when in the presence of the Pahana. And Hayden Mayer, the white man with the long blond hair, *was* the Pahana. Big Man was sure of it. Mayer fulfilled prophecy. All the prophecy, and Big Man was willing to do anything for the man.

Anything to bring in a new age of peace.

It was time.

As Mayer strode purposefully past Big Man, the big Hopi did all he could to ignore the blond man, despite the fact that the hair on the back of his neck was standing on end. He read from the paper—or pretended to—and when the Pahana had gone around a corner Big Man waited a beat, then casually folded his newspaper, stood, and made his way to the elevators.

The blond man was waiting for him, kindly holding the

elevator door open. With a subtle nod of his head, Big Man stepped inside, and the two men rode up together in silence. Big Man's heart wasn't so silent. It beat powerfully in his chest like a war drum. Big Man eyed the Pahana's old hand-carved, hand-painted Hopi cane, with a sharpened metal tip on the end—a favorite of the Pahana's.

When the elevator reached the 3rd floor, both men stepped out and walked down the empty hall. At room 314, Big Man inserted a card key into a door and opened it. He stepped aside as Mayer swept passed him. Big Man glanced down the hallway—confirmed they were still alone—and stepped inside the room. He double-locked the door behind him, and when he turned, the Pahana was standing directly behind him, waiting. With the blond man's piercing steely eyes boring into him, Big Man nearly jumped.

"Do you have it?" asked the Pahana in a calm voice.

Big Man looked away from those piercing eyes and stepped around the thin man. He sat in a chair at a small desk and removed a brown envelope from the inside of his jacket. He handed it to Mayer.

"It's all there," said Big Man, again avoiding eye contact. He always averted his eyes when he spoke to the Pahana. "Schematics, security procedures, map of the plant, guard shifts—everything you asked for."

The Pahana smiled, though his eyes still looked like cold chips of blue ice. They always looked like blue ice. And they always appeared to somehow see inside Big Man. The Hopi sensed that there was no secret he could hide from the Pahana.

The blond man put a hand on Big Man's shoulder. The Hopi shuddered. "Excellent," said the Pahana. "You have served us well, my brother."

Big Man grinned. The Pahana's approval was important to him, perhaps the most important thing in the world. He reveled briefly at pleasing the Pahana—their savior—then decided to go ahead and express a concern weighing heavily on him.

"But all that information will do us no good if we can't get past the security."

"We have an answer for that." The Pahana carefully set his briefcase down on the small table in front of Big Man and snapped it open. Inside was a long tube surrounded by a bank of capacitors.

"What's that?" questioned Big Man.

"An FCG—a Flux Compression Generator."

"What does it do?"

"It will take care of our security problem."

"How?"

"It sends out an electromagnet pulse that fries any and all electronic equipment within a certain radius."

"You mean an EMP weapon?" asked Big Man. He was aware of such devices. He also knew these devices were extremely difficult to come by. But he also knew that nothing was too difficult for the Pahana, as the man had already proved countless times before.

"Close," said the Pahana. "This is far less sophisticated and far less expensive. The effects, however, are the same.

"But how did you get such a weapon, and where did you find the money to purchase it."

Mayer laughed. "My stout brother, we have supporters that range far a field from simple environmentalists. I have a friend on, let's say, the technical side? He built it for us. Four hundred dollars in parts and the plant security problem is solved—if we get close enough."

He paused a moment. "And once the security problem is solved, we shall move in, and," there was a noticeable gleam in the Pahana's icy eyes, "purify the area." He looked directly at Big Man. "That's your job."

Mayer noticed a sign of doubt in Big Man's eyes. "But are you sure it will disable their sophisticated security system? I mean, after all, this is post 9-11."

The Pahana clapped him on the shoulder again, sending an electric thrill through the Hopi. "The more complicated the plumbing, my friend, the easier it is to stop the drain."

Big Man could literally feel warmth spreading from where

the Pahana's hand remained on his shoulder. Perhaps it was his imagination, but Big Man doubted it.

The man continued, "We must fulfill our charge tomorrow, my brother. Do you believe I am the Pahana?"

Big Man nodded immediately, without hesitation.

"Good," said the blond man. "Be strong, my brother. Purifying the Four Corners is the first step of the coming New Age. Remember the words of the old Hopi Shaman." He lowered his voice a pitch and said solemnly, "*Prepare the land to purify the earth. Prepare it for earth's end and a new brotherhood of man.*"

A shudder coursed through Big Man.

A very good shudder.

Roswell, New Mexico

The trip from Albuquerque to Roswell was long, slow, and wet. The long night of driving through the worsening weather left Jeremy Nash exhausted. He had to fight not only the dark road dimly lit through the heavy rain, but the sleep that threatened to overtake his mind. He should have pulled off somewhere and stayed the night, or at least slept in the car, but the concern in his sister's voice drove him onward. He tried several times on the way to reach her by cell, but all he received on his cell phone was, *All circuits busy. Please try again later.*

He also cursed his decision to rent a sports car. The Corvette was no match for the strong storm winds blowing off the high desert.

So, hours later, as he approached Roswell, he was physically and mentally drained—and beyond thankful that daylight was peering through the clouds ahead. As morning approached, the weather had greatly improved.

There is a God, he thought. Then added—*But it's doubtful.*

He was, after all, a professional skeptic and debunker of myths, legends, and conspiracy theories. He currently published a successful magazine, and his website had hits well into the millions. His three books debunking everything from crop circles to 9-11 conspiracies had all hit high on the bestsellers lists. And the fact that Nash was born and raised in the UFO capital of the world—Roswell, New Mexico—was an ironic twist of fate that was not lost on his colleagues.

Or just about anyone else, for that matter.

Growing up here, Nash had discovered something curious about himself. He was different. He didn't automatically believe that aliens had crash landed here. Even as a child he wanted to see the proof. He wanted to see the bodies. When it came to religion, he wanted to see God firsthand. He wanted to witness miracles. Show him an alien or a man walking on water, and he would be a believer.

Until then, he reveled in his role of skeptic, and early in life he believed he had to be the voice of reason. Growing up in UFO country cemented that belief. He had been exposed early in life to the highly delusional, and perhaps on some level he wanted to help them. Give them another answer.

Yes, he knew that people wanted to believe in the supernatural. Such beliefs were an escape from their reality. Nash understood the psychology of it all, but for those who were on the fence, for those who didn't know who or what to believe, Nash wanted to be the voice of reason.

He was also aware that had he not grown up in UFO country, this personal quirk of his might not have ever manifested itself. He was thankful, therefore, for having been witness to the loonies of the world. The loonies carved his career path.

And that was the real epiphany for this great debunker and skeptic—his drive to prove everyone else in his crazy city wrong.

With the rising sun settling just above the distant rocky crags to the east, Nash entered the city of Roswell, New Mexico. A city he at once loved and rejected. A city that held many good memories for him—and many more strange ones.

Too strange.

As he drove along the main thoroughfare, he passed the International UFO Museum and Research Center, where the infamous—and bogus—alien autopsy had been performed on TV several years back. Orchestrated by Fox News, it was a brilliant publicity scheme, if nothing else. Nash had been on the team of skeptics that had blown the whistle on it.

He pulled the Vette up to a stop light a few blocks from his sister's house. As he waited for the signal to turn green, he noticed a short man in what looked like a dingy robe with long dirty brown hair flowing down his grimy bearded face and on to his stubby shoulders. The homeless-looking street prophet held a sign that read, *Prepare for thy doom. The purification is coming.*

It wasn't so much the sign that unsettled Nash. Rowell was known for its kinky combination of alien believers and religious freaks. No. The man stared icily at him from a set of burning, bloodshot eyes.

The light changed, thankfully, and Nash drove on to his sister's.

A few minutes later, he was knocking on her door.

Alyson Nash opened the door, gasped at the sight of her older brother, then threw her arms around him. Nash grunted and did his best to not fall off the front porch.

"You made it!" she squealed.

"Barely," he offered, and when she pulled away and frowned, he added, "I'll tell you about it later, sis. For now, I came as fast as I could."

Though they were five years apart, Nash had heard all his life that he and his sister could have been twins. They were both medium height with auburn complexions, hazel eyes, and straight dark brown hair. Anyone could see the influence their Native American ancestry—Chiricahua Apache—had on their appearance.

"Your timing couldn't have been more perfect," said Alyson anxiously. "There's someone here to see you."

"Who?"

"Just follow me."

He grumbled as she led him through her modest-sized home, along a hallway filled with her own desert paintings—Nash had always thought his sister had missed her true calling—and into the living room. There, sitting on the couch, was a young Native-American woman. A very attractive Native-American woman. Nash caught himself staring. He couldn't help it.

Her olive skin was flawless. Eyes almond shaped. Cheekbones high and proud. Her face was framed by pitch black hair, stylishly cut, hanging to her shoulders. She was sitting alone on the couch and looked up anxiously as soon as Nash entered the room. Despite his hellish night, despite the fact that he felt like something the cat had dragged in, he found himself grinning like a fool at her.

She stood immediately, and he took note of her dark blue designer jeans and tasteful Ann Taylor white blouse. The only nod to her obvious Native-American heritage was the intricately beaded red and blue cloth belt tied around her slim waist.

"Jeremy," said his sister. "This is Kaya. She drove all the way here this morning from the Hopi Reservation to see us."

Nash recognized and respected the Hopi in her. After all, he had spent a lot of his childhood on Hopi reservations with his father. In deference to her Hopi heritage, he turned his smile down a notch or two and extended his hand, careful to not make eye contact. "Hello, Kaya. Nice to meet you."

She gave a firm shake that matched her firm athletic body. But was her handshake too firm? Perhaps overcompensating? And was there a slight sense of anxiety—fear—about her?

Or just his imagination.

As the trio sat, Nash caught a whiff of Kaya's Calvin Klein perfume, a heady scent, very unHopi-like, that forced him to remind himself of why he was here in the first place. A reason that still baffled him. Then again, not much would have baffled him after the surreal night he had experienced.

So he sat forward and got right to the point. "Excuse me if I sound rude, Kaya, but what exactly is going on?"

The young lady nodded, and, in a very un-Hopi like manner, spoke directly to him. Many of the Hopi Nash had known were often passive, working their way slowly—almost poetically— around a subject.

Mercifully, she didn't mince words. "I have something that will lead you to the people who murdered your parents," she said sadly.

Nash opened his mouth to speak, but nothing came out. His brain, he knew, was still somewhere in Rome. And his stomach was still somewhere on the plane.

He looked over at his sister and she had an uneasy look on her face. He looked back at Kaya, who waited for him patiently. "Go on," he said lamely.

She nodded. "Your parents—your father, to be exact—found something in the Hopi end-times prediction, the *sipapu*, the place where our ancestors emerged from the previously destroyed world to this one. Your parents were silenced before they could reveal it."

Sipapu? Nash knew of it. His father would talk of it often.

"Let's back up a bit," Nash said. "What makes you think our parents were murdered?"

The intensity of Kaya's gaze made Nash sit back a bit. Never had he known a Hopi to be so direct.

Or beautiful.

She spoke evenly, never taking her eyes off him. "Because my grandfather said so. And he spoke only the truth."

"Who was your grandfather?" Nash asked.

"Grandfather David Alo. He was the shaman of our Hopi village."

The name sounded familiar to Nash. He was certain his father had mentioned it but couldn't recall in what capacity. Then again, in his current fatigued state, he could barely recall his own name.

Kaya continued, "One day when I was ten years old, two men pulled up in a truck and beat my grandfather senseless, crippling him both physically and emotionally for life. They might have just put a bullet in his head, considering the end result. He never spoke of the beating and admonished me severely whenever I brought it up. He was afraid. For the first time ever, he was afraid."

Nash could perceive a deep sense of anger in her. Or was it one of revenge? Very unlike a Hopi.

She withdrew an aged piece of paper from her Coach designer handbag. "On his deathbed he gave me this and told me to give it to the eldest son of the Nash family." She looked squarely at Jeremy. "You are the eldest son of the Nash family, correct?"

Nash nodded. "*A* Nash family, certainly. Perhaps you have the wrong—"

"No," she said sharply. "Grandfather knew your father well. He even knew you, Jeremy."

Nash had a fleeting image of an old man sitting in a rustic room—perhaps a hotel room. A blond man was in the room. There was an argument. And Nash remembered running.

And then he remembered the dead bodies. A horrible night. One of the worst of his life, and one he had done his best to block out entirely.

"Grandfather died two days ago," Kaya said solemnly.

"I'm sorry," offered Nash softly.

"*Asquali*," she said in Hopi. "Thank you." She handed the piece of paper to Nash. "This was your father's."

Nash took the folded paper, surprised at how hard his heart was suddenly thumping against his ribcage. It was, after all, a note from his deceased father. A message from the grave.

He carefully unfolded the aged paper and eagerly looked it over, breathing hard. He missed his adventurous father, and such a note—any note—was more valuable to Nash than any earthly treasure.

And then his heart sank.

The *note* was nothing more than a sales invoice. Confused and disappointed, he said, "It's just an invoice...for something called a Mana Kachina Doll."

"Let me see that," said Alyson. She snatched the paper from Nash's hand so quickly that she might have given him paper cuts. "The doll wasn't for you," she exclaimed. "The assignee is for someone named Velvalee Dickinson."

As she showed him the name, he grabbed the invoice back and gave his sister a look of scorn. She ignored him. Typical. He read the invoice again, saw the name she had mentioned, and looked over at the Hopi girl in front of him. "My Kachinas are a little rusty," he said. "What, exactly, is a Mana Kachina?"

"She was a warrior woman, or He-he-he," said Kaya. "Mana represents the warrior spirit."

Alyson frowned. "A warrior Hopi? But I thought Hopis were a peaceful people."

"To a large extent," said Kaya, "but we have a history of violent conflict with the Navajo over disputed land. Today, thankfully, that dispute is fought in the courts."

"What's the significance, then, of this Mana Kachina?" asked Nash.

"According to our legends, He-he-he was a young Hopi girl who, while out in the desert, witnessed enemies sneaking up on her village. She snatched up her father's weapons and raced to the village to warn the people. She then led the defense until the men returned from the fields to rout the enemy. He-he-he is held in high esteem."

Nash nodded. As he did so, he spotted two strange annotations typed next to the name of the doll. The first read, 'This is from the Banzai collection and speaks from the small singer.' And the second, 'Turkey rain whale long bee to run away sandy hollow in the deer ice strict.'

He showed them to the others and asked Kaya if she knew what they meant.

The Hopi shook her head and shrugged. "I am sorry, but no."

Alyson squeezed next to him and read the invoice sheet from over his shoulder, which somehow bugged the hell out of him. She pointed to the bottom corner of the invoice where there were three red ink dots in a circle. "And what are those?"

Nash had no idea. He tried to move over but was firmly wedged between his sister and the arm of the couch. She smiled sweetly at him and pointed to another section of the invoice where a sequence of numbers and letters were printed: 2-7-3 470NM.

"What do you think those mean?" she asked.

Nash shrugged. "Maybe it's the invoice form number."

"Or some kind of code," said Alyson. She nearly shivered

with delight. His sister, like his grandfather, was a sucker for a good puzzle.

"I doubt it," Nash replied shortly, rolling his eyes at his sister's enthusiasm for intrigue. "Dad wasn't into cryptography. He was a cultural anthropologist. Codes, as you well know, were our grandfather's shtick."

Not to be deterred, Alyson said, "Still, Dad wouldn't have placed that consignee's name and those annotations on the invoice unless they were important."

"Your father was a cultural anthropologist?" asked Kaya suddenly.

"Yes," said Nash. "He studied many Native-American cultures. My mother, Tracy, was a physicist." Nash paused to reflect. "Everyone asked if they lobbed brain teasers at each other over the kitchen table. But, in fact, they loved each other very much and especially loved sharing the knowledge of each other's work. I guess it disproves the thesis that science and social science can't co-exist."

"C.P. Snow," said Kaya. "The Two Cultures."

"You've read C.P. Snow?" asked Nash, stunned.

"Studied him at Radcliffe," said Kaya. "While getting my own anthropology degree. I never agreed with him about the gulf between scientists and intellectuals, though."

"Neither did I," Nash replied. "In fact, I always believed that—"

"Hey! As interesting as this is," said Alyson, cutting in, and sounding a bit agitated, "I think this invoice should be our main focus."

Kaya nodded. "Yes, of course. Grandfather also told me to tell you that your parents hadn't died in a cave accident." She waited, staring at them both intently. "That they had, in fact, been murdered."

"Why?" cried Nash.

"Grandfather did not know the details, and was too afraid to dig too deeply, but he did know this. Your father had uncovered something about the Hopi End Times prediction. He thought he found something relating to Sipapu."

Nash was about to ask what when Kaya continued, "And, no, Grandfather did not know. Your father was flying out to meet with him the very next day to discuss what they found. Your father—and mother—never made it."

Nash sat back and stared at the invoice. That was a lot of information to absorb. A lot of bizarre information. Nash, who made a living debunking stories half as crazy, found himself not so willing to write this one off as insanity. He knew of his father's research in Native American eschatology. What he didn't know—and this had always bothered him—was of his parent's sudden newfound interest in caving.

The caving accident had been shocking news to him. He had always suspected there was more to the story. And now this woman, a stranger, was telling him that his parents had been murdered.

Nash took a deep breath. He looked again at the paper in his hand. "So what does this invoice have to do with the murder of our parents?"

"Grandfather didn't know," said Kaya. "Just that your father mailed it to him prior to his death, with strict instructions to give it to you upon his death."

"It has to be important, Jeremy," Alyson emphasized.

He nodded his agreement but was still nonetheless baffled. "Well, Dad obviously put this Velvalee Dickinson's name on the invoice for a reason. I guess we should first track her down and see what she knows. Let's google her name." He pulled out his cell phone and jacked into the Internet—or at least tried to. "Damn. No service. Alyson, try your provider."

"Forget it," said Kaya. "The weather is causing havoc with the cell signals."

Nash shook his head. "But that doesn't make sense. I thought cell towers were impervious to weather, no matter how severe."

"All I heard on the radio was that there's something different about these storms," said Alyson. "Something intensely electrical—even magnetic about them."

Nash sighed and gestured to Alyson's laptop. "No matter. We'll use your computer."

She shook her head. "No-go. Wireless been down all day."

"What about your library computers? They have a land line."

She shrugged. "Sure. We can give it a try."

"Can we get into the library this early in the morning?" he asked, doubtfully.

Alyson stood up, crossed her arms under her chest and stuck out a hip. "You're asking if the Director of Archives and Research has a key to the front door?"

"Right," said Nash. "Dumb question. Let's go."

"I'm coming, too." Kaya said decisively. "I want to know who nearly killed my grandfather, and I bet whoever did are the same people who murdered your parents."

Nash was about to say this was a family matter when Kaya said, "Look. How well do you know Hopi culture? You too, Alyson."

"Well, I know a lot—" Nash started to reply.

Kaya cut him off. "I bet I know a helluva lot more than you do, and that knowledge might be significant to solving this puzzle."

Of course, how they were going to need her, he had no clue. But one thing was for certain. He sure as hell wanted her around.

"So that leaves my Corvette out," he added. "We'll take your Bronco, Sis."

Roswell, New Mexico

The appearance of the morning sun was short-lived. As the trio walked up the broad stone steps to the Roswell Public Library, sipping steaming cups of Starbucks, Nash noticed more dark clouds approaching from the west. Worse, they ominously stretched from horizon to horizon, reminding him of an endless advancing army.

At the door, with the wind kicking up, Alyson searched her over-sized purse for her library keys.

"Why didn't you have them out before we got here?" Nash groused impatiently, sipping his drink and tucking his hand inside his jacket pocket.

"Because I was driving," Alyson hissed.

Nash was about to make a comment on the black hole of women's purses but decided discretion was the better part of valor and shut up. He also knew he was cranky as hell, having been awake now for well over twenty-four hours. It took all his will to just close his mouth and wait for his sister as she continued rooting around in her purse like a forest animal searching for grubs.

He smirked at the thought.

While he waited, Nash glanced over his shoulder and saw a robed figure standing on the opposite street corner behind them.

Watching them.

Nash frowned, certain it was the same prophet holding the sign he had seen at the streetlight earlier that morning. This time there was no sign. Nash knew that crazies were abundant here in

Roswell. But seeing the same crazy inside of an hour or so was pushing it.

He touched his sister's shoulder and pointed to the man behind them. "Hey, have you seen this guy before?"

Alyson ignored him and continued hunting through her damnable purse, then triumphantly held up a jingling set of keys. "A-ha!"

"Good for you, Sis. We're really quite proud of your accomplishment."

"Oh, shut up. Now who were you talking about?"

Nash turned around to point out the prophet—but the guy was already gone. Nash frowned again, searching. There was a handful of pedestrians around, but the guy had slipped away in the interim.

Damn.

"Never mind," he said, irritated. "No big deal. Just open the door."

"Yes, sir," Alyson replied, saluting.

As he turned around, he caught Kaya watching him. Normally, being studied by such a beautiful woman would have sent a thrill through him. But in this case, he caught her distinct look of concern. She smiled weakly as Alyson unlocked the library door.

The trio walked through the darkened entrance, lit only by the security lighting. They were soon passing row after row of bookshelves.

"So, where do you keep the Roswell history books?" Nash asked, smirking. "Under fiction?"

Alyson threw him a nasty look.

A few minutes later, they were all crowded into Alyson's small office. She logged into her computer and called up one of the library's research databases.

"Hey, it works! We're in," she said excitedly. She held up her palm for a high-five, but no one reciprocated. She turned back to the computer. "You guys are no fun. Anyway, if this Velvalee Dickinson exists, we'll find her—or him—in here."

She typed the odd name into the search window, hit enter, and waited. The group watched the status bar creep along the bottom of the screen until the computer found what it was looking for. Up popped an FBI database and displayed a page titled *Famous Cases* and a picture of a woman. Under the picture was a name: Velvalee Malvena Dickinson—The Doll Woman.

"Son of a bitch!" said Nash. "Click on that."

"Like I wouldn't have thought of doing that," Alyson replied sarcastically, rolling her eyes.

"What does it say?" Kaya said pushing her way past Nash and into Alyson to get a better view of the screen.

"Don't shove," growled Alyson. "I'll read it aloud."

She summarized from the page. "Says here that during World War Two, Dickinson owned and managed a doll shop in New York City. She catered to wealthy doll collectors and hobbyists interested in obtaining foreign, regional, and antique dolls. Oh, this is interesting! She used correspondence about dolls to conceal information about U.S. Naval forces she was attempting to convey to the Japanese via South America."

"Wow! She was a spy," exclaimed Kaya. "What else does it say about her?"

"Patience, my dear," admonished Alyson. She scrolled down the page. "Okay. There's lots of info here on her background… where she was born, who she married, yada, yada, yada—ah, here. The FBI's interest in Mrs. Dickinson stemmed from a letter about dolls intercepted by wartime censors because of its unusual content. It was brought to the Bureau's attention in February 1942. The letter, purportedly from a Portland, Oregon woman to an individual in Buenos Aires, Argentina, dealt with a 'wonderful doll hospital,' observing that the writer had left her three 'Old English dolls' for repairs. Also mentioned in the letter were 'fish nets' and 'balloons.'"

"Fish nets and balloons?" questioned Kaya incredulously. "What the hell does that mean?"

Hell indeed, thought Nash. *She definitely was not your everyday Hopi.*

"I'm getting to that part. Cool your jets, or whatever Hopis do."

Nash stepped between them. "Okay ladies let's calm down. What else does the page say, Sis?"

Alyson shifted her frame in the chair and continued her summary. "Says here the FBI laboratory cryptographers examined the letter and concluded that the 'three Old English dolls' probably were three warships, and the doll hospital was a shipyard where repairs were made. They further concluded that the fishing nets referred to submarine nets protecting ports on the West Coast, and that the reference to balloons was intended to convey information about other defense installations on the West Coast."

"What does this have to do with the invoice?" asked Kaya.

Nash stepped back from the computer and settled into one of the plastic chairs in front of his sister's desk. For some reason, the cheap plastic chair felt unusually comfortable. Too comfortable. He felt his eyelids drooping.

"Please tell me you are deep in thought and not sleeping," said Alyson sharply.

"A little of both," said Nash, jolting upright. An idea had occurred to him from the black depths of his subconscious. "Let's say, for the sake of argument, that the invoice from our father is an example of a coded message like that from Dickerson. Ones she used in World War Two. And let's say the specific doll on this invoice points to some Hopi warrior tradition. If so, where does that lead us?"

"May I see the invoice again?" asked Kaya.

Nash handed her the crumpled sheet of paper. As she scanned it, Nash caught himself staring at the beautiful Hopi. She suddenly looked up at him—and promptly caught him staring, too. For some damn reason, his face burned crimson.

She smiled shyly and said, "The only Hopi involvement that I am aware of during World War Two were the Hopi Code Talkers."

"Right!" said Nash, perhaps louder than he intended. "The military used Hopi, Navajo, and other tribal languages as encrypted codes, mostly to keep the Japanese from understanding orders to and from GIs in combat." Nash suddenly paused and looked directly at Kaya. She returned his stare, and he said, "Your grandfather was a Code Talker, wasn't he?"

She held his gaze for a beat or two, then the corners of her lips slowly turned up. "You are no fool, Mr. Nash. Yes, both my grandfather and his brother were Code Talkers."

Nash stood and paced his sister's little office, thinking out loud, as he was prone to do. "Yes, that makes sense. And our father's invoice makes even more sense now."

"Could the annotations be Code Talk?" asked Alyson, looking up from the computer. She positively shivered in anticipation.

"There's one way to find out," said Kaya. "Come back to the reservation with me and attend my grandfather's funeral. He would have wanted you there. He considered your father a great friend. Besides, there's someone there I want you to meet."

Nash paused in front of her, looking down. "Your great uncle," he said. "The Code Talker."

She dipped her head once. "Like I said, Mr. Nash, you're no fool. But we must hurry. The funeral is tonight. We have a nine-hour drive ahead of us."

Morgan Lake Reservoir, Arizona

The two windsurfers glided silently over the dark waters of the Morgan Lake Reservoir. Dressed in black wetsuits and wearing night vision goggles, they were aided by strong winds that rippled the surface of the water. Above, a vast moonless sky helped them move undetected towards one of the largest coal-fired generating stations in the United States—the Four Corners Power Plant.

At the south shore of the reservoir, the two windsurfers rode straight up onto the smooth sandy beach. There, they ditched their blacked-out boards and worked their way carefully along the electrified outer perimeter fence, keeping to the shadows as much as possible.

Before them, the massive power plant hummed with life, steaming and puffing its toxic fumes into the night sky. Flood lights illuminated the area around the security fence, and security cameras, mounted high upon the electrified fence, continuously scanned the area. Dressed in matte black wetsuits, the two figures could have been nothing more than creeping shadows. Or so they hoped. A hundred yards before them, a lone man sat in a guard shack, his face silhouetted in a small square window. He appeared to be asleep.

The two figures, a man and a woman, stopped and removed their backpacks. Ryvre, a short, plump hippie with hanging scraggly hair, pulled a long copper tube wrapped in condensers from his backpack. Rainbow, a thin, braided, pig-tailed woman with a hint of a mustache above her upper lip, withdrew a timing device and detonator from her own pack.

"Make sure you insert that detonator like they showed us," Ryvre instructed, keeping his voice low. Nearby, crickets chirped loudly. "That piece goes into the—"

Rainbow cut him off. "You know, for a liberated man you can be such a chauvinist pig." Her nostrils flared, and she waved him off with a flick of her wrist. "I know what I'm doing. Now fuck off."

Ryvre muttered something about *unshaven underarms* and *that time of the month* as he turned back to his work.

Despite the heated exchange, the two worked quickly and efficiently together, and soon they had the FCG device ready to detonate.

"Set it for five minutes," Ryvre ordered.

Rainbow gave him a cold stare and crossed her arms. As she did so, her polyurethane wetsuit squeaked.

"Please," he added, rolling his eyes.

"I'll set it for three," she replied emphatically. "That'll give us more than enough time to distance ourselves from the detonation."

Rainbow dialed in a hundred and eighty seconds, and with their mission accomplished, the two slid back along the fence, keeping to the shadows. They took cover in the sand behind some desert scrub brush and a fallen mesquite tree. As they did so, Ryvre's chubby frame accidentally dropped on top of her.

"Watch it, you idiot," she hissed.

"Sorry."

They peered anxiously over the fallen tree and waited. A few moments later, the hairs on their arms raised, and their skin tingled like a million ants crawled over them. Then a blinding flash of light seared Ryvre's eyes. When they cleared again, he momentarily wondered if he had gone blind.

After all, the entire area had gone black.

Four Corners Power Plant, Arizona

From afar, the plant looked entirely dark. The FCG had done its job. A broadband, high-intensity, short-duration burst of electro-magnetic energy had extinguished the lights at the Four Corners Power Plant, plunging the entire area in near total blackness.

"Let's go!" ordered the tall blond man sitting in the passenger seat of the Jeep.

Big Man, behind the wheel, did as Mayer told him. Big Man hit the gas hard and the Jeep reacted by kicking up dust and swerving to the right. The Hopi regained control and aimed the vehicle down the center of the narrow road. Leaning against his leg and gleaming under the dashboard lights was the barrel of a silencer-equipped XM8 Lightweight Assault Rifle. Behind them, the second and third Jeeps followed, all their drivers and passengers equally armed.

Showtime, Big Man thought, and grinned. It was the first time he had grinned in many days.

As they drove under the imposing high-tension wires of the electrical towers, Big Man, as planned in excruciating detail, turned sharply off the access road and headed straight for the main gate. As he did so, he hit the brights and the Jeep's hi-beams cut through the inky night as the main road to the power plant lit up before him.

Just ahead, he could see a security guard trying, unsuccessfully, to make a phone call with one hand and aim a fumbling flashlight with the other. The man jerked his head around and stared into the hi-beams of the oncoming Jeep. To Big Man he looked liked the proverbial deer in the headlights. The guard fumbled at his hip, going for his gun.

"Shoot him!" Mayer shouted.

As the Jeep slammed hard into the metal entrance gate, bursting it open, Big Man, after regaining control of the vehicle, lifted his rifle and took aim. Before the guard could bring up his pistol, the Hopi calmly fired a muffled burst from his automatic rifle. Bullets ripped through the guard shack—and two or three ripped through the man, as well. He fell in a heap. Big Man looked at him impassively as they drove on.

My first kill, he thought. *My first kill for the Pahana.*

One by one, the other Jeeps followed into the blacked out power plant. Big Man had the details of the plant memorized. He had studied charts of it for weeks and could have driven blind through its main roads and back alleys. For now, the headlights were more than adequate, and he tore through the plant with the other two Jeeps right behind him. He turned again, skidded around a corner, and stopped in front of the dark administration building. The other vehicles swarmed around him. Big Man silenced the vehicle and the lights, and the others followed suit.

This night had been chosen to sync perfectly with the new moon. And with the moon completely hidden in earth's shadow, the night sky was almost completely black, with only a smattering of twinkling stars.

The Pahana slipped on a pair of night vision goggles, and Big Man promptly did the same. The two men stepped outside into the cool night air. The other men followed suit, all wearing night vision goggles—and all holding semi-automatic weapons.

"Ready?" barked Mayer.

The others nodded at the Pahana in response, and Big Man led the way into the building. The security door, as expected, was unlocked. Once inside, Big Man shot the only man they came across—a janitor. Big Man knew the elder man, having spoken to him briefly on a couple of occasions.

Bad night to work the late shift, thought Big Man. *Kill number two.*

"Split up," commanded Mayer to the group. "Check every office. We don't want any interruptions. Kill anything that moves." He turned to Big Man. "Lead the way to the pulverizer."

The Hopi nodded, leading the way through the building and out to the massive adjoining warehouse. Inside, it was pitch dark. Luckily, the night vision goggles worked well enough. Big Man could see, in fuzzy green detail, the plant's pulverizer. The vicious-looking machine did exactly as its name implied. Day and night, it ground coal into a powder the consistency of flour, which was used to run the turbines generating the electric power.

Now, it sat silent. A hungry beast denied.

Mayer looked around the vast interior. "We need the mechanical controls now that the computers are knocked out."

Big Man nodded and led the way up a narrow ladder. High above the floor, the two men made their way carefully across the narrow catwalk to the mechanical hand controls of the pulverizer. Seized by sudden vertigo, Big Man refused to look down.

Mayer surveyed the imposing piece of equipment. "This is your gig," he said to Big Man. "Work your magic."

Magic. The Pahana's words lifted the Hopi's spirit. Chest swelling with pride, he reached for the lever attached to a turn wheel. There would be no programming finesse needed here. Just old fashioned gears. He grasped the lever and turned the wheel slowly, straining with the effort. The reluctant creature creaked and groaned, and eventually Big Man had it turned all the way to the right.

The wheel controlled the chemical composition of the air inside the pulverizer. Too little oxygen and the coal wouldn't burn efficiently. Too much oxygen and—Big Man smiled for the second time this night.

He turned to the Pahana. "Now all we need is a spark." He pulled a timing detonator out of his pack. As determined, he set it for fifteen minutes. "Let's go."

The two men dashed out of the building and found the rest of the team waiting in the parking lot. All was quiet.

But not for long, thought Big Man. This time, he did not grin.

They climbed into their respective Jeeps and drove quickly off the plant grounds, passing no one. At least, no one alive.

Nearly a mile away on the access road, they came across two figures dressed in wet suits. Big Man promptly picked them up.

And just as their doors slammed shut, a giant explosion split the night air. The group turned and felt a searing heat on their faces from an immense fireball rising high over the center of the plant.

In the eerie light, a wicked smile crossed the face of Mayer.

"The purification has begun," he announced solemnly.

Oraibi
Hopi Indian Reservation

Nash dropped off his rental car and, with Alyson and Kaya, headed off to the Hopi reservation in Alyson's SUV.

The weather had finally cleared, and they drove straight through the hot day. It was a miserable, grueling trip out of New Mexico, across the Four Corners, and into Northern Arizona to the Hopi Nation.

The sun had not quite set behind the smattering of distant flat mesas when the trio pulled into the Hopi holy city of Oraibi. They parked in front of a row of flat, adobe structures—buildings and homes constructed in the traditional style of the Hopi. Nash knew these structures were, in fact, perfectly adapted for the harsh, dry environment, and that the mud adobe walls offered surprising relief from the desert heat.

"You live here?" asked Alyson.

Kaya nodded kindly, and Nash saw the pride on her face. "Born and raised right here in Oraibi," she said. "But I live in San Antonio now. Many of us have decided to move on beyond the reservation, although it will always be our ancestral home. It may not look like much, but many of my best memories are from here."

"Yes, of course." Alyson somehow managed to sound sheepish, although the way she held her hand over her mouth made it rather evident that she still didn't think much of the place.

Nash stepped in, cleaning up after his sister.

As usual, he thought.

"My father brought me here often," he said softly. "We would watch the sunset behind those distant buttes. Sometimes I would hear a soft throb of drums pounding in the distance—although my father claimed he never heard them."

Kaya turned her head around, and Nash caught her staring at him. Her eyes, he decided, were perfectly almond-shaped, and about as big as he had ever seen. What had he said? The part about the drums? Nash always assumed he had made them up. In fact, he was certain of it. Just a child's wild imagination.

He continued, "The village, if I recall, is quite old."

She nodded slowly, keeping her eyes on his. "Yes, it was founded sometime around eleven hundred CE and is considered one of the oldest continuously inhabited settlements within the United States."

Nash and Alyson followed Kaya through the dusty streets of the aged village to an even more ancient looking Hopi multi-story pueblo building. He looked up at the mud-colored structure. "Why here? What about your grandfather's burial?"

"My grandfather's burial will be in about an hour, near sunset. Meanwhile, I want you to meet someone."

The trio stood in what Nash could only describe as unbearable heat—and this coming from a native New Mexican. He wiped his brow and followed Kaya up a narrow path to a shorter than average door recessed into the adobe mud brick wall. Almost immediately, an old Hopi opened the door.

Not old, thought Nash. *Ancient.*

"Hello, Grandfather," said Kaya respectfully, keeping her distance.

The old man nodded and cast his surprisingly lively eyes over to Nash. Nash instinctively nodded. The elder simply watched him, his expression unchanged and, for the most part, completely unreadable. He wore a white, long-sleeved shirt, jeans, and a huge turquoise bracelet. Nash eyed the bracelet—drawn to it, reminding him of his father's.

Kaya introduced him as Grandfather Martin. As soon as she mentioned Nash and Alyson were friends of hers, the old man smiled brightly. "Welcome to my home," he said in halting English. "Please come in."

As they stepped into the pleasantly cool entrance, walking under a low ceiling comprised mostly of mud and bits of twig, Alyson whispered a question to Kaya that was loud enough for Nash to hear: "I thought you said your grandfather was dead."

The queen of tact, thought Nash, shaking his head again.

In response, while Grandfather Martin shuffled deeper into the squarish room, Kaya paused at the peeled log beams in the entry way and answered, "We use the word *Grandfather* as a sign of respect for our elders. He's my grandfather's brother."

"Oh," replied Alyson.

"Please, please. Come in," implored Grandfather Martin from what appeared to be a small sitting room.

It was. And as Nash ducked under the wooden archway, he almost tripped on an ornate Hopi cross rug. No surprise there, as the room was very dark, with only a smattering of dim light making its way through the tiny windows that were dotted within the structure. A heavy musk hung in the air. Nash suspected the smell was from the different rugs strewn about.

"Please sit here—by the fireplace," invited the old man. He took a seat in a wicker chair, which creaked so badly Nash thought the old man just might plunge through to the dirt floor.

The fireplace was in the corner, surrounded on both sides by small niches in the mud-plastered walls. Each niche contained rather ornate clay pots.

When all were seated in the creaky wicker chairs—each more rickety than the next—Kaya got right to the point. "Grandfather, we need your help." She motioned to Nash to hand her the invoice. When he did, she continued, "We wondered if you might be able to shed some light on this puzzle."

"Puzzle?" queried the old man, brightening considerably. And

Nash realized the man—who had once been a Code Talker during World War Two—obviously had a taste for riddles and puzzles.

She handed the invoice to her great uncle, who took the old piece of paper eagerly in his gnarled fingers. How the old man could read in the dim light, Nash had no clue. With the room darkening each advancing minute, the man slowly and carefully read the invoice.

Outside the adobe home, Nash could hear children playing. If he concentrated hard enough, he thought he could hear the faint pounding of a drum. He wondered if the others could hear it. He almost asked his sister when the old man finally looked up, a hint of a smile crossing the man's thin lips.

"I haven't seen words like this since the war," he whispered thoughtfully.

"Code talk?" asked Nash.

Martin looked at Nash, seemed to weigh his answer, then replied, "Yes, Mr. Nash. Code talk."

"Can you tell us what they mean?" asked Alyson.

"If I did, I'd have to kill you," he said.

Alyson blinked, saw that the old man was actually joking, and laughed nervously. Nash held back his own laughter. He liked this old guy.

Martin continued, "I'll do my best to help, young lady. But first, someone needs to tell me what this is all about."

And they did, all three of them chiming in together. When finished, the old man nodded and looked at Nash and Alyson with deep compassion in his eyes. "Your father was a good man. He was always welcome here. His and your mother's death was a tragedy."

He held up the bill of sale. "This receipt refers to the Banzai Collection and something called the small singer. In the War, we used the word Banzai to mean *fool them* or *to keep secret*. I suspect the words Banzai Collection were deliberately chosen since the word itself, Banzai, has nothing to do with Mana Kachinas."

Nash liked the way Grandfather Martin's brain worked.

Obviously, the man hadn't lost much—or any—of his reasoning powers. He said, "Deliberately chosen—to mean this invoice was an attempt to fool whoever was looking for something."

Martin nodded his head.

"What about the words *speaks from a small singer?*" asked Nash.

The old man nodded. "We used code words to represent different military items that were not part of the Native-American languages. Iron fish for submarine. Hummingbird for fighter plane."

"But how is that a code?" said Alyson dismissively. "Even I could figure that one out."

Grandfather Martin smiled patiently. Nash rolled his eyes.

"It was in original Hopi, Alyson," he said. "A language that at the time had never been written down. Outside of the Hopi Nation, no one on the planet could have broken that code. It's one of the reasons why we won the war in the Pacific."

Alyson merely shrugged.

Grandfather Martin continued, smiling patiently. "Small singer could mean some kind of broadcast or communication apparatus like a radio or walkie-talkie or—"

"Or a musical device," interrupted Nash. "Stereos or even audio tapes."

"Yes," Martin agreed. "That's very possible."

"Dad kept quite a selection of DATS, digital audio tapes, and what may be relevant here, many of them contained original recordings of different tribal chants he recorded on his many research trips."

"Seems like a stretch," said Alyson, shrugging.

"Of course it's a stretch," noted Nash, finally frustrated by his sister's negativity. "All of this is a stretch, Alyson. For all we know this is just a bill of sale with some strange notations on it."

"But Father wanted us to have it," Alyson persisted.

"Exactly," said Nash, exasperated.

Kaya leaned forward, her smooth features catching the last of the setting sunlight that filtered into the small home. Nash caught his breath. She frowned. "You think the code words mean a tape?"

Nash shrugged. "Why not? DATs are small, and they certainly *sing*. If Dad had something to do with creating this invoice—which is turning out to look more and more like a series of clues-—then it could make sense."

"Still seems like a stretch," repeated Alyson. Nash was about to counter more of his sister's negativity when her face suddenly brightened. "You know," she added, "I have many of Daddy's things back home. There were some DATs with them."

"Bingo," said Nash. "That's probably them."

"But there's more," said Kaya, looking at her grandfather. "What about the other code words?"

He nodded and read aloud from the paper. "*The whale long bee to run away sandy hollow in the deer ice strict.*" He looked at the group, his face heavily shadowed—and wrinkled—in the diminishing light. "In Code Speak, the word whale referred to *battleship*, long bee means *belong*, run away meant *abandoned*, and the words sandy hollow stood for *bunker*."

"What about *deer ice strict*?" asked Alyson.

Those words stood for *district*." So, all together these words in Code Speak mean B*attleship belong to abandoned bunker in district*." He shrugged. "I'm sorry to say that I have no idea what that means."

"Well," suggested Nash, "we have half a solution. Let's act on that."

The old man looked out the window as the last of the light highlighted his worn and lined face. "It's time," he said softly. "Your Grandfather's funeral will begin soon."

Oraibi
Hopi Indian Reservation

The darkened sky was threatening rain as the funeral procession entered the kiva belonging to Kaya's clan.

Nash ducked into the small ceremonial room, blinking, waiting for his eyes to adjust to the dim light. At the far end of the squarish room was a fire pit complete with a weak, wavering flame. Next to the pit was a narrow opening in the floor that led down into total darkness. An elder Hopi Shaman, adorned in ceremonial robes and jewelry, was already in the room and surrounded by several members of Kaya's family. The prostrate body of Grandfather David lay on a large woven blanket near the black hole in the floor.

Kaya, Alyson and Nash stood quietly at the back of the room while the shaman muttered an indecipherable prayer. Nash had a very strong feeling that he didn't belong here. That he was intruding on something sacred. In fact, he was certain of it. He had to keep reminding himself that he was an invited guest.

"I've never been to anything like this," Alyson whispered to Kaya.

Leave it to Alyson, Nash thought, *to talk at a Hopi funeral.*

To his surprise, Kaya answered back, speaking quietly while the shaman sprinkled something over the inert body. "The Hopi burial ceremony is very solemn and formal," she said. "For us, life is connected to death."

"How do you mean?" whispered Alyson.

"See that small hole next to the fire pit?" Kaya whispered. "That represents the *sipapu*—the Hopi word for *place of emergence*. The Hopi dead are believed to return to the Underworld through the *sipapu.* It represents the place where our ancestors emerged from the previously destroyed world to this one."

The sipapu? thought Nash. Was this what his parents were killed for finding? He wished he knew.

"Previously destroyed?" whispered Alyson.

"Yes. Hopis believe that there were several worlds before this one—each created and destroyed, and our current world will be destroyed too."

"And you believe that?" asked Alyson. Nash could hear the doubt in his sister's voice.

Kaya dodged the question. "Anyway, in the Underworld, the dead are in original communion with the Kachinas where they carry on both a ritual and secular existence that is a replica of Hopi life on earth."

"Are you saying that this *sipapu,* this hole in the earth, has a physical manifestation somewhere?" asked Nash.

"Yes. Legend has it," Kaya replied.

The three watched as Grandfather Martin approached the body of his brother, solemnly knelt down, and tied a prayer offering to the hair of the deceased. Nash saw the tears in the old man's eyes. His heart went out to the older man. Despite being in a nearly constant state of irritation with his younger sister, Nash could not imagine life without her.

Well, it would be much simpler, he thought, trying to suppress a grin.

The shaman now knelt over Kaya's grandfather and covered the man's face with cotton fabric. Nash took a step closer. The material was, in fact, a sort of mask with openings for the eyes, nose and mouth. A string attached to the material was passed around the top of head and tied at the forehead.

The image was decidedly bizarre.

Yeah, thought Nash. *I don't belong here.*

"Why is he doing that?" whispered Alyson.

"The mask is used to hide themselves in," replied Kaya.

Nash wasn't entirely sure what that meant, and he was certain his sister didn't either. Amazingly though, she had enough tact not to press the matter further.

The shaman stood, raised his arms, and directly addressed the body before him. "You have become a Kachina, old friend. Aid us now in bringing rains to fertilize our farms." The others in the room nodded gravely.

Next, Grandfather Martin dipped his fingers in a clay bowl filled with what appeared to be black paint. He carefully lifted the cotton fabric and proceeded to make black marks under his brother's eyes, along his lips, across the forehead, cheeks, the palms of his hands, and the soles of his feet.

Next to him, Alyson's mouth dropped open. Nash prayed to God his sister kept silent. To his relief, she did.

A young girl brought Grandfather Martin various items—prayer feathers, food, and a small container of drinking water. He carefully placed each on his brother's chest. He stood slowly, then stepped away as three men proceeded to wrap the heavy blanket around the body, covering it completely, and securing it with rope.

Once done, the men moved away, and Grandfather Martin picked up his brother in a feat of strength that made Nash gasp. The old man hoisted his brother over his shoulder and walked slowly out of the room.

The burial took place on the outskirts of town, at the foot of a rocky mesa. The burial ground itself was a small area encircled with upright rocks. Nash and Alyson watched silently as Kaya's grandfather was lowered into the ground. The moment Grandfather Martin and some of the other men had finished covering the grave with native clay soil, something remarkable happened—something that briefly clouded even Nash's skeptical mind.

It began raining. Lightly at first. But as the winds increased, so did the rain, until it was driving hard into their faces.

The women instantly began to weep. The children danced and played, and the very old man who had just covered his brother with dirt simply stared up into the sky with his eyes closed and mouth open.

"Your grandfather answered the shaman's prayer," said Alyson gently, her voice filled with awe and respect. She took the other woman's hand. "He brought the rain."

Nash found himself looking at his sister in stunned silence. Her surprising depth at times blew his mind. She looked at him, shrugged, and continued to hold Kaya's hand. A sense of unease filled Nash, radiating out from his core to his extremities. Mostly, the sensation affected his chest and seized his breathing. He looked for a place to sit but saw none.

As the rain continued to fall, and the dirt turned into mud, and small puddles turned into rivulets that snaked down from the mesa above, Nash's inner skeptic finally won out.

He could never believe—would never believe—that the spirit of a deceased could actually influence the weather.

Unless, of course, he was shown undeniable proof.

And with that thought, Nash's uneasiness abated, leaving him breathing freely and comfortably.

Despite being soaked to the bone, Nash made no attempt to prod Kaya, who seemed content to stand there in the rain and gaze at her grandfather's grave. Most of the tribe had gone, and Nash was actually enjoying the feeling of standing in the rain. He wasn't so sure about Alyson. She fidgeted next to him.

Her compassion and understanding, he knew, only went so far. He expected his sister to say something any minute now.

But before that happened, a lone figure emerged from the wet shadows and stepped over to Grandfather David's freshly dug grave. Next to him, Nash heard Kaya gasp. She then marched forward, slogging through the deepening puddles.

"You have lot of nerve showing up here," she said, spitting the words at the big figure.

Nash and Alyson looked at each other and shrugged, then dashed after her.

The man in front of her said, "I do it out of respect for my people and our grandfather." And with a hint of animosity, he added, "I can't say the same for you."

"Respect?" she hissed. "You don't know the meaning of the word. You've done nothing but belittle the elders."

"And you disgrace our people with your white man ways."

Although there was little light to make the man out, Nash could tell he was big. Damn big. So big that he was beginning to wish that Kaya would keep quiet.

"This sounds like a family thing," Nash said, backing up and stepping into a deep puddle that reached past his ankles. He ignored the unpleasant sensation. "Perhaps Alyson and I should meet you back at the—"

"No, stay," Kaya implored. "I'm sorry. I forgot my manners." She turned to the man, unsmiling. "This is my half-brother, William Big Man. William, these are my friends, Alyson and Jeremy Nash."

Big Man nodded, his face expressionless. He turned back to Kaya and said, "Let me pay my respects and leave. We have nothing else to say to each other."

"Fine," Kaya replied. "Alyson, Jeremy. Let's go."

Kayenta, Arizona

They were seated at a McDonald's several miles from the reservation. Outside, the driving rain pummeled windows painted with oversized Big Macs and French fries. Inside, each sipped coffee. Nash snacked on a small bag of fries, enjoying each and every one.

"I'm sorry you had to hear that back there," said Kaya for perhaps the third time. "I so apologize."

"I guess you and your brother don't get along," Alyson said.

Kaya smiled weakly. They were all exhausted from the long drive. Nash couldn't remember when he slept last. The coffee was barely keeping him functional.

"William and I come from two different worlds," said Kaya.

"What do you mean?" Alyson loved family stories.

"When I went off to college and followed my career, I dropped many of my people's traditions and ways. I was ostracized for that."

"You were ostracized for going to college and improving yourself?" said Alyson, not masking her disdain. "That doesn't make sense."

"Think of it this way," said Nash. "What if you abandoned everything your mother and father held dear? On second thought, let's take it a step further. What if you abandoned everything that our parents, grandparents, and all those we know and love held dear and adopted all new beliefs?"

Alyson opened her mouth, then closed it. She tried again. "Well, if the new beliefs were better..."

"Let me stop you there, Sis. How do you know the new beliefs are better? Just because they're modern? Modern does not make better."

"May I speak now?" asked Kaya. She smiled easily at Nash and reached out and touched the back of his hand, sending a thrill coursing through him.

Despite himself, he blushed, realizing he had been speaking for her. "Yeah, sorry."

"Thank you," she said. "First off, I did not abandon my entire culture. I am a Hopi now and forever. I just feel there is room for both worlds."

"And there are those who don't agree with your assessment?" asked Nash.

"Yes," she answered.

"And your half-brother is one of them?"

"Yes." She took in some air and gathered her thoughts. "I've taken up the path of a researcher. A researcher, in fact, of my own people's culture. For that, I must remain objective and not let any previous enculturation interfere with my study. My objectivity, the discounting of my own enculturation, is seen by some in my clan as a rejection of my culture."

"And by some," said Nash, "you mean William?"

Kaya nodded. "William, among others, is a deep believer in what I told you at Grandfather's funeral. He believes in the ancient legends of worlds being created and worlds being destroyed. William believes that we are at the end of this world and the beginning of a new one."

"So, how's that different from what the Hopis believe in?" asked Alyson.

"It's not so much the what, but the when." Kaya took another breath. "Let me explain. Although The Elders disagree, William believes that all the requirements for fulfilling the Hopi prediction for the end times have come to pass."

Alyson blinked. "Say again?"

Nash stepped in. "The Hopi prophesy of the emergence of the future Fifth World."

Kaya's eyes widened with surprised.

"Very good, Jeremy. You know the prophesy?"

"I'm writing a book on the history of apocalyptic predictions. I cover the Hopi end of times predictions in one of my chapters." Nash thought for a moment. "If I recall correctly, there are nine signs that herald the end of this Fourth World and the emergence of the next—the Fifth World."

"That's correct," Kaya agreed.

Nash had to admit, he loved impressing her. He felt like a school kid showing off for the pretty girl in class. His fatigue briefly disappeared.

"What signs are those, Jeremy?" asked Alyson.

Nash looked at Kaya. "May I?" he asked.

Kaya nodded. "Please."

Nash cleared his throat. "The first sign tells of the coming of the white men. The second sign tells of the white men bringing their families in wagons across the prairies. The third sign tells of the coming of the white men's cattle, and the fourth tells of the land being crossed by the railroad. The fifth tells of the land being crisscrossed by a giant spider's web. Some interpret this as the internet, or, perhaps metaphorically, as the oppressive web of the white man. The sixth says the land will be crisscrossed with rivers of stone that make pictures in the sun. Many feel these are our modern freeways. The seventh sign tells of the sea turning black and many living things dying within it. We can all guess what that is—the destructive effects of massive oil spills. The eighth sign tells of the time when the youth who wear their hair long come and join the tribal nations to learn their ways and wisdom."

"Hippies," Alyson noted.

Nash continued. "Finally, the ninth sign—the death of the Blue Star Kachina."

Nash looked at Kaya and winked. "How'd I do?"

Kaya clapped her hands together, applauding. "Very good. Very good. That is, for a man with white blood, of course."

Alyson's mouth was hanging open. "Good God, Jeremy. Now

I know why you can't keep a girlfriend. You spend way too much time with your books."

Nash wanted to kick his sister under the table. He decided against it. Still, what she said was true. It had been far too long since Nash's last real date, and even farther back since his last relationship—not counting a brief interlude with a stunning Mossad agent just a few short days before. Indeed, far too much time was spent traveling, researching, writing his books, and running his magazine.

He glanced at Kaya. She smiled at him warmly, and his heart seemed to leap for joy in his chest.

Far too long, he thought.

"Do you discuss the Pahana in your book?" she asked him.

"The Pah-who?" asked Alyson.

"The Pahana," said Nash. "When he appears to the Hopi people, the Fifth World will emerge, and mankind will be led into the next."

He turned to Kaya. "Yes, I mention him."

"What about him?" asked Alyson suspiciously, sipping her coffee.

Outside, the rain seemed to intensify. The windows in the McDonald's rattled. They were the only customers inside. Behind the counter, a young kid with far too much acne flirted with a young girl with the same teenage affliction.

"Hopis believe," Nash said, "that the true Pahana—the Lost White Brother or Elder Brother—left centuries ago for the east. At the same time, the Hopi entered the Fourth World, or the physical world of earth. According to Hopi legend, the Pahana will return, and at his coming the wicked will all be destroyed—and a new age of peace will be ushered into the world.

"William believes the Pahana has appeared," Kaya replied. "Like I said, The Elders disagreed."

Nash sat up. "And when was he supposed to have appeared?" he asked.

"Twenty-one years ago at a Blue Star Kachina ceremony at

the Hopi House at the Grand Canyon," Kaya replied. "I was just a child then."

"Wait a minute," said Nash. "Twenty-one years ago? The Grand Canyon?"

"Yes."

"I was there."

"What!" Alyson and Kaya said in unison. The response would have been almost comical if Nash's insides suddenly weren't churning.

"I was there with Dad. He wanted to show me the Blue Star Kachina dance-—but at that dance something happened...something very, very bad."

"What?" asked Alyson, sitting forward.

Nash took a deep breath. "It began when I witnessed an old Hopi arguing with a young man—a young white man—in the El Tovar. The disagreement ended when the white man picked up a clay pot and smashed it on the floor."

Kaya's eyes widened. "Really? That's part of the prophesy! The legend says that the Pahana would pick up a clay pot and smash it to the ground, thus identifying himself to our people."

"Was that it?" Alyson asked, clearly disappointed. "Someone smashing a pot?"

"No," said Nash. "And it's something Dad and I promised we would never tell you. At least, not when you were a kid."

"Well, I'm hardly a kid now."

Nash let the first response that came to mind pass. Instead, he took a deep breath and said, "During the ceremony, the Blue Star Kachina removed his mask..."

"That's also the prophesy," Kaya interrupted excitedly. "It's said that the end of all Hopi ceremonialism—and of this world—will be signaled when a Blue Star Kachina removes his mask during a dance in the plaza before uninitiated children. That's you, the general public."

"What happened after he removed his mask?" asked Alyson.

Nash hadn't talked about this for years. The last person he had talked about it with was his father. And both of them had struggled to come to terms with it. He looked at his sister and said simply, "The dancers died in front of us. All of them. Instantly."

For the first time in a long time, his sister was struck into silence.

Kaya said, "I had heard rumors of this growing up."

"It's more than rumors," said Nash. "There was a huge investigation. Tribal police. FBI. Local sheriffs. Forensics. You name it. Father and I were quarantined nearly a week for fear that we had contracted a rare disease."

"How did they die?" Alyson finally asked.

"Brain hemorrhage," said Nash. "At least, that's what they said."

"Jesus!" Alyson responded. "No wonder you were so weird growing up."

Despite himself, Nash laughed. It was just the levity he needed. "Well, at least I had an excuse for being weird."

"Oh, shut up."

"So, what's next?" asked Kaya.

Alyson pulled the invoice out from her purse. "Back to Roswell and my father's DATs."

Oraibi
Hopi Indian Reservation

After William Big Man left the grave, he walked slowly through the small, empty village to his truck. The rain only seemed to have increased, drenching him. Big Man didn't care. In fact, except for the Pahana, he didn't care much about anything.

As the puddles turned into streams, cutting patterns into the muddy streets, Big Man turned off the main road and approached his truck parked behind a decrepit building. Almost immediately he sensed a presence behind him, stepping out of the shadows.

Big Man ignored the presence, whoever it was. Big Man was good at ignoring things. Still, he opened his soaked jacket a little, revealing the stock of his bone-handled knife.

He continued to his truck.

Once there, as a strong wind whipped through the empty back lot, Big Man spun around, unsheathing the long knife in one fluid motion.

As he held it out before him, a man holding a gun and sporting a bemused expression materialized out of the rain about ten yards behind him. He was big man with a scar running down from his right eyebrow to his cheek—scar tissue sealing his eye shut.

"Nice knife," said the man, his voice thick with a heavy Mexican accent. He stepped closer, raising the small weapon. "Remember me, my friend?"

Big Man did. And he immediately wished he had something more threatening than a knife. "You're no friend of mine. You tricked me. You said you were a follower of the Pahana."

"True believers are the easiest to fool, my big friend."

A sneer crossed Big Man's face. "You said you wouldn't hurt him."

"Things change."

Big Man turned away and opened his car door. As he did so, he couldn't help but feel as if a big fat target had blossomed on his back. The man's name was Garcia. Big Man knew little of him. And what he did know, he didn't like.

"Leaving so soon?" asked Garcia. The Mexican had stepped around the Hopi's truck and appeared at the passenger door. "Let's chat inside. It's a little wet for my taste."

He stood there briefly, thought about his chances of bolting, and didn't like them. The Mexican was unpredictable. Big Man knew that firsthand.

The big Hopi nodded and at Garcia's instruction, dropped the knife outside. The two men slid into the front seat. With the engine off and the wipers silent, the rain should have been comforting. But having a deranged man holding a gun on him was anything but comforting.

Big Man was silent, staring straight ahead.

"Ah, the stoic Indian," said Garcia. "So quiet, so strong. I like that."

"What do you want?" hissed Big Man.

He sensed the Mexican grinning at him. A few seconds later, the man asked, "Who were those people with your sister today?"

"Friends of hers."

"Did you get their names?"

Big Man was silent, wondering just how much to reveal. As he pondered the question, Garcia said, "I suggest you speak up, my friend. Obviously, you don't give a shit about your miserable existence, and no doubt death would be a welcomed relief for you. But how would you feel if your family found out that you had a hand in your grandfather's beating?"

"Nash," said Big Man immediately. "Jeremy and Alyson Nash."

Big Man noticed an expression of surprise on Garcia's face—which quickly passed.

"Now that wasn't so hard, was it?" Garcia said with a sarcastic smile.

"I don't want to see you again," Big Man said.

Garcia opened the truck door and stepped out into the rain. "If you're a good boy and keep this to yourself, you might not."

The Mexican grinned and slipped away into the rain.

Project KRATOS

Reuben Prescott sat in his glass office overlooking KRATOS's cavernous interior, waiting for a phone call. A very important phone call. He tapped his $2,000 Mont Blanc pen impatiently on his chrome and Plexiglas desk, keeping time with the steady beat of the particle accelerator below.

Above and in front of him, outside his glass-enclosed office, he could see the main holographic panel displays that loomed over the heads of the techs and engineers. All were working on the particle accelerator floor behind heavy Plexiglas panels peppered with large workstations holding an array of small wide-screen monitors. The displays kept track of the progress and output of Project KRATOS.

Too much was going wrong too fast, and now an old threat that was deemed gone may be surfacing again.

His phone rang. He snatched it up immediately. "What did you find out?"

"You were right," said Garcia. "She did contact someone. Two people, actually. And you won't believe their names."

"Who?"

"Jeremy and Alyson Nash."

Prescott sat straight up in his chair. *Nash!* Prescott knew the name well. Damn well, and whatever that Hopi woman told Nash was not going to be good for Project KRATOS—or for him.

Shit! First the failed missile attack on Somerton's plane—now this.

"Sir," said Garcia. "What do you want me to do?"

"Nothing. Go back to your primary surveillance. Leave the rest to me."

Prescott knew what he had to do.

He hung up, unlocked his desk drawer, opened it, and pulled out a small card that contained a series of code numbers in non-sequential order. He chose a number third on the list and punched it into his phone. After a series of beeps and buzzes emitted from his receiver, a deep voice came on the line.

"Parker here."

"I have an assignment for you," said Prescott. He looked at his watch. "How soon can you get to the Four Corners area?"

"Within the hour."

"Good. Here's what I want you to do—and do it quietly."

Four Corners Power Plant
Arizona

FBI Special Agent Steven Yarnell knew all too well that the Arizona heat could be brutal on most days. Today was no better. And worse, something unprecedented was happening to the weather. Arizona and record-breaking temperatures were definitely two things you never, ever wanted to hear in the same sentence.

I really need to be stationed somewhere else, he thought as he stood outside of what was once the Four Corners Power Plant Administration building—now a heap of charred smoking rubble. The smoldering ruins only made the heat that much worse.

Can't buy a break, he thought.

The place was a beehive of activity, with federal investigators, police, and plant workers everywhere. It was Yarnell's job to take control of this mess.

Lucky me.

As Yarnell continued surveying the damage—and sweating through his dress shirt—a short, balding man who carried too much weight around his midsection rolled towards him. It was one of the Arizona Public Service crew. Although the police kept most of the workers away from the destruction, Yarnell had allowed one or two of them to be his guide through this tangled mess, some of which he couldn't make heads or tails of.

"What is it?" barked Yarnell.

"There's some people who want to talk to you. They say they need permission to begin their investigation?"

"Damn right they need my permission. Who are they?"

"They're from the EPA."

"EPA? What the hell?" That's all he needed now was some bureaucratic pencil pushers taking up his time and trotting around where they didn't belong. "Tell them to go play with their paperwork somewhere else," Yarnell snorted.

"We're not here to do paperwork," said a stocky 40-ish man with thinning red hair, suddenly appearing behind Yarnell. His face had a five o'clock shadow, which made him look unkempt for a man in his position.

"Who the hell are you?" said Yarnell, now completely and thoroughly annoyed.

Appearing with the man was a rather attractive young woman with a flowing blonde mane and the face of a serious lioness to match. Yarnell was a professional in every sense of the word, but he knew his eyes must have bugged out a bit. He tried not to openly stare at the woman, but she was wearing her official pant suit a little tighter than regulations probably permitted.

She pulled out a wallet and flashed an official looking credential in Yarnell's face. "I'm Paige Chandler with the EPA Criminal Enforcement Division. My partner here is Zack Safford with Homeland Security. We're here to investigate the explosion." She was all business in that suit, and the tone of her voice reflected her government ranking in the EPA. Beautiful or not, to Yarnell she was very much a bureaucratic cog.

He studied the two, perspiration slipping steadily down his cheeks and into his shirt collar, as heat from the fires of the explosion still came at him in waves. He briefly wondered if he should report this to his command field office or, perhaps a better option, let them do whatever they were here to do and just pray they stayed out of his hair.

He sighed, wiped the sweat from his brow, and made an executive decision. "Fine. Just try to stay out of the way. I'll assign an agent to show you around. And for the love of God, please don't disrupt the crime scene."

71

"You've already classified this as a crime?" asked Chandler.

Yarnell pointed to a semi-charred body a few dozen yards away lying in the parking lot. The sight of it, once again, made the bile rise in the back of his throat. "The victim was shot three times. If anything, this appears to be a terrorist crime."

Safford glanced at Chandler and replied, "Then we have work to do. Your cooperation is very much appreciated."

Yarnell dismissively pointed to a field agent currently conducting an interview with a plant worker. "That's Agent Kearny. He'll show you around."

Safford nodded, and as he and Chandler were about to turn away, he paused, and said, "Oh, by the way. The press will be here soon. Perhaps we shouldn't use the word *terrorism* in their presence. Makes them nervous."

Yarnell was about to tell him he would use any damn word he wanted, but he knew the little bureaucratic prick was right. Best to keep this as low-profile as possible.

Chinle, Arizona

The briefly cleared skies over the stretch of highway from the Hopi Reservation to the Four Corners area turned threatening once again. Massive gray columns stacked high into the stratosphere, shouldered out the blue skies, and Nash knew they were in for a hideous thunder and lightning storm. Indeed, as the Ford Bronco approached the town of Chinle, a small outpost town at the edge of Arizona, flashes of lightening illuminated the underbellies of the swollen clouds.

Nash drove past a dusty, bullet-riddled sign on the side of the road that read: *Welcome to Chinle—Where the Water Flows Out*. Nash would later learn that the small town was located right at the mouth of the Canyon de Chelly, whose towering walls dropped to the level of the Chinle wash.

"I don't know about you," Alyson said as they entered the sleepy town, "but I'm hungry."

"You're always hungry," flipped Nash.

"I'm also hypoglycemic, and you know it."

"I think you're just addicted to cheeseburgers," said Nash.

"I'll pretend I didn't hear that."

"We'll stop for some food," soothed Kaya in the backseat. "And be nice to your sister, Jeremy. I like her."

"She knows I'm kidding."

"Unfortunately, I'm used to it," laughed Alyson, glancing back at Kaya. "He's teased me all my life."

"Well, we're going to have to break him of some bad habits," said Kaya, and both women laughed. Although Nash felt his face redden, he had to admit he enjoyed Kaya taken an interest in him, even if it was to playfully protect his sister.

"There's an A&W in the center of town," added Kaya. "It has a drive-thru."

"Mmm," Alyson said, smacking her lips. "Root beer and burgers. Perfect!"

Nash just shook his head. Except for the guilty pleasure of a McDonald's milkshake now and then, he was not a fan of fast food, but it appeared the women had ganged up on him, and he had little choice.

A few minutes later he found the A&W, and ten minutes after that they were back on the road again. Everyone had a burger in their hands, and the Bronco smelled like heaven.

They all downed their burgers quickly, and Nash idly sipped his root beer while anxiously watching the rapidly darkening sky. Bold streaks of lightening tore through the gathering blackness.

"The storm ahead is getting worse. I think we're in for some serious rain."

"Should we break for a commercial now, Mr. Weatherman?" asked Kaya, and now both women snorted with laughter.

Nash shook his head. As he did so, he saw something in the road. Something burning. Flares. *What the hell?*

As Nash approached, he saw that there was some kind of road work in progress.

At night?

A tall workman holding a "Slow" sign appeared out of nowhere, and Nash dutifully slowed down. As they drove closer, a tall workman, standing next to a black Lincoln Navigator, waved them down.

Nash pulled up to a tall strapping man with a cropped haircut wearing a bright orange road worker's vest over his rippled arms. Nash couldn't make out if he was Asian or Hispanic. *Probably Eurasian,* he thought. Whatever he was, he had a natural tan, was buff—and imposing.

Nash frowned and rolled down his window.

"What's up?" he asked.

"You have to detour," ordered the worker. "The highway is washed out up ahead. Take the dirt road there on your left and follow the detour signs back to the highway."

Nash nodded and turned the SUV onto the dirt road as instructed, frustrated by yet another set back. He drove cautiously along the graded dirt road, as small, skeletal twigs and branches from various scrub trees and bushes slapped the side of the Bronco. As the road grew darker and the dirt road became narrower, Nash grew increasingly anxious.

"So, where's the detour sign?" Alyson asked, sitting up.

"We might have missed it in the dark," Nash said, although he doubted that. Still, it could have been hidden behind a gnarled tree, or blown down in the storm.

"I see lights ahead," said Kaya, leaning forward between the two front seats and pointing.

Indeed, from around a bend in the road, two lights had appeared.

"Headlights," observed Nash. "Maybe they could tell us how to get back on the highway." Although it was encouraging to see some signs of life in the total darkness, Nash was wary about approaching anyone out here.

Something's not right, he thought.

"It's coming toward us," said Alyson. "Fast!"

She was right. The headlights were rapidly approaching, and as the vehicle came within the range of their own headlights, Nash could see that it wasn't a car. Indeed, it had six wheels—two in front and four in the rear—supporting what looked like an armored modified Humvee.

There wasn't much road, and the damn thing was driving right down the middle of it—and fast. *Sweet Jesus.*

"They're going to hit us, Jeremy!" screamed Alyson.

He could see that. And he could also see someone leaning

out the rear driver side window and aiming something at them. A weapon of some kind, and Nash's instincts were immediate.

He turned the wheel hard to the right, into the twisted brush, and screamed "Everyone! Down!"

He caught a brief flash from the weapon, which silently spit out a stream of objects that peppered the windshield and the driver's side of the Bronco. Whatever the hell it was spitting out, Nash didn't want to know. He continued plowing through the underbrush, lifting his head just high enough to see. The massive Humvee rocketed by, too big and cumbersome to stop on a dime. As it passed, it fired again sending a sporadic blast of what seemed to Nash to be small darts, but he had no way of knowing since he was busy dodging the smaller trees and massive boulders.

When the Humvee was a safe distance behind him, Nash pulled back onto the dirt road, looking in the rearview mirror. The damn thing was turning around, crushing anything in its way. Nash accelerated, kicking up dirt and debris. The way before him was black, and it appeared one of his headlights had been lost, either hitting a bush or maybe from those odd dart things.

Either way, he was out a light and it took all of his concentration to navigate the darkened back road.

He glanced quickly in the rearview mirror but could see nothing except a cloud of dust and a massive set of headlights. And they were getting closer.

"What's this road?" Nash asked, yelling above the strained roar of the Bronco's engine.

"It's the road to the Canyon de Chelly," Kaya replied, sticking her head between the two front seats.

"So, you know where the hell we're going?"

"Yes."

"Good. Now stay down, they're gaining on us."

And just as he said that something crashed through the rear window, zipped between the seats, and out the front windshield.

"Holy shit!"

Nash briefly lost control of the vehicle, but somehow kept it from flipping. If Kaya had still been sitting between the seats, she would be dead.

He glanced briefly at Alyson, who was curled in the front seat, head down.

Nash set his jaw, aiming the vehicle into the darkness, but this time he swerved a little hoping to keep from being such an easy target for the shooter. The dirt road turned suddenly rocky, and despite the darkness, Nash sensed massive walls rising up on either side. The dirt road had entered the canyon as a light rain began to fall.

Not a good place to be, he thought, *with a storm coming.*

Behind him, he saw the Humvee enter the canyon as well, bouncing over the rock-strewn path and dry wash gullies. The military vehicle was better equipped to handle off-road driving, but so far, the Bronco was holding up.

Nash patted the steering wheel. *Hang in there, old boy.*

Within a few seconds, the rain turned into a downpour. Nash strained to see ahead, fearing that if a massive boulder suddenly appeared out of the dark, he would have little chance to avoid it.

"Pray that we don't hit anything," Nash intoned, fighting the wheel. "Pray hard."

"They're getting closer," reported Kaya.

Despite himself, Nash risked a glance into his rearview mirror and saw their pursuers had appeared in a cloud of dust at the mouth of the canyon, headlights blazing towards them.

Just then a twisted stump of a lightning-blasted oak tree appeared out of the darkness before them. Nash yanked the wheel hard, just narrowly avoiding it.

"Turn off your lights," cried Kaya suddenly.

"What?"

"Turn out your lights. Let's not give the bastards anything to follow."

"If I turn out the lights, we'll die, and we'll have done the job for them."

"Trust me," she begged, leaning forward through the seats. "I have a feeling about this. I always trust my feelings."

"Well, I have a feeling that if I turn out the lights, we'll all die in a horrible fireball," yelled Nash, fighting the wheel again as they dipped down into a narrow gully, "It's pitch black."

"No, it's not. We can use the lightening flashes to navigate," she reasoned. She put a hand on his shoulder. "Trust me, and trust The Great Spirit."

Nash would have laughed if he wasn't so focused on picking his way through the rock-strewn canyon floor. He risked another glance behind them and saw that the big machine was getting closer. Although the Humvee was bigger and less agile, the smaller obstacles in the canyon would pose less of a problem. The Humvee could plow right over those, whereas Nash had to twist and turn picking his way.

Which meant, Nash knew, that they were gaining. And rapidly.

Nash sighed heavily and would have prayed hard himself had he believed prayers worked. He turned out the lights, and immediately the canyon plunged into darkness.

Bad idea, he thought.

"Keep going," ordered Kaya. "Trust me."

Just as Nash was about to throw the lights back on, his heart hammering with fear, a sheet of lightning rippled across the sky in front of him, illuminating the canyon. Nash, to his great relief—and perhaps awe—saw that there appeared to be no major obstacles directly before them.

"Keep going," breathed Kaya, resting a hand on his shoulder. Admittedly, her touch had a calmly effect on Nash. "Follow the dry riverbed."

"The river?" asked Alyson. "In this rain? I don't think that's a good—"

"Trust me," Kaya replied firmly.

This time, both Nash and Alyson sighed. Kaya patted his shoulder, and he had a sense she was actually smiling in the back-seat behind them.

Amazing, he thought.

With their pursuers still on their tail, Nash forgot about Kaya's soothing touch and focused on keeping them alive. As lightning continued to illuminate the sky, almost on command, Nash followed Kaya's next instruction and cut hard across the canyon. Soon, they were following an offshoot canyon down a riverbed that, miraculously, was still dry.

"It's dammed," informed Kaya, smiling in the rearview mirror at Nash. "No flooding."

Nash just shook his head. Within moments, the lights of the Humvee disappeared somewhere behind them, completely unaware that Nash had veered out of the main canyon.

He shook his head again.

This woman was unbelievable.

Highway 191
Outside Chinle, Arizona

Just after the Bronco had pulled off the main highway and onto the bogus detour, Addison Parker removed an ultra high-tech device from his pocket. It was a Senao unit, a 'low probability of interception' device that would block any type of covert or overt surveillance of his phone communications.

And in Parker's line of business, he could not afford to ever have his communication intercepted.

Parker punched a series of letters and numbers into the device, spoke orders into it, and then waited.

Parker's team was good. No doubt his targets were dead at this very moment. At that thought, he smiled inwardly. Parker would not deny that he drew a lot of pleasure from taking life. He knew that made him a sadistic sociopath, as modern psychologists called it. Parker just thought of it as sport. Hunting humans. His trusted, hand-assembled team all had similar attributes. Granted, the trust extended only so far. He knew each would kill the other for a cheap thrill. That is, if there wasn't so much money on the line. They were assassins, hired killers, and this was just another contract paid for by a client.

Tonight was special. Tonight they were testing a new shoulder held AA-12 electromagnetic rail gun on their latest target. It was virtually silent—and very deadly—using a pulsed power system utilizing electromagnetic energy similar to what powers many modern roller coasters. He was interrupted in his thoughts when his Senao unit squawked to life.

"Team A," said a gravelly voice.

"Status?" Parker asked.

"We lost them."

Parker frowned. Quite honestly, he had not expected that reply. Rarely did his team fail. But, like any good assassin for hire, Parker always had a back-up plan. "I'll send in Team B."

"Ten four," was the reply, and Parker clicked off.

Canyon de Chelly, Arizona

The rain was coming down in sheets now, making it even more difficult to see the road ahead. "We need to get out of here," said Nash. "This is a flash flood waiting to happen."

"There's a trail coming up that off-road vehicles sometimes use. It leads up to the high desert."

"Sure. Just let me know when you see the exit sign," said Nash sardonically.

"It's next to the gas station," commented Kaya.

"Gas station?" questioned Nash.

Kaya actually laughed, and Alyson shook her head. "For someone who's a world-renowned skeptic, he sure is gullible."

Now both women laughed, and Nash could only shake his head. *Women*, he thought. *I'm doing all I can to keep them alive, and they're cracking jokes.* "When you two are done making jokes, could you keep a sharp eye out for the Humvee. I doubt they've given up."

"There's no sign of them anywhere," informed Alyson, turning in her seat. "So can we still make fun of you?"

Nash shook his head again and willed himself to see through the inky blackness. Although the lightning still came, it was doing so with less frequency, forcing Nash to slow down. Luckily, Alyson was right—the Humvee was nowhere to be seen.

"I wish we had more light," he said.

And just as the words left his mouth, the road before them lit up like it was daylight. Nash stopped the Bronco and all three looked up into the sky.

Kaya spoke first. "Be careful what you wish for..."

It was a small black helicopter, and it was descending out of the low, dark clouds like a bat out of hell, shining its light over them. And just as the light found them, something else found them as well.

"They're shooting at us!" screamed Alyson.

Indeed, more of those *whooshing* projectiles peppered the top of the Bronco. Nash instinctively yanked the Bronco to the right. At least he had some light, and he could see where he was going.

"Who the hell are these people?" he cried out, alternately scanning the rock-strewn canyon and looking up at the racing chopper.

"Just keep going," ordered Kaya, "and keep your lights off!"

"Why? We're already lit up like a Christmas tree."

"Trust me," Kaya replied as the pings of small darts continued to hit the roof above her head. "And drive as fast as you can. Deeper into the canyon."

She sounded more confident than Nash felt, and so he complied, wondering what the hell Kaya had up her sleeve.

The chopper stayed on their tail as Nash swerved the Bronco back and forth, although he wondered if it was doing any good. The black chopper seemed to easily keep pace with them. Indeed, it seemed to drop even lower, hovering just above their vehicle. Nash expected to hear its landing skids hit the roof of the Bronco at any minute

It was bad enough driving in the dark through the driving rain, but now the dust and rocks kicked up by the low-flying helicopter dropped visibility to near zero.

Like driving with your eyes closed, thought Nash, leaning forward over the steering wheel, peering through the windshield. He knew at the reckless speed they were going that if they hit a boulder or a tree, the steering wheel was going through his chest.

But he pressed forward, using the occasional glimpses through the rain and dust to pick his way around the rock debris field of the canyon wash. His knuckles, he briefly saw, were bone white.

"Keep going," yelled Kaya. "Faster!"

"Faster? You've got be kidding."

"Trust me, please!"

Nash shook his head, but there was something about Kaya that he did trust. The woman seemed to know this country like the back of her hand.

He hit the gas, flooring it, kicking up a massive plume of mud behind them. Above them, the helicopter followed suit, flying low and fast, keeping pace. Little darts still peppered the roof.

"Where the hell are you taking us—*Holy shit!*"

Then he saw it.

The canyon took a sudden, almost ninety-degree turn, and looming before them was a stone obelisk reaching hundreds of feet into the sky. The 800-foot-tall red sandstone Spider Rock, as it was called, seemed to rise straight up out of the wash and into Nash's path.

"Hit your brakes!" yelled Kaya.

But Nash was already in the process of lifting his foot from the gas to the brakes. He mashed it hard and slid sideways toward the monolith's base. In a hail of debris and driving rain, they stopped with plenty of room to spare.

The black helicopter wasn't so lucky.

It's pilot had been focused entirely on the SUV and had neglected to spot the threat looming before it. Nash saw the chopper try to steer around the red obelisk, but to no avail. Its tail section clipped the side and threw the distressed chopper into a wild spin. After just a few wild gyrations it smashed headlong into the adjoining canyon wall—and exploded into a massive flaming ball.

"That did *not* just happen!" cried Alyson, and Nash saw the burning glow reflected in his sister's eyes. "Should we try to help them?"

"Help? Help what? Whoever was in the chopper..."

Above the sounds of the burning chopper, Nash heard

something else. Something thunderously loud that caused the very ground to shake.

"What's that?"

"Flash flood!" cried Kaya.

Nash looked east to where Kaya pointed and saw it. Through the lightening flashes and dagger-like rain, a great wall of water roiled and churned towards them. The ten-foot wall of water pushed before it uprooted trees, rocks, boulders—and anything it could pick up along the way.

"There's our exit!" shouted Kaya, pointing toward a trail that seemed to lead up and out of the canyon. The dirt was heavily rutted through years of use by all-terrain vehicles.

The only problem was that it was going to be a race to the dirt ramp.

"Go, go, go!" shouted Kaya.

Nash turned on the Bronco's headlight, aimed the vehicle at the dirt ramp, and stomped on the gas as hard as he could.

They hurtled recklessly down the rapidly-filling riverbed. At least now he had a headlight. Which was a good thing. The path here was heavily strewn with boulders and tree stumps. Once a coyote dashed madly away, its wild yellow eyes glinting in the high beam.

They were now racing directly across the wide river. To Nash's left was a sight too horrible to contemplate, and certainly a sight he never wanted to see again.

Ever.

The wall of water growing exponentially the closer it got to them, pushed more debris of all sorts before it. Utter destruction for anything in its path.

And they were in its path.

If it were possible for Nash to mash on the gas even harder, he would have. As it was, he was already flooring it, hurling fast enough to barely give himself time to dodge the various obstacles that appeared in his path.

Rain continued driving sideways across their windshield. The ground was no doubt shaking, but the Bronco was bouncing and turning so much that it was impossible for Nash to tell.

They hit a smooth patch of ground, and Nash aimed the vehicle at the rapidly approaching trail. Next to him, in his peripheral vision, he could sense the water nearly upon them.

We're not going to make it!

Alyson screamed next to him. So did Kaya. Nash couldn't look. He knew the water had risen above him. It was only a matter of nanoseconds before they would be swept away, to be pulverized into a million pieces.

But he could see the trail ahead of him. And if he could still see the trail, and if they were still on four wheels, then Nash was going to do everything he could—

Slam!

A massive wave of water crashed behind them. Behind them, because Nash miraculously shot up the steep dirt trail and above the towering wall of water, which surged below them, continuing on through the canyon.

About halfway up the canyon wall, Nash eased up on the gas. He still couldn't believe they were alive.

"Remind me to buy you something nice for your birthday, big Bro," breathed Alyson. "That was some seriously awesome driving."

"No," replied Nash. "That was some desperate driving."

"Either way," offered Kaya. "I could kiss you."

And Nash nearly said, *"Please do,"* but the path before him suddenly forked and he was forced to make a decision. To the left, the road seemed to lead up through a rough chasm, although the road wasn't much more than a narrow game trail. Before them was a wider and better maintained, although still deeply rutted, canyon trail.

Kaya saw his hesitation and pointed up the main path. "Keep following this road."

Nash had gone up perhaps fifty feet, with the sounds of the flash flood surging beneath them, when he was suddenly blinded by a pair of oncoming headlights.

Heading straight for them was the six-wheeled, armored Humvee.

"Jeremy!" cried Alyson.

"Hang on!" he yelled.

Nash slammed the Bronco into reverse, feverishly backing down the steep dirt trail. The Humvee followed, bounding easily over the deep ruts.

Veering dangerously close to the trail's edge, and easily a fifty-foot wall to the surging river below, Nash made it back to the fork in the dirt road.

He threw the vehicle back into first, gave the screaming machine a lot of gas, and soon they were crashing up the narrow trail and into the wooded ravine. Tree branches slapped the body of the Bronco, which bounded over smaller rocks. Nash prayed like hell that the vehicle would hold up.

Behind them, in his rearview mirror and through the tangle of branches, he saw something amazing. Horrifying, certainly, but amazing. The Humvee had turned into the ravine as well, its lights blazing, but it appeared stuck. One moment it was there, lights blazing, engine growling, and then the next it was gone.

Then Nash saw why. The rising river, which even now was flooding into the ravine, had swept the massive machine away.

Sweet Jesus, he thought.

He pressed forward through the tangle of undergrowth.

For now, they had escaped, but Nash gloomily wondered what else lay waiting for them above.

Highway 191
Outside Chinle, Arizona

When Parker saw the red fire ball appear down the Canyon, he feared the worst. He tried to reach the chopper but received nothing except static on his LPI unit. He next tried the Humvee, but it too wouldn't respond. He couldn't believe this was happening.

Four of his team were likely lost.

He clicked off his LPI unit, climbed back into his Lincoln Navigator, and drove off. He wasn't looking forward to the conversation he was going to have with his client. He made a mental note to make sure that whoever this Jeremy Nash was, he would pay for his unit's embarrassing performance.

This was no longer business.

Now it was personal.

Phoenix, Arizona

It was hot.

Too hot, thought Bryan Henderson as he sat in his second-floor office of MultiPhase Limited, a network security company he had founded ten years earlier. He was poring over the reports from the latest run of the Web Bot program left for him by his assistant—even as he was pouring sweat.

He loosened the buttons of his sport shirt as he scanned the printout. His spacious office building was equipped with solar energy panels that made it almost energy self-sufficient in the Arizona sun. However, the building was now drawing from the power grid, due to the constant overcast, muggy, and rainy weather Phoenix was experiencing. The air conditioning was not doing its job due to the high humidity in the air. The offices were deliberately kept hotter than the IT room downstairs to keep the computers and network servers from overheating.

He would have said screw the computers if his livelihood wasn't dependent upon them.

Henderson's large office looked more like an architect's drafting room than a traditional executive office. That is, until someone looked at the wall directly to his left, a wall that contained a detailed poster of the Mayan Calendar showing the Mayan Long Count, along with a Time Wave Zero graph projecting the end of time.

Not your traditional executive's office, and Henderson liked that about himself. He was *free to be me*, which was one of the reasons he had started his own company a decade ago.

On the wall to his right was a large schematic and interpretation of the Hopi Prophesy Rock, and spread across two drafting tables was a half-year's result of his specialized Web Bot program. A book on Nostradamus was presently being used as a paperweight to keep one end of the long printout from rolling back up...along with a Bible to hold down the other end.

Contradictions, he thought. *Life was full of them, until you dug a little deeper and saw the beauty of the Grand Design.*

Henderson irritably wiped the small beads of sweat from his brow and scanned the highlighted words on the printout. These were associations of target words that his Web Bot Program had uncovered on the internet. The web bot was particularly adept at finding key words kept hidden on obscure servers.

Henderson was the first to admit his obsession with the end times predictions. *Hell,* he thought, *we should all be obsessed with the predictions.*

"My God," he often told friends. "What if they are right?"

But Henderson wasn't a scholar, and he wasn't even a novice archaeologist. He was just a businessman with an obsession, an obsession that attracted hundreds of thousands of people to his monthly *End Times* blog.

Turns out I'm not the only one obsessed with the end of the world, he mused. Ultimately, he hoped to do some good with his research. What that good would turn out to be, he didn't know.

But he was going to find out.

Hell, we're all going to find out soon.

Now, with the afternoon sweltering and sweat dripping down the center of his back, he studied this latest set of search results. The resulting words and phrases were of no surprise to Henderson; after all, they were like the results of the target words he'd used in the past year: *Hopi, Hopi Stones, Prophecy Rock,* and *Purification.*

Prior runs on these very target words acted as a baseline for the Web Bot predictions. There was nothing new on this latest search, but Henderson whispered the phrases and words as he read, almost out of reverence—then stopped. He had come across an entirely new word. And not necessarily a word, but a name.

"Nash?" he said under his breath. A name he knew well. *What the hell is he doing in the search results?*

Henderson didn't know, but he was going to find out.

Roswell, New Mexico

Whor the fortunate three arrived in Roswell, they spent some time at the sheriff's office reporting the attacks. They all made statements, and photographs were taken of their damaged Bronco. Because people had likely been killed, the sheriff asked for the three of them to stay in town, as there would be follow up questions. But for now, they were free to go.

As they pulled off to Alyson's suburban home, the full weight of the night hit them all. Within minutes of arrival, they all crashed hard for three or four hours.

Nash's last thought, before a desperate need for sleep overtook him, was that someone had spent a lot of time and energy trying to kill them.

But who? And why?

Hours later, each holding a steaming mug of freshly ground and brewed coffee, Nash and Kaya watched as Alyson rummaged through a small trunk in the attic. Nash thought Kaya looked cute with bedhead. They all had bedhead, and after the night they had had, they each had dispensed with personal grooming upon waking.

"I'm pretty sure I saw same digital audio tapes here somewhere," Alyson said. She alternately searched through the trunk and sipped from her coffee mug, some of which splashed over the back of her hand. If it hurt her, she didn't seem to mind or notice.

"Aha! Here they are."

She removed a small metal box and set it on the wooden floor, sitting cross-legged next to it. She set her coffee down and opened the box. Inside, Nash saw that it contained several credit card sized cassette tapes. She picked up the cassettes—or the DATs—and began reading the descriptions written in her father's handwriting.

"Let's see. Navajo ceremonies. Zuni chants. Apache incantations—oh, here—Hopi chants."

"Good," said Kaya. "Where's your father's DAT player?"

"I don't know," Alyson replied. "It wasn't in his things."

"Where can we find one?"

"In a place you find all things archaic," said Nash, who was quite familiar with the machines, since he often used them in his own research. "The public library."

"Then let's go," said Kaya.

"Can I at least finish my coffee first?"

"Bring it with you," said Nash. "C'mon. We'll take my rental."

Once at the surprisingly large and quite modern Roswell Public Library, Alyson led them to the archive room. Nash located a DAT player, which was connected to a computer in a small cubicle. When they were all seated around it, he expertly inserted the small cassette and pressed *play*.

The three listened as each track of the tape played through different Hopi chants, and over the next twenty minutes, Kaya named each chant as it played—Father Sun chant, Arrow Dance, and Eagle Dance.

"Nothing unusual in them," she said, shrugging.

"There's one more," said Nash.

As it was coming to an end, Kaya shrugged. "That was the Snake Dance chant. It sounds as it should to me."

"Nothing out of the ordinary?" asked Nash.

She shook her head, but then frowned. "Actually, play it again.

Something is standing out now that I think about it. It's been a while since I heard the Snake Dance Chant."

Nash played it again, and near the end of the recording Kaya suddenly sat forward. "There! Stop it there!"

Nash did as he was told. "What did you hear?" Admittedly, to his uninitiated ears, one Native American chant sounded much like all the others he had heard, with only slight variations.

"The sound at the end. It's wrong."

"Wrong? How?"

"At the closing of the Snake Dance, the War Priest is supposed to whirl a bullroar in the air."

"What the hell is a bullroar?" asked Alyson.

"It's a thick tablet, pointed or terraced on one end, with a cotton string tied to a handle. The War Priest swings it in the air to create an awesome groaning sound. And that sound we heard was not the sound of a bullroar. It was something else."

Nash had heard it, too. "Like the sound of crickets."

"Yes! Something like that."

Nash didn't believe in a *sixth sense* or *gut feelings* or anything else that couldn't be scientifically proven but, in that moment, he sure as hell felt like someone was watching them. He glanced up sharply over the cubicle wall—and saw a man.

A disturbingly familiar man.

"Hang on," said Nash, and dashed down the long row of mostly empty cubicles, to the surprise of his sister and Kaya. He heard Alyson whisper harshly after him, but Nash was already halfway down the row.

The man dashed off, and Nash picked up his pace. As he rounded the aisle of cubicles, he found himself hemmed in by a long row of bookshelves. Through the shelves, he saw the robed figure dashing away through the library. Nash hung another left at the end of the fiction aisle, flashing past two teenagers necking against a row of Tom Clancy novels. The girl gasped and adjusted her blouse. Nash passed them and dashed into the front of the library. A surprised desk clerk looked at him. Nash smiled at her weakly, gasping for breath. The mysterious man was gone. He took a quick peek out the smoky glass door, but the street was empty. No use following. The man could have easily gone in any direction and disappeared down the alleys to either side of the library.

"Is everything okay?" asked the elderly librarian.

Despite himself, Nash jumped. She had appeared directly behind him.

"Yeah," said Nash. "Just fine."

Back at the cubicles, both women looked at Nash curiously. "What the hell was that all about?" asked his sister.

Nash filled them in on the robed figure watching them—the same robed figure he had seen before.

"You think that nutjob is following us?" asked Alyson.

"Hard not to," said Nash.

"Forget him," said Kaya. "Alyson had a revelation just after you decided to play hide-and-go-seek."

Nash was about to defend himself but looked at his sister instead. "What revelation?"

"Ever heard of Nine Inch Nails?"

"Nine what?" asked Nash.

"Nine Inch Nails. A famous hard rock band."

"Maybe. I don't know. And what are you getting at?"

"Patience, brother. A while back, as part of the launch of a new album, the group hid clues for their fans to find promoting their new songs. One such clue was hidden on a flash drive left in the rest room at one of their concerts."

"This is a side of you I never knew, Sis. Both a square librarian and a hard rock groupie?"

"I'm a fan, okay? Anyway, the drive had a previously unknown music cut at the end that trailed off with the sound of crickets."

Nash perked up. "What was the significance of the crickets?"

"The crickets were really some kind of cipher, and when it was decoded, it gave a phone number for fans to call."

"Great," said Nash disdainfully. "Maybe there's a Hopi Hotline somewhere that we can call in."

"You're impossible," said Alyson.

"No, I'm realistic. Even if there is something in this recording, which I seriously doubt, how do we decode it?"

"Hey, you're the one with all the contacts, big brother. Don't you know someone who can help?"

Nash thought about it, and a name did come to mind. As he pulled out his iPhone, he found himself shaking his head. *How the hell does someone like me—a known skeptic—approach a respectable scholar with something like this?*

It had to be a trusted scholar—a scholar with some technical resources—and Nash knew just the guy.

He tried make the call. "Damn. Battery's dead." He walked over to his briefcase, snapped it open, rummaged through it, and found his charger. A moment later, his phone was plugged in, and the moment he turned it on his cell phone beeped. He had a text message.

He pulled it up. It read: *Call me, Bryan.*

"Shit."

"What's wrong?" asked Alyson.

"It's Bryan Henderson. I promised him I would go to his father's funeral last week. I was stuck in Europe and forgot to call him."

"How unlike you," said Alyson sarcastically, and Nash knew he had a sort of bad reputation among his friends and family for not getting back to people. Nash, after all, could lose himself for days in his research. He thought it was a unique quirk. Apparently, other people found it annoying.

Nash ignored her comment. Instead, he checked the text message. Three hours ago. Nash didn't know how long his phone had been dead, but obviously his friend had texted during that period.

He quickly typed out a short apology, told his friend he would get to him when he got a chance, and sent it off. Then he scrolled through his phone book, looking for his contact. "Actually," he said, "I just might know someone who could help—"

His phone rang. It was Bryan Henderson. Nash debated not taking it. There were, after all, people trying to kill them. Surely Bryan would understand.

"Aren't you going to get it?" asked Alyson.

"It's Bryan—"

"Just get it. It might be important."

Nash sighed and clicked over. "Jeremy. This is Bryan."

"Hey, I'm sorry I—"

But his friend cut him off. "I need to see you."

"I can't. I'm in the middle of—"

"I have to talk to you, man."

Nash frowned, noting a level of hysteria in his friend's voice that normally not there. "What's going on?"

"I've found something about your family concerning the Hopi End of Times."

Nash was certain he hadn't heard correctly. His face must have registered his bewilderment because Alyson leaned forward and mouthed *"What?"* But Nash irritably waved his nosy sister off.

"Say again?"

"You heard me right the first time, Jeremy. And the less we say over the phone, the better."

"Bryan, you're not making a lot of sense."

"I know. But we can't talk about it over the phone. I need to show you. How fast can you get to Phoenix?"

Tucson, Arizona

Reuben Prescott looked impatiently at his watch.

He didn't like to be kept waiting, and Addison Parker was doing just that. He was sitting anxiously at his desk at the headquarters of E-Squared, a *green* research and development company. They implemented alternative energy initiatives employing solar, wind, and geo-thermal sources throughout the Southwest and Four Corners States.

Prescott needed confirmation of Nash's death to assuage the mounting pressure from the Chairman of The Committee—pressure he didn't need.

The Committee was nothing to fool with. Its black hand reached into every aspect of the marketplace—technology, agriculture, food processing, consumer goods, banking, and a host of other markets, including energy.

And energy was Prescott's responsibility—a responsibility that paid enormously well. Project KRATOS would supply an endless supply of almost free energy, soon to be controlled by The Committee to secure its far-reaching goals and objectives.

Far-reaching and, some would argue, nefarious.

Prescott thought of the ramifications of failure and the Committee's reaction, but it was something he didn't want to dwell on. And now, a name from the past had resurfaced that could place in jeopardy over twenty years of work by Prescott and The Committee.

Waiting for confirmation of the death of a man—two women as well—was hell on the nerves.

Prescott needed a drink. He also needed to hear good news. Good news in this case would be hearing that the problem had been eliminated.

His cell phone rang on the encrypted line. He answered.

"Go ahead," he said.

"The target escaped."

"Escaped?"

"Yes, sir. And I lost some men in the process."

Prescott could barely believe what he was hearing. "We hired your team because of its reputation. But I'm wondering now if that reputation was a bit exaggerated."

"Tread carefully, sir."

Prescott realized he might have gone a little too far. Parker was, after all, a notorious hired killer—a killer who had apparently just lost some team members.

"Fine, do you know where the target is now?"

"I lost him."

Prescott held his tongue. Instead, he said, "The target will surface again soon." Prescott leaned forward over his desk. "And when he does, I expect you to do your job."

Nash picked up his Cirrus SR 20 that he kept in a hangar at the Roswell Airport and left there when he went to Europe. He submitted his flight plan, did his usual preflight inspection of the plane, got everyone on board, and waited for clearance. Once it came, Nash taxied out onto the runway, and soon they were flying at five thousand feet.

"So, who is this guy, anyway?" asked Alyson. She was staring out the passenger side window. Ceiling and visibility were unlimited. The desert below looked majestic and endless. Kaya sat silently in the back, looking pale. The Hopi girl had made it known that flying was not one of her favorite past times.

"Bryan is a good friend. He was also my drinking buddy in college."

Nash went on to explain that Bryan Henderson was a tall gangly Welshmen who could drink anyone—including the massive football players—under the table. He was also a mathematical genius with a warped sense of humor. Like the time he wrote code that posed as a security exploit—a program that identifies security flaws in a computer system—to all the workstations at the University. Being a supposed security exploit, it slipped by IT security and seemed to erase the hard drive of every University workstation. It was just a spoof. The drives were not erased, only looked like it, but it threw the entire school into a tizzy—and Bryan was nearly dismissed.

"Sounds like a barrel of laughs," said Alyson, rolling her eyes.

"Too many laughs, actually. He was always looking for a good time, and during his senior year in college he got into psychedelics—mushrooms, to be exact—and immersed himself in all kinds of native esoteric philosophies." Nash paused briefly as he adjusted their direction. "The drugs and his search for some higher meaning of life burned him out the last year of college. He never graduated. We hooked up several years later, and he seemed to regain a sense of balance. He went on to become a mathematician and a damn good one, studying, on his own, ciphers and codes—especially how they were applied to numerology and ancient numbering systems."

"And he knows something about our parents' deaths?"

"That's what he said."

"I don't know," said Alyson, who was never one to mince words. "Sounds like a flake."

Nash grinned and looked back at his other passenger. Kaya was sitting there rigidly. Her pretty face was drained of color. "How you doing back there?"

She shook her head. "When do we land?" She sounded nothing like the confident woman who navigated him through the canyon.

"In about ninety minutes," Nash said. "Look out at the scenery below. You don't get to see scenery like this every day."

"Thanks," she replied weakly. "But I'd rather not. And for the love of God keep your eyes pointed forward."

"What do you think I might hit?" Nash asked. "A UFO?"

He complied with her request as he didn't want to make her any more anxious. Nash never enjoyed flying with nervous passengers. They had a way of bringing down the natural high he had when he flew.

"Not funny," said Kaya.

"Not even a little?" asked Nash.

"Not even a little."

Yeah, she was definitively blowing his high. Nash sighed and aimed the plane west towards Phoenix.

Phoenix, Arizona

Nash landed at Sky Harbor Airport without incident—to the utter relief of Kaya. After making arrangements for his plane, the three caught a cab outside the general aviation terminal and headed for the offices of MultiPhase.

"You two sure keep things interesting," said Kaya on the cab ride over.

Nash never meant to keep things interesting. Truth be told, he preferred dusty libraries and working at his computer over running for his life.

Twenty minutes later they were in the MultiPhase company lobby. Nash had phoned ahead, and Henderson was waiting for them. The tall Welshman was dressed yuppie casual—pressed khakis, slip-on moccasins, and a green Izod sport shirt. The two old friends exchanged pleasantries as Nash introduced Alyson and Kaya.

Nash could have been mistaken, but it appeared his sister and his old college friend, judging by the broad smiles they shared, seemed quite taken by each other.

Great, thought Nash. *The last thing I need is a lovestruck sister.* Then he thought of Kaya and the eye contacts they had shared. *Fine, so I'm no better.*

As Henderson led them back to his office, through a maze of polished floors and mirrored walls, a heavy-set Latino man in his early forties appeared from a side office. The man approached Henderson determinedly, and Nash couldn't help but notice the deep scar running from the man's right eyebrow down to his cheek. The scar virtually sealed his right eye shut.

Nash found himself staring. *Sweet Jesus.*

"Here's the report, Mr. Henderson."

Nash's friend absently took a thick file folder from the man and clapped him heartily on the back. "Let me introduce you to Mike Garcia," Henderson said. "He's been my assistant ever since I started the infamous Web Bot Project. I don't know what I'd do without him."

The big Latino looked directly at Nash with his one good eye, and Nash was damned if he didn't feel a shiver run up his spine.

You're just stereotyping him, Nash thought. *Just because the man has a scar, that doesn't make him evil.* Still, it brought back unpleasant memories of the last scarred man he had the misfortune to meet.

Interestingly, the man cocked his head slightly, and Nash thought he caught a glimmer of recognition on Garcia's face.

No way I forget a face like that.

But Garcia didn't say anything, and soon they were once again following Henderson's lanky frame. He led them through a maze of cubicles and finally into a massive corner office. Nash couldn't help but notice the plethora of charts and diagrams plastered all over the walls.

"Most offices I've seen have those cheesy motivational posters," said Nash. "This is a nice touch."

Henderson grinned. "These are a hobby of mine."

"Collecting graphs and charts?" said Alyson, walking over to one. "Nice, um, hobby."

The tall man shook his head. "Boy, I'm getting it from both of the Nashs!" Henderson slipped over and stood next to Alyson.

A little too close, thought Nash.

As Nash's friend pointed to the chart directly in front of Alyson, he gently rested the palm of his other hand on the small of her back. Alyson seemed to move even closer to him. Nash rolled his eyes. As he did so, he caught Kaya's eyes. She smiled at him and shrugged.

Love is in the air, thought Nash.

Henderson continued. "They're a distraction from my network security business. You see, I'm combining a number of different eschatology tools to predict the timing of the Eschaton."

"And what's an Eschaton?" Alyson cooed.

"The End of Time," Henderson replied. "The end of everything, really. The final destiny of the world."

She immediately looked over at her brother, no doubt expecting a sarcastic look. He gave her one on cue.

"Many different eschatology tools, seers, and cultures predict an End of Time," commented Nash. "It's all bunk."

"Spoken like a true skeptic," said Henderson. "But luckily, the world isn't full of skeptics. If it were, nothing would get done."

He laughed, and so did Alyson—and even Kaya.

"Sure, laugh at the rational one," said Nash grumpily.

Henderson laughed again and pointed to another chart, smoothly walking Alyson over to it. "Irrational or not, I find it great fun. Take this Mayan Calendar here. It's a prediction of the end of the world."

"Sheesh. Is everyone predicting the end of the world?" asked Alyson.

Nash began, "There are many such apocalyptic stories deeply engrained in the fabric of most—"

Alyson held up her hand. "Give it a rest, big bro. It was just a rhetorical question."

Nash opened his mouth again, then promptly closed it. Henderson was already speaking again, pointing to another section of the wall, and another image. "And over here we have the Time Wave Zero chart.

"And what would that be?" Alyson asked with a dazzling smile.

"Time Wave Zero was created by a man named Terrence McKenna, who found an unrecognized pattern in the sixty-four hexagrams of the I-Ching. What he created was a mathematical graphing of the I-Ching and turned it into a map of time. He found intriguing correlations of events over the four thousand years of recorded history. The map correlated time and history with the ebb and flow of novelty points like the atomic bomb, the Neanderthals, the rise of homo sapiens, the birth of language, the Black Death, the Enlightenment, the agricultural revolution, etcetera.”

“Amazing!” breathed Alyson.

“Coincidence,” added Nash.

Henderson ignored him and went on. “A peculiarity of this correlation is that at a certain point, a singularity in the Time Wave Zero chart, the pattern of history ends. When we combine this with the predictions of Nostradamus and the Bible Code, the Mayan Calendar and the visions and beliefs of certain Native-American tribes, we see that they all point toward the Eschaton arriving on December twenty-first, two thousand and twelve.”

Nash rolled his eyes. “Yes, people, we have yet another two thousand and twelve myth. They seem to be coming out of the woodwork these days.”

Henderson grinned and gave Alyson a knowing smile. “Who invited your brother to come along?” he asked.

“You did, love bird,” said Nash. “Now what do you know about our parents.”

“I was coming to that. This way.” Henderson led them over to his work bench and pointed to a long printout unrolled on the table. “This is the latest run of the Web Bot program. This is why I asked you here.”

Alyson muscled her way in front of Nash and looked over the printout. “You said something about a Web Bod in the lobby—”

“Not Bod. *Bot*.”

“And what’s a Web *Bot?*”

Nash rolled his eyes. “It’s an Internet prediction program, right?”

“Right,” said Henderson. “The Web Bot taps into the collective unconscious of the universe and its inhabitants.”

"Come again?" said Alyson.

"It predicts the future up to ninety days out. The Web Bot looks for changes in language that precede large emotional events. The larger the emotional impact of an event, the more advance notice the Web Bot gives."

"And how does it do that?" asked Kaya.

Henderson looked at Nash. "I bet Jeremy knows the answer. You've written about eschatology, right?"

Nash nodded, studying the print-out as he spoke. "The Web Bot is like any other intelligent bot on the Net. It's a spider or software agent similar to the ones used by internet search engines. It looks for particular keywords in the content—any and all content like discussion groups, web sites, and blogs—on the Net. When a keyword or what's called a target word is found, the Web Bot takes a small snippet of surrounding text. It takes these snippets or phrases and sends them to a computer program."

"Very good," said Henderson. "And then the collected data is filtered, and the words or phrases are reduced to their essence."

"Essence?" asked Alyson.

"Think of how the lowest common denominators work in fractions," said Henderson, clearly enjoying educating Alyson, who was a most eager student. "The Web Bot process is, in fact, like looking for the least common denominators among *groups of words*."

"So, what you're saying is that you're a geek like Jeremy."

"Geeks rule the world," said Henderson, laughing.

Nash was growing impatient with their nauseating flirtations, and slight digs at him. "Can we get on with it?" he pushed.

Alyson shot him an irritated look. Nash raised his eyebrows and pointed to his watch. Henderson caught the gesture.

"Yes, of course, Jeremy," he said. "I know you guys are anxious, but I think you will find what I discovered is well worth your time." He pointed to the printouts again. "Okay, once the Bot run does its thing, we then use the essence of these phrases to decipher possible future events. The technology, of course, doesn't come out and say *Buy AT&T* or *the Cowboys will win the Super Bowl*. But it does base its prediction on web chatter which ultimately represents the collective conscious of society."

"The Web Bot's predictive qualities are not proven," interjected Nash.

Henderson chuckled. "Always the skeptic. People like you keep the rest of us honest, Jeremy."

"Just doing my job."

"With that said, the Bot's predictive abilities have, in fact, been proven! Take its run in June, two thousand and one. The Web Bot predicted a life altering event would happen within the next sixty to ninety days. And it was spot on! The Twin Towers fell in September of two thousand and one!"

It was easy for such claims to be made, Nash knew. Harder to back it up with clear-cut evidence. He was about to point this out when Henderson, on a roll, thundered on. As he spoke, he ticked off points on his long fingers.

"Additionally, the Web Bot predicted the two thousand and one anthrax attack on Washington D.C., the East Coast power outage in two thousand and three, and the earthquake which led to the December two thousand and four tsunami. It even predicted the events that would follow hurricane Katrina. I have the proof!"

Nash almost laughed at his friend's unbridled enthusiasm. "Fine, send me the proof another day. But what does any of this have to do with our parents?"

Henderson nodded. "Yes, of course. It's easy to get carried away with this stuff." He scanned the sheet before them and then brought their attention to a few snippets of phrases in the latest Web Bot results. "Okay, I've been running groupings of target words through the Web Bot now for almost two years. These are words that generally center around an idea or possible event that I want clarity on."

Nash read aloud the groupings of words indicated in this

section of the Bot report: "These say, *Hopi, Hopi Stone, Prophecy Rock,* and *Purification.*"

Kaya snapped her head up. "Why those words?"

"Not just those words, remember," said Henderson. "I do lots of search clusters, but that is one of my clusters. Why? Why not? They often yield fascinating results. Case in point. Look at this first snippet."

Henderson directed their attention to a series of phrases on the printout.

> *"Many think that the [day of purification] has been described as forces of mankind's future...according to our Native Prophecies he unfolded the story of the five [Hopi stone] tablets while they... interpretation of the carving on [Prophecy Rock] thought to be end of times compared to...the words seem to reflect a [Purification] theme of Native American myth including the [Hopi] combined with other 2012 end of time...missing piece of the [Hopi stone] tablet and see if it can give...petroglyph known as [Prophecy Rock] which symbolizes many Hopi prophecies...."*

"There's nothing new there, granted," Henderson said, almost dismissing the phrases. "Only confirmation of previous runs over the last year or so that repeatedly picked up the same chatter on the target words."

He moved his finger further down the printout. "But these are what caught my attention, and the reason why I called you immediately, Jeremy."

> *"...great day of [purification] has also been described as a mystery egg...anomalies accompany the sipapu as foretold on [Prophecy Rock]...oldest center study of consciousness in southwest believes the [Purification] of the mind...told him that the keeper of the secret would hold it until such time when [Hopi Stone] would reveal... end of times related to the sipapu as to pertains to a mystery egg...*

*included such predictions and myths like the [day of purification]
pointing to the program of KRATOS advanced by conspiracy
hacks...interpretations of the enigmas [Prophecy Rock] by a half-
white half-Sioux Somerton is seen as...."*

Henderson paused. "Let me stop here for a moment. This is
new material—surprising material never reported on previous Web
Bot runs. It must have some significance over the next ninety days.
Especially the reference to a mystery egg and something called
KRATOS." He looked gravely at Nash. "But the biggest surprise
of all was in this last phrase."

*"...research on the esoteric meaning of the [Hopi stone] tablets
including Nash's interest in 2012...end of times to be brought forth
by the sipapu and mystery egg...Nash who with his wife studied the
confluence of...reported cipher expert Bryan Henderson's attempts
at decoding the meaning of [Prophesy Rock] in the area of..."*

Alyson had gasped at the mention of their parents. Nash
admittedly felt his own heartbeat increased in tempo. But what
did this all mean? He hadn't a clue. Not yet.

When Henderson finished reading, he looked up at Nash.
"Your parent's name and my name. Combined together on this
run. That is significant."

Nash thought a moment and decided to take Henderson into
his confidence. He explained how they believed their parents might
have been murdered because of what they may have discovered
about the Hopi End Time Prediction. Nash went on to tell his old
friend about the Kachina doll invoice and the mysterious *chirping*
noise on his father's DATs.

"Incredible," Henderson replied when Nash had finished. "But
remember, the Web Bot predicts ninety days out from the run." He
smiled at Nash. "If you read closely, I think the run is also about
you and what *you* will do—or, at least, be a part of."

Nash studied the print-out again. Bryan was right. The ambiguous wording of his name could have been referencing either him or his parents.

"So, what does this all mean?" asked Alyson. The flirting in her voice was gone. She sounded as perplexed as Nash felt.

"It's too soon to know," said Henderson. He looked at Nash. "Tell me more about this *chirping*."

"We think there's a hidden code or message of some kind embedded in the chirping," said Nash. "We'll probably need a spectrograph to see if there's anything really there."

"No problem," said Henderson. "We have one here at the company. We use it to look for clandestine messages used with steganography."

"You boys like to use big words," said Alyson.

Henderson laughed lightly. "Digital files—like sound recordings and images—contain unused areas of data. Steganography takes advantage of these unused areas by replacing them with information. The files can then be accessed and exchanged without anyone knowing what really is inside them. For example, an image of a fighter plane could contain a private message. A wave file might contain an image or map, or even the plans for a building or telecommunications network. And it's all relatively easy to do if you have the right software. Now, let's take a look at that DAT."

Alyson opened her purse and handed it to him. Henderson called for Garcia on the intercom to set up a terminal and DAT player in the IT room below.

Henderson headed for the door. "Be right back. I'll copy this over onto a flash drive."

Several minutes later, he returned with a flash drive in his hand. "Okay, done. I'll load the cut into my laptop and run the chirping through the steganography software."

The four watched as the software program changed the sound

spectrum at the end of the cut into a series of pixels on the screen. The pixels slowly transformed into an image that became clearer and clearer as more pixels were added until a well-defined set of visual images appeared.

"Holy shit!" cried Henderson. "I figured we'd might find something but..."

An image of a swastika inside a circle appeared on the screen, along with a third image—a series of red dots inside a circle.

Nash blinked, stunned.

"I know those images," said Kaya, standing back. "They're the same images found on the Hopi Prophesy Rock."

Phoenix, Arizona

Once Henderson left the IT room, Garcia pulled out his cell phone and punched in a number. It rang twice, and then a voice answered.

"What do you have?" Prescott asked.

"It's not what I have. It's what you don't," Garcia replied.

"Explain."

"It's Nash. He's supposed to be dead, but he's here at MultiPhase."

The response was instantaneous. "Kill him."

"There's one other thing," Garcia said.

"And what's that?"

"The latest Web Bot run."

"Did it make any mention of The Project?" Prescott replied

For once, Garcia caught real concern in Prescott's voice.

"Affirmative. It mentioned KRATOS."

"Terminate your surveillance. Terminate it all," was Prescott's abrupt reply.

"Understood."

Garcia hung up and walked over to a computer terminal and punched in a username and password. He clicked on a software application, and once in, he scrolled through a list of reports, found the latest run of the program, and ordered a printout. A few moments later he ripped the report off the network printer, rolled it up and stuffed it into his shirt.

Next, he made his way to the Halon suppression system, found the console, and flipped off a few switches. That done, he shredded a mass of computer paper and placed it in the center of the room for kindling. He pulled out his Bic lighter and lit the corner of a piece if paper. As the flame caught hold, he smiled.

He loved fire.

Phoenix, Arizona

"You know, there still might be some other images behind these," said Henderson, excitedly. "That happens sometimes. Let me grab another application and—" He stopped short. "Does anyone else smell smoke?"

Kaya pointed to the air duct near her feet. The other three followed her finger. Dark smoke was issuing out.

"We've got a fire," said Nash as calmly as he could.

And at that moment the air duct exploded from the wall. Tongues of flame flicked through, lapping at the air. Alyson screamed, and Nash pulled her hand and grabbed Kaya around the waist moving them immediately to the door. "We've got to get the hell out of here," he shouted. "Now!"

"The IT room below us is on fire," Henderson shouted. "But that's impossible. That room has a Halon fire suppression system!"

"I don't give a shit what it has," shouted Nash. "Let's get going. Go! *Go!*"

Nash felt the office door and was dismayed to discover it was quite warm. He opened it anyway—and saw that the hallway directly before them was ablaze.

"Shit!" He slammed the door shut. "It's everywhere."

Nash was eying the massive office window, knowing they were three floors up, when Henderson yelled, "Into the closet, I have an idea."

"Are you nuts?" cried Kaya, coughing into the nook of her arm. Smoke, pouring in through the air duct and under the door was rapidly filling the big office.

"We can break through the drywall on the inside," Henderson said. Tears were openly flowing from his reddening eyes. "It leads to our neighbor's offices."

"Then let's go," Nash said, trying to shield his mouth and nose from the smoke. He grabbed one of the small, metal client chairs sitting in front of Henderson's massive executive desk. Already the flames from the vent had lapped up to the ceiling, where they were spreading rapidly.

Nash ducked into the closet with the others. He sure as hell hoped Bryan's idea was a good one. The last thing he wanted to do was to be burned alive in a small closet.

Or burned alive, period.

Turns out it wasn't so small. It was bigger than a walk-in closet. It also housed some electrical and data storage equipment. Nash had the others move to one side, and he and Henderson proceeded to pound the hell out of the drywall in front of them.

Sections of the wall broke off in large chunks, as the legs of the chair repeatedly punched through the drywall. When there was a gaping hole, Nash tossed aside the chair, and with Henderson's help, tore away the rest of the loose drywall.

Fresh air came pouring through. Beyond was a dimly lit room. *Henderson, you're a genius.* Nash could have kissed his friend.

Luckily the studs separating the two rooms were aluminum and not wood. Nash pulled them apart, grunting, and when there was enough room to pass through, he urged Alyson and Kaya through. He turned and was dismayed to find his friend racing back into his flaming office. Smoke poured into the small closet.

"What the hell are you doing?!"

He cursed Henderson as he coughed, and a moment later his friend returned, coughing, and retching, and holding the flash drive triumphantly.

"We may need it later," gasped the tall man between fits of coughing. Nash slammed the closet door shut behind him and

hurriedly pushed his friend through the opening, following immediately behind.

And what waited for him beyond made Nash's heart sink. As
he wiped the streaming tears from his eyes, he shook his head and
said, "You have *got* to be kidding me."

Phoenix, Arizona

They were in a large storeroom filled with boxes.

And under the glare of a single, dusty bulb, Nash could clearly read the labels on most of the boxes. *Propellant Slugs.*

"*Good Christ!* Bryan. What kinds of neighbors do your have?" Nash exclaimed.

Additionally, the boxes were all marked with the same diamond-shaped sign, the universal indicator of hazardous material—or highly *flammable* hazardous material.

Maybe his friend wasn't such a genius after all.

Henderson just stared in disbelief at the floor to ceiling boxes in the storeroom. "Jesus, I forgot! They're a model rocket company. They make solid propellant similar to that used in the solid rocket boosters of the space shuttle—"

"There's no time for that. Go, go, go!"

Just then, he felt a flash of searing heat behind him. Nash turned, gasping. The closet door had burst open. Flames whipped through the makeshift doorway and into the storeroom.

Jesus, this whole thing's going to blow.

Nash dashed to the closet door and was relieved to discover it wasn't locked from the outside.

At least something's going our way.

He threw it open, only to be faced with a roaring wall of fire that seemed to be coming up through what had once been the floor.

Spoke too soon.

Fires on both sides, with explosives in the middle. That didn't leave much wriggle room. Luckily, a hallway ran to either side of the door.

"Cover your mouths with your shirts. Breathe through the fabric and follow me."

The group did as they were told, and Nash, protecting his mouth with his shirt, hung a right and led them down the smoke-filled hallway. Amazingly, the sprinklers were on, drenching the four of them—but to no avail. The fire was too much for the water. With his eyes rapidly tearing up and smoke working its way even through the fabric of his shirt, he was greatly relieved to find a metal door leading to a service stairway. He felt it. It was still cool. He yanked the door open.

"C'mon, c'mon!" he urged, waving the trio in.

Once inside, as he nearly ran into Henderson's lanky frame, he saw they had another problem. A big problem. Black smoke was billowing up from below. The route was cut-off.

"We go up!" shouted Nash.

They climbed up through the rapidly engulfing smoke of the stairwell to the roof level. Henderson pushed open the door into the gloriously fresh air. Nash sucked in hard and then staggered in a fit of coughing. The acrid smoke was deep in his lungs. The others hunched over, coughing violently, tears streaming from their eyes.

They weren't safe yet. After all, they were trapped on the heat-baked roof of an office building that was sitting on a storeroom of explosives.

When he had forcefully regained some control of himself, Nash shouted, "We've got to get out of here before that storeroom blows."

Nash looked around. There had to be a fire escape or a ladder somewhere, but he could barely see through his streaming eyes. Luckily, Henderson had a plan.

"Over there are the dumpsters," said his friend, pointing, and hurriedly led the way over the flat roof to the south side of the building. Once there, wiping his eyes, Nash carefully peered over the edge. Two massive dumpsters filled with black trash bags just below them were sitting in the alley. What was in those trash bags were anyone's guess. In the near distance he heard a cacophony of sirens.

Just then, the building seemed to buckle. Nash knew what that meant, and there was no time to wait for help.

The propellant slugs had ignited.

Safely watching the burning structure, a half block away, Garcia sat on his Harley Roadster and gloated over the glorious flames leaping high into the air.

God, he loved fire!

The fire crew was on its way, and so far, Garcia had seen no signs of Nash and the others escaping. How many innocents died in the fire was of no concern to Garcia. They were the very definition of collateral damage.

The fire churned and raged, and Garcia smiled to himself.

No one could survive that.

No one.

Phoenix, Arizona

In one swift movement, Nash pushed both Alyson and Kaya off the roof together. Then he grabbed a startled Henderson and jumped.

Even as Nash and Henderson plummeted the three stories to where his sister and Kaya lay inside the open dumpster, the building exploded around them. Bricks and glass and twisted metal blew in every direction just as Nash and Henderson miraculously avoided landing on the women. The plastic bags were plentiful and filled mostly with cardboard. Not the softest of landings but Nash wasn't complaining since he was fairly certain he hadn't broken anything and hoped the others were as fortunate.

He didn't waste a second. With fiery debris raining down, Nash ordered Henderson to follow his lead and soon both men had reached around and pulled down the heavy metal lids, sealing them in the dumpsters.

Another explosion followed, this one blowing out the sides of the building, slamming hard into the dumpster. The metal container, with its cargo of humans, was hurled across the parking lot only to slam into God knew what.

The wind burst from Nash's lungs as he lay somewhere underneath the others. His last thought before blackness engulfed him completely was a sarcastic one—he was happy to have provided a cushion for the others.

And then he blacked out.

It was hours later, and Nash and the others had been thoroughly checked out by the paramedics. No one had any serious injuries other than some bruises and a sore ankle here and there. Nash was the beneficiary of the sore ankle.

Sitting across the street under blankets, each gave a detailed report to the various police and fire investigators. In front of them, the building lay in smoking ruins. Nash watched gloomily as body after covered body was wheeled out from the rubble.

Those could have been us, he thought.

When the group was finally alone, Nash looked at all of them.

"Everyone okay?" asked Nash.

The general consensus was, *good enough.*

Nash looked at his old friend. "I'm afraid that fire was no accident," he commented, keeping his voice low.

"But you just got done telling the fire inspector that you had no clue what happened," asserted Alyson.

"I don't have a clue what happened," Nash replied, "and I don't know who's responsible, but someone out there is determined to kill us."

"Maybe you should fill me in," Henderson said.

Nash did, with help from Alyson and Kaya. When they were finished, Henderson said, "And you have no clue who the men in those vehicles were?"

"No," said Nash. "But you said something earlier that's stuck with me. Who could have turned off the fire suppression system?"

"Just a handful of my own staff."

"Wasn't your employee, Garcia, in the basement?" asked Kaya. Nash was sitting next to her, their legs touching. The feeling was more comforting than anything. Nash noticed his sister was sitting exceptionally close to Bryan. He didn't blame her. Strength in numbers.

"Yes, he was."

"Would he have known how to turn off the suppression system?" asked Nash.

"Maybe. And if he didn't, he would certainly know how to

figure out how to do it." Henderson looked sharply at Nash. "You're not seriously suggesting Garcia caused the fire."

"Maybe, I don't know, but something turned off the suppression system, and now a lot of people are dead. Where do you know him from?"

"Garcia? He came to me the day after my former assistant died."

"Died?" queried Kaya.

"Yes. Died of a heart attack. Was only twenty-five. I was in the middle of a big project and needed someone right away. Garcia showed up for a job, so I hired him on the spot."

"Didn't you check his references?" asked Nash.

"Of course. They were impeccable."

They were silent for a few minutes while emergency workers swarmed everywhere, helping the wounded, carting away the dead, keeping away the curious public.

"I would kill for an Advil," sighed Henderson, rubbing the side of his head. "The printout of the run was burned in the fire. We could have used it for further analysis."

"What good what that do?" asked Alyson.

"It might have given us some clue as to what will happen next."

"Assuming this print-out of yours has any merit, could this Garcia had gotten a copy of it?"

"Certainly. My Web Bot runs weren't a secret. The print-outs were generally left in my office."

"Maybe your Web Bot came across something it wasn't supposed to come across," volunteered Alyson.

"Or predicted something that you weren't supposed to know about," added Kaya.

Henderson looked from them to Nash. "If so, then that something is going to happen in ninety days—or sooner."

"I'm guessing sooner," predicted Nash. "Based on the attempts on our lives."

Henderson nodded. "Okay, then. We have little time to lose. Where do we go from here?"

"To the Hopi Cultural Center," Kaya replied confidently, surprising Nash with her conviction. "We go to Old Oraibi. My uncle is one of the caretakers at the Center and knows quite a bit about Prophesy Rock."

"Then let's get moving," agreed Nash. "We'll use my plane."

Scottsdale, Arizona

Garcia pulled his Harley Roadster into the parking lot of a biker bar called the Dirty Dawg Saloon in Scottsdale. He knew he would blend in there, and no one would ask any questions if they overheard the phone call he was about to make.

He punched a series of letters and numbers into his LPI device and waited for a reply.

"Prescott here. What have you got?" came the immediate reply.

"The program was terminated," Garcia said into the device. "They'll be no possibility of KRATOS exposure."

"Good. And the others?"

Garcia hesitated a moment then said, "Both Henderson and Nash are still alive." Garcia went on to quickly explain the utterly inexplicable sight of watching Nash, Henderson, and the two women crawl out of a badly damaged dumpster from halfway across the parking lot.

"The man has nine lives," growled Prescott. "Have we lost him, then?"

Garcia, fearing he was now a suspect in the fire, had to flee the area. He admitted as much, but added, "But I'm sure we can track them."

"How?"

"I have the only printout of the Web Bot run. I can analyze it and project where they may be going. Not precisely, and not in sequence, but I can get close."

"Then do it," Prescott ordered. "Call me when you find them."

The line went dead.

Garcia, sitting on his Harley in the hot sun, hoped like hell those projections were accurate.

Arizona
Over the Mogollon Rim

Before going to the airport, the quartette stopped at Henderson's condo to change out of their smoke-stained, torn, and rancid-smelling clothing.

"There are jeans and shirts in the bedroom closet," Henderson offered. "Take what you want." He pointed to the guest bedroom door. "My ex-girlfriend left some clothing. Check the back of the closet. You two should fit in them."

"You did say ex, right?" queried Alyson.

"Six months ago," said Bryan, nodding, "she left me for my second cousin."

"You poor baby—"

Nash threw on a pair of jeans that were far too long. He rolled them up three or four times and tossed on a t-shirt that swam on him. While the two women changed, chattering on and on about Bryan's ex's taste in clothing, he went over to the remote on the coffee table and jabbed at few buttons. The TV came on in the middle of a Fox News Alert. The TV screen was snowy and pixilated but Nash could see that a woman—a pretty blonde clone like most female Fox News anchors—was just finishing up a news item about the latest atmospheric disruptions. The screen split, and a staff person at the National Oceanic and Atmospheric Administration by the name of Walter Payson appeared.

"Turn that up," Henderson asked, walking in while stuffing a shirt into his pants.

Nash raised the volume on the remote.

The anchorwoman explored, "Dr. Payson, about these atmospheric anomalies that we have been experiencing. Some scientists think that we could be, in fact, experiencing a pole reversal."

Dr. Payson wore wired rim glasses and an honest-to-God pocket protector full of pens. The scientist nodded. "That's certainly one theory."

"For the benefit of our viewers, just what is a pole reversal?"

"The scientific name is a geomagnetic reversal—a change in the orientation of Earth's magnetic field. The positions of magnetic north and magnetic south become interchanged."

The pretty anchor woman tried to put on a competent face. "And if we are experiencing, what you call, *a geomagnetic reversal,* what should we expect?"

"Many things. Compasses would be affected as would our navigational instruments which depend on them. Migratory animals such as birds and fish would become greatly disoriented. Such creatures would no doubt wander far from current feeding and breeding grounds into areas not suitable for them."

Nash remembered the news item he saw at the Executive Terminal at the Albuquerque Airport about beached whales and freezing Canadian geese.

Payson continued. "Large scale fluctuations in magnetic fields would knock out power suppliers, and all electromagnetic communication could conceivably be disrupted for long periods of time."

The pretty news anchor, despite her professionalism, seemed to turn pale. Nash's own mouth went instantly dry.

"Additionally, some of my colleagues theorize that we can also expect to see violent geological events in unlikely places. Earthquakes in New York City; hurricanes hitting the Northwest."

"You are certainly painting a scary scenario."

"These are scary times."

"Scarier than the disasters they were warning us about for the Millennium Bug in two thousand?"

"Unlike the Y2K scare, this one is real, and involves natural disasters, rather than just man-made. Earthquakes, volcanic eruptions, tidal waves, nuclear winter, and a migratory herd of caribou taking up residence in your backyard."

Nash clicked off the TV just as the lovely announcer looked like she was going to get sick—and quite unlovely.

Nash felt sick, too.

What the hell was happening?

At that moment, Alyson and Kaya appeared in the living room, dressed in clean clothes that fit remarkably well. *Perhaps too well,* Nash thought. Still, he couldn't help but notice the way Kaya's jeans hugged her waist. She had also tied off the hem of her t-shirt, revealing a smooth, well-toned tummy.

A perfect tummy.

Nash hadn't meant to stare, but her curves just threw him off. He was certain she had caught him staring, and he felt himself redden. He immediately looked away and said, "Now that the fashion show's over, we should get going."

Two hours later, they were flying over the deserts of Arizona. Nash was in heaven, and the others seemed to be relaxed and enjoying themselves. Everyone, that is, except Kaya. Sweat beaded her brow, and as he glanced back at her, she seemed to be having some difficulty breathing. Flying was definitely not her gig.

And this latest batch of turbulence didn't help, either, as hot thermals from the desert floor bounced Nash's small plane up and down. He made small talk, with the hopes of easing her anxiety.

"So, Kaya, could you tell us more about Old Oraibi," he quietly, turning back as he spoke.

She blinked, shook her head, and focused on him. He smiled at her warmly. He wished like hell he could reach out and take her hand.

"Yeah, sure," she said, swallowing hard. "Let's see. Well, for centuries, the Hopi have lived in Hopiland, located on three mesas which rise above the desert floor of northern Arizona. Oraibi is located on Third Mesa and is the oldest continuously lived-in settlement in North America. As I said before, archaeologists date it back to eleven hundred CE."

The plane made a violent move, pushing it down and then quickly back up. Kaya gasped, and so did the other three.

"Tell us more about Third Mesa," said Nash as calmly as he could, as if nothing happened. It was important for the pilot to remain utterly calm. Truth was that a little turbulence never bothered him. It was all part of flying.

"Third Mesa, yes," said Kaya, clearly distracted by her own fears. Nash gave her credit for plunging forward despite her obvious anxiety. "The mesas are called First Mesa, Second Mesa, and Third Mesa. Farming is done on the desert floor surrounding these mesas. When the clans of the Hopi ancestors migrated to Old Oraibi so many centuries ago, they were seeking a destination which, as told to them by the Creator, was *Earth Center*. It would be a place where all of the Hopi clans would settle to take care of the land and practice their ceremonies. This place is Oraibi, although its original name was Sip-Oraibi, which means *rock solid and anchored down into the Earth*."

"And Prophesy Rock is located there?" asked Alyson.

"Yes. Prophecy Rock, which is known to the Hopi as the *Life Plan*, is located on Second Mesa. That's where we'll be going."

"I assume you know how to get there," Henderson asked.

"Of course."

"Jeremy!" squealed Alyson suddenly.

Despite his calm, Nash jumped, "Jesus, what, Alyson?"

"Look up there!"

She pointed up through the windshield, and they all followed her finger.

"Is that what I think it is?" asked Henderson.

"The aura borealis," said Nash, stunned. But the beautiful, streaking colors that alighted the upper atmosphere were different than anything he had ever seen before. The colors were pale, washed-out.

"What the hell is the aura borealis doing this far south?" asked Alyson in disbelief.

"No clue," Nash replied, shaking his head. "Maybe it's something else. There's the San Francisco Mountains up ahead. We're approaching Flagstaff. We'll be landing soon."

Alyson pointed out the window to the northeast. "What's that down there?"

Henderson looked to where she was pointing. "That's the Cinder Lake volcanic field."

"Volcanic?" Alyson replied.

"Yes. The whole area up here was once volcanic," Henderson said.

"Looks like a moonscape," Alyson replied.

"Pretty close," Nash remarked. "In fact, back in sixty-three NASA trained astronauts up here to prepare them for their trip to the moon. Dad told me that on one of our field trips up here. Look over there."

Nash pointed to a cone shaped object in the distance. "That's Sunset Crater. The Bonito Flow in Sunset Crater National Park appeared to be similar to flows on the lunar surface, so a field of artificial impact craters was created in the Cinder Lakes area to create a surface similar to the proposed first manned American landing site on the Moon."

"Sunset Crater last erupted about a thousand years ago," Henderson blurted out, trying to be inclusive.

"Were people living around there then?" asked Alyson.

"Yes," Nash replied. "A small tribe of Native Americans."

"Probably moved to a better neighborhood after that," Alyson remarked with a laugh.

"You know," Kaya said, "There's a story that goes with the astronauts training up here."

"What's that?" asked Alyson.

"Well, as the story goes, about nineteen sixty-six or so, a nearby

Navajo sheep herder and his son were watching the astronauts train. The Navajos were noticed and approached by the NASA personnel. Since the old sheep herder didn't know English, he asked his son to ask the NASA personnel what they were doing."

"And they told the son they were training for a flight to the moon," Alyson interrupted.

"Correct. Now the old man became very excited and asked if he could send a message to the moon with the astronauts. The NASA personnel thought this was a great idea, so they rustled up a tape recorder. After the old man recorded his message, the NASA people asked his son what he said. The son refused to answer."

"What *did* he say?" Nash asked now very curious.

"Well, later they asked several people on the reservation to translate the message, but all refused. And everyone they asked only chuckled and walked away."

"Did they ever get it translated?" Alyson asked.

"Yes. Finally, cash in hand, someone translated the message."

"And...?" asked Nash.

Kaya grew a wide grin. "It said, *Watch out for these guys. They come to take your land.*"

Alyson and Henderson burst out laughing.

Nash smiled to himself. A great story whether it was true or not!

Hopi Indian Reservation
Second Mesa

After landing at the Flagstaff Pulliam Airport, they rented a CJ-5 Jeep, the only off-road vehicle left at Avis, and headed once again to Hopiland.

An hour or so later, dusk began to encroach on the bright glare of the day.

Nash looked over his right shoulder and asked, "Bryan, you said something back in your office about images *behind* images."

"Yeah. I wanted to run the images through another steganography program. There might be further information in those. But I need access to the Net to download the program I need."

"There's Net access at the Cultural Center," Kaya replied.

"We'll do it there, then," said Nash. His stomach growled. "I don't know about you guys, but I'm hungry as hell. Where can we stop for a bite to eat?"

"There's a restaurant and inn at the Hopi Cultural Center where my uncle works. We can eat and get a room for the night. Then we can see him in the morning."

"As long as they have cheeseburgers!" Alyson piped up.

Nash and Kaya looked at each other and grinned.

After checking in and getting settled in their rooms—one for the women, and one for the men—they walked together to the restaurant for dinner. As they were seated, a young Hopi maiden dressed in typical blue and white waitress garb handed them menus. Printed clearly in bold letters near the top of Nash's menu were the words: **Welcome to the Center of the Universe**.

"You weren't kidding," said Henderson jovially to Kaya, pointing to his own menu.

The table next to them was filled with what seemed to be locals. They were enjoying Hopi tacos—which Nash knew were exactly like Navajo tacos—big fry bread with beans, lettuce, cheese, and onions on the top.

"Yum!" smiled Alyson, sniffing the air almost smacking her lips. "That's for me."

"Make it four," said Nash to the waitress. Then double-checked with his companions. "Okay by you two?"

Kaya and Henderson both nodded.

As they waited for their food, Nash turned to Kaya, who was sitting next to him. "Tell us more about your uncle, if you don't mind."

She nodded, "His name is Joseph Ahote. He's the curator of our museum here and one of our Elders."

"I've heard of him," offered Henderson. "He comes up often on my Web Bot searches. He knows everything you want to know about the Hopi Life Plan and Prophesy Rock."

Nash inadvertently made a noise, which got the attention of everyone at the table.

"Is there a problem, Jeremy?" asked Kaya.

Alyson reached out and took her brother's hand. "You two do realize that you're eating dinner with the world's foremost skeptic on *everything*," Alyson said, laughing good naturedly. "Tell her what's bugging you, Jeremy."

Nash released his sister's hand. "Look, Kaya, I don't want to insult your heritage, but these prophesies of the Native Americans are verbal stories, passed down from storyteller to storyteller, generation to generation. The problem with Native-American oral stories is that they are just that—*verbal*—and thus they can change with time. I just don't trust them."

"And I suppose you believe that the Native-American story-tellers are charlatans, too?" asked Kaya icily.

"No, of course not. I just don't put much merit into them. They are, after all, just stories."

He saw Kaya wince, and Nash knew he was being a bit harsh. In fact, everyone at the table winced. Henderson looked away and whistled lightly. Alyson gaped at him openly. But Nash held firm. Being a skeptic in today's world took guts. Almost as much guts as being openly spiritual or proclaiming to the world one sees aliens. Now *that* took guts, Nash knew.

But he might have pushed too hard and been a bit too abrupt. Kaya wasn't a loony claiming to have seen UFOs or Elvis. This was part of her culture, and he knew he had deeply wounded her. The pride in him kept him from openly apologizing, but he did decide to temper his words.

"Look, we're all tired and cranky," he said. "To say that we've been through hell together is an understatement. Let's just have some drinks, enjoy our dinners, then get some rest and come out swinging in the morning." He reached out and gently took Kaya's hand. She flinched slightly, then warmed a little toward him, relaxing. "I'm truly sorry if I offended you."

The Hopi woman nodded and gave him a small smile. God, he loved her smile.

"Alright then," said Henderson. "Now that we've made nice-nice, let's eat and hit the hay."

The next morning, after Nash had a fitful night's sleep dreaming of fires, Humvees, and helicopters, the tired-looking group enjoyed a filling late breakfast of huevos rancheros. Then they drove the short dusty distance to the Hopi Cultural Center Museum.

They entered the small gallery of Native American art and found the office of the curator.

"How do we know your uncle is in?" asked Alyson.

"He's here every day. When I was growing up, I would run here after school to visit and hear his stories."

"Run?" asked Alyson.

"Yes. Running is a Hopi tradition. We are well known for running great distances at high speed."

"Seriously?" Alyson asked.

Kaya grinned. "Seriously."

"But why?"

"Centuries ago, Hopis didn't own cattle, sheep, or burros," Nash answered, jumping in. Nash, admittedly, was hoping to make points with her and get back on her good side. "They had to rely upon game-capturing, which required them to cultivate the practice of running. Besides running for gaming purposes, Hopis also ran in search of food. When there were no horses for transportation, running obviously helped to cover great distances."

Kaya looked suitably impressed, and Nash felt himself beaming.

I'm nothing more than a girl-crazy schoolboy with a crush. A big crush, he admitted to himself, smiling.

"Your father taught you well about our Native American traditions," she said, and Nash was certain the remaining ice from last night had surely melted. She squeezed his arm lightly, and a thrill of pleasure coursed through him.

The group stopped before an office door. Kaya knocked gently on it, and immediately a soft voice from inside said, "Enter." She waved the group in.

Seated behind a rough-hewed desk was a small, elderly man with a round face and slits for eyes. To Nash, he looked ancient. His face was heavily leathered and lined. Pure white hair cascaded down over his shoulders onto a bright white shirt under a white vest stitched with traditional Hopi designs.

"*Um pitu*, Uncle," Kaya said in traditional Hopi.

The old man's dour face lit up brightly at the sight of his niece. "*Um pitu*, my child! It has been a long time since you visited."

"Too long," she replied. She went over and hugged the man deeply as he remained hunkered down in his heavily worn executive chair.

Ahote then motioned to them to have a seat on the large well-worn cowhide couch and chairs beside his desk. Kaya introduced Nash, Alyson, and Henderson. The grave old man nodded warmly to all of them.

"So, tell me, child," he said, "what brings you here? Surely not just to visit an old man?"

"We need your help, Uncle." She paused, seemed to gather herself, and then plunged forward. "We need an interpretation of the Hopi Life Plan on Prophesy Rock."

With her uncle listening patiently, she quickly outlined the reason behind the request, leaving out the parts of their near-death experiences. She then pulled out a pen and a scrap of paper from her purse, and quickly drew the image of a swastika inside a circle with a circular pattern of red dots next to it. Nash thought she did a hell of a good job. She handed it to her uncle.

"Ah, yes," Ahote said. "The Mystery Egg."

"And what would that be, if I may ask?" said Nash.

"The Mystery Egg, or the Great Day of Purification, is when the forces of the swastika and the Sun plus a third force symbolized by the color red culminate either in total rebirth or total annihilation—we don't know which," the old man replied.

"Did you say *red?*" Henderson asked.

Ahote nodded. "The color red is of great importance."

Henderson turned to Nash. "Didn't you say there were red dots on your father's invoice?"

"Yes," Nash said, biting his lip. He turned to the old curator. "Mr. Ahote, would it be possible for you to show us Prophesy Rock?"

"I cannot show you the actual rock, my friend. Our icons are restricted only to Hopi religious leaders. But I can show you a life-sized reproductions here at the museum."

Nash agreed. Kaya then made arrangements with her uncle for Henderson to use the museum's equipment. A few minutes later, with Henderson seated in front of a computer with the intent to analyze the mysterious images on his flash drive, Nash and the women followed Mr. Ahote through the museum.

Second Mesa
Hopi Cultural Center

The Prophesy Rock reproduction was a plaster cast standing about eight feet tall. It appeared unremarkable at first glance, but upon stepping closer, Nash could see crude Hopi hieroglyphs angling across the surface of the faux rock.

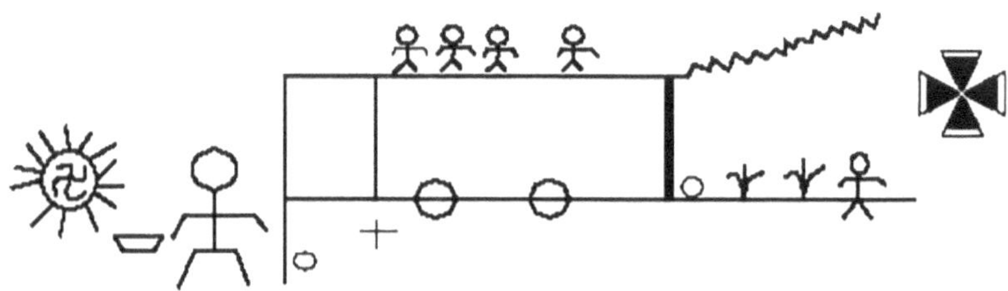

Nash leaned in closer, careful not to touch the hulking piece of plaster. They were in the far corner of the museum, alone in a fairly empty wing. Pleasant flute music played over the speakers. The hieroglyphs, as far as Nash could tell, consisted of a series of human figures, circles, and lines all angling up toward a ragged zigzag tapering off into nothing. On the left side of the glyph was clearly the image of the sun with a swastika engraved within it.

To Nash, it didn't look like much of a prophecy.

Mr. Ahote now became their tour guide, reciting a speech Nash suspected he had no doubt repeated hundreds of times before.

"The large human figure at its left is the Great Spirit. The vertical line to the right of the Great Spirit is a time scale in

138

thousands of years. The point at which the Great Spirit touches the line is the time of his return."

"The line seems to diverge," Alyson observed.

"Indeed," agreed Kaya's uncle. "That's the Life Path established by the Great Spirit. It divides into the lower, narrow path of continuous life in harmony with nature and the wide upper road of white man's scientific achievements. The bar between the paths, above the cross, is the coming of white men. The Cross is that of Christianity. The circle below the cross represents the continuous Path of Life."

"What do those circles and small figures mean on the two paths?" Alyson asked.

"On one level, the four small human figures on the upper road represent the past three worlds and our present world. On another level, the figures indicate that some of the Hopi will travel the white man's path, having been seduced by its glamour. The two circles on the lower Path of Life are the *great shaking of the Earth*—World Wars One and Two."

Nash, admittedly, didn't see it. He saw circles and lines and crosses and suns, and it looked like gibberish. In fact, he was fairly certain that anyone, anywhere, could concoct whatever story they wanted out of the figures, lines, and shapes.

Mr. Ahote continued, and Nash kept his mouth shut, listening. The elder Hopi point to another line. "This short line here that, as you can see, returns to the straight Path of Life, is the last chance for people to turn back to nature before the upper road disintegrates and dissipates." He pointed to a jagged line moving away from the white man's scientific path. "If we continue only on this upper path, we will come to destruction."

"You said something about a Mystery Egg?" asked Nash.

"As I said before, the swastika in the sun, plus a third force associated with the color red, is a seed or Mystery Egg. This seed comes from the core of the earth through caves called the *sipapu*."

"Sipapu," exclaimed Nash.

He looked at Kaya and Alyson. "Your grandfather's funeral and our parents' murder!"

The three stood there silently, thinking.

"This Great Day of Purification that comes from the Mystery Egg, or seed, as you call it," Alyson said, "how and when will this occur?"

"The Hopis believe the human race has passed through three different worlds since the beginning of time. At the end of each world, human life has been purified or punished by the Great Spirit due mainly to corruption, greed, and turning away from the Great Spirit's teachings. Our Fourth World shall end soon, and the Fifth World will begin. Our elders know this. All the signs for the Great Day of Purification have come to pass, save one. The return of the Pahana."

The word once again struck a deep chord in Nash, and he was once again that little boy witnessing a nightmare beyond nightmares.

No boy should ever have seen what I saw, he thought.

Mr. Ahote was still talking. Nash forced himself to focus on the elder man's words and push aside the gruesome images. For now. The images always returned.

Lucky me.

"The swastika in the sun and this Celtic cross represents the two helpers of Pahana, the True White Brother. The return of the Pahana will be the beginning of the Great Purification—total rebirth of a new world or total annihilation of this one. We shall see what man chooses."

The elder Hopi paused a moment, perhaps to see the reaction of his words on Nash and Alyson. Nash, of course, knew most of this already. But hearing the stories spoken by a Hopi Elder—and spoken so matter-of-factly—made them come alive in a way they never had before. He almost felt like a Boy Scout sitting across a campfire, listening to wondrous tales that fired the imagination.

Mr. Ahote continued, "And we are not alone in our vision. The

Cherokee, Lakota, Onondaga, and Mohawk tribes, for example, all believe we are on the cusp of the Fifth World."

"And this Fifth World can only happen after the Purification of this world, the current Fourth World?" asked Alyson.

"I'm impressed," Nash whispered.

His sister elbowed him sharply.

The elder Hopi nodded, and when he spoke again, he did so quietly, almost reverently, "The world shall rock to and fro and all the suffering going on in this country with tornadoes, floods, and earthquakes is carried on the breath of Mother Earth because She is in pain."

Kaya spoke up after a short moment of silence. "These Four Corners are particularly sacred because we believe these lands literally hold Mother Earth's internal organs—coal and uranium which the Bureau of Indian Affairs has, unfortunately, allowed to be mined."

"They are killing Her for money," said the old Hopi quietly. "They are ripping out Her liver and heart and lungs." He suddenly looked fiercely at Nash. "You do not believe, I can see. But your beliefs matter not, my friend. Turtle Island will turn over two or three times, and then the oceans will join hands and meet the sky. We are in Koyaanisqatsi."

"What does that mean?" asked Alyson.

"World out of balance," Kaya explained. "It speaks of the axial poles as twins that hold the Earth in place. At the end of each age these twins are instructed to leave their position and let the world plunge into chaos. After this, a new world is born, and the whole cycle repeats itself again and again and again."

"But first," stated Mr. Ahote, "we await the Pahana—our lost White Brother. When He returns, the wicked will be destroyed, and a new age of peace will be ushered into our world."

Second Mesa
Hopi Cultural Center

They found Henderson where they had left him, in front of a computer terminal in a side office. Kaya's uncle had given his niece a warm hug, told her to be careful and to come to him if she needed anything. Now the group was huddled around Henderson's computer.

Henderson sat back and laced his fingers behind his head. "So, did you kids learn anything new?"

Alyson was the first to speak up. "The Hopis believe that the poles will shift."

"I told you! A polar shift fits one of the scientific scenarios."

"Oh, bunk," exclaimed Nash, perhaps a little more irritably than he had intended. "There's nothing scientific about your Web Bots, Bryan. It's nothing more than computerized guess work."

His friend was up to the challenge and gave him a big grin. "Face facts, Jeremy. The world is a loaded gun and it's just waiting to go off." The lanky man looked at Alyson and winked. "But some of us are doing something about it, like the IHC."

Nash rolled his eyes. Why was he always the only rational person wherever he went?

"The IHC are a bunch of kooks," he grumbled.

"What's the IHC?" asked Kaya.

"The Institute for Human Continuity," answered Henderson. "They're developing underground shelters at safe zones all over the planet to be ready for Doomsday two thousand and twelve."

"Enough," said Nash. "I have a massive headache, and the last

142

thing I want to talk about are billionaires who don't have anything better else to do with their money."

"Fine," said Henderson, and he gave Alyson another wink. "I think we won that round."

Nash pretended he didn't hear that. "Did you find anything else in the image?"

Henderson nodded and reached for a printout. "I downloaded a steganography program from the Net, ran it through the image of the swastika in the sun and this is what I came up with." He handed it to Nash.

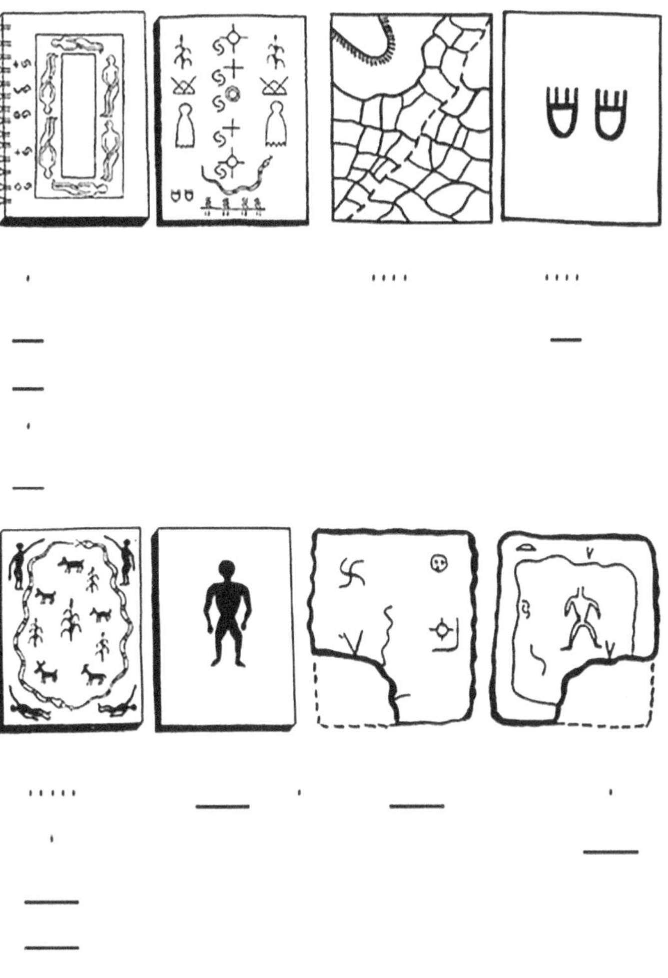

Nash held it up. On the printout was an image that contained eight rectangular boxes, with a series of dots and dashes below each box. "Any idea what this means?"

"Haven't a clue," shrugged Henderson.

Alyson plucked it out of Nash's hands. She glanced at it. "Me either."

"Big surprise there," he said dryly taking it back from his sister and promptly handing it over to Kaya. "What do you think?"

She studied it for a heartbeat or two. "These eight images look like the front and back of the four Hopi Sacred Stones."

"Four Sacred Stones?" asked Alyson. "Have we talked about Sacred Stones yet? I'm getting confused."

Kaya smiled and laid a gentle hand on her forearm. "I don't think we have. You see, Hopis believe that at the beginning of this current Fourth Cycle, the Great Spirit came down and made an appearance to the human beings. He then sent humans in the four directions of the world and gave each of the four groups a stone tablet. The Sacred Stones. What you see here are the front and back of the four stones. Then, over time, he changed the groups into four different colors."

"By four colors, do you mean four races?" asked Henderson.

"More or less. To the East, The Great Spirit gave the red people, the Native-Americans, one of the Sacred Stones. They were to be the guardians of the earth. To the South, He gave the yellow race of people the Guardianship of the wind. To the West He gave the black race of people the Guardianship of the water, and finally, to the North, He gave the white race of people the Guardianship of the fire."

Nash was looking again at the image. "This Hopi stone on the right seems to be missing a piece."

"Very good, Jeremy. The missing piece was broken off by the Great Spirit and given to the True White Brother."

"The Pahana," exclaimed Alyson, snapping her fingers.

"Correct. And as my uncle has said, when the Pahana returns, we will know him by the missing piece of the Hopi Stone he carries—and the Great Purification will begin."

"And the Hopis are in possession of one of these Sacred Stones?" asked Nash.

"Of course," said Kaya patiently. "The Earth Stone."

Nash ran his fingers through his hair. "I think we need to see this Stone. Would that be possible?"

"Perhaps, but I cannot guarantee it. The Hopi Stone is in possession of the Hopi Fire Clan." Kaya replied. "Grandfather Martin Kikmongwi leads the Clan and lives in the village of Hotevilla. Just a short drive from here."

"Well," observed Nash. "I guess that's our next stop. Maybe the Fire Clan could shed some light on why these stones are in my father's message. But it's late. Let's bunk down for the night and get an early start in the morning."

White Mountains, Arizona
Ecotopian Compound

After the attack at the power plant, Hayden Mayer, the Pahana, sent Big Man to the offices of the Department of the Interior in Phoenix on a secret mission. As with all the blessed missions the Pahana had bestowed upon him before, Big Man was more than willing to comply.

The secret mission completed, with pride in his heart, Big Man was now returning to the Pahana's mountain compound.

There was no freeway between Phoenix and the White Mountains. It took Big Man almost three hours into the late morning, in inclement weather, to reach the Ecoptopian's compound in the eastern part of the State.

To the casual observer, the compound looked like any hippie commune—dancing circles of hippies beating drums and enjoying life in the middle of the wilderness. But the wooded area below the mountain tops also served as a secure place away from prying eyes. The compound, in fact, contained a series of caves dug out from the mountain terrain and used to store militia supplies.

As Big Man approached over a winding dirt road, he could see dilapidated tree houses peppering the property. Big Man was grateful to the disgruntled old environmentalist who gave the property to the Pahana before he died.

Once inside the compound, Big Man drove to the main house—a large geodesic dome—in the center of the compound. There he parked his Jeep, climbed the short steps to the deck of the house, and entered the main room.

The Pahana was sitting on an ornate Navajo rug in the middle of the room, legs crossed and eyes closed. Beside him were two young women, a blonde and a redhead in their early twenties, both dressed in hippie garb. They sat quietly. To Big Man, they seemed to be meditating.

Big Man did not speak. He stood there patiently. Always patiently. He never disturbed the Pahana. Ever. A few minutes later, the Pahana opened his eyes, as did the two young women. With a sharp wave of his hand, he dismissed the females.

As soon as they left the room, the Pahana looked up at Big Man and said, "Come and sit, Brother."

Big Man did as he was told and sat in front of the Pahana, crossed his legs, and waited quietly for him to speak.

"Tell me, Brother. Do we have access?"

"Yes." Big Man was proud that once again he was able to serve the Pahana. "We have the permit."

The Pahana smiled. "And the Sierra Club didn't suspect anything?"

"Not a thing," confirmed Big Man, proud of the Pahana's ability to execute such a complex plan. "They welcome us to the demonstration. The reputation of the Ecotopians, which you have so carefully nurtured, drew the Sierra Club's praise for our involvement. And based on their endorsement, the Interior Department complied."

"Good, good. It's time. We must prepare. Inform Ryvre and Rainbow. They're preparing the Ultralights. They know what to do."

The Pahana stood smoothly. The white man's tall stature towered over the sitting Big Man. "This will permanently prepare the way for the Great Purification." He placed a hand on Big Man's shoulder. "You have done well, my Brother. Now go. You have work to do."

Four Corners, Arizona
Hotevilla

As they drove through the historic village of Hotevilla, which consisted of a small cluster of adobe buildings, Kaya instructed Nash to park in front of a large structure about halfway down the narrow dirt street.

Kaya rapped lightly on the wooden door, and they were greeted a moment later by an elderly Hopi man. He and Kaya exchanged, in Hopi, what to Nash seemed to be pleasantries. Then she mentioned the group behind her and said something else. The man listened quietly, nodded once, and then simply led the way inside the dark structure.

Kaya motioned for them to follow, and Nash found himself moving along a dimly lit hallway. To Nash, the lingering scent of old rugs and burnt wood hanging in the air was not unlike the scents in Kaya's uncle's home in Oraibi.

Silently, they were shown into a small room where a fire crackled in a fireplace that probably wouldn't have passed most fire codes. An even older looking Hopi man sat unmoving in a cushioned wooden chair. Kaya greeted the man and then made introductions. Grandfather Martin Kikmongwi, wearing a red cotton shirt and faded blue jeans that looked almost as old as he was, nodded to each person in turn.

Kaya then spoke to him earnestly in her native tongue, no doubt explaining the reason for their unusual visit. Like the old gentleman who greeted them at the door, Grandfather Martin said nothing while she spoke. When she finished, he asked her a question. She answered. The old man nodded and directed them to sit down in the wicker chairs scattered throughout the room.

Nash leaned over and whispered to Kaya, "We came here to ask him for help, Kaya. Not sit through another lecture. Remember, there are people trying to kill us. We need answers, and we need help."

Kaya touched his arm, and a thrill raced through him. "Please bear with me, Jeremy. It has to be done this way."

At that moment, Nash would have done anything for her. He nodded and sat back. The old man had closed his eyes, and Nash thought that was a pretty damn good idea. He seemed to be nothing but exhausted these past few days.

No surprise there, he thought. *Running for your life has a way of doing that.*

As the old man seemed to gather his thoughts, and as dim patches of daylight filtered through the small windows, a phantasmagoric haze created by the fire drifted across the small room and reflected some of the angling light. Nash could have slept. At the very least, he felt comfortable in this small, warm dwelling. A fit setting for storytelling.

Finally, the old Hopi spoke in broken English, and as he did, his voice seemed to carry the timbre of legend. "I am entrusted with the sacred Fire Clan tablet of the Hopi. The tablet represents our ancient title to this land, which existed long before the arrival of Columbus. The land has never been relinquished. It was entrusted to me under the highest authority, to be held until the last stage of our prophecies has been completed. The signs that we have entered that final stage are now clear."

Henderson looked triumphantly at Nash as if to say, *See?*

The elder Hopi then went on to describe the Sacred Hopi Stone. It was apparently very small, perhaps four inches square and made of a dark-colored stone. The small tablet had a piece broken off of one corner. One side of it was marked with several symbols, and on the other side was the figure of a man without a head.

Grandfather continued. "The Four Corners area of the Hopi

is bordered by Four Sacred Mountains. The area contained within these four mountains will serve a special purpose for the survival of mankind during the coming apocalypse. It is vital that this area be left in its natural state. All nations must protect this spiritual center. In accordance with the Great Spirit's instructions, our ancestors have established sacred shrines upon each of these four mountains. From within this spiritual center, surrounded by these Four Sacred Mountains, our religious leaders serve as caretakers of all the land and life in the Western Hemisphere. Drilling for gas, oil, gold, uranium, water, or any combination of these will directly affect everyone on Mother Earth."

"Apocalypse eleven eighteen," Henderson remarked. "The time has come to destroy those destroying the Earth."

Still angling for the 2012 myth, thought Nash.

The old Hopi rose slowly and walked noiselessly to the window. He gazed briefly at the intense sun before he said, "My good friend Lame Deer predicted many, many years ago that the day is coming when nature will stop the electricity. A young man will come, who will know how to shut off the electricity. But there is a Light Man coming bringing a new light. The Light Man has the power to stop all atomic power and to stop wars."

Nash nearly rolled his eyes. Granted, this was his natural reaction to hearing anything that lacked solid, scientific evidence, but out of deference to the holy leader and the others, he kept his eyes locked firmly ahead at the old man.

Grandfather Martin turned from the window. To Nash's utter amazement, there were tears in the old man's eyes. "Mother Earth is in pain, brothers and sisters. The signs are all around us. It is coming to pass. The Great Purification will soon be upon us when the white man's electro-power goes off."

They all were quiet for awhile. Then Kaya spoke. "Grandfather, would it be possible for us to see the Hopi Sacred Stone?"

"We do not have it, my child," he said. He spoke with heart breaking sadness. "It is gone."

"Gone?" Nash blurted.

"Yes," replied Grandfather Martin.

"But I don't understand," said Kaya.

The old Hopi now moved carefully over to the fire in the corner and stoked it with a long iron rod. He stared intently into the fire. Tears still shone on his wide cheekbones.

"A young man by the name of Hayden Mayer came to us several years ago. He claimed to be the Pahana and said that he held the missing piece of our sacred stone."

Henderson sat forward. "What happened then?"

"He was very persistent. Very, very persistent. He visited the reservation on three occasions, and each time he was turned away. Then..." He closed his eyes and hung his head.

"Then what?" asked Kaya.

"He came back with others and said that the Hopis were denying his destiny as the Pahana and that he would usher in the next world himself." The old Hopi turned and looked at each of them, one at a time, thoughtfully. "They forcibly took the sacred stone from us. We don't know where it is now."

"I never knew," said Kaya, shaking her head.

"The elders didn't speak of it, child, and I shouldn't be speaking of it now." He then looked at Nash. "But perhaps there is hope of it returning to us someday."

He held Nash's gaze for a good heartbeat or two, and then turned his heavy gaze to Kaya. "Perhaps it's time you make a visit to the Keeper of the Secret."

Kaya blinked. "Who?"

"His name is Peter Somerton," said Grandfather Martin, sitting again in his cushioned chair. "He resides in Sedona, near the Spiritual Life Center. He has knowledge of the missing piece and of our tablet."

Nash thought a moment. *Now where have I heard that name before?*

Flagstaff, Arizona

Addison Parker flicked his cigarette away into the empty parking lot. A small breeze made its way through his open SUV window. His partner sat silently next to him. Both were sweating profusely in the heat of the car. Mercifully, storm clouds had begun gathering in the sky, providing some relief from the Arizona sun.

Parker and his partner had spent the past forty-eight hours on a wild goose chase searching for Nash, based on information provided by Prescott from Garcia. Nash wasn't here, and Parker silently fumed. Garcia was proving to be useless.

But Parker was a man on a mission. Not only did he have a job to do, but he had a score to settle with the man who soiled his professional reputation.

As his henchman munched on a dried-out liquor store hot dog, Parker gazed at the picture of Nash on his cell phone that Prescott forwarded to him. He stared at it intently, burning the image into his mind.

The buzzing of his LPI phone pulled him from his dark thoughts. He pocketed his personal cell and brought the secure phone up to his ear.

"Parker here."

"Where are you?" It was Prescott.

"Northern Arizona. Near Flagstaff."

"Remember. The conference is tomorrow."

Parker knew what Prescott meant. Rumor had it that the conference was going to announce to the world the real reason behind the current geologic and climatic chaos, and it could expose the Project.

The Project, Parker knew, was covering all its tracks, real or imagined.

"And Parker?"

"Yes."

"This small weapon of yours...can it do the job?"

"A handful of them can take out a Navy Cruiser," replied the hired killer. "There will be little to worry about from the conference."

"Good. Get on with it then," Prescott ordered, and hung up.

Sedona, Arizona

As the skies cleared and the sun set over the towering southwestern rim of the vast Colorado Plateau, the massive rust red rock formations of Sedona lit up into a beautiful orange hue.

"Fantastic," breathed Alyson in awe.

"Never been here before, I gather?" Henderson asked.

Alyson shook her head, her lips parted with awe.

"The New Agers claim Sedona is an important spiritual center," said Henderson. "That its rocks, mesas, and canyons emanate a mystical force."

Nash rolled his eyes. "You know, why can't anyone ever go to Sedona and simply enjoy its beauty without being bombarded by its supposed vortexes and energy and mystical bullshit?"

"The same way you can't go to North Pole, Alaska and not hear about Santa Claus, Jeremy," quipped Henderson, laughing. "Just roll with it, Jeremy. Roll with it."

"I will never roll with whatever *it* is."

His sister, obviously, had latched onto only one word. "Did you say *vortex?*"

"Should have kept my mouth shut," said Nash, glumly.

"Yes, energy vortexes," Kaya answered. "There are dozens of them here in Sedona. They are believed to be locations of energy flow that exist on multiple dimensions. The energy of the vortexes interacts with a person's inner self. It is not easily explained—only experienced, which is why such vortexes are ideally suited to facilitate prayer, mediation, and healing."

"And to drive skeptics crazy," chuckled Henderson. "Sedona is considered to be one of the most energetically supercharged locations on earth, in fact. Remember the nineteen-eighty-seven Harmonic Convergence?"

"The what?" asked Alyson.

"Jesus, Bryan," Nash groaned. "Please. Give it a rest."

But Henderson plowed forward, clearly enjoying seeing his friend's discomfort. "On the weekend of August sixteenth and seventeenth, the great Harmonic Convergence was to take place. At the time, some believed the Earth would start slipping out of its time beam and risk spinning off into space. A great many people believed this—and not just prominent leaders of the New Age movement like Shirley MacLaine, but also millions and millions of others."

"Shirley MacLaine," Nash groaned. "Now there's a prominent testimonial for you."

"Quiet, Jeremy," his sister said. "I want to hear what Bryan has to say." Her voice became genial. "Go ahead, Bryan."

Nash noticed that his sister was becoming more and more enamored with Henderson, and less and less with logic.

Maybe she's not my actual sister, Nash mused. *Maybe she's adopted. One can hope.*

Henderson shot a toothy smile at Alyson and happily continued. "Now, only by the psychic efforts of the human race could the earth be saved, or so some believed. And if enough people gathered at sacred places around the globe and concentrated hard enough, the earth would stay in place. A New Age would begin, and a new era of harmony and love would be inaugurated."

Nash groaned once again, slumping his shoulders.

"And with Sedona being such a sacred place, it hosted the biggest of the gatherings. Ultimately the earth did not slip away and spin into space, as you might have noticed. The convergence of people in Sedona obviously saved mankind."

Henderson winked at Nash, and the skeptic was seriously

wondering if Henderson—perhaps, as a result of all those psyche-delic drugs in college—had turned into some kind of New Age flake. Nash also didn't know how much Kaya bought into this New Age claptrap, but it seemed he was outnumbered three to one. He sighed. He was clearly going to have to *roll with it*. For now.

Still, he managed to change the subject. "Alyson. See if the radio is working. Let's see what's going on in the news."

Alyson and Henderson exchanged a knowing smile, and then, to appease her brother, she promptly turned on the radio. She scanned through stations mostly filled with static, until she found one that came in fairly clear. It was a talk show, and the host was speaking to a book author.

The host was saying, "In your new book on the twenty-twelve end of days, Mr. Benson, you made some dire predictions. How do they jive with the recent geologic and environmental events we have been experiencing? Especially over the last twenty-four hours?"

"Unfortunately," said the author, a deep-voiced man. "They *jive* far too well. Let's take the aurora borealis, for example. It has now occurred at latitudes unheard of in human history. And volcanic eruptions, hurricane level storms, and earthquakes have happened in some of the most unlikely places—"

"Like the hurricane that hit Anchorage last night?"

"Yes," he said. "Like that."

"So how do we prepare for these end times?" the host questioned.

"In my book, I list the ten ways you can prepare for the twenty-twelve disaster."

"Probably invest in tin-foil hats," Nash blurted out sarcastically and scanned for a new station.

Alyson shot him a dirty look. "Hey! We were listening to that."

Nash ignored her plea. Alyson was about to protest again when the radio settled on another station in the middle of another interview.

"...guest is Professor Peter Somerton..."

"Hey!" shouted Henderson. "That's him! The Secrets guy."

"Quiet!" hissed Kaya.

"Mr. Somerton," the female interviewer continued, "your background on Native American culture is impressive. You're fluent in sign language used by many of the tribes. You have written a number of books that deciphered the hidden meanings of American petroglyphs—particularly, the Hopi. How did you become such an expert on codes and symbols?"

"For starters, as you may or may not know, I'm half-Sioux and was raised traditionally by my Native American mother." Somerton spoke eloquently and precisely, his smooth voice reaching them as easily as if he were sitting in the car with them. He went on, "And while in the military working as an officer with the Army Security Agency, I was trained in the science of crypto analysis."

"And that gave you the foundation to decipher Native American prophesies, too?"

"Yes."

"Like those of the Hopi?"

"The Hopi prophesies are a hot topic these days."

"What can you tell about them, professor?"

"It's a vast subject—"

"How about in relation to the end times, in particular, what the Hopi might have to say about current climatic phenomena happening in our world today?"

There was a pause, as the professor was no doubt collecting his thoughts. Then he said, "Like the Maya, Aztec, and other Native American tribal wisdom traditions, the Hopi tell of a series of worlds which have come into existence then disappeared. Each of these worlds may be thought of as a cycle of civilization. And according to the Hopi, we are currently at the end of the Fourth World—the fourth cycle of civilization."

Nash looked in the rear-view mirror and saw Henderson nodding his head, eating this stuff up. Alyson was wide-eyed, too.

"What were the other worlds?" asked the female radio host.

"Well, as the Hopi believe, the First World ended when the world's volcanoes erupted as one. The Second World ended when the poles shifted, and the earth was covered in ice. The Third World was very corrupt and was destroyed through water. A great deluge drowned the earth as large continents sunk and broke apart into smaller islands. When dry land appeared again, those that had survived the massive flood found themselves in the Fourth World. This is our world today, the world that many Native Americans believe is soon coming to an end."

"There's been speculation that the extreme climatic and geological events we are currently experiencing are precursors to this world's end. Do you agree? Is there anything in the Hopi prophesies about such changes?"

"Indeed," said Somerton. "They very much believe that Nature will speak to us with its mighty breath of wind, and there will be earthquakes and floods and great disasters. The Hopis warned the world of this in nineteen fifty-nine."

"Nineteen fifty-nine?"

"Yes. A delegation of six traditional Hopi leaders, led by the late spiritual leader, David Alo, traveled to the United Nations Building to fulfill a sacred mission in accordance with ancient Hopi instructions."

Kaya sat straight up, excited. "That was my grandfather! Grandfather David. Please turn the volume up, Jeremy."

Nash complied.

"And what was their mission?" the interviewer asked.

"It was foretold that the Hopi leaders would go east, where a house of mica, the United Nations Building, would stand at this time. There, great leaders from many lands would be gathered to help any people who are in trouble. The delegation was to go when the lands of the Hopi and other Indians were about to be taken away from them, and their way of life was in danger of being completely eradicated."

"That must have been quite an event."

"That's putting it mildly. I don't think the United Nations knew what hit them." Somerton chuckled lightly. "David Alo invoked the Hopi prophecies about the consequences of living out of balance with nature and spirit. He predicted floods, earthquakes, extinction of animals and birds, climate changes, hailstorms, and many damaging hurricanes. These, he claimed, were the loud voices of his ancestors' warnings. And on the evening of their appearance at the United Nations, heavy rains, strong winds, and the worst floods in New York's history assailed the New York City area. Major highways were closed, and the UN Building's lower sub-floors flooded, forcing a shutdown of its heating and air conditioning. This is all recorded fact."

"What happened?" asked the woman breathlessly.

People came to their senses and realized it was just a coincidence, Nash wanted to say, but kept his mouth shut and his thoughts to himself.

"Native peoples attending the General Assembly considered these events more than coincidental, of course," said Somerton. "The Hopis called on all the participants, including UN officials, to form a great circle in a symbolic act of prayer. One participant reported feeling a sense of safety within this circle. Others noted that no further storm damage occurred in Manhattan after the circle had gathered."

Nash snorted. He hadn't meant to, but he seriously could not control himself. Kaya promptly shushed him. Nash sighed and continued driving while the radio host plunged eagerly forward.

"Professor Somerton, there's a report that a conference is about to be held in Arizona attended by dozens of esoteric experts to discuss two thousand and twelve."

"That's true. The conference attendees will present their particular theory of what will happen on December twenty-first, two thousand and twelve and its significance for mankind. Because of the growing natural disasters and climate changes, the major seers around the country are meeting in Sedona, known as the capital of the New Age movement. There, they will discuss a wide variety of topics, including spiritual, health, economic, and historical facts that apply to the twenty-twelve predictions. They will investigate the coming shift of the ages, as revealed by many world traditions, scholars, thinkers, and philosophers."

"Can you tell us what, exactly, will be discussed, Professor?"

"Many topics, of course. The completion of the thirteenth B'ak'tun cycle in the Long Count of the Maya calendar, the prophesies of Nostradamus as they apply to twenty-twelve, Native American prophesy, the predictions of Edgar Cayce, Terence McKenna's numerological novelty theory, *Bueno de Mesquita* forecasts, and many, many other topics pertaining to the subject."

"Will you be attending the conference, Professor?"

Somerton became circumspect. "Let's just say I'll be monitoring the activities."

"Thank you, Professor. And where can people reach you?"

"I can be reached through the Spiritual Life Center in Sedona, Arizona."

Nash quickly turned the radio off. "Bryan, you know this area. How much farther to this Spiritual Life Center?"

"Should be up the road a bit. And Jeremy?"

"What?"

"Let's keep our skepticism under our hats. Try not to piss off this Keeper of the Secret, okay?"

Nash sighed, shook his head and just took in the breathtakingly beautiful landscape.

Project KRATOS

Prescott was watching CNN's live report on the hurricane in Alaska while at the same time trying to reach Parker on his phone.

After several attempts, frustrated, he gave up. Had the assassin found Wilcox? Had he disposed of him as ordered?

Prescott sat back in his chair and tried to relax. He interlaced his hands behind his head and closed his eyes, and almost immediately he detected a musky scent in the air again. He made a mental note to order the environmental air handler to be re-calibrated. Though most of the men working there were comfortable with the atmosphere, he still couldn't get use to the constant flow of moist cool air that hung like a heavy blanket that circulated throughout the miles of the Project infrastructure.

Relax, he thought. *All will be taken care of.*

He was about to pick up the HVAC remote on his steel desk in his soundproof room to turn down the air when it suddenly began to shake and vibrate. Remarkably, the remote moved just out of his reach. Calmly, he looked up and could see the hanging fluorescent lights swinging back and forth; the visible I-beams of the ceiling from which they hung undulated, then shimmered, rattling the pipes they supported.

The vibrations had just stopped when Alfred Laveen entered his office. Laveen, a short man with a nervous smile, was now the top scientist at Project KRATOS, with advanced degrees in molecular energy and quantum physics—second only to Jackson Wilcox when the Project was conceived.

Prescott could see that Laveen was concerned. Prescott didn't have to ask why.

"What did we get from that last run?" Prescott asked.

"Mr. Prescott," Laveen stammered, "We need to consider what—"

"I asked, *what* did we measure from the last run?"

Laveen took in some air and looked down at the report in his hand. "Energy was point zero zero one percent of output."

Prescott's eyes brightened and a thin smile crossed his stern face. "But that's incredible!" Prescott knew the best they could ever get from a centrifuge technology was .07 percent.

Although Laveen nodded gravely, his slightly sweating forehead was creased in worry. "Sir, Wilcox could still be right about the vibrations—"

Prescott waved the man's fears off. "We have the energy engine of the universe nearly in our grasp, Mr. Laveen. We are not going to stop now. Is that clear?"

The professor sighed heavily. "As you wish."

"Good. Now, what about the Hawking radiation?"

"We were correct on that," Laveen answered. "As we theorized, the total amount of energy released during the final seconds of evaporation is equivalent to a billion megaton hydrogen bombs."

Prescott could hardly contain his delight. This was fantastic news. Now, if they could only harness that engine...

"What about the collector?" Prescott asked. "Where are we on that?"

"We're making progress, sir. The collector shows an increase in the absorption of the electromagnetic-spectrum radiation that is propelled by the Hawking radiation. We're almost there."

"Good. Back to work. I want that engine harnessed, and I want it harnessed soon."

Leveen nodded solemnly and left, and Prescott immediately turned his attention to another lingering problem. Hayden Mayer. He and his Ecotopians needed to be found. And if Prescott's intel was correct, Mayer could be a real threat to the physical existence of the Project.

Prescott picked up his phone and once again called his EPA contact.

Phoenix, Arizona
Environmental Protection Agency Field Office

Special Agent Paige Chandler was sitting at her desk at the EPA's Phoenix field office staring at an old picture of her parents. She didn't hear her office door open until someone cleared his throat.

She gasped and looked up through her dishwater blonde locks to see the Field Office Director, George Tolleson, standing in her doorway. He was not a big man—maybe an inch or two taller than Paige—and he always wore a neat suit, even during the hottest of days. His expression, as usual, was dour. Paige always suspected he had a crush on her, sometimes offering her furtive glances. But the man was a professional, and he always kept things on a comfortable level.

He pointed to the neatly organized stacks of papers on her desk in front of her. "You're behind," he noted patiently. "I asked for that report on the Glenn Canyon Dam protest three days ago."

"They're kooks," she replied.

"True. But it's a well-organized protest. So there's crowd control to consider and sanitation requirements and—"

"Then let some lower bureaucrat handle it," she said, waving him off. "They're good at paper pushing. Or the local police."

Tolleson stepped into her office and pulled the door closed behind him. He grabbed a cushioned client chair and pulled it around her desk. As he sat, their knees nearly touched.

"Look," he said calmly, "the country and the whole damn world, for that matter, is going nutzo over these geologic and climactic anomalies. Every wing nut with a cause is blaming this on everything from the Mayans to cow farts and global warming is high on the agenda of the culprits."

"They're not my prob—"

He held up a hand and opened a green folder he had been holding. "See this? Now these *kooks* as you call them are blaming the world's dams for causing global warming. They believe, in fact, that dams are the largest single source of human-caused methane emissions. Not only that, but they actually believe the world's dams have shifted so much weight that they have altered the speed of the earth's rotation, the tilt of its axis, and the shape of its gravitational field."

"Like I said," she pushed, "kooks."

"Look, Paige, this protest at the Glenn Canyon Dam is attracting every eco-group in the country. They'll be shouting and waving signs demanding that dams be removed. I need you there."

"To do what? Crowd control? George, we already have people there. Good people. They, and the local police, can handle it." She paused and reached out, putting her hand on his forearm. She could almost see him shiver with her touch. Her calculated touch. "Please, George, I think I'm onto something here."

He glanced down at the open file on her desk. It was, of course, her parent's file. Their **Pending/Unsolved** file. At an early age, Paige had lost both parents to a massive house fire. Officially, the fire was ruled a homicide, as there had been evidence of gasoline being used. Unfortunately, the police (and the FBI, since her parents had been working secretly with the government on various nuclear energy programs) had exhausted every lead, and the file had been relegated to the *unsolved* stack. Paige herself had been spared, since she had been away at a friend's slumber party, an act which had saved her life.

Later in life, once she grasped the nuances of the case, once she learned that her parents had received death threats from various eco-terrorist groups, Paige became devoted to bringing those responsible for her parents' murders to justice. Which was how she eventually came to work as an inspector for the Criminal Enforcement Division of the Environmental Projection Agency pursuing those who used violence to advance their ecological agenda.

But secretly—and sometimes not so secretly—she pursued her parents' killers.

Tolleson made some sympathetic noises as he glanced down at her parents' open file. Paige knew the man worried about her, and he had given her a fair amount of leeway to pursue her parents' killers—perhaps too much leeway.

"Paige, you know we have no proof that the Ecotopians are behind these latest attacks."

The Ecotopians were, of course, her number one suspects for setting the horrific fire that took her parents' lives.

She crossed her arms under her chest. They had gone through this argument—and similar arguments—countless times. "If there's proof, George, I'll find it."

"I have no doubt about it, Paige, but once again, the Ecotopians have a sterling reputation. General knowledge is that they're as much a terrorist group as the Sierra Club."

Paige looked up sharply. "If so, then why is their leadership so secretive, George? Who is this, Hayden Mayer? Why is there so little information on him? I tell you, it stinks, and you know it."

Tolleson sighed and sat back. He appeared to be debating something. Finally, he sat forward. "Okay, I'm pulling you from the dam protests."

"Thank you, George."

"And I have some news for you. I think we have a lead on the location of the Ecotopians."

Now she grabbed both his arms. Completely unprofessional, she knew, but she didn't care. George was a good friend, and they were close. "What kind of lead?"

"There's a man in Arizona. Rumor has it—and this is just a rumor, granted—that he knows where Mayer and the Ecotopians are."

"Great! Give me the four-one-one and I'm out of here."

Paige bolted up from her chair and reached for her suit jacket.

"One minute, young lady," Tolleson said, stepping in front of her. "I want you to wait for Zack Safford. He called from HomeSec in Washington and will be here shortly. He's going with you."

Zack Safford, she knew, was a good man to have on an investigation. Ex-FBI, he was a great help with the Four Corners terrorist incident.

"Okay. I'll wait. I'll be across the street getting some coffee."

He watched her don her jacket. As she shoved her parents' file in her briefcase, he said, "Paige, if this pans out, maybe you can put your obsession behind you."

Paige glanced at him. "I suppose so, George."

She had been obsessed with her parents' murder for so long she had never, admittedly, looked much beyond it.

Once outside the building, she looked up into the darkening sky. Pulling her jacket up around her shoulders, she walked towards the corner Starbucks.

She didn't notice the robed, derelict man watching her from a beat up sedan.

Spiritual Life Center
Sedona, Arizona

Nash and the others arrived at the Spiritual Life Center in the late afternoon. Henderson explained that the rocks, trees, and shrubs often took on a special look at that time of the day—a favorite time for photographers. Despite his reservations about Sedona's mystical powers, Nash could appreciate the incredible beauty of the quaint city nestled in this high wilderness.

Presently, the lowering sun in the sky cast a cool light, full of yellows and reds that made the desert landscape almost glow. Teddy Bear cactus seemed to be surrounded by a sort of shimmering aura. Nash rubbed his eyes. Surely this was a trick of light.

They parked the Jeep in front of the center, and a few moments later the quartet was standing in front of the welcome desk.

"May I help you?" asked a sour-looking senior citizen with white curly hair. Reading glasses hung from her rubbery neck.

"We're looking for Mr. Somerton," Nash answered quietly. No need to announce to the world their intent. After all, the center was fairly busy.

"Mr. Somerton isn't here," she replied curtly.

"Where would he be then?" asked Henderson. "We have urgent business with him."

She frowned and made a show of putting on her glasses. She studied the group suspiciously from behind thick lenses. "We have no way of getting in touch with him. He contacts us."

"Fine," said Nash. He pulled out a business card and wrote a short message on the back. "Could you please give him this when you do hear from him? Like my friend said, it is quite important for us to speak with him."

She took the card and placed it near the phone. "I can make no guarantees, young man, but I will give him your message if and when we hear from him again."

Nash thanked her, and as the group stepped away, momentarily stumped, Nash caught Kaya staring intently across the room. He followed her gaze. She appeared to be looking at a short, round man in his late forties with a graying beard. The man was in the process of moving several large boxes from the next room to a small display area behind the welcome desk. He must have been part of the center staff.

"I know him," she said. "Hang on."

And Kaya, to Nash's surprise, walked right past the front desk, unhooked a velvet rope, re-hooked it, and then continued on. All to the shocked consternation of the elder front desk clerk.

"Miss, you can't go in there without buying a pass. Miss? Miss!"

But Kaya kept walking, heading straight for the rotund gentleman. Nash dashed over to the front desk and pulled out a $20. He handed it to the clerk. "We'll take four tickets, please."

A few minutes later, after a brief introduction, Nash found himself in a cramped office filled to the brim with Native American art and artifacts. The little man was Professor Ian Clarkdale, and it turned out Kaya knew him quite well. He had been one of her college professor.

"How long has it been, Kaya? Five years? Are you back to do some research? asked the professor jovially, sitting comfortably behind his desk. He obviously enjoyed visitors. He had smiled warmly at each, shaking hands with all of them as introductions were made. The professor was quite familiar with Nash's own work—and impressed.

Nash liked him already.

Kaya said, "In a way, yes. And what are you doing here, Professor? I thought you were still teaching at Northern Arizona University?"

"Yes, I still teach at NAU. But I also spend time as a docent here at the Center leading tours and teaching visitors about the Native American cultures we have here in Arizona." He smiled warmly at Kaya. "Now tell me...what brings you to the Center?"

"We came to see Peter Somerton, but we were told he's not here."

"Ah, Peter Somerton. Well, you were told right. He's rather difficult to get a hold of."

"Professor," Nash implored, sitting forward. "It's important that we see Somerton. A matter of life and death. *Our* lives and my *parents'* deaths."

Clarkdale raised an eyebrow. "Perhaps you better tell me what this is all about."

Clarkdale sat silently and listened to Nash—with Alyson and Henderson occasionally interrupting—tell him what had transpired over these past few days. As Nash listened to himself explaining everything, it sounded crazy even to his ears.

When he was finished, Clarkdale sat back and stared at him openly. "That's some story."

"I assure you, sir, it's all true."

He nodded, but Nash noted some uncertainty in the man's eyes. "And you feel Somerton can shed light on the problem?"

"Grandfather Martin thought so," replied Kaya. "That's why he sent us here."

A mischievous smile suddenly appeared on Clarkdale's face. The mention of her esteemed uncle seemed to remove all doubt in the man. He suddenly stood from his desk and clapped his hands. "Well, I've often wondered how it would feel playing Indiana Jones." He walked over to Kaya and took her hand. "Let's go see Somerton."

"But I thought he was difficult to find—"

Clarkdale winked. "Some of us know his secrets."

Parker could give a shit about Sedona's mystical history. He had a target to find. Two targets to find, and it rankled him to no end that he had been pulled off the Nash hit to take care of some eccentric old professor.

Take care of Wilcox, then take care of Nash, he told himself as he drove slowly through the center of town. He and his men needed to regroup and come up with a plan. Apparently, Wilcox was difficult to locate.

Parker liked a challenge.

Luckily, he had his connections.

Everywhere.

He and his partner stopped outside a rundown motorcycle shop, a shop that looked like a blemish in this pristine city. He knew a man there—an ex-biker with a horrific past—and the man owed him a favor.

Enchantment Resort
Sedona, Arizona

It was cramped in Nash's Jeep now that Clarkdale had joined them. They drove west through the town of Sedona. The sun was low on the horizon and in their eyes.

Clarkdale pointed to a sign that read Boynton Canyon. "Somerton has a condo at Enchantment."

"So, the curse of Long Canyon doesn't bother him?" said Kaya, and Nash caught a rare mischievous look in her almond shaped dark eyes.

"Curse?" asked Alyson, perking up. "What curse?"

"Why don't you inform your friends, Kaya, about the Long Canyon Curse?" said Clarkdale, smiling. "You did a class paper on that, did you not?"

"Right, and you gave me a C."

"But an A for originality."

"What's this curse?" asked Henderson.

"Boynton Canyon, or Long Canyon, as the Hopis call it," Kaya replied, "is sacred ground for Native Americans. Medicine Men from various tribes could go into it and do their prayer ceremonies at certain times of the year, which they still do to this day. Developers wanted to build casino back in the canyon where the Enchantment Resort stands today."

"Tell them about the skeletons," Clarkdale said, and Nash heard the amusement in the man's voice.

"What skeletons?" piped up Alyson excitedly.

"Skeletons had been dug up when the casino developers were

trying to build. Shortly thereafter, the site started experiencing accidents and strange happenings. People vanished. Workers got sick. The owners eventually decided to sell, claiming they couldn't build there. The next couple of building attempts resulted in bankruptcy for the developers. The latest attempt, Enchantment, has stuck it out...so far."

"Quite a story," Nash quipped, knowing his voice dripped with sarcasm.

"And a *story* it is," exclaimed Clarkdale. "That's why I gave Kaya a C." He patted the Hopi woman on the knee and grinned. "But the paper was very entertaining."

The group laughed, but Nash noted it was a nervous laughter.

Nash could go on and on about the improbability of curses, but he decided to use it as a theme for his next book. He even had a tentative title: *Curses: Pure Bunk.*

He nodded to himself. The title had a certain derisive ring to it. He liked that.

The paved road turned into a dirt road, and several minutes later they passed through the gates of the resort. Clarkdale directed them to the main building which was overlooked by impressive towering red rocks soaring up from the canyon floor directly behind the building.

Nash whistled. Curses or not, this was a helluva beautiful place to live.

"You four wait in the lobby," Clarkdale directed. "I'll be right back."

Henderson and Alyson strolled through the lobby together as Nash and Kaya, alone for the first time in days, walked past the quaint shops and distinguished art galleries. He led her out onto a sun-drenched deck.

"Awesome," Nash exclaimed, looking up at the soaring scarlet rocks.

"Yes," Kaya agreed. "We always have something beautiful the white man wants."

"Well, there is something beautiful that this white man wants," said Nash.

Kaya frowned and turned her head toward him. Her frown quickly left when she saw the look in his eye. "Oh, you are a charmer, Mr. Nash."

"Call it what you want," he said, "but it's true."

She looked at him for another heartbeat, and the faint lines around her forehead softened. Nash fought a nearly uncontrollable urge to reach out and take her hand and caress her.

The moment passed, and Nash took in some air and looked out beyond the balcony, at the many different Adobe-shaped casitas spread out throughout the property. Each was snuggled between the ancient red rocks, and lush green brush and trees. To Nash, this was a veritable paradise. If someone like Somerton wanted to be anonymous and get away from it all—this would be the place.

"I can see why medicine men believed this was a holy place," offered Nash, just to be saying something. His voice sounded harsh and throaty even to his own ears. He wondered if Kaya noticed.

"You put their belief in past tense, Jeremy. Trust me, our medicine men will always believe this is a holy place."

They both turned when they heard people step out onto the deck behind them. Clarkdale was followed by Henderson and Alyson. And with them was a gray-haired man wearing a tweed jacket and faded blue jeans.

Nash recognized the gray-haired man immediately. "You!" he exclaimed, flabbergasted. "We sat together on the plane from Rome."

Somerton looked Nash over and said, "Yes, yes. That was quite a flight, no? And this is quite a coincidence. So, Grandfather Martin thought I could be of help, eh?"

"Yes," said Nash. "He said you might know where the missing piece to the Hopi tablet might be. He said you were—" and Nash had a hard time saying the next words, but he fought through it, "—he said you were the *Keeper of the Secret*."

Somerton smiled pleasantly, as pleasantly as he had when

Nash sat with him on the airplane ride from hell. "I'm sorry to disappoint all of you, but I don't know where the missing piece is."

"With all due respect, Mr. Somerton," said Henderson a little impatiently, "what secret is it that you keep?"

Somerton leaned a hip on the balcony rail. He studied each of them in turn, finally settling on Henderson. "I'm only one of the Keepers."

"Who are the others?" asked Alyson.

Somerton studied them some more. Nash wondered if they were looking at a crazy man. But Somerton hadn't sounded crazy on the plane, Nash thought. Somerton had sounded rational and calm in the face of great danger. If anything, the man had sounded *too* calm.

Somerton said, "Let's go to my condo and discuss this in private."

Parker was happy. The first time he had been happy in some time. His contact had proved invaluable. He glanced down at the address in his hand as he started his vehicle.

Little did the man on the list know that his days were not only numbered, but his minutes alive on this earth.

Parker grinned, nodded to his partner, and put the car in gear.

Enchantment Resort
Sedona, Arizona

They were in Somerton's elegant living room. *The man certainly knows how to live well,* thought Nash, admiring the scientist's vast collection of Native American artifacts, especially the Kachina dolls. Understandably, Nash had developed quite a fascination for Kachina dolls. Somerton explained that many of the Native American artifacts and paintings were given to him by different tribes in appreciation for his help in bringing their cultures and traditions to the public.

When everyone had settled in with either an ice cold bottled Heineken or glass of water, Somerton spoke from his corner of the couch. "The Keeper of the Secret is, in fact, a select group of cultural anthropologists, scientists, and Native-American shamans. We believe that the Hopi End Times prediction is coming true—and that there is, in fact, a scientific basis for it."

"The recent geological and climatic disturbances and disasters we are experiencing," Henderson commented, jumping in excitedly.

Nash didn't bother rolling his eyes. He was sick to death of rolling his eyes at this group.

Somerton nodded. "There was a rumor many years ago that a socio-scientific paper existed that confirmed we were entering The End Times. It was supposed to have been submitted to several cultural and scientific journals, but no one could find any record of it. However, a partial abstract of the paper eventually fell into our hands a couple of years ago."

"So that's the secret, then?" asked Henderson.

"No. The partial abstract did, however, confirm what we had long suspected. So, we decided to go to the Rome conference on climate change to present our findings."

"And how were your findings received by other scientists?" queried Nash.

Somerton turned his head toward him slowly and said, "You saw first-hand the response to our findings on the plane, Mr. Nash."

"What do you mean? What response?"

"You remember the missile attack, don't you?"

Nash knew his mouth was hanging open. He didn't care. Actually, he didn't know what to think. The missile attack had been so surreal, so strange. To Nash, the attack felt as if it had happened to someone else or had happened a long time ago. In reality, it had been only a few days. Nash had been so busy with the life-and-death events of the last few days, he had not stopped to think about it.

He finally managed to speak. "You're saying that the attack was because of you? Because of your revelations at the Rome conference?" Nash shook his head. "Do you know how crazy that sounds?"

"Jeremy!" hissed his sister, but he ignored her. Enough was enough.

But Somerton only smiled calmly at him. "As crazy as a missile attack, young man?"

Nash didn't know what to say to that. Hell, everything was just so goddamned crazy these days. He sat back and drank his beer in silence.

Somerton went on. "Since the attack on me, we began looking into some very disturbing events."

"Such as?" Henderson asked.

"People have been turning up dead," said the scientist. "People who we believe had gotten too close to the truth."

"What truth?" questioned Alyson breathlessly.

Somerton looked straight at Nash. "We believe that someone, or some group, is triggering the End Times."

Nash nearly choked on his beer. "You have got to be kidding me."

"Quiet, Jeremy!" snapped Alyson. "Go on, Mr. Somerton."

The elderly scientist looked nonplussed. "We believe that there is a real physical emanation of the End Time. A *man-made* emanation, and it's coming out of the Four Corners area."

"What kind of emanation?" asked Henderson.

"We believe, and our scientific and cultural research proves it, that something within the planet—some powerful force—is slowly ripping the earth apart."

Henderson leaped out of his seat, spilling some of his beer across his lap, which he ignored completely. "The Hopi mystery egg! The seed," he shouted.

"Precisely," Somerton said. "We need to find exactly where these disturbances are emanating from."

Kaya placed her hand on Nash's arm. "Show him the invoice, Jeremy." She looked at Somerton. "We may have a clue."

Nash motioned to Alyson who reached into her purse and pulled out the now shopworn piece of paper. She handed it to Somerton and said, "You said people were being murdered who came close to the truth. Well, I believe my parents were two of them."

Enchantment Resort
Sedona, Arizona

With the sun setting, anointing the surrounding red rocks in a fiery display of magnificence, Somerton politely asked Clarkdale to leave for the evening, saying he didn't want to place his friend in any more danger. Clarkdale, seeing a chance for adventure, protested, but Somerton would have none of it.

Although Nash wasn't sure he believed any of this—in fact, he was certain he didn't—he didn't like the connotation that it was okay for the rest of them to remain in mortal danger.

As the professor departed, bidding them all safe hunting, Somerton made a pot of Green Thread—Hopi Tea—in the kitchen. While they sipped their tea, Nash brought Somerton up to date on what had happened to them so far. In particular, Nash recounted how they believed the invoice and missing piece of the Hopi Stone would lead them to the people who murdered his parents.

Somerton absorbed all of this impassively, sipping his tea as Nash spoke, with Alyson occasionally chiming in. When Nash was finished, the gray-haired man studied them all carefully and said, "These other clues—in particular, the code words that mean *the Battleship belong to abandoned bunker in district* and the image of the Hopi Stone—do you have any idea what they mean?"

Nash shook his head, and so did everyone else. Nash wasn't sure how he felt seeking help from Somerton—someone Nash was quickly adding to the *kook* category. But he was desperate for help. Any help, obviously.

"Mr. Somerton," asked Alyson, "Grandfather Martin mentioned something about a Light Man coming. Who did he mean?"

"Ah, yes. Lame Deer's end of time prediction. Lame Deer was a Sioux shaman who lived in the last century. He predicted two things: First, a young man will come and shut off the white man's electricity. The result would be very painful. Second, a Light Man will follow bringing a new light, a new electricity. We don't know for sure who or what Lame Deer was referring to."

"Could they be referring to the Pahana?" asked Alyson.

"Would be my guess," said Somerton.

"We were told by Grandfather Martin that the Pahana now has the missing piece," offered Kaya. "What do you know of that?"

Somerton took a sip of his tea. "Not much, I'm afraid. Apparently, a young man was cutting firewood on a farm near the Pacific Coast and found a broken piece of a tablet nestled in the decay of a giant cedar stump. The piece itself was carved with images that were themselves made up of smaller images, figures, and faces, and within those were still smaller signs—figures, designs, symbols. Amazingly, within even those were tiny etchings, so tiny that it was difficult to tell where the carving left off and the natural pattern of the rock began. This man claimed to be the Pahana and visited the Hopi reservation on three occasions. Each time he was turned away."

"And the Hopi elders examined this broken piece?" Kaya added.

"Correct, and they decided it was *not* the missing piece of the Hopi Stone."

"Would you have any idea where this Pahana is now?" asked Nash.

"No, sorry," Somerton replied. "But there is someone here in Sedona who might know. I can contact him now if you like."

Nash and the others nodded. Nash spoke for everyone. "Yes, of course."

Somerton reached inside his pant pocket and removed his cell phone, and scrolled through what Nash assumed was his phone book. The older man found the number he was looking for and made the call.

Somerton asked for a *Samuel Douglas*, and then was apparently told that Samuel Douglas wasn't available. Somerton told whoever was on the other end to inform Douglas to expect the four of them tonight.

Somerton abruptly ended the call and explained, "Samuel Douglas is the director of the Consciousness Research Center in Oak Creek. Apparently, he's attending the 2012 conference here in Sedona. Tonight, is the pre-conference mixer at Tlaquepaque. I'm told Samuel is quite familiar with this fellow who calls himself the Pahana. Perhaps he can tell you where you can find him."

"Then we better get going," said Nash. "Is the conference open to the public?"

"Yes, of course."

Nash idly wondered why Somerton wasn't in attendance but decided, in the end, he really didn't care. As the group got up to leave, Somerton asked Nash, "May I look at that invoice while you're gone, Jeremy?"

Nash blinked. "Sure." He pulled it from his pocket and gave it to Somerton.

Tlaquepaque
Sedona, Arizona

As Nash drove the group toward *Tlaquepaque*, Henderson explained that this was a thriving arts community in Sedona modeled after an authentic Mexican village. They were stopped by a construction worker flagging down traffic before a small bridge. Nash slowed down and leaned out his window, wary that this could be another trap.

But if it is a trap, thought Nash, *it's a hell of an elaborate one, with dozens of workers and a major street shut down.*

"What's up?" he asked the construction worker.

"You can't cross here. The bridge isn't safe. Oak Creek is swollen, and Soldiers Wash is rising here. Lots of rain up north."

Henderson sat forward from the backseat and pointed to the beautiful, Mexican-inspired architecture of the buildings just across the street. "We're just going to *Tlaquepaque*."

"No problem, then." The worker waved them through.

Once they were parked, Henderson led the way through the West entrance of the plaza. Alyson picked up a brochure on the way.

"It says here," she said, reading from the small colorful pamphlet, "that *Tlaquepaque* means the *best of everything*. Tasteful galleries and unique shops live in harmony with *Tlaquepaque's* lush natural environment where giant sycamore trees stand in testimony to the care taken in preserving the timeless beauty of the *Tlaquepaque* grounds." She put down the pamphlet and said excitedly, "And there's shopping!"

"Are you quite done," said Nash, shaking his head and grinning.

He could always count on his sister to lighten the mood. "Let's find this convention."

Kaya pointed to an information booth. "They should know."

A guy with a long grey ponytail directed them to the *Patio de las Campanas* where the pre-conference get-together had their mixer. "Just follow the *Mariachi* music," he added.

Together they walked through the authentically designed buildings filled with elegant shops and restaurants. A few moments later, they were standing in line in front of a registration desk manned by two elderly women. Sure enough, a *mariachi* band was striking up a festive tune on the patio behind them.

A silver-haired lady checked off names on a list while a tall one with horned rimmed reading glasses handed out pre-made name tags.

When their turn came, the first woman said, "Names please."

"We're here to see Samuel Douglas," Nash said smoothly. "He's here at the mixer and is expecting us. Could you direct us to him."

The second lady shook her head. "We have room for only two more, I'm sorry."

"Then we'll take them," said Nash quickly. As the elderly woman nodded, filling out two temporary name tags—one for Nash and one for Kaya—Henderson suggested that he and Alyson stroll the grounds.

Alyson clapped. "Good, we can get some shopping in! Come on, Bryan." She left with a suddenly worried-looking Henderson in tow.

Nash shook his head, grinning. "The poor sap has no clue what he's gotten himself into. My sister's ability to shop is second to none."

Kaya ignored him; instead, she directed a question at the two women. "Could you tell us what Mr. Douglas looks like?"

"You can't miss him," replied the first lady. "He's short with nappy red hair, bald at the top, with long sideburns flowing into a long light red beard." She grinned. "Sort of a cross between Dr. Andrew Weil and Timothy Leary."

"Thank you!" Kaya said, amused at the description.

"And he'll have his Chihuahua with him," said the second lady, giggling. "Never leaves home without it."

Nash and Kaya walked into a cobblestoned courtyard framed by two-story arched buildings on either side. Nash took a chance and reached out, taking Kaya's hand. She flinched slightly at first, perhaps surprised by his gesture. But she immediately relaxed and held his hand warmly. Nash knew he was smiling from ear to ear.

We're supposed to be finding our parents' killer, he thought. *Not acting like love struck school kids.*

But he didn't care. Holding her hand felt good, felt right, and together, hand-in-hand, they worked their way over to some arches and stone pillared railings. A white canvas was stretched above the courtyard between the rows of buildings to keep out the intermittent rain. Elegant strings of white light dangled below the canvas, glowing warmly. Nash, in his present frame of mind, thought he had never seen such a romantic place in his life. He suspected, of course, that his present company no doubt influenced that amorous thought.

At the far end of the patio there stood a long buffet table filled with many varieties of food and drink. Behind it was yet another mariachi band playing its lively south-of-the-border street music. Directly above them, Nash noted, was a tall bell tower.

Kaya looked over the crowd of approximately a hundred people. "For a professional gathering," she observed, "most of the people here are dressed pretty casual."

"That's the Southwest for you," Nash remarked. "No slaves to haughty tradition." He looked over the crowd. "There. I think I see our man." He pointed to a short, balding man with kinky red hair holding a small dog.

"You think?" asked Kaya, grinning, and giving his hand a squeeze.

They approached Douglas, who was standing by the *hors d'oeuvres* table holding a small light-brown Chihuahua in one hand and a glass of red wine in the other. The little dog immediately growled at Nash. To Nash, Douglas looked a lot like a jolly old elf, talking jovially to a small group of people who seemed to be hanging on to his every word. It sounded like quite a heated exchange.

Nash stood by and waited for a break in the conversation. Meanwhile, the little dog eyed him suspiciously, growling under its breath, raising its black lips, and showing him its teeth.

"I don't think he likes you," whispered Kaya, giggling. Nash almost laughed.

Together they waited patiently for an appropriate moment to to speak. When it finally came, Nash jumped in, "Mr. Douglas. My name's Jeremy Nash—"

"Yes, Mr. Nash! Peter Somerton phoned my office."

"I'm glad you got the message. We were hoping you could help us."

"You want an address, correct?" The rotund man set down his wine—not his dog—and pulled out his cellphone.

Nash glanced at the others around him. They were all watching the exchange with degrees of impatience and interest. "Actually, no, Mr. Douglas. May we, um, speak to you in private?"

"Certainly. But not now." He pointed to a man with wire rim glasses, a pasty complexion, and a dour expression. "This gentleman here holds the opinion that the Mayan Calendar does not really *end* in 2012, but rather, all the cycles turn over and start again. I subscribe to the more realistic forecast of *Bueno de Mesquita*. At least his predictions are anchored in game theory and rational choice theory, not the flighty theories of the prognostications of soothsayers and seers."

The little man with the wire rim glasses responded with a squeaky, agitated voice. "It does not take Mayan soothsayers to see that we are moving to an age of peace and harmony, Mr. Douglas. Besides, other spiritual movements have similar traditions—the tradition of a transformation of consciousness."

At that moment a young woman, wearing a peasant madras

blouse and bell-bottom jeans, jumped in. "Just think what we are bearing witness to: peace, harmony, sharing, community, caring for Mother Earth and each other—a global sense of community and the spirituality of Love. Wow!"

Nash rolled his eyes and was about to jump in himself when Kaya beat him to it. "Mr. Douglas. Please, this is important. We don't have a lot of time—"

"Time?" Douglas interrupted. "Slow down young lady," he smiled. "The night is young, the weather has cleared, and the conversation is enlightening. Here, have some wine." He picked up a glass from a tray and handed it to Kaya then did the same for Nash. "I hope you like red."

He laughed warmly and turned back to his small audience. "Now, I'll let you all in on a secret. As you know, tomorrow I will be giving the opening speech at the conference. At that time, I will announce that my committee has definitive proof that a real physical emanation of the End Time is coming out of Northern Arizona and proves our prognostications." He gave his rapt audience a wink. "As you know, there have been many psychic disturbances in the Four Corners region over the last dozen or so years. Not to mention several here in Sedona alone at the Consciousness Research Center, which I head. We've proven it without a doubt."

Just then, Alyson appeared around the corner, out of breath, and seemingly running for her life.

Tlaquepaque
Sedona, Arizona

Fifteen minutes earlier, Alyson and Henderson had left the patio and made their way around the back of the buildings down the *Avenida de la Constitucion*. As they did so, Alyson noticed a black Lincoln Navigator pull slowly into the lot, heading towards the *Tlaquepaque* bell tower.

Her eyes widened when she saw the driver. "Hey! That's one of the construction workers we saw back in New Mexico."

"What do you mean?" asked Henderson, squinting at the guy.

"Don't look at him!" She quickly pulled Henderson over to the shade of a juniper tree. "He's one of the guys who diverted us off the main road. You know, then we were chased by crazies shooting us."

"You sure?"

"I never forget a thug," she sneered.

Henderson set his jaw. "Then let's see what they're up to."

The two altered their course and strolled casually through the parking lot, keeping to the cover of some planted trees. They watched as the Navigator pulled behind the bell tower.

"C'mon," said Henderson, pulling her along, and picking up their pace to a light jog.

Alyson silently wished she was wearing more than her flat-bottomed shoes, but she did the best she could. When they rounded the corner to the bell tower, slowing down, they saw two young men and a woman unloading food and wine from a panel van labeled **Red Rock Catering.**

The Lincoln Navigator, Alyson noticed, had pulled up directly behind the catering truck.

"What's going on?" she whispered.

Henderson brought his finger to his lips to shush her; he then pulled her behind a dumpster where they carefully peeked around the corner. What they saw next terrified Alyson to her core and sickened Henderson to his stomach.

Three men got out of the Navigator—one of them was definitely the man who had waved them off the road.

Alyson watched in horror as the man she recognized removed something black and small from inside his light jacket. It was a gun.

"Oh shit, oh shit," whispered Henderson.

The man said something, and all three employees turned, each holding a tray of food. The man raised the gun and the girl screamed. In a blink of an eye, the man calmly shot the two male workers in the head, the shots muffled. Both men jerked back as blood sprayed against the side of the white van.

Alyson choked back a scream as Henderson covered her mouth with his hand. The young woman was saying something, begging, holding her hands up in front of her.

The man turned his lip up into a wretched smile—then shot her between the eyes. She fell face-first into the gravel, and Alyson, unable to restrain herself, gasped into Henderson's hand.

The killer and his men looked calmly around as Henderson yanked her deeper behind the dumpster. *Jesus, did the killers see us?*

Alyson waited, struggling to control her breathing. She heard crunching feet nearby. Next to her, Henderson reached out and snagged a long wooden fragment of a shipping crate.

The footsteps grew louder. Alyson could hear a man breathing.

Henderson quietly eased himself into a crouch, holding the splintered wood out before him. She surmised his simple plan. If someone stepped around the dumpster, he was going to spring into action. What happened after could only end badly for them.

The footsteps drew closer, and she heard someone else—probably the shooter—bark an order to toss the bodies inside the van.

Someone above them, just around the corner of the dumpster, grunted and turned back.

Alyson nearly cried with relief.

Killing the three workers had elevated Parker's mood. Killing always gave him a natural high. Luckily, they were alone in the alley, but they had to act quickly.

He ordered his men to dispose of the bodies in the catering van and wipe the blood off the vehicle. Once done, he ordered them to find some clean catering aprons.

The henchman complied, digging through the van and turning up some more aprons which all three men quickly wrapped around themselves. Parker hated making plans up on the fly. Such plans were what got you caught—or killed. For all he knew, another catering van was coming, or their boss was inside somewhere, waiting.

They had to *move*, and they had to move *fast*.

He quickly reached inside the Navigator and pulled out what looked like a small floodlight the size of a coffee can. He placed it and a battery pack on a catering cart. He next attached a small tripod to the base and handed it to his henchman.

"Set this up in the tower," he ordered. "Point it directly at the utility room at the other end of patio."

The man nodded and left.

Parker knew the utility room had thick walls to protect the hydrogen storage tanks residing there. But the Krakatoa, a MEPS device—modular explosive projectile system—similar to a shaped charge, could propel a plate-like explosively formed projectile. Basically, a lethal copper bullet that would easily penetrate up to two inches of steel at a hundred yards. A concrete wall would offer little resistance. The projectile would continue through and cut easily into the large hydrogen fuel cell that powered the shopping center—with devastating results.

Parker took one last look around to make sure they weren't noticed, grabbed a tray of nachos, and walked towards the bell tower.

Tlaquepaque
Sedona, Arizona

Nash was just about to forcibly separate Douglas from his New Age admirers, when a horror-stricken Alyson came rushing up to him. Henderson was close behind, looking equally terrorized. Even odder, they were both coming from the rear of the open space, through what appeared to be a side service door.

"What the hell's wrong?" Nash asked when his sister was close enough to hear. Already, she and Henderson had attracted the attention of most everyone in attendance.

"We've got trouble, Jeremy," she gasped, almost inaudibly. Nash saw that she was shaking uncontrollably. "Big trouble."

He pulled her aside, after excusing himself from Douglas. When they were out of earshot of everyone else, he said, "Slow down, Sis. What are you talking about?"

She and Henderson both started talking at once, babbling incoherently about people getting killed and gunshots and caterers.

"Whoa! Slow down. One at a time."

Alyson took a deep breath, doing her best to calm herself, and spelled out to Nash what had happened. "Three murders. The killers are here. Disguised as caterers. The same men who ran us off the road at Canyon de Chelly."

Nash fought a brief wave of panic and then got hold of himself. First, he checked to see that his sister was okay. She appeared to be, although she was clearly in shock. Next, he glanced around and verified with Henderson and Alyson that the killers weren't there on the patio.

191

"Okay," he said. "This is the plan. You girls are going to get Douglas out of here."

"How?" asked Kaya, endeavoring to calm herself.

"Any way you can, but I would suggest you discretely point out to him that his life is probably very much in danger, along with everyone else here."

The women nodded, and Kaya led the way to Douglas.

Nash turned to his friend, "Bryan, where do you think those SOBs went?"

"One of the men was carrying something that looked like a small spotlight to the bell tower behind us."

Nash scanned the patio and found what he was looking for—a flight of stairs.

"We need to see what they're up to," said Nash. "I'll head up those stairs to the second floor and see what they're doing in the bell tower. You try and find some security people and call the police. Just be quiet about it. Don't incite a panic."

Henderson nodded and dashed off.

Nash glanced briefly at Kaya and Alyson, who were both urgently speaking to a very confused-looking Douglas, and then slipped quietly away. A moment later, he was creeping up the white alabaster stairs to the second floor, and shortly after that he was looking down at the canvas-covered patio below. Now he moved quickly along the walkway to the far end of the building which, he reasoned correctly, would give him the best view of the bell tower.

From there, the pleasant sounds of the reception reached Nash's ears, the party-goers clueless that a heinous act of brutality had been perpetrated just a few buildings away. Alone for now, Nash kept to the shadows of the various columns and studied the bell tower, which rose majestically from across the busy courtyard.

A small, hot wind whipped Nash's hair, and he suddenly realized how exhausted he was. This quest to find his parents' killer had proven to be much more than he bargained for.

And now killers were on the loose. But who were their

intended victims? The people at the reception? Or just Nash, Alyson, Kaya, and Henderson.

In the far distance, Nash heard the sound of a siren. It appeared Henderson had done his job and alerted the authorities.

But, if someone were trying to kill the four of them—or perhaps just Nash and his sister—then what the hell was going on with the bell tower?

Almost in answer to his question, Nash watched a man appear on the far ledge of the tower. The man was dressed in an apron and appeared to be positioning a spotlight of some sort over the wall.

Nash didn't know what it was, but his instincts told him it was something ominous. It didn't look like any bomb he had ever seen, but these guys had already proven to be very creative with their attacks.

Whatever it was, it wasn't good, especially if they were willing to kill innocent people in the process.

Nash turned and dashed away, intent on finding his sister and clearing the area.

As Parker arrived at the top of the bell tower, breathing in the warm air, he savored the hypnotic flood of adrenalin that coursed through his veins. After all, he was about to kill a lot of people. More than he had ever killed at any one time before.

I'm moving up in the world, he thought, and grinned to himself.

"Is the Krakatoa ready?" he asked, unable to hide the excitement from his voice.

"Yes, sir."

"Good. Set the timer."

Parker was about to leave when his LPI phone buzzed. He paused high up on the bell tower, frowning.

"Parker here."

"It's Prescott. Garcia figured out one the references on the Web Bot run. The one mentioning a *consciousness research center.* The

center is in Sedona. Find someone named Douglas. He's there at the mixer. It's important. Do not harm him. Find him and bring him to me. Repeat, do not harm him."

"What about the mission?" Parker asked. He felt his heart sinking. He had been so close to killing so many people.

"Once Douglas is found and is out of harm's way, then complete the mission." Prescott paused. "Terminate the conference attendees."

Prescott gave Parker a description of Douglas—a short, balding man with a dog. Piece of cake.

"Set the timer," Parker ordered. "Don't worry about me. Continue with the countdown then get clear. I'll meet you at the car in ten minutes."

Tlaquepaque
Sedona, Arizona

As the sun set over the patio and the strings of lights gave a warm glow under the canvas tent, the crowd below seemed to be growing exponentially with the amount of food and wine being served.

From the upstairs landing, Nash looked feverishly around for the girls and Douglas, but they appeared gone.

Good, he thought, relieved. Hopefully they were safely back at the Jeep waiting for him.

In the near distance, Nash heard the sirens approaching. Now it was up to him to clear the area.

He dashed recklessly down the stone stairs, skipping three and four steps at a time. How he didn't break his neck, he had no clue. He maneuvered his way around and between the partying crowd towards the stage and live band in the far corner.

To the shock of the upbeat Mexican band, whose lead singer was crooning a lively, traditional song, Nash bounded up the wooden steps along the side of the stage. In a few quick strides, Nash crossed the stage and grabbed the microphone that was on a stand in front of a stunned guitarist.

"Hello ladies and gentlemen," said Nash, his own voice blasting from the surrounding speakers. Almost everyone turned and looked expectantly at him. Nash suddenly wondered if this was a good idea. After all, he didn't know for sure that anything unfortunate was about to happen. The men were killers, he reminded himself, and they were clearly setting something up in the tower, something ominous and threatening. If he were wrong, then fine, he could live with himself for ruining their party. But if something terrible happened and Nash didn't warn these people...well, he knew he could never live with himself.

"Ladies and gentlemen," he said again, "as orderly and as calmly as you can, you must exit these premises immediately."

People immediately jumped to their feet, gasping, and talking excitedly. A heavy-set security guard was now running at Nash.

"Why?" a half dozen people yelled at him.

Nash briefly debated how much to say. There really weren't enough people here to cause a full riot but he wasn't sure.

"I think there's a bomb in the building."

And that did it. Those who hadn't already stood, leaped to their feet, and bolted for the exits. Behind him, he heard one of the musicians translating to the others in the band. The band members scrambled off the stage, grabbing what instruments they could. All around him, to Nash's great relief, the mass exit was done in a fairly orderly way with no one getting hurt or left behind.

"And please warn anyone you see along the way!" yelled Nash loudly into the mic. He noticed the security guard had done an about-face and dashed off with the others.

Smart man, thought Nash. *Now, let's get the hell out of here!*

Parker couldn't believe what he was seeing. He had just dashed down the stairs and was sprinting through the outdoor shopping center, when he heard a loud voice speaking urgently into a microphone.

A few seconds later, Parker heard the screaming. And immediately after that, like so many threatened ants pouring out of an anthill, the whackos at the 2012 Conference were madly running from the outdoor gathering.

Shit! Somebody tipped them off.

Now how the hell was he supposed to find his new target in this melee? Parker didn't know, but he pulled out his gun from inside his light jacket. No one noticed, and no one cared. Everyone was running in a blind panic, surging around him.

Like a bull in a China shop, Parker rushed forward, shoving aside anyone in his way. He ran toward the only place he could think of, where he had heard the voice issuing the warning, where the conference had been.

A young woman appeared before him, and he threw her aside. She saw his gun and screamed, stumbling with the force of his impact. He considered shooting her, but realized his window to find his new target was rapidly closing.

Parker glanced briefly at his watch. Six minutes before the weapon went off. Parker could kill a lot of people in six minutes. The very thought gave him a shot of energy.

He lowered his shoulder and continued charging ruthlessly through the crowd.

Nash had just leaped off the stage when someone appeared at the far end of the outdoor pavilion. Nash expected to see his sister, or perhaps Henderson. He did not expect to see a man with a gun, the very man he had seen arming the apparatus at the top of the bell tower.

The man had dashed partway into the now empty space before pulling up short.

Now closer, Nash immediately recognized the figure as the same man who had directed them off the road. Nash also realized this might just be his last thought on this earth.

The buff man appeared stunned to find Nash alone. His surprise turned into satisfaction as he grinned and raised his weapon.

Nash had nowhere to run or hide. He was fully exposed and had no doubt that the man was a hired killer, capable of easily shooting him from across the open space.

Nash had just decided to run like hell when another man suddenly appeared behind the killer.

It was Henderson and he was holding a folded medal chair by the leg. He swung the chair as hard as he could, and the resulting metallic *thunk* was music to Nash's ears. The hired killer was forcefully launched onto a portable table which promptly collapsed under his weight. The killer's gun skidded to a stop a few feet away.

In a flash, Nash scooped up the gun. The man seemed to be out cold. Blood dribbled from his scalp. He could care less if the man were dead or alive.

"Good work," gasped Nash to his friend.

Henderson looked down at the now badly dented chair. "I came back for you when I saw the crowd pouring out and saw this asshole running up. He's the guy who killed the caterers."

Sirens filled the night air, and Nash was just about to tell Henderson they needed to get the hell out of here and fast, that something devastating was about to happen, when a deafening cracking sound echoed behind them.

Nash had no time to turn to see what it was when a searing heat slammed against his back, hurtling him and Henderson forward.

Tlaquepaque
Sedona, Arizona

For Nash, the next few horrible seconds moved in slow motion.

Like sandcastles on a beach, the buildings to his left and right collapsed in a surreal wave of destruction, collapsing into a cloud of dust and flying debris. A cloud that was fast approaching them.

He grabbed Henderson's shoulder. "Go! Go!"

Both men turned and dashed forward, with Henderson stumbling. Nash grabbed him and forcibly hurried him along, feeling an intense heat scorching the back of his neck, forcing him to move even faster as he pulled Henderson along with him.

Parker shook his pounding head, flinging blood in every direction. Something—or someone—had hit him hard.

And something else had stirred him to consciousness from the black oblivion he found himself in.

And that something was the ground shaking beneath him.

Parker tried to sit up.

Shit! The device had detonated.

Then he saw a site that chilled him to his bone. The world around him was collapsing.

He crawled on his hands and knees until he found his feet, and soon he was stumbling and running...

Nash and Henderson joined the hysterical crowd in the parking lot.

The scene was chaotic. People crying, holding each other. Others watched in stunned silence. Nash knew not everyone could possibly have made it out. Some had perished. Perhaps many lay dying now under the crumbled debris. Sirens filled the air and so did choking dust. Nash was determined to go back and help anyone who was trapped, but first he had to find his sister—and Kaya.

Jesus, what if they didn't make it out?

For the first time in a long, long time, Nash felt completely lost. If he had to, he would look under every fallen wall and pile of debris—

Henderson, who had been anxiously scanning the parking lot—a parking lot that now looked far different than it had just thirty minutes earlier—suddenly pointed. "I see them! They're at the Jeep."

Relief flooding over him, Nash followed the long-limbed Henderson through the crowd and the choking dust. When they arrived at the Jeep, Nash saw Kaya attending to his sister's leg. There was blood on her knee where her pants were torn. Nash ran up and threw his arms around his sister and Kaya. Despite himself, he felt tears come to his eyes.

"What happened to you, Alyson?" he finally asked when he could find his voice.

"She's fine," Kaya assured him. "Some jackass nearly ran her down. She has some scraps and bruises, and I think she sprained her ankle."

Nash yanked open the Jeep's passenger door and helped his sister inside. Only then, with his sister safely inside and Kaya tending to her, did Nash see Douglas, the little man who was the reason why they were here tonight. The red-haired man looked deeply distraught and lost. He was literally wringing his hands. Hands, Nash suddenly realized that had recently been holding a mean little dog.

"My dog," said the man emptily, hollowly. "Did you see him?"

There were people dead, people dying, people who needed help now. Nash was about to ignore the weird little man and dash back to the rubble to help and do his part, when a faint yipping sound came from the nearby brush. At least, Nash thought it came from the nearby brush. As more and more dust drifted down, Nash found seeing anything beyond twenty or thirty feet increasingly difficult.

Douglas perked up, much as a dog would have done after hearing a high-pitched sound. "There's my Amigo!" cried the man, and dashed off toward the brush, nearly disappearing into dust-clogged air.

Nash was inclined to leave the man be and help those who truly needed help, when a strange sound erupted from the brush. The sound, he was certain, was coming from an animal. The other sound Nash heard was distinctly human, and it was coming from Douglas. The sound, remarkably, seemed to fade as well.

Confused and irritated, Nash dashed off into the haze where Douglas had disappeared. As he approached the brush, Nash realized a fast-flowing river lay just beyond, down a steep embankment.

Soldiers Wash!

And there, through a gray cloud of dust, was Douglas. The little man was being pushed down the wash, holding his dog above the surging currents. If Nash had to guess, he would have guessed the red-haired man had misjudged the steep embankment and tumbled down into the flood. The very wash the work crew had warned them about.

Instinctively, Nash clambered down the embankment as fast as he could.

Soldiers Wash
Sedona, Arizona

Henderson, who had followed Nash to the edge of the steep embankment, couldn't believe it when his friend disappeared over the edge. Through the choking dust haze, Henderson watched his reckless college friend maneuver alongside the rushing river, and then dive in after Douglas.

In a blink of an eye, Jeremy and Douglas were gone, swept along by the surging river.

Henderson turned and ran back to the Jeep.

Swimming furiously, Nash was able to gain on Douglas.

The water was ice cold and moving far faster than Nash expected. The skeptic also realized, far too late, that jumping into a swollen, overflowing river was probably not the smartest idea.

About twenty yards ahead, Douglas appeared to be having a hard time keeping both his head and his little dog above the churning surface. Directly before him was a narrow foot bridge, the very bridge the construction crew had warned them about. Nash, struggling to keep his own mouth above the frothing surface, almost cheered when he saw the little man grab hold of one of the wooden pylons that plunged straight down into the river.

Nash steered himself toward Douglas, and fighting the currents, soon grabbed hold of the very same pylon.

Both men held on for dear life, gasping. When Nash finally got his wind, he said, "Do what I say, and I'll get us out of this."

Douglas nodded, holding his pooch tightly to his chest.

That was when Nash heard something crashing nearby. Something big. Impossibly big.

Douglas pointed behind him and screamed.

As Henderson started the Jeep and threw it into gear, he told the girls what he had seen. A few seconds later, tires squealing, he fish-tailed out of the parking lot, praying like hell there wasn't someone hiding in the thick clouds of dust in front of him.

"Where are we going?" gasped a nearly hysterical Alyson.

"We'll cross that bridge and parallel the street on the other side next to the wash and see if we can get to him."

Kaya, sitting in the backseat, suddenly leaned forward and pointed through the haze. "Look at that!"

Surging down the river was something broken and battered. Henderson could barely believe what he saw coming through the dust-filled air. Like a ship appearing through a dense morning fog, the jagged remains of a house—or perhaps a shack—rushed down the overflowing river towards the bridge.

The damaged remains, obviously a victim of the torrential flooding, were heading straight for the highway bridge—a bridge they had to cross to get to the road that fronted the wash. A road Henderson knew they needed if they were to continue following the raging water and rescue Nash and Douglas.

Henderson punched the gas.

The jeep bounded forward, scattering the dust clouds. He turned the wheel and aimed for the bridge. At the moment, he was about ninety percent confident the bridge was empty of any pedestrians or vehicles.

And only about fifty percent sure he would beat the damaged house to the bridge.

Alyson grabbed hold of the sissy bar in front of her. Kaya disappeared behind him, probably throwing on her seat belt.

Henderson gritted his teeth and aimed for the center of the bridge.

To Henderson's left, he could see the surreal sight of a battered house coming at him, hurled along by the force of the overflowing river.

A second later, just as the front wheels hit the concrete pad of the bridge, the front porch of the house slammed into the bridge pilings. The structure shuddered.

The Jeep lurched. Something gave out beneath him.

"The bridge is collapsing!" cried Alyson.

Indeed, great chunks were disappearing in front of Henderson, falling to the river below. Henderson swerved as a massive hole appeared before them—and nearly swerved them off the bridge. He fought the wheel hard, and a heartbeat later, miraculously, the trio burst across the bridge to land safely on the other side.

Behind him, in his rearview mirror, Henderson watched with a pounding heart as the entire bridge collapsed down into the fast-moving water.

Nash looked up and couldn't believe his eyes.

Could this day get any stranger?

It looked like a part of a house, and it was bearing down on them rapidly, swept along by the swollen unrelenting wash. It was headed directly for them.

Nash knew they had no choice. He reached over and grabbed Douglas still clutching his beloved dog.

"C'mon!" he yelled above the roar.

Nash kicked off and soon they were swept once again downstream. Behind them the foot bridge shuddered with the impact from the hurtling broken house.

The raging water swept them along. As Nash fought to keep his head above the currents—and hang on to Douglas—something slammed into him hard. It was debris from the house—a massive wooden plank—and it promptly dislodged Douglas from his grip.

Nash watched in horror as the exhausted, red-haired man sank below the surface. His little dog, amazingly, had found a perch on the very plank that rocked Nash. Calling out the man's name and searching wildly, there was little Nash could do other than swim over to the plank and the little dog as they were swept wildly along.

Henderson was relieved at the lack of traffic paralleling the wash. Fortunately, the further away they got from the collapsed buildings, the better the visibility.

As he drove, reaching speeds nearing a hundred, Alyson and Kaya scanned the wash. Alyson suddenly yelled, "Stop! Back there! I think I saw him."

The Jeep screeched to a halt, and Henderson kicked it into reverse.

"There! There!" Alyson screamed, pointing to the far side of the wash. "That's him!"

Kaya and Henderson looked to where she was pointing and saw Nash holding onto a metal bar attached to the inside of a culvert. He looked half dead.

Henderson stopped the Jeep and scanned the rushing water. There, lying on his back, with a little dog on his chest, was Nash. Henderson had no clue if his friend were alive or not. There was no indication that Douglas had made it.

Henderson and the two girls piled out of the Jeep. They stumbled down the mild embankment, and before he could stop her, Alyson ran recklessly toward her brother, screaming his name.

It had taken all of Nash's strength to swim to shore. As he lay gasping for breath, going in and out of consciousness, he felt something cold and wet on his nose. He also heard a voice reaching him from a great distance.

It was not just any voice. It was his sister, screaming his name.

Nash opened his eyes to find the little dog licking his nose and his sister running down the muddy embankment toward him with Henderson and Kaya close behind.

Nash dropped his head again, exhausted, relieved, and thankful beyond words.

Enchantment Resort
Sedona, Arizona

As Nash slowly recovered on the shoreline, Henderson and Kaya scoured the river for any sign of Douglas. The man was gone. Nash knew the man was probably miles from there by now.

With the destruction at *Tlaquepaque*—an epic terrorist act rarely seen on American soil—and the chaos of rescue workers, police, firemen, and the military swarming everywhere, Nash and company decided to deal with the loss of Douglas at a later time.

For now, they all agreed, they needed to get to Somerton ASAP, for his life might very well be in danger.

When the group returned to Somerton's villa, with the little dog in tow, much worse off and bedraggled than when they had left, Somerton had already heard of the destruction at *Tlaquepaque*. Apparently, the whole country had at this point, as well.

The reclusive scholar made them all hot tea and listened to their story, making sympathetic noises as he poured more tea while the little dog sniffed around the condo. When they were finished, Somerton stood at his sliding glass door and gazed out at the towering rock above. "I know these people are killers—but to murder hundreds of innocent people...and for what reason?"

"I think I know," ventured Nash. His body ached in places he never thought possible. "Douglas echoed what you said today that there is a real physical emanation of the End Time. You said from the Four Corners area. Douglas claimed that his study committee found that the emanation was coming from Northern Arizona. He was going to announce it at the Conference."

"Then we could be closer than we think to the truth," Somerton speculated.

Nash stood and peered out Henderson's living room window. The surrounding red rock was still visible, lit up by the lights of the resort throwing out colors that Nash could only marvel at. He wished he had time to enjoy its beauty. "You must leave this place, Mr. Somerton. If these killers knew about Douglas and his research, you can bet they're onto you, as well."

"You're probably right," Somerton sighed, glancing sideways at Nash. "I always knew it might come to this. I was leaving for Flagstaff, anyway."

"What's there?" asked Alyson.

"I think I may have a solution to your father's clues." Somerton went over to his corner desk and picked up the printout of the four Hopi tablet images, front and back, and showed it to the group. "Did you notice the series of dots and dashes under the different tablets?"

"Of course," said Nash, now suddenly eager to get moving again. "What of it?"

"Any idea what they are?"

"We have no time for speculation, Mr. Somerton. If you have some idea what they are, then please tell us."

"I thought they might be Morse Code, but now I'm inclined to believe they represent numbers."

"What kind of numbers?" asked Nash, perking up. Anything to do with his parent's murder had his undivided attention.

"Numbers based on the Mayan counting system. I'll show you what I mean."

Somerton moved swiftly across his living room to a shelf packed with books. He chose one, and once back with the group, he placed it on a large hewed-wood coffee table. He opened the book, flipped through some pages, and stopped at a colorful table that depicted the Mayan counting system.

"In our English system," he explained, "there are ten symbols that are used to create numbers. One, two, three, four, etc, etc. When we count past nine, we have to start using combinations of these symbols, correct?"

Everyone nodded, Nash perhaps more impatiently than the others.

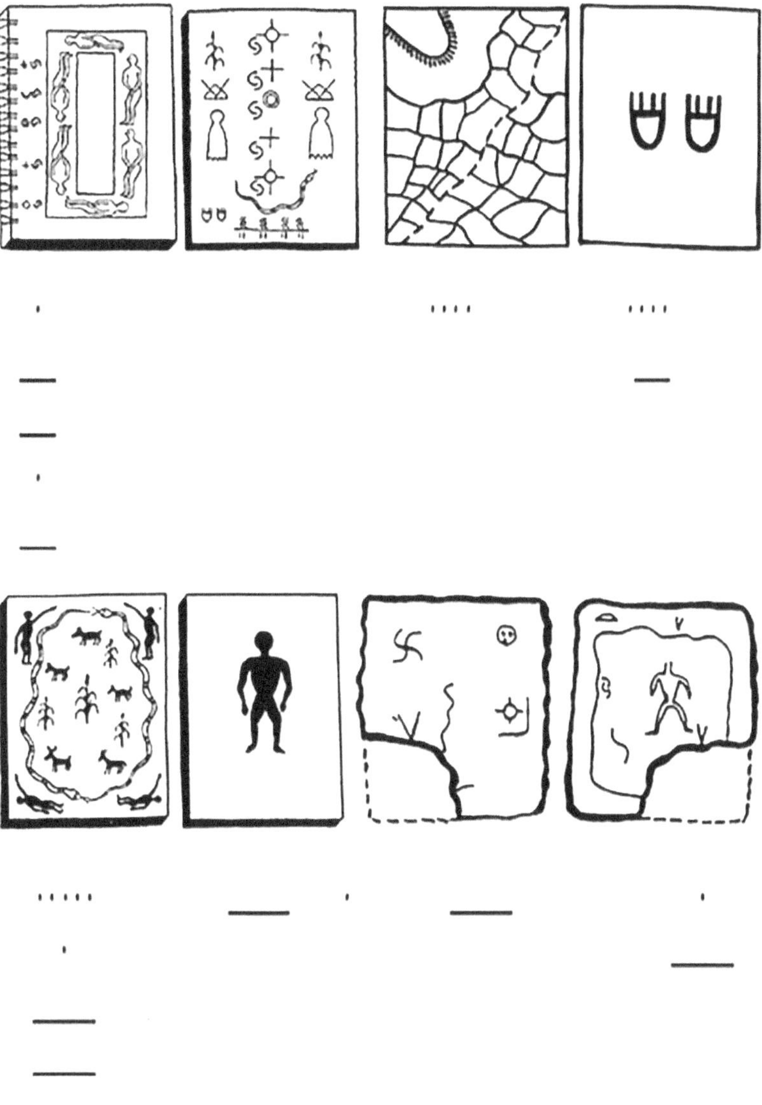

Somerton went on. "Take the number forty-six. In this case, the four is in the tens place and represents four sets of ten. The six is in the ones place, representing six sets of one. With that we get forty-six. With our current system, we can create every whole number possible."

"And how did the Mayans do this?" asked Kaya.

"The Mayan system was similar, but instead of having only ten symbols, like we have today, there were twenty. So instead of combining two symbols together after reaching nine, they started after reaching nineteen. Because the Mayan system is based on twenty and not ten like the English system, there is a twenties place instead of a tens place. Look here at the example of the number forty-six written in Mayan."

The historian pointed at two dots that represented the twenties place, indicating two sets of twenty. Additionally, there was a bar with a dot in the ones place indicating six sets of one. He pointed to another diagram to illustrate his point.

"And this base twenty system is still in use today by such tribes as the Inuits—and the Hopi."

"So, what do the dots and dashes mean?" asked Alyson.

"Based on what I see here below the tablets, I come up with the numbers thirty-five, nine, seven, three, one hundred and twelve—and one, two, and five."

Nash waited. "And?"

"And that's all I have," said Somerton. "But I think it means something."

They were silent for awhile, thinking through the possibilities. Nash gazed out the glass door. He was admittedly intrigued by the numbers. Nash loved numbers, as any good skeptic would. Numbers were always a good way to prove anything conclusively, unless such numbers were distorted and not based on provable facts.

Rapidly turning the numbers over in his mind, Nash was the first to speak. "These numbers. Could they be, in fact, two sets of numbers?"

"What do you mean?" asked Somerton.

Nash pointed to the printout of the tablets. "There is a row of numbers on the top and another row on the bottom."

"Two separate sets of numbers?" queried Kaya.

"It could be," agreed Somerton. He glanced over at Nash. "If I recall, you're a pilot like me. Perhaps these numbers represent sets of coordinates.

"Right!" Nash exclaimed. "GPS!"

"I don't get it," said Alyson.

"The first number is a longitude," explained Nash. "And the second is a latitude."

"We can find the locations online," offered Henderson.

Nash turned to Somerton. "Does your internet connection work?"

Somerton shook his head. "Been down for days." He thought a moment. "But I have a detailed atlas. We can use that."

Somerton went back to the same bookcase and extracted an atlas. Within minutes he and Nash settled on a location. It was along the south rim of the Grand Canyon Park, in an area called Tusayan.

"The Tusayan ruins," intoned Kaya.

"Ruins?" said Alyson.

"Eight-hundred-year-old Pueblo Indian ruins," informed Kaya. "Excavated back in the early part of the Twentieth Century."

"Nineteen-thirty, I believe," added Somerton.

"And what significance would these ruins have to the image of the tablets on the printout?" asked Nash.

"Legend has it," Kaya replied, "that the missing piece to the Hopi tablet may be buried there. It's one of several places where the missing piece is supposed to reside. Of course, it's only legend. They've been excavating that place for close to eighty years. If anything were there, they would have found it by now."

"Not necessarily," Somerton said. "The archeologists left areas of the site undisturbed so visitors could view an unexcavated site."

"Well," Nash replied. "I guess we should chase this out."

He turned to Somerton. "You said you were headed for Flagstaff."

"I have a reason."

"What's that?" Nash asked.

Somerton pulled the invoice from out of the drawer of the table next to him. "These red dots on the invoice. Any idea what they signify?"

"We think the dots have something to do with the Hopi legend of the mystery egg," Kaya replied. "The final stage of the Great Day of Purification."

Somerton nodded. "The final stage of the end times has been described by the Hopi as a Mystery Egg or *seed*."

"Yes." Kaya added. "The forces of the Swastika and the Sun, my uncle told us, plus a third force symbolized by the color red will culminate either in total rebirth or total annihilation."

There was aloud noise outside, and they all turned towards Henderson at the widow. He looked at them and just shook his head.

Somerton pointed to the invoice. "Do any of you know what these numbers, 2-7-3 470NM, mean at the bottom?"

Nash and the others admitted to having no clue.

Somerton picked up the computer printouts that Henderson had made from the steganography program. He examined them focusing on the Hopi tablet with its missing corner piece. "And did any of you notice the three dots in a circle on this tablet, second from the right, that match the pattern of the dots on the invoice?"

"We see the connection," said Nash. "We just don't know what it means."

"Years ago," Somerton said, "when I was with military intelligence, we read about barely noticeable dots like these being placed on common everyday documents. Those dots held secrets. Secrets that were placed right in the open."

Nash had heard of this. "They were called microdots, and they were used in World War Two."

"Microdots?" said Alyson.

"Text or images that were substantially reduced in size to

prevent detection by unintended recipients," said Somerton. He stood suddenly and went over to his liquor cabinet, which was filled with an impressive array of booze. Nash briefly wondered if the eccentric historian was going to pour himself a shot of the hard stuff, but instead, Somerton returned with a crystal shot glass, which he promptly placed on top of the invoice—atop the red dots. "Aha!" he said a moment later. "There's something strange about these dots."

"In what way?" asked Nash.

"There's something here—something odd—but I'm going to need lab equipment at Northern Arizona University to see what it is." Somerton motioned to the invoice. "May I have this for a while, Jeremy?"

"Certainly, but how will we find you again?"

"You and your friends go to the ruins. See what you can find there. When you're done, meet me at Northern Arizona University, Physics Department. I'll leave a note with the secretary there as to where I'll be."

Nash turned away from the sliding glass door. "You know, there's one thing that bothers me about all this," queried Nash.

"What's that?" asked Somerton.

"All of this high-tech stuff. These complex clues and microdots and such. They were beyond the knowledge of my parents, even if my mother was a scientist."

"You think they had help," Somerton remarked.

Nash nodded. "*Sophisticated* help."

Somerton packed some belongings in a small suitcase—including the invoice and printouts—and grabbed his laptop. He also grabbed the little dog. "I guess he's mine now," said the historian and gave the bewildered dog a scratch between the ears.

The group headed out. In the far distance, Nash could see helicopters circling the scene of the destruction. So much pain and misery. For what? Nash didn't know, but he was going to find out. After all, it appeared more than likely that his parent's murders were somehow mixed up with all of this.

In the villa's parking lot, Nash saw Somerton off, and as the elder man disappeared, Nash turned immediately to his sister. "You're going home to New Mexico."

His sister blinked. "Say again?"

"You're going home," he said again. "And I'm taking you to the airport. This is getting too dangerous for my little sis."

"Oh, no you don't, Jeremy Nash. I'm not about to—"

"I agree with Jeremy," said Henderson sheepishly, obviously not wanting to get on Alyson's bad side.

She spun on him. "And who said *you* had any say in this?"

"Ouch," said Henderson, wincing.

She marched over to her brother, who was getting in the Jeep. "You don't control me, Jeremy. I'm a grown—"

"You're going home," he said with finality. "And that's that. We're going to the airport now. I would die if anything happened to you. Do you understand? I almost lost you once in the Holy Land. Besides, things are only going to get crazier, and I will rest easy knowing you are safe."

And with that, the quartet left the villa, although one of the four silently fumed in the passenger seat, occasionally casting her brother venous looks.

Sedona Airport
Sedona, Arizona

Nash dropped Alyson off at the airport and arranged for a charter to take her back to Roswell. To Nash's surprise, she seemed to have resigned herself to her fate and had stopped her protests. She even quit casting him nasty looks.

At the airport security gate, which was swarming with police and armed SWAT members, Nash gave her a kiss on her icy cheek, and Henderson attempted an awkward hug and promised to meet up with her soon. She said sure, shrugging. Kaya gave her a hug as well and told her she would get in touch with her soon. Alyson smiled a little more warmly at the beautiful Native American, but remained silently detached.

And as Alyson watched the trio leave the building, she turned, and immediately looked for an opportunity to stay in the game.

It came from a most unexpected place.

Sedona Airport
Sedona, Arizona

It was a rough flight.

Flying in from Phoenix over the Mogollon Rim, the small government Gulfstream V had nearly been knocked out of the sky by violent thunderstorms. Special Agents Paige Chandler and Zack Safford did all they could to hold their dinners down as the small EPA jet was pushed up and down through incessant air pockets. The hour or so trip felt more like an eternity.

As the wheels of the EPA's Gulfstream thankfully touched down at the Sedona airport, red and blue lights flashed across the wet tarmac.

"I wonder what's going on," Safford remarked, looking out the small windows of the government jet while popping a handful of Tums into his mouth.

Chandler shrugged. "Are you sure Douglas is there?"

"Yeah. I checked before we left Phoenix." Chandler thought her partner looked green. "He's at the pre-conference mixer at Tlaquepaque."

She nodded, then looked concerned. "Hey, are you okay?"

To answer her question, Safford swallowed another handful of Tums and nodded.

The Gulfstream pulled into the small terminal, and the two disembarked. As they walked from the jet towards the terminal, they noticed two National Guard Blackhawk helicopters surrounded by heavily armed soldiers. Next to them was a large medivac chopper with two more circling above, apparently waiting to land.

Chandler looked at her partner. Safford shrugged.

Inside, the terminal was in utter chaos.

There were armed soldiers and a number of SWAT teams roaming about. An EMT team rushed by them ferrying two wounded people, bumping Chandler almost off her feet. They were followed by more EMT teams pushing bloodied men and women with IVs dangling above their heads towards the tarmac.

As a stunned Chandler and Safford watched, the second and third medivac landed nearby.

"What the hell's going on?" asked Chandler.

Safford didn't answer, but someone else did, a young woman who was standing behind them. "A terrorist attack, or something close to it. Someone blew up a shopping center in Sedona."

Chandler turned to look at the woman speaking, first registering surprise at the woman's voice, and then was surprised as hell that she recognized the woman herself.

"So, what brings you here, Paige?" asked Alyson.

Seeing her old sorority sister from the University of New Mexico was like a breath of fresh air to Alyson.

"Alyson? Alyson Nash? Oh my God, I haven't seen you in, what, ten years?"

The two old friends hugged deeply, chatted briefly, and then got right to the point. "Ally, what's this about an attack?"

Alyson told her old college sorority friend what she knew and ended up breaking down in the process. Alyson hadn't realized how emotional she was, but it made sense. So much had happened in the past few days, let alone the past few hours.

After much sobbing and hugging, Alyson eventually got around to why they were in Sedona in the first place—to meet with Somerton and Douglas.

"This man, Douglas," asked the handsome man with Chandler. "Where is he?"

Chandler jumped in. "Oh, I'm sorry, Alyson. This is Special Agent Zack Safford, FBI."

Alyson blinked. "FBI?"

"Yeah. He's attached to my division of the Environmental Protection Agency, Criminal Investigation Division."

"You're a cop now?"

"Sort of."

"Would never have thought that when we were in the sorority together. You were always the anti-establishment type. Always had your nose stuck in some book trumpeting this cause and that."

Chandler laughed then became subdued. "Things change, Alyson. Things change."

Alyson realized she shouldn't go any deeper and just took both of Chandler's hands. "So, why is the EPA here in Sedona?" Alyson looked at Safford. "And to answer your question, Mr. Douglas is dead."

The handsome agent's mouth dropped. So did Chandler's. Alyson went on to tell them what had transpired in the creek, and her brother's efforts to save Douglas.

Both agents took a few seconds to absorb this, and then Safford said, "That's just great. There goes our lead."

"What lead?" asked Alyson.

"We were told that this Douglas knew the location of a man we want to question."

"Would that man happen to be Hayden Mayer?" Alyson asked.

Safford's eyes narrowed. Alyson noticed the man had stopped breathing. "How do know about him?"

"It's a long story," said Alyson, suddenly wary of the man. Safford was too intense, too demanding.

"What are you doing at the airport?" Safford asked. "And where's your brother now?"

Alyson decided not to mention the ruins. She probably could trust Chandler, her old sorority sister, but Safford was a little too demanding for her taste. Besides, she planned to catch a plane alright—but one to Flagstaff, not Roswell.

"I'm flying to Flagstaff to meet Jeremy."

Chandler looked out of the terminal at the pouring rain. "Not in this weather, Ally."

When Safford spoke again, Alyson felt she were being interrogated. "And why are you and your brother interested in Hayden Mayer, Ms. Nash?"

Alyson thought better of answering, wondering just how much she should reveal to the man. But with the scene in the airport being so chaotic, and recent events leaving her an emotional wreck, she decided that if she couldn't trust the FBI, who the hell could she trust?

"We thought he might have a clue to the death of our parents."

Paige Chandler frowned. "Wait. You told me they died in, what, a caving accident?"

"Yes, but now we think they were murdered."

"Murdered? But why?"

"We think because of something they found in the Hopi End Times Prophesy. Someone, or some group, might have thought they were getting too close to something, or some truth. But we don't know what. Not yet." She paused, thought about how much she should say, and decided to stay neutral. "But based on the information we have already, we think we're getting close to their killers."

"What information is that?" demanded Safford.

"My brother knows," she said. She folded her arms over her chest. "And if you take me to Flagstaff, you can ask him yourself."

"Her brother may be on to something," Safford said to Chandler. "Might as well find out what he knows. We're at a dead end here."

Chandler agreed.

Alyson smiled. *I'm back in the game.*

"We need a car," Safford said. "I'll check the rentals." He dashed off, leaving the two girls to chat about old times.

Sedona, Arizona

P arker and his partner sat in a small bar at the west end of Sedona listening to the endless sirens screaming by outside. The bar was mostly empty. The owner sat glued to the TV set. After knocking back a few beers, Parker decided it was time to give his client the good and bad news. He punched in a series of numbers into his LPI phone. Prescott promptly answered and Parker gave his client a status update, in particular, that he could confirm that both Nash and Douglas were dead. He added, "I saw them both tumbling down the wash among heavy debris. I couldn't go downstream to confirm, but nothing could have lived through that flood."

There was a long silence on Prescott's end as Parker held his breath. Then, "We needed Douglas, but what's done is done. We'll have to find another way to locate Mayer."

Parker was relieved. "Orders?"

"Leave Sedona as soon as you can then wait for instructions."

Prescott leaned back in his plush leather chair. This was a setback. He knew the Ecotopians were up to something—something that would endanger the very existence of Project KRATOS. But what?

He placed a call to his EPA contact. Two rings later, a man's voice answered.

"Yes, sir?"

"Douglas is dead."

"I know. But I have news."

Enterprise Rent-A-Car
Sedona, Arizona

While Paige Chandler made arrangements for a rental car, Zack Safford excused himself to make a phone call. He came back in the office just as the Enterprise worker was handing over the keys. He promptly snatched them and told Chandler to finish the paperwork; that he and Alyson would pull the rental car around front.

Alyson soon found herself virtually dragged along by Safford, who ordered her into the front seat, which Alyson thought was odd and started to protest. Surely, she should sit in the back, especially when accompanying two FBI—

But Safford would hear none of it. He barked another order, and Alyson promptly sat like a schoolgirl being disciplined by a particular nasty teacher. She realized her instincts about this guy were right. There was something about him she didn't trust. And there was definitely something about him she didn't like.

Yeah, she thought. *He's an asshole.*

A few minutes later, they drove from behind the rental office in a brand new Ford sedan and found Chandler waiting for them. She stepped off the curb when she saw them.

Then Safford did something very, very odd.

He sped up. Worse, he turned the steering wheel and aimed the vehicle directly at his partner.

"What the hell are you doing?!" screamed Alyson.

The dark look Safford gave her chilled her to the bone. Now he slammed the accelerator down to the floorboard. The car briefly fishtailed, headed straight at Chandler who stood in the middle of the windshield. Alyson could see her friend's confused expression.

Alyson, at first, was too shocked to move then reached over and grabbed the steering wheel with both hands. Safford growled and drove his fist into the side of her face. The force of the punch rocked Alyson, and stars appeared inside her skull, but she held on. Safford hadn't been able to put his full weight behind the strike, and now Alyson yanked hard on the steering wheel, fighting him.

The sedan, still hurtling towards Chandler, slewed sideways. Tires squealed. Alyson saw that her friend was no longer directly in the center of the windshield. There was a chance they would pass her, but at the last second, Safford drove an elbow hard into Alyson's temple and yanked the wheel hard in Chandler's direction.

Before blackness briefly swallowed her, Alyson heard a massive thump and then saw her college sorority sister careen off the side of the vehicle.

Yanking the wheel hard at the last second had done the job. He had hit his intended target. Whether or not he killed her, he didn't know, but he would worry about that later.

For now, he had more pressing matters.

That final yank had sent the vehicle spinning out of control. Safford fought the wheel and hit the brakes. And when a massive propane tank appeared before them, he screamed and covered his face.

The vehicle hit the tank hard. The propane tank ruptured. Hissing propane filled the air.

A moment later, sparks from collision take ignited the propane, catching the vehicle on fire.

Tusayan Ruins
South Rim of the Grand Canyon

The drive from Sedona to the South Rim of the Canyon through torrential rain took almost three hours longer than it normally would. Nash's nerves were frayed by the time they reached the ruins a little after two in the morning.

Nash passed out flashlights, and in the driving rain, Kaya led them past the main excavation site, which was roped off, and towards the unexcavated portion of the village. They found themselves standing in the ancient ruins, with the rain hitting them full in the face, and their flashlights illuminating broken stone walls. Nash could not have imagined a more surreal moment.

"Now what?" asked Henderson.

Kaya thought for a moment. She slowly scanned the area with her flashlight looking for something. She stopped on a small mound of brush and mud. "That area over there. Let's take a look."

"Sure," said Henderson dryly. "Let's take a look at a pile of mud. Sounds exciting."

Kaya threw him a withering look, and Nash found himself chuckling. She threw him a similar glance, and he promptly shut his mouth and followed her.

She led the two men to the small pile of dirt and debris and knelt, brushing aside some branches and various sopping wet organic debris.

"Let's clear this area," she said.

"I'm all for digging randomly in dirt," said Henderson. "Hey, who isn't? But could you at least tell us why?"

"Because this looks like the remains of a hidden kiva. An underground ceremonial room. If there's anything here to be found at this site, it'll be found in here."

Nash dashed off and quickly went through the archaeologist's site and found what he was looking for—a shovel and trowels. He returned, handing the trowels to the others.

"You expect me to dig with this?" Henderson said, holding up the small digging apparatus.

"Yes," said Nash, grinning. "Now get to work."

With Henderson grumbling to himself, the three got to work clearing the area, which went quick enough, although digging through the mud proved to be challenging. The constant rains had turned the stuff into a thick, brown syrup, which tended to ooze back into the hole they were digging.

"Isn't this illegal?" asked Henderson.

"Highly," said Kaya.

"That's good to know," said Henderson. "That makes me feel a whole lot better."

An hour later and a lot dirtier, they hit pay dirt. Or, in this case, solid wood. Thick beams of burnt wood seemed to span what appeared to be an opening. A few splinters later, Nash and Henderson pulled free the wooden beams.

Henderson whistled. Nash stood back in awe. Before them was a dark opening. A very ancient and musty smell issued out.

"This is it," Kaya said excitedly, dropping to her knees and shining her light inside. The others joined her.

The kiva appeared to be a small, round room. To Nash, it also looked scary as hell, but he never believed in ghosts or curses or things that went bump in the night. But here in this abandoned village in the middle of the night, during a driving rainstorm, and looking for the first time into a ceremonial room that had not been opened for centuries, Nash couldn't help but feel a small shiver of apprehension.

Excitement, he corrected himself. *A shiver of excitement.*

"See that bench there?" said Kaya, shining her light on a long wooden plank that circled more than half of the interior. "That's a banquet bench. The charred wood is what remained of the posts that supported the upper structure."

Kaya sat at the edge of the opening, swung her feet inside, braced herself, and then fearlessly dropped down into the dark room. She did all of this with her flashlight in her mouth.

Henderson looked at Nash, raising his eyebrows. "I'm sure as hell not going in there."

"Suit yourself," said Nash, and promptly followed Kaya into the dark maw.

"Wait! Don't leave me!"

A few moments later, the gangly Irishman was hunched behind Nash. The ceremonial room was obviously not built for six-foot, eight inch scaredy cats.

Kaya ignored them both. She ran her hand between the banquet bench and what looked like a fire pit. Occasionally she brushed dirt and debris away. Nash moved next to her. There was something cozy about this creepy little room. Perhaps it was the thunderstorm outside. Perhaps it was Kaya's company and her intoxicating hint of perfume. Perhaps it was all of these things. Nash regretfully pushed those thoughts aside. They had work to do.

"What are you looking for?" he asked, now on his hands and knees next to her.

"The *sipapu*," was all she said.

"Oh, God," moaned Henderson. "I think something just hissed at me from somewhere in the corner."

"Maybe it just wants you to be quiet," snapped Kaya.

Nash stifled his laughter as he and Kaya carefully brushed away the loose dirt that filled the hole. Shortly, they hit something solid. Kaya outlined in the dirt something flat and hard, digging at the edges.

Now this is a girl I could love, Nash thought. *A woman who is unafraid of damaging her nails.*

225

A moment later, Kaya carefully withdrew a flat stone object, looked at it, paused, and tears sprang from her eyes.

"What?" said Nash, the beam of his flashlight reflecting off the tears that now streamed down her high cheekbones. "Is that it? Is that the missing piece?"

That got Henderson's attention, too, and the tall man was now squatting next to them in an instant.

Kaya nodded reverently and gently handed it to Nash. "It is beyond belief. Even more amazing, your parents actually found the missing piece to our sacred stone."

Nash examined the broken section of stone. Admittedly, it wasn't much to look at, especially in the near total darkness of the kiva. He ran a finger over it, acutely aware that his father had touched this very relic. A shiver ran through him, and then he set his jaw.

"And next we need to find who killed them."

"And my grandfather."

Nash had just started to nod his agreement when a voice spoke above them.

"Not quite," a voice said behind them.

Nash snapped his head around, swinging around his flashlight. Kaya gasped. Henderson slammed his head on the low ceiling. Standing above them silhouetted against the lighter darkness of the cloud-filled night sky, was a lone man. When Nash's light hit the man in the eyes, he squinted, and aimed a gun directly at Nash's face.

"Drop everything," said the man. "Hands where I can see them."

Nash did as he was told, setting his flashlight and the broken section of the stone tablet down. The brief glimpse he saw of the man was a strange one. He looked like a plump hippie, with long scraggly hair and a tie-dye shirt that was soaked through and through from the rain. Another figure appeared silhouetted in the opening.

A woman.

Both figures dropped down into the Kiva, and Nash had a good look at them. They were both hippies. They even wore peace sign hemp necklaces. The gun in the man's hand, of course, was the ultimate peacemaker. The irony was not lost on Nash.

"We'll relieve you of that," said the woman. She motioned to the man to retrieve the stone from Nash's hands.

The man held his gun on Nash, who was still kneeling next to Kaya over the open *sipapu.*

Nash waited for his moment. When the man bent down to retrieve the piece of tablet, Nash scooped up a handful of dirt and threw it in his face.

The man yipped, stood straight up, smashed his head, and rubbed frantically at his eyes. He swung the pistol around dangerously, and Nash knew it was only a matter of seconds before an errant shot was fired.

Nash lunged on the man, jumping on his broad back. Like a cornered tiger, the man screeched and reached up, clawing at Nash's face. Nash held on, tightening his grip around the man's throat. That did little to stop this maniac. The man swung around violently, waving his gun.

He's going to shoot, thought Nash.

The man slammed Nash hard against the kiva wall. Air burst from Nash's lungs. The man backed up, and prepared to slam Nash back into the wall, when Nash released his grip on the man's throat, dropped down, and tackled the man to the ground. It was an old high school wrestling trick, and it worked perfectly. The man went down hard, and the gun went flying.

With the flailing man pinned to the ground, Nash looked desperately over his shoulder. "Grab the gun, Bryan! Grab the gun!"

The woman had made a mad dash for the weapon. Nash couldn't have been happier when he saw Kaya take a flying leap at the woman, completely knock her off her feet.

Holy shit!

When Henderson retrieved the pistol, Nash literally sighed

with relief. *Jesus, who were these people? And where did they come from?*

"Hold the gun on them, Bryan" Nash said, getting up carefully from the guy, who finally seemed to calm down.

"I don't think so, old boy," Henderson said. Nash looked at his friend. There was a strange smile on his face as he pointed the pistol at Nash and Kaya. "Let my friends go."

Sedona Medical Center
Sedona, Arizona

"You're a lucky lady," the young freckle-faced intern said as he held Paige Chandler's hand to check her pulse.

Chandler wondered if her interest in his hazel eyes, boyish face, and well-toned physique might have made her heart beat a little faster.

Priorities, she reminded herself. After all, she had found herself in an explosion, and as of this moment she had no idea what had happened to Alyson Nash.

"No bones broken or muscles torn," he went on, "just small cuts, scrapes, and bruisers." He winked at her.

She tried to wink back but it hurt, so she settled for a crooked smile instead.

"Did they catch whoever, um, hit me?"

"I hope so, but I don't have any information on that."

"Can I be released?"

"Any time. Is there anything else we can do for you?" he said in a flirtatious voice.

"Yes. Please lower the TV, leave, and close the door behind you."

With an air of disappointment on his face, the young intern shrugged his shoulders, got up, and left.

When he was gone, Chandler picked up the phone by her bed and asked to be connected to her EPA office in Phoenix. A minute later she was talking to Tolleson and explained what had happened.

"I don't believe it. Why?" asked Tolleson.

"I have my suspicions but first, check him out with HomeSec and the FBI. I'll hold."

As Tolleson went to work, Chandler thought back over the meeting with Alyson at the airport. Alyson was reluctant to tell where her brother was, and Safford seemed only to be interested in his whereabouts. Alyson's instincts proved right. The big question was, *Where were they?*

Tolleson came back on the line. "HomeSec knew only that he was with the FBI and had the credentials to prove it. So I checked with the FBI in Washington, and get this, they have no record of a Zack Safford as an agent or anything else at the Bureau."

Chandler felt sick. She was certain she was going to vomit. As she took a few deep breaths, her door opened, and a tall scraggly man dressed in a threadbare robe entered.

On the other end of the phone, she heard Tolleson asking for confirmation on what he had said. But she couldn't speak. Her mouth had dropped open and was hanging there on its hinges. When she found her voice, she could respond only with, "I'll call you back," and abruptly hung up.

She turned her full attention to the ghost standing at the foot of her bed, and when she spoke her voice sounded tiny and confused.

"Uncle?"

Jackson Wilcox walked to her side. He took her shaking hand in his. "It's been a long time, child."

"I...I thought you were dead?"

Her uncle, who had played a major role in taking care of her when her parents had been killed in the fire, had disappeared a few years ago. Paige had exhausted all her leads looking for the man—a man she had grown to love and care for. She had assumed, since her uncle was on the front lines of a radical environmental protection group, that he had met with an unfortunate demise at the hands of a ruthless private company that he had probably seriously inconvenienced. She had thought regretfully at the time, he had died doing what he loved. Protecting the earth. She had learned much from her uncle, and she had missed him greatly.

Seeing him now, especially after the traumatic events of the past few hours, was surreal at best.

"Am I dreaming?"

"No, sweetie."

"Maybe I'm hallucinating. A bad reaction to the pain killers."

"You're not hallucinating, and I have much to tell you, but now is not the time. Soon, I promise."

"But where were you, uncle?"

He sat next to her. "I've been in hiding."

"From what?" she asked. "From whom?"

"Please. I promise to tell you everything. But first, we need to find Jeremy Nash."

Again, with Alyson's brother?

"I'm not going anywhere, Uncle, until you tell me what the hell is going on?"

Wilcox sighed and began to speak.

Twenty minutes later, finished and emotionally exhausted, he sat back in silence. "And that's the whole story, lass."

Paige knew her mouth was hanging open again. Finally, she found the only word she could think of. "Unbelievable!"

"Believe it. And we're running out of time. Things are about to get a lot worse."

"Then why your interest in Nash?"

"He's the only person who can locate the Project. He has the clues to do so. His parents found the clues and were killed for their discovery. His father left him the clues to locate and stop the Project."

"And how do you know this?"

"Child, I have devoted my entire life to knowing this. Besides, I have been keeping an eye on Jeremy and his sister. What's going down now will have global implications. Deadly implications. We need to act now."

Chandler was silent for a moment. "I know where Nash will be. Alyson told us. He'll be in Flagstaff. At the University."

Wilcox smiled. "Good. I have a car. Now let's get you out of here."

Ecotopian Compound
White Mountains, Arizona

The sun was rising over the White Mountains in eastern Arizona as the two Jeeps drove through the Apache Indian Reservation to the Ecotopian's compound. Nash could only fume and stare at the back of Henderson's head in the lead Jeep all the way from the Grand Canyon.

What the hell is going on? Why is Bryan doing this?

But Bryan Henderson wasn't talking. He made it clear to them, as well, that they were to remain quiet during the drive. Nash did discover that the weirdo holding the pistol was named Ryver, and the woman was named Rainbow.

Hippy freaks, thought Nash, and he was relieved all over again that he had sent Alyson home.

As they drove through the compound, Nash looked to his right and saw a half dozen flying machines with long Mylar wings and a bare undercarriage on wheels. Nash knew the aircraft well. They were called *ultralights* or *trikes*, designed to carry two people. He wondered what they were doing with so many.

His thoughts were cut short when they suddenly pulled up in front of a large geodesic dome.

Nash and Kaya were led into the dome—or Main House, as Nash soon discovered it was called. The inside of the Main House was sparse except for the many Native-American rugs and two or three Aspen tables scattered about. The smell of incense hung in the air, and hookah pipes sat on two of the low wooden tables.

Henderson, who had been avoiding all eye contact with Nash,

peeled off into another section of the camp while his hippie hench-man, Ryver, led Nash and Kaya through the vaulted space and into a small room in the rear of the structure. The room was lit by sunlight streaming through a small triangular window ten feet above their heads.

"You'll wait here until the Pahana requests your presence," said Ryver. The hippie locked the door behind them with the sound of a heavy bolt firmly seating itself.

"Now what?" said Kaya, standing in the triangular beam of light and looking, Nash thought, utterly radiant.

He sat glumly in the center of a throw rug, since there was no furniture in the small room. "I guess we wait for the Pahana. Meanwhile, I'm going to think of every conceivable way I'm going to wring Bryan's neck."

Ecotopian Compound
Main House

It was late afternoon as Hayden Mayer, the self-described Pahana, sat on an ornate Navajo rug in the middle of the Main House with his legs crossed. Next to him was his hand-carved, hand-painted, metal-tipped walking stick which he considered his regal scepter.

He was, after all, the Pahana.

Sitting in front of him were Henderson, Ryvre, Rainbow, Big Man, and another young Ecotopian.

But most important of all, sitting in front of him on a folded silk cloth, was the broken piece of the Hopi tablet. He reverently fingered the broken stone.

I am the Pahana.

He had waited a long time for the missing piece to the Hopi stone tablet. All was playing out as the Hopi predictions had said. He was the long-awaited white brother, and now he had the proof.

I am the Pahana.

There would be no mistake this time. The missing piece he brought to the Hopi elders many years ago was rejected even though he had fulfilled prophesy by breaking a clay pot at the feet of an elder at the El Tovar hotel. To Mayer, the Hopi had not adhered to the way of life faithful to their religious beliefs.

Ah, but this piece of broken stone was different. Mayer ran his fingers over it again, shivering. On one side was an image of a man with a tail. The man, thought Mayer, looked more like a tadpole. The little *y* on the Hopi Stone matched the fingers of the man's right hand. On the other side of the broken piece were four wavy lines and a V above an oblong symbol around a man's reflection in water.

The missing piece...

Unlike the images on the piece he showed the Hopi years ago, Mayer knew in his heart that the translation of the symbols on *this* piece—the true missing piece—would surely point to where the *Sipapu* was located.

The sacred point of emergence—the point where the Fifth World will emerge.

Mayer had come to fulfill prophesy, but the Hopi had turned their backs on him. Not all Hopi. Not Big Man. Not Mayer's other faithful followers.

And soon they will be rewarded for their faith in him and witness proof of his true calling—with a little help from Nash and Henderson, of course.

"Bring me the Hopi Stone," he commanded firmly. Mayer learned early on that he never needed to raise his voice. Raising his voice was a sign of weakness. The Pahana was not weak.

Big Man hastened over to an ornate turquoise and silver studded box and reverently withdrew a small stone tablet—a tablet with a broken corner. He handed the stone to Mayer.

The Pahana always felt a rush when he handled the sacred Hopi Tablet, a tablet he had stolen to fulfill prophesy. As his four faithful followers watched him in silence, most with their mouths slightly unhinged, Mayer held up the broken stone tablet in one hand, and the recently acquired broken corner in the other.

He brought them slowly together. The Pahana smiled triumphantly. They were a perfect fit.

He turned to Rainbow and Ryver. "It's time to meet our guests."

The two hippies jumped up and moved quickly to the small room in the rear of the building.

A few minutes later, they returned with Nash and Kaya.

"William?" Kaya said when she first entered the room. "What's going—"

"Silence," ordered a thin blond Caucasian who sat before them.

Whoever he was, Nash ignored him. Instead, he looked at his one-time college buddy. "Bryan, what the hell is going—"

But Nash's question was cut short by a sudden blow across his back from Ryver, driving him to his knees.

"You don't play well with others," said the white man, standing smoothly from a lotus position. And using a bizarre-looking cane, he walked steadily over to Nash. "I know this, Mr. Nash, because I read all your work." He lowered his face until he was just a few inches from Nash's own. "You see, I feel it's important to know your enemy. Allow me to introduce myself. My name is Hayden Mayer. I am the Pahana."

Nash knew that face. Although young—perhaps just a few years older than Nash—the face was heavily creased with lines. And not laugh lines, either. Worry lines. Stress lines. From the depths of Nash's memory, surfaced recognition. It was the young man he had seen in the room with the Hopi shaman at the El Tovar hotel.

Mayer studied Nash some more, cocking his head slightly, then retreated to his lotus position and sat before them.

"But even a skeptic like yourself will soon be convinced that The End Times are here." Mayer pointed to Henderson. "Bryan was a tremendous help. His research on the Omega Point has given us collaborative proof we need to move forward." A creepy smile crossed the man's face. "Bryan also informed us of your father and the clues he left for you while you went to Prophesy Rock. Once he saw the images of the sacred stones on the printout, he knew you might be able to lead us to the missing piece—with your father's help."

"Way to go, Bryan," said Nash. "You betrayed your friends to help a lunatic."

Henderson dipped his head down sheepishly, and Nash felt nothing but disgust for his former drinking mate.

Mayer, who had been watching the interaction between the two former friends with a greasy, creepy smile—the kind of smile that you'd expect to see on a serial rapist—said, "One man's lunacy is another's prophecy, Mr. Nash."

"Sure. Remind me to write that down later," said Nash. He turned to Henderson. "I guess those psychedelic cocktails in college really did fry your brain, chump."

Eyes flashing, Henderson became indignant for the first time since turning on Nash and Kaya. With self-righteous conviction, he reminded Nash that the Hopi prophecy fit his research into the Omega Point perfectly and that he wanted to be part of the coming New World.

Nash looked at Hayden Mayer. "What's a New World for some is an insane asylum for others."

Mayer smiled again. "Clever, Mr. Nash. Anyway, do not be too hard on your friend. He did what he thought was right. Remember, there is something greater at work here then mere mortal friendships."

"If you call that something brainwashing, then you might be right."

"All my followers are here on their own accord. Because they believe in the cause. They believe in me. And as you can see, my followers are very dedicated."

Nash held his tongue as Mayer stood again. Using his ornate-looking cane, he walked behind the male hippie who was standing to Nash's left. The hippie, Nash noted, was looking increasingly nervous.

"But some of my flock have become, let's say, a little overzealous and have lost any semblance of discretion. Some have broken direct commands from their Pahana."

Nash had a bad feeling about this. Hayden Mayer, Nash noted, was sounding increasingly deranged.

Mayer next ordered the man to his knees. The young hippie dropped instantly, obediently. Beads of sweat had broken out on the young man's forehead.

Nash glanced at Kaya. Kaya raised her eyebrows in alarm. Behind them, Rainbow and Ryvre were still holding their guns.

The young man began stammering. "I-I was only proud to be accepted by you, O Great Pahana. I didn't mean to—"

"Of course you didn't *mean* to," said Mayer. "You didn't *mean* to brag that our involvement in the dam protest would usher in the next world."

"I shouldn't have—"

"Yes," said Mayer, raising the crazy-looking staff behind the young hippie. "You shouldn't have."

And with that, jammed the metal tip of the stick deep into the base of the young hippie's skull. The kid convulsed wildly, like a speared fish, and then fell flat on his face as blood spurted from the deep wound in the back of his head.

Kaya muffled a scream with her hand, and Nash grimaced and looked away, his knees suddenly weak. Nash was certain he was going to vomit.

Mayer, whose face had flushed into splotchy red spots, looked excitedly down at the now dead young man. Nash made a decision right then and there that he was going to go down swinging before he let this piece of shit drive the tip of his cane into either him or Kaya.

The Pahana took in a lot of air, seemed to center himself, and next turned to the silent Hopi Indian standing next to him. "Of course, even my fine disciple here makes mistakes. For instance, he made the mistake of providing an unknown group of thugs—thugs he erroneously thought were followers of mine—with information that was responsible for a shaman's brutal beating."

Kaya sat straight up. "William! You?"

"I-I'm sorry, Kaya."

"Because of you," Kaya snarled. "Because of you my grandfather was left a broken man. He didn't speak and hardly ate again. He was dead to me, my family, and my clan. You sentenced him to death!" Her eyes burned deep into Big Man's.

Nash would hate to have Kaya look at him like that. Big Man, he realized, had acquired an enemy for life.

"Your grandfather is of no consequence," said Mayer, waving his hand dismissively. "I forgive Big Man for his impetuousness." Hayden paused as Kaya fumed. The self-proclaimed Pahana looked dispassionately at the dead body lying prostrate on the floor before him. He said, "Now, the Great Purification that the Hopi's predicted is upon us. We will cleanse the entire sacred Four Corners Area deeded to the Hopis and usher in the Fifth World—the New Age."

Nash's head hurt. He felt he was trapped in the very insane asylum he had mentioned early, and all the inmates were just that, utterly insane—and utterly dangerous.

"And how do you plan to cleanse the Four Corners?" he asked, knowing he was encouraging the little crazy bastard, but also eager to buy more time for them. Nash, as he spoke, constantly looked for ways to escape.

"By washing away the sins of the white man—and with *his* help, of course."

"His help?" said Kaya. "What does that mean?"

Before answering, Mayer reached into his wrinkled white muslin shirt and pulled out a small copper box. He opened it, took a pinch of the white powder within, and inhaled it deeply through his nose. He shook his head like a wet dog, then continued.

"There is a flaw in the Glenn Canyon Dam—a fatal flaw. And we will use it to remove the dam." He paused in thought. "Glenn Canyon faced the same problem in 1983 when a twenty-five-year flood—what they called a *relatively small flood*—corroded the spillways and almost brought down the entire dam. We will, in effect, use Nature to purify itself. Poetic justice, no?"

"I don't understand," Nash said. "How will you use nature to bring down the dam? Those things are built to resist the forces of nature."

"With the recent rains, the dam operators are running out of options," Mayer said. "These rains are sending millions of gallons of water each second down the Colorado River. The dam's two giant spillways are built to control high water building behind the dam by discharging the water from below. But the water pressure is too much, and such pressure is eroding through the concrete spillway linings and into the rust-colored bedrock below. The same bedrock that holds up the massive dam." Mayer leaned forward; his eyes alive with something close to insanity. "The corrosion is turning the water red. A sea of red, so to speak. Almost Biblical."

A self-proclaimed Hopi deity dipping into the Hebrew Bible. Now Nash had heard everything.

"Only a few hundred feet of soft, porous sandstone separate the spillway tunnels from the base and sides of the dam. If the spillways continued to erode, water could exploit even the tiniest opening in the weak rock, like a supersonic water-pick drilling through a loaf of bread. As the opening widens, pressure would force still more water through the opening, enlarging it, until the nine trillion gallons of water in Lake Powell bursts through."

Nash didn't know much about dams, but he did know what such an uncontrolled release would do. A tidal wave would blast through the Grand Canyon, inundating its steep walls and leaving nothing alive. Three hundred miles downstream, a wall of water seventy feet high would no doubt surge over the parapet of Hoover Dam, causing it to collapse. Then, each of the smaller dams below Hoover on the Colorado River would topple in turn. From Glen Canyon to the Gulf of California, the river would have destroyed each obstacle that Man had placed in its path, just as it had destroyed many natural obstacles in its five-million-year history.

"Surely, the dam operators know this and are taking the necessary precautions," Kaya said.

"Of course," Mayer replied. "That's why we're going to give Mother Nature a little help."

"How?" asked Nash with a sickening feeling.

"We will, of course, speed up the erosion of the spillways that nature has already started. Have you ever heard of ASR—or Alkali Silica Reaction?"

Nash and Kaya shook their heads. Nash noted that Henderson was looking increasingly uncomfortable. He wondered if his ex-friend had been aware that he had signed on for such epic, full-scale murder and mayhem.

Mayer indicated for Big Man to explain, which the Hopi did in a dispassionate, monotone voice. "ASR is a chemical reaction within hardened concrete, which causes the concrete to expand over time. The reaction can continue indefinitely if sufficient alkalis are available to sustain the reaction. The expansion eventually causes cracking in the cement paste and aggregates which adversely affects the mechanical properties of the material."

Mayer smirked. "And by adverse, we mean corroding the concrete."

"You're going to pour alkali into the water rushing through the spillway," Nash said.

"You get a gold star, Mr. Nash," answered Mayer. "A simple thing to do, really. Take one reactive aggregate—or, in this case, a concrete spillway—add some hydroxyl and alkali, and we have the conditions required for ASR. All we need now is access to the inside of the dam and then the spillway itself."

The man sounded insane, but he had obviously thought this out. Nash knew that a well-prepared lunatic was the most dangerous lunatic of them all.

"And how do you plan on getting such access?" asked Kaya.

Mayer grinned. "The Ecotopions are a major participant at the dam demonstration today. Such a demonstration, with perhaps a distraction here and there, will provide my team an opportunity for access. Big Man has worked out the details."

"And this is the Hopi way, William?" challenged Kaya. "Through violence?"

Big Man was about to speak when the Pahana cut him off. "Enough of the science lesson. There is one more thing to complete." He picked up the piece of broken stone and showed it to Kaya. "What do the symbols mean to you? Where is the point of emergence?"

"Even if I knew, I wouldn't tell you," she spat. Her voice was filled with contempt.

The Pahana smiled, his hideous, serial rapist smile. "We will see, Hopi. When we return from purifying the Four Corners area you will tell us where the *sipapu* is located so that I can lead us all into the Fifth World. And if you fail me, you will be eliminated."

He turned to Rainbow. "Lock them up. Big Man, come with me. We have much to do."

Mayer walked with Big Man giving him last minute instructions. When he was finished, Big Man asked for permission to speak. Mayer nodded and Big Man spoke in a low hushed voice.

"You will not get the Hopi woman to give you the translation. I know my sister. She is very stubborn. And I doubt Nash knows. They're both a liability now."

Mayer paused in thought. A few moments later he said, "Agreed. Have Ryvre eliminate them. Once done, they can join us at the dam."

"Shall I help him?"

"No. I need you to gather our people. It's time to do our sacred work."

"I'm sorry I got you into this," Nash said to Kaya again.

They were in their make-shift jail cell once again. He reached over and took her hand as they sat on the hard floor, their backs against the hard wooden wall. His exhausted mind wandered over all that they had been through together, all the crazy places, the near-death experiences. It had been a wild ride.

A helluva way to get to know a girl, he thought, almost grinning.

"Don't be sorry," she said after a few moments, snapping Nash out of his scattered thoughts. She sounded as tired as Nash felt. She squeezed his hand. "It was my decision to follow through on this. Remember, I brought your father's message to you. Nobody made me do this." She moved close to him, laid her head on his shoulder, and closed her eyes.

Nash closed his eyes, too, and imagined they were far away together, faraway from all this craziness, and if he ever heard the word *Pahana* again, it would be too soon.

A few minutes later, jolting Nash out of his reverie, the door to their prison banged open. They both sat up as Ryvre stalked towards them. Another hippie followed close behind. Both men were carrying side arms. Ryvre stopped just a few feet short of Nash and Kaya who were still huddled on the floor. The young man's upper lip turned up in a scowl, and his bloodshot eyes burned with hate. Something else burned there too.

Blood lust.

Ryvre raised his Glock and aimed it at Nash's forehead.

Resigned to his fate, Nash put an arm around Kaya, pulling her to him, cradling her head on his chest. No need for her to see death coming faster than the speed of light in the form of 115 grains of jacketed lead.

Nash closed his eyes and held Kaya closer to him, waiting for death to come. A moment later there was the sound of the slide being pulled back and a round being chambered.

A shot rang out, followed immediately by Kaya screaming. And as another shot echoed painfully in the small room, Nash wondered what death would feel like.

So far, death wasn't such a big deal.

A moment later, something hit his right leg. *Kaya?*

Nash opened his eyes to see Ryvre's corpse sprawled on the ground before him, the top of his head blown off, blood pooling on the floor, soaking his pants legs. Blood had splatter all over the wall behind them, as well as a fine mist of brain matter and blood on their clothing.

The other hippie hadn't fared much better. He lay motionless in a pool of blood on the floor, and in the dimming light, Nash saw a man standing over them both. In his hand he held what appeared to be an Army regulation Colt .45 pistol.

Henderson, face ashen and eyes wide, stepped forward and said, "I didn't sign up for mass murder."

And then he promptly vomited.

As they walked through the deserted Ecotopian camp Nash, who was still holding Kaya's hand, said to Henderson, "Jesus, Bryan. What the fuck did you get us into?"

Henderson was still pale. "I'm so sorry I got you two into this. I don't know how you could forgive me. I have no excuse other than I fell for Mayer's delusion. I'm so sorry. So, so sorry."

"Fine, you're sorry," said Nash. "Let's just get the hell out of here, unless you plan on going bi-polar on us again."

"Ouch," said Henderson. "I guess I deserved that. Look, I'm not all bad."

He paused in mid-step, reached into his baggy pant pocket, and pulled out a folded white handkerchief, ladened with something heavy. He handed the folded material to Nash with a sly smile.

Nash frowned and unwrapped the handkerchief. Inside was the Hopi Stone, complete with its missing piece. Nash blinked, stunned. Then he quickly refolded the white kerchief and pocketed the stone.

"You did good, Bryan. Granted, I'm still fairly certain I hate you, but you did good."

Kaya reached over and placed her long-fingered hand on Henderson's shoulder. "You saved our lives, Bryan. We're thankful for that. Let's just move on."

Nash gazed around the empty compound, which he found eerily and disturbingly quiet. It was morning now, and the sun was rising above the distant craggy peaks. "Tell us what they plan to do, Bryan."

"They're using the demonstration at the Visitor Center at the dam as a diversion."

"Yes, but they still have to get inside the dam, don't they?"

"Not *inside*," Henderson replied. "*On top of*." He pointed to the lone ultralight sitting under a patch of trees fifty feet in front of them. "They plan to land an assault force on top of the dam, overwhelm the distracted guards, and gain entry into the dam."

"The guy is nuts," said Nash. He almost commented that his one-time friend was equally nuts to go along with Hayden Mayer, even if briefly. It was all Nash could do to hold his tongue.

"We have to stop them, Jeremy," said Kaya anxiously.

Nash paused and turned to Bryan. "Did you see any cell phones or any type of communications equipment lying around here?"

"None."

Nash chewed his lip. "So, alerting the authorities is out."

"Then it's up to us," Kaya said emphatically.

"What do you mean *us*?" Nash said. "I don't want you involved in any of this. Not anymore. Not after what nearly…" His voice trailed off. *Good God, had they really been within seconds of being executed?* "Anyway, it's just too dangerous. I'm sending you—"

"Listen, Jeremy Nash," said Kaya, cutting him off, her voice rising an octave or two. "I have more at stake here than you. That's my brother who's desecrating our tribe, and that loony white man is defiling our most scared traditions. I have, what you white people call, a dog in this fight."

"She has a point," Henderson added.

"Okay," Nash resigned. He pulled the two Glocks from his waist belt that they retrieved from Ryvre and the dead hippie and checked the clips. Both had eight bullets in them. At least they were armed.

He handed one to Kaya. "Do you know how to—"

Kaya snatched the Glock from his hand, pulled back the slide and chambered a round. Nash's jaw dropped.

"Varsity shooting team," she quipped.

Nash grinned, then turned to Henderson. "Okay. Now. How do we get to the dam?"

"The Jeeps are still here. We can use one of them," Henderson replied.

"No. Too slow," Nash said. "Wait a minute." He turned to Kaya. "How much do you weight?"

"First of all, sir, that's not a question you ask a woman."

Nash rolled his eyes. He pointed a thumb behind him at the ultralight. "That's our ticket. It can hold just over 400 pounds."

"Fly to the dam in that?" Kaya said. "All three of us?"

"Why not?" Nash replied. "Mayer and his loonies did."

"And you can fly one of these?" asked Henderson skeptically.

"Piece of cake. Have one in my garage."

Kaya nervously eyed the two-seated open cockpit and remarked, "But it has only two seats."

Nash gave her a lopsided, devilish grin. "I guess you'll just have to sit on my lap, then."

Glen Canyon Dam
Arizona

It was dusk as the ultralight carrying the three approached the dam several hundred feet below. As they drew closer, fingers of black smoke reached high into the sky, and soon Nash could see dozens of small fires burning in various locations around the Visitor Center. As they flew further, a swarming mob of people seemed to be clashing violently. It was, Nash realized, a full-scale riot consisting of protestors and security forces. The scene was one of utter chaos.

A helluva diversion, thought Nash grimly.

Flying over the dam, it was obvious that an explosion of sort had occurred. Most of the windows in the Visitor Center had blown out, littering the area with sparkling glass shards.

"There," Kaya exclaimed, pointing to the top of the 710-foot-high dam where several ultralights were sitting on the roadway. Many bodies lay scattered around them. Earlier, as they had just gained altitude in the little flying craft, Henderson had explained that Mayer's had trained a highly capable assault team consisting of many ex-military vets.

Looking down at the bodies, Nash didn't doubt their efficiency.

"Poor bastards," said Henderson. "I bet they never heard—or even saw—Mayer's assault team."

"Thanks to the riots below," added Kaya bitterly.

Nash maneuvered the ultralight for a closer look. "I count five Trikes. Assuming two Ecotopians to a Trike, I guess ten all told in the assault team."

248

Henderson nodded. "About right."

When Nash landed their Trike, Henderson immediately stepped out and examined the bodies strewn around the dam. Nash and Kaya followed.

With the eerie orange glow of light from the fires at the Visitor Center as a back-drop, Henderson said, "I count five of the assault team among the dead."

"You sure?" asked Kaya.

"Yes. I recognize them. The others are dam security."

"Then that leaves five to deal with," said Nash. He didn't exactly know how to deal with them, and the more he thought about it, the more he wanted to get the hell out of there. But maybe, just maybe there was a way to get through this without any more bloodshed—especially his own. He looked at Henderson. "So where do we go from here?"

The tall man scanned the lifeless area. "Mayer told us their objective was the east spillway since it had been more damaged than the west during the eighty-three flood, and its concrete would be the weakest."

"Good," Nash replied. "Then let's go."

"Wait," Henderson said. "Some of his men would also be in the control room. Once the ASR is planted in the spillway cave, they'll release the water from the dam and..."

"And that's all she wrote," said Nash. He turned to Kaya. "And there's no way I can talk you into waiting somewhere safe?"

"No."

He sighed. "Okay, fine. You and Henderson go to the control room. I'll go to the spillway cave alone."

Kaya took his hand. "Jeremy. If you find William..."

"I know. Give him your regards."

"Please, be careful, Jeremy."

Nash couldn't help but wonder if he would ever see either of them again. He nodded and said to Henderson. "Keep her safe."

Glen Canyon Dam
Galleries

After a 528-foot descent deep into the interior of the dam, Kaya and Henderson exited the east elevator and walked towards the control room. Nash turned away and entered the galleries to the east spillway.

The atmosphere in this labyrinthine of dam galleries was cold and damp—a constant 50 degrees Fahrenheit year-round. As Nash wondered if he would ever find his way out of these cement tunnels again, he remembered from his visits to Hoover Dam the purpose of dam galleries. They provided an area for boring holes and grouting into the foundation of the dam during construction, then later, provided a space to monitor and inspect the structural behavior of the dam. This far down into the guts of the dam it was comforting to know that more than 100 feet of concrete lay between him and Lake Powell.

As he walked through the dim cathedral-shaped galleries, only the yellow emergency lights were on. He looked for the spillway cave that Henderson had described during the elevator ride down into the heart of the dam. Shortly, more through accident than anything else, Nash found the east spillway cave marked by a plaque embedded in the wall.

This had to be it because as he approached the entrance he saw that the heavy metal door to the spillway was ajar. Nash fingered the Glock in his hands. Hardly a comfort against a handful of heavily armed ex-soldiers.

I'm not cut out for this hero shit, he thought, and considered his options again. If he turned and ran, many people were likely to perish. If he stayed and fought, he was likely to take a bullet in his head—and accomplish nothing.

Knowing his probability of success was undoubtedly low—very, very low—he pulled the heavy door open and peeked into the long spillway cave. The tunnel, which was lit by a handful of flickering yellow service lights, appeared empty.

Mercifully empty.

Nash carefully peeked down the nearly vertical spillway which disappeared straight down into nearly total blackness. As he peered over the ledge, Nash saw what appeared to be a half dozen foot-long metal canisters attached by D-rings to the handholds on the inside of the spillway. He could guess what was in them.

The Alkali Silica.

He knew what he had to do.

From within a long, concrete hallway, Kaya peered cautiously through the glass of the control room door. Henderson was directly behind her, nearly breathing down her neck.

"What do you see?" asked Henderson.

"Mayer and that hippie woman are waving a gun in the face of another man, who looks like a control room tech. The man's scared shitless and seems to be explaining things to them. Now he's showing them around the control room and pointing out gauges on the status panels on the circular wall."

"What else?" Henderson asked.

"Now they seem to be distracted by something." She strained to get a better view through the small glass in the door.

"Do you think we can barge in and surprise them?"

Kaya shook her head. "Doubt it. It's a long way from the door to the control panel. Maybe if—oh, shit!" She yanked her face away from glass and stepped back. "Mayer is coming this way."

The two quickly retreated around a nearby corner and listened as Mayer exited the room. His footsteps, mercifully, echoed away from them, toward what Kaya knew were the elevators.

"There's better odds now," Henderson whispered.

Kaya nodded and led the way back to the control room, her pistol drawn and held out before her. Kaya looked back at Henderson. Although the tall Irishman was sweating profusely, he looked calm enough. Good. She needed calm. She didn't need a trigger-happy basket case accidentally shooting her in the back.

She nodded to him and then quietly opened the door to the control room. Inside, Rainbow's attention was firmly fixed on something on the security monitor to her left as Kaya slowly opened the control room door.

The little tech, a balding skinny Asian man in his mid-fifties, was sitting quietly in a chair against the far wall, no doubt clearly intimidated by the pistol Rainbow was casually pointing at him.

The tech looked up sharply as Kaya and Henderson slipped into the room. Kaya motioned for him to be quiet. The man nodded once, clearly cool under pressure.

And then he cleared his throat loudly.

Kaya stopped. Henderson nearly bumped into her. But the Hopi immediately saw what the tech was up to—distracting the hippie woman. Rainbow immediately glanced over at the tech, raising her weapon threateningly, and as she did Kaya moved fast.

In five quick strides she was at full speed and a half second later she hurdled herself at the sitting woman. Rainbow turned in her seat, swinging the gun around, but Kaya's shoulder hit the woman hard, driving her head into the console.

Rainbow slumped beneath her, spilling onto the polished floor, her dirty hair spreading out beneath her like an oil slick. The hippie was out cold.

Kaya looked at her only briefly before turning her attention to the security monitor on the controller's desk—the same monitor Rainbow had just been studying.

"Damn," she said.

On the screen, to her amazement, was Nash. He was hanging in the spillway cave reaching over something long and metallic. What he was doing, she didn't know, but it was obvious that Mayer—and no doubt some of his loonies—were on their way to deal with Nash.

Glen Canyon Dam
East Spillway

This is insane, thought Nash as he hung precariously from the spillway's metal handholds.

Sweat stung his eyes. The rusted metal was oddly slippery, which frustrated Nash to no end. Wouldn't the designers of the dam use something easier to hold onto? Below him was a straight drop into a black abyss.

No, not entirely black. There was someone below him, working from a metal cage, attaching canisters to the spillway. His light flashed every now and then, and Nash occasionally heard the squeak of wheels and a chain. It was a lift, of come sorts, a lift that dropped straight into the black depths.

For now, the man hadn't noticed him, and for every canister he attached, Nash intended to detach them. And what happened when the two finally met? Well, Nash could only hope he could take the man by surprise.

And what happened after that? Well, that was up to the gods of fate. That is, of course, thought Nash ruefully, *if there is such a thing as "gods" and "fate."*

Nash took a deep breath and then climbed down another rung. His breathing echoed around him. From somewhere far below he heard the sounds of a creaking metal cage. He reached another canister, steadied himself, unclipped it and clipped it to his belt. He continued down.

As he reached the next canister, Nash realized he was actually gaining on the man in below. Nash looked up. The spillway's opening was many dozens of feet above and just as Nash unhooked the canister, a flood of light washed over him from below.

Shit. Even though Nash was doing all he could to remain silent, the bastard still must have heard him.

"Hey!" shouted the man from below.

Momentarily blinded, Nash fumbled with the canister in his hand, then lost his grip on it altogether. It plummeted like a missile and, with a sharp metallic *clunk*, slammed into the basket below, just missing the Ecotopian. The light from the startled guy's helmet swung wildly.

And in the light, Nash watched as the man drew his pistol.

Crap!

Nash had just decided to pull the Glock from his belt when two bullets *thunked* deep into the wall next to him, pelting his eyes and face with shards of concrete.

Sweet Jesus!

As the creaking cage began to rise, Nash fumbled desperately for the Glock at his waist. But just as his right hand gripped its stock, another shot was fired from below. Searing, white-out pain exploded over the back of his left hand as the bullet left a deep, bloody furrow.

Nash yelped and involuntarily released the rung.

With his hand nearly useless, Nash found himself falling—and screaming.

Nash contorted his body just enough to brace himself for the impact that was to come.

And it came quickly.

The metal cage rushed up at him. Nash raised his hands, protecting his head and face, then slammed hard into the eco-terrorist. The force of the impact drove the man straight to the bottom of the basket, which swung wildly out into the gaping spillway. Nash, who had the benefit of landing directly on the man, had a brief glimpse of the terrorist's pistol flinging over the rail and into the abyss below.

As the mesh basket continued to rise, the two men fought like caged animals. Although the Ecotopian was much bigger, Nash soon got the upper hand, leveling blow after blow into the man's face and body.

That is, until the hulking bastard grabbed Nash around the waist. Before Nash knew what was happening, he found himself lifted off his feet and dangling over the edge of the basket, staring down into nothing.

Nash drove an elbow straight down into the man's face, crushing his nose. Blood splattered. Nash had hoped to get the man to let go.

He got his wish. The man let go, heaving Nash over the railing of the basket.

Glen Canyon Dam
East Spillway

Flying through the air, Nash frantically scrabbled for a handhold.

He found one, his desperate fingers ensnaring the meshing of the metal basket. The weight of his body continued down, slamming him hard against the bottom of the cage. Air burst from his mouth.

The cage, which continued to rise, swung wildly.

Nash was certain a finger had broken, twisted grotesquely as he hung there, and supporting his entire weight. With his already injured right hand, he reached up and took some of the weight off his left hand.

And as Nash looked up, grunting, he was dismayed to see the thug had found his footing—and Nash's Glock in the bottom of the basket. The man grinned and pointed the Glock at Nash's head.

Game over, he thought and prepared for the muzzle blast that would end his life.

Instead, he saw something else—a shadowy figure just above the cage on the spillway door landing, about twenty feet above them. The figure had his arm outstretched and seemed to be pointing at them. Nash realized the man was holding a gun.

Nash closed his eyes and felt his damaged fingers slipping.

A sharp *crack* echoed down the spillway. Something slammed into the cage, followed by a grunt. Nash opened his eyes just as the thug flipped over the cage railing and plummeted past him, down into the dark chasm of the spillway.

Holy shit!

A familiar voice from above rang out. "That's the second time I saved your ass today, buddy. Are you okay?"

It was Henderson. And as the basket continued to rise, Nash clambered up its side, ignoring the excruciating pain in both his hands. When he had flopped back into the rising basket, Nash examined his hands. Where the bullet had grazed his left hand, it was bleeding steadily. The finger in question to his right hand seemed to be only badly out of joint.

Gritting his teeth and crying out, he torqued his finger back into place. The intense pain almost had him retching. And as the basket drew closer to the surface, Nash lay at the bottom of the cage, gasping and bleeding.

When the basket was nearly parallel with the landing, Henderson reached out a hand and steadied the world's most dangerous elevator.

"You've seen better days, pal," said Henderson, grinning.

Nash was about to respond when Henderson suddenly withdrew his proffered hand and reached behind him. His face instantly went white. Henderson turned slowly around, pivoting, as if performing some bizarre dance. And as he turned his back to him, Nash saw the bone-handle knife protruding from the back of his friend's neck. Blood spilled over his shirt.

The tall Irishman stumbled and fell face first in front of Big Man, who stood looking down at Nash. The silent Hopi curled his upper lip—and leaped from the landing into the basket with Nash.

Not again, thought Nash, as the basket swung wildly out over the black depths.

Big Man, with an oddly empty look to his dark eyes, went straight for Nash's neck. And as Nash struggled, his hands nearly useless, the big Hopi managed to slip a forearm around Nash's throat.

Nash struggled against the Native American's powerful grip, but it was a losing battle. The man was coming into this fresh, and Nash was battered and bloodied.

As the skeptic began losing consciousness, as the lights dimmed around the edges of his vision, his dropping hands landed somewhere near his belt, where he had clipped a half dozen of the metal canisters of alkali silica.

Darkness encroached rapidly. Nash, nearly unconsciousness, managed to unclasp one of the canisters. With numb fingers that didn't seem to quite heed his command, Nash fumbled briefly with the end of metal tube, and was pleasantly surprised when he seemed to have opened it.

How he managed that, he didn't know, but he wasn't going to stop and ask questions. In one quick movement, Nash closed his eyes and flung the contents behind him where Big Man had a ridiculously strong choke hold on him.

The effect was miraculous.

Big Man screamed and released his hold. Nash, sucking wind, immediately scrambled across the cage, and hauled himself over the railing and onto the landing, where he dropped down next to his friend's bleeding body.

As the Hopi swiped at his eyes and stumbled across the cage, Nash pulled Henderson's body out of the doorway—no mean feat for someone with a severely dislocated finger—then slammed the door shut and bolted it behind him. Through the door, he heard the big Hopi bellowing in pain and rage.

Gasping, Nash caught his breath. How he had made it out of the deathtrap, he had no clue. But he was alive, which was more than he could say about his friend.

He had to find Kaya and leave the dead where they lay. He also needed weapons. Grimacing, Nash reached down and slowly pulled the bloodied knife from between his friend's shoulder blades. The meaty sucking sound it made would stay with him forever. Nash wiped the blade on his friend's shoulder, then tucked it, along with Henderson's Glock, in his belt.

With the sounds of screaming still coming from behind the locked spillway door, Nash dashed off, limping badly.

And as he reached the service elevator, two ear-splitting gunshots exploded behind him. Instinctively, Nash ducked and rolled as two bullet holes punched through the metal elevator door.

These guys never quit, he thought, and he kept on rolling until he had found cover.

Glen Canyon Dam
Control Room

Kaya and the control room tech watched the scene at the spillway play out over the security monitor. There had been no way to warn poor Bryan. Kaya had adverted her eyes when she watched William creep behind the tall Irishman with the bone-handled knife. When she looked again, Henderson lay sprawled on the concrete, bleeding profusely.

That didn't just happen, she thought, horror-stricken.

With bated breath and a very bad feeling, she had watched William leaped into the spillway tunnel. There was no movement for many minutes, and Kaya expected the worse. Nash was surely dead at the hands of her Hopi brother.

And then, miraculously, Nash had appeared in the doorway, dragging Henderson's body away, and slamming the door. He grabbed the knife and the gun and, clearly hurt, stumbled down the concrete hallway toward one of the cameras. A moment later, in another security screen, she watched as he desperately punched the elevator's up button.

Unfortunately, Nash was unaware that Hayden Mayer was roaming the catacombs. She saw the bastard just around the corner. She prayed the elevator would arrive before Mayer saw Nash. But too late, the self-proclaimed Pahana had turned the corner and spotted Nash.

He leveled his gun—and fired. Two shots.

Luckily, Mayer was a bad shot. Both missed Nash, who had now ducked and rolled and took cover.

Oh, sweet Mother, thought Kaya, clutching her heart. She was going to have a heart attack just watching all this play out on the security monitors.

Rainbow waited patiently for her chance.

The tech and the Hopi woman were heavily distracted with the events on the monitors. Rainbow watched them, too, and when she saw the beloved Pahana appear on one of the monitors, firing two shots at the hated enemy, she saw her chance.

When both the tech and the Hopi woman gasped, Rainbow lunged forward, pouncing on the weaker of the two—the tech, in this case. Rainbow, who had been heavily trained by the Pahana's warriors at their desert compound, easily disarmed the little Asian tech, driving her elbow hard into the man's face. And this she did within seconds.

When the Hopi woman turned, Rainbow was already using the tech as a buffer and holding his weapon before her.

"Drop your gun, bitch," she commanded.

Kaya did as she was told. Next, Rainbow commanded her to kick the weapon over, which Kaya did. After picking up the weapon, she dragged the little tech with her to the control desk. "Now we'll continue where we left off." She forced the tech to sit before her. When he did so, she said, "Good, now set up the controls to open the east spillway."

The little tech complied. He pushed some buttons and turned some dials. Almost immediately an alarm reverberated throughout the room.

"Good," Rainbow said. "Now sit down over there with the Hopi bitch and shut up."

The two sat a few moments against the wall under the status boards when the tech whispered to Kaya, "We have to do something. We can't let this happen."

And suddenly, without warning, the little tech stood up.

"What are you doing?" whispered Kaya.

The tech held up his finger, gathered himself, and then walked boldly across the room towards Rainbow.

"Hey!" Rainbow barked, snapping her head up. "What the fuck are you doing? Sit down!"

"You're forgetting one thing," said the little guy, still approaching Rainbow.

"I said sit the fuck down!" Rainbow ordered. She raised her pistol, tracking him from behind the status boards.

The little tech now slid in front of her, forcing Rainbow to inadvertently turn her back on Kaya. He crossed his arms confidently over his chest. "The water flow will not execute unless a sequence of commands are given."

Kaya realized what he was doing and quietly found her feet, moving silently.

"What commands?" ordered Rainbow. "What are you talking about?"

"I know those commands, and I'm not telling you."

She stepped forward. "You will tell me, little man, or I will shoot you."

"If you kill me, the codes die with me."

"I didn't say I would kill you."

She lowered the gun and shot him in the right thigh. The tech screamed and fell to the ground, grabbing his legs. Blood poured over his hands.

No doubt realizing, she had lost track of Kaya, Rainbow turned—

But was met immediately with a fist to her face. She reeled back and Kaya stepped forward, hoping to pounce on her before she could get another shot off, but too late. Firing wildly, the flailing Rainbow snapped off two more shots. The bullets went wide and, although they missed Kaya by a comfortable margin, they slammed into the status boards on the far wall.

Sparks immediately erupted from several electrical shorts.

Kaya pounced on Rainbow, swinging her fists like a cornered hellcat, but the brutish hippie was stronger than most men. Rainbow stood, screeching, and drove Kaya over the control desk. Kaya's breath burst from her lungs. But she knew how to fight, and she knew how to fight dirty. From that position, she shoved both her thumbs as deep as they would go into the eye sockets of the dirty bitch.

Rainbow roared with rage.

Amazingly, she picked Kaya up with one hand and drove her back toward the smoking and sparking status board. As the crazy bitch did so, she brought the pistol up and towards Kaya's face.

Kaya grabbed Rainbow's pistol hand by the wrist, using all her strength to keep the weapon away from her, even while spitting hot sparks scorched the back of her neck. Smoke filled her nostrils. Coughing, Kaya fought the devil woman as she was pushed further back toward the now burning wall.

Heat seared her neck. Smoke billowed everywhere.

As Kaya fought, she managed to get both her feet planted firmly below her, and instead of resisting Rainbow's momentum, Kaya pivoted and turned her hips away from the smoking status board, slamming Rainbow's back into it.

With sparks flying and fires smoldering behind her, the enraged hippie continued to fight, intent on leveling the barrel of the weapon at Kaya's face.

Alarms sounded everywhere. Smoke filled Kaya nostrils and eyes. She could smell something meaty burning, and realized it was the hippie's own flesh.

My God!

When the gun was nearly level with her face, Kaya did the only thing she could think of. She drove her knee hard into the woman stomach and, when the woman doubled over, slammed her hand into a glass gauge above. The gauge shattered, and when the metal pistol made contact with the exposed wiring, something horrific happened.

Kaya leaped back as the hippie shook and contorted. Smoke poured out of her mouth, and Kaya turned away, horrified, as the screaming woman was electrocuted to death in front of her.

Kaya turned her head and covered her mouth. The sound of crackling skin and popping fat continued for many minutes. A second later, she vomited hard. And when she was done with that, she averted her eyes and tended quickly to the technician. She found his light jacket on the back of a chair, wadded it up, and had him press it as hard as he could into the wound.

But she had more pressing matters. She knew that William was still in the spillway. She scanned the monitors before her, doing her best to ignore the horrific smell of charred human flesh, and spotted Big Man replacing the canisters removed by Nash.

The bastard is finishing the job—willing to kill untold thousands of people.

Kaya hated the man, the one responsible for her grandfather's beating to near death, and was ashamed to call him a brother Hopi.

Seething, she looked over the control panel and saw the release valve switch for the spillway still in the *ready* position.

William needed to be stopped.

At all costs.

If he succeeded in attaching enough canisters in the spillway cave, she would be unable to prevent Mayer and his goons from storming the control room and sealing the dam's fate.

And so she acted.

Perhaps more out of revenge then she realized and not logic. But that wasn't her concern right now.

The security monitor showed William methodically lowering himself down the spillway in the service basket, attaching more and more canisters as he went. He still had a few of them littered at the bottom of the basket. What he had attached now would surely cause damage to the dam, but would it cause the catastrophic damage Mayer had hoped for?

She didn't know, but the more canisters William attached,

the more that outcome was likely. She turned to the little tech. "What's the code sequence?"

"There is none," he replied. "It was just a ruse."

With little or no emotion on her stoic face, Kaya flicked the release valve switch.

Another alarm immediately went off.

The water-flow gauges on the status board in front of her spiked into the red as they recorded the surge of the water through the spillway—a surge of 104,000 cubic feet per second of water plunging through the forty-one-foot diameter spillway.

Over the din of the alarms, the control room started to vibrate, along with everything in it. The vibrations increased, the room began to shake, and the whole dam itself groaned like something ancient and alive.

Kaya sat back, the full scope of what she had done suddenly hitting her.

God! What have I done?"

Glen Canyon Dam
East Spillway

Big Man knew he had to hurry and finish attaching the remaining alkali canisters. He knew they were running out of time—and he was far from finished. Some kind of security team was sure to show up at the dam once the authorities were aware that dam security had been breached.

Sweating profusely as he worked quickly in the dank vertical shaft, Big Man was about to lower the service basket further when he felt the contraption shudder. His stomach jumped up to his throat. It was a long way down if this thing gave...

The shuddering basket was soon joined by a rumbling sound from above his head.

A rumbling? he thought. *Just what in the hell is Rainbow doing?*

He raised his flood light above his head—and screamed.

Barreling towards him was a deluge of water.

A moment later, the swelling deluge overwhelmed the big Hopi, blasting him and the service basket down the spillway tunnel in a maelstrom of water now laced with crimson ribbons.

Glen Canyon Dam
Subterranean Cathedrals

Nash had just emerged from around a corner when he was met by the Pahana.

Mayer was quicker, bringing his weapon up before Nash could react.

And that's when the whole dam shook violently, as if a massive locomotive was rushing down the concrete hall. Nash fell to his knees as Mayer was tossed back against the wall of the cathedral. And when the rumble subsided enough for Nash to regain his balance, he found his feet and dashed off through the labyrinthine guts of the dam.

The lights flickered and then dimmed. Something was going on with the dam, something big. Nash just didn't have any clue what. The rumbling was still there, but it was more of a controlled rumbling, vibrating up through his feet.

He had other things to worry about, though. Like a psychotic nut who thought he was literally the Second Coming.

As Nash worked his way through the poor lighting and the network of cathedrals tunnels, certain he was lost, but also certain he had finally ditched the creepy bastard, he came across a promising door. He pushed it open and found himself in what appeared to be a mammoth power room, fueled by eight massive generators.

Nash could hardly hear himself think over the roar of the generators around him, which seemed to vibrate the very teeth in his skull. And as Nash dashed along a metal catwalk, which rose high above the skull-rattling machines, he could not have been more surprised when, as he rounded a corner, he found Mayer waiting for him. How that S.O.B. beat him here, Nash had no clue.

"Drop your weapon," ordered the Pahana.

Nash did as he was told.

"No one interferes with the Pahana's destiny," hissed Mayer, looking thoroughly insane.

Insane enough to shoot, thought Nash. Weaponless, his only thought was to launch himself with Big Man's knife, which was tucked in his belt.

I'll be dead before I'm halfway to him, he thought. *But better than being a sitting duck.*

"Destiny is a fickle mistress," Nash quipped, just to be saying something—anything—to distract this asshole enough from pulling the trigger. "I was destined to be a rock star and look where I'm at now."

Mayer grinned and leveled his weapon at him.

He's going to shoot. Nash was reaching for Big Man's knife when bullets suddenly peppered the metal catwalk around them. He looked down to see Kaya firing from below. Mayer returned fire, ignoring Nash for the moment, who watched as the stupid son-of-a-bitch launched several rounds into one of the generators.

Oil burst from the machine, spraying across the hot turbine. Within seconds, the generator and turbine caught fire. Noxious smoke and fumes quickly permeating the power room. So much so that Nash was able to retreat back across the catwalk and down the metal stairs to the generator floor below.

Now the smoking turbine began vibrating wildly.

What Nash didn't know was that the burning generator's vibration had increased four times more than the other turbines due to the rushing water flowing through the spillway. The rushing water, which moved quickly through the now-damaged turbine, pushed powerfully against the turbine's blades. The blades, which rotated like a pinwheel, were connected by a large vertical shaft to the rotating assembly of the generator. A generator that now was vibrating out of control.

And as the mammoth machine's vibration increased, it forced the rotor inside the turbine up, which put an astronomical amount of pressure on the turbine cover, a cover which was kept in place by eighty massive bolts. The heavy cover shook, straining against the pressure. Seconds later the turbine cover blew off in a thunderous explosion, hurling the nine-hundred-ton rotor straight up into the air. Unfortunately for Hayden Mayer, he was standing on the walkway directly above the turbine. Mayer and the turbine cover where hurled into the air and smashed against the concrete and steel ceiling.

The explosion was thunderous. Nash, who had just reached Kaya, was blown backward.

They slammed into something hard and lay there briefly stunned as the entire dam seemed to collapse around them. At that moment, the lights went out, plunging the generator room into total darkness. As chunks of ceiling rained down around them, Nash grabbed Kaya's hand and pulled her towards what he remembered to be the exit door.

His memory was mercifully correct.

He pushed them through the door—and they found themselves along the far edge of an 86,000 square-foot grassy area that lay at the base of the dam.

Glen Canyon Dam
Dam Base

Once outside, Nash filled his tortured lungs with fresh air, alternately drying his eyes with his sleeves. Thankfully it was windy and still raining hard, which helped clear the smoke and fumes from their nose and eyes.

Nash took in the surreal surroundings. Water roared from the spillway beneath them, and a heavy windy rain began to come down, increasing in intensity.

"My God," Kaya said looking back at the generator room. "Mayer..."

Nash didn't give a shit about Mayer. Instead, he looked up apprehensively at the dam above them. All the lights had gone out, even the security lights. Everything was nearly pitch black. The dam had stopped vibrating, but water was still gushing out of the east spillway nearby.

"I think when that turbine blew," Nash yelled above the din, "it released the pressure on the dam. At least, I hope so."

"But the water is still pouring out," Kaya said over the roar of the water rushing out of the four eight-foot-wide outlet tubes just below them. "It can still undermine the dam."

"Yeah. But we..." Nash's comment was cut short when they were both lit up by a spotlight from above. Almost immediately the spotlight was accompanied with automatic gunfire.

Nash grabbed Kaya and they both ducked down in front of the steel powerhouse door for protection.

"Who the hell is attacking us?" yelled Kaya.

Nash caught movement above them and pointed. Amazingly, coming directly at them from above, was an ultralight, obviously flown by one of the last Ecotopians. The spotlight on its nose jerked wildly as the pilot was clearly having a difficult time steadying the craft in the wind, rain, and updrafts.

"You stay here," Nash yelled.

"Where are you going?!" she cried.

Nash gave Kaya's a quick squeeze. "Stay near the door. It will give some protection. And don't look so concerned. Sometimes I actually know what I'm doing."

He dropped her hand and ran as fast as he could towards the base of the dam. The ultralight's erratic spotlight came around again and trained on the sprinting Nash. Nash put his head down and, praying he didn't snap an ankle or get shot in the back, led the ultralight closer to the bottom of the dam.

And the closer they got to the base of the dam, the more erratic the ultralight became. Its spotlight swung wildly.

Like a running back on crack, Nash zigzagged left to right to left as he ran, doing his best to not give the bastard a clear shot. And just like that the shooting stop. The pilot must have realized his dire situation, and buffeted by growing winds, he pulled on the controls and turned away, back up the dam to gain altitude and stabilize the ultralight.

But it wasn't meant to be.

Immediately, the ultralight was caught in what must have been a powerful downdraft. It paused in mid-air, and then its nose dipped down. Nash watched with grim satisfaction as the out-of-control craft dropped like a rock straight into the grass.

Nash carefully approached the wreck and peered into the cockpit.

The pilot was obviously dead. His body was sprawled over the front of the cockpit, his neck clearly broken—and probably every other bone in his body. It had been a hell of a fall.

And I caused it, thought Nash grimly, and then added. *Well, it was either me or him.*

Nash felt a hand on his shoulder and jumped. It was Kaya.

"Sweet Jesus, you scared the shit out of me." But Nash's voice was mostly lost to the sounds of water roaring below. Nash noticed Kaya kept her eyes adverted from the body in the cockpit. He didn't blame her.

"Sorry," she said, shouting above the din. "So now what do we do?"

Nash thought about it, then said, "We should—"

But at that moment the roaring water from the spillway started to quiet down, and quickly. Within moments, there was an eerie silence in the mostly empty river basin.

"Someone turned off the water," Kaya said.

"That means the calvary has arrived." Nash suddenly frowned.

"What's the matter," Kaya asked.

"We're not in the position—nor do we have the time—to answer a lot of questions."

"You mean just leave?"

Nash walked around the broken ultralight and gave it a quick inspection. "Only the gondola and engine are unusable. The actual sail is still in good shape."

"What are you getting at?" Kaya asked suspiciously.

Nash didn't answer. He detached the sail from the gondola then withdrew Big Man's knife. He cut the webbing of the pilot seat into strips after unceremoniously dumping the pilot out of the gondola. He proceeded to make a makeshift cradle and attached it to the useable sail.

Nash positioned himself under the sail, and said, "Climb on my back."

"I was afraid you were going to say that. There ain't no way in hell—"

"Look, it's the only way to get out of here and avoid a lot of questions from the authorities." He motioned at the growing activity above them, which was now swarming with people and flashing lights.

Kaya obviously didn't like it. In fact, it was clear she hated it. But she nodded and, whimpering, climbed on his back and closed her eyes. "Go," she squeaked.

Nash walked over to the edge of the grass area below the dam and jumped. Kaya screamed, nearly choking him.

They immediately dropped like a rock.

Nash fought the makeshift glider and stabilized it, and a few seconds later, with Kaya burying her head between his shoulders, they were gliding down the Colorado River.

Project KRATOS

"It could get out control, sir."

Those were not the words the Chairman of The Committee wanted to hear. He drummed on his fingers on the desk before him. "That's unfortunate."

"Orders?"

"We may have to cut our losses." The Chairman paused a moment. "If deemed necessary, follow your back-up plan."

"Plan B?" There was a chuckle in the Chairman's phone.

He smiled. "Yes. If you want to call it that. You have your orders. Understood?"

"Affirmative" came the reply.

The news of the attack on the dam and Mayer's death reached Prescott just before his evening conference with Laveen and his techs. Mayer's death was damn good news and one less threat to the Project—despite Laveen's constant worrying about the effects of KRATOS.

Prescott smiled inwardly. Now they could get on with harnessing the energy of the universe—and fulfill Prescott's responsibility to The Committee.

En route to Flagstaff, Arizona

After a nerve-racking landing, Nash and Kaya ditched the make-shift ultralight glider several miles down river. And as dawn broke, Nash saw they had landed just outside the city of Page.

At a small cafe, with each covered in road dust and looking like hell, Nash got information on a shuttle that was to leave soon. While scarfing down a massive breakfast, Nash listened to the locals go on and on about the crazy events at the Glen Canyon Dam. Dozens of people had been killed. The military had been called in.

Nash caught Kaya's eye. They had to get the hell out of there.

They had finished their last refill of coffee and boarded the shuttle bus to Flagstaff. It pulled away shortly, and Nash couldn't have been more relieved. He also couldn't have been more tired. He closed his eyes and slipped instantly into sleep.

Nash awoke to find a melancholy and pensive Kaya staring out the side window.

"Something bothering you?" he asked, yawning. Amazingly, he was already hungry. *Saving lives*, he noted, *burns some serious calories.*

She looked at him. "I've never killed anyone before."

So far, they hadn't talked much about what had happened back at the dam. "Tell me about it," he said.

And she did. She went on to tell Nash about Rainbow and her decision in the control room.

Nash nodded. "So you were the one who released the water?"

"Yes, but I don't know if I did it out of revenge for William or—"

"Look, Kaya. You did what you had to do to save lives. Big Man placed himself in harm's way. Trust me. He would have killed hundreds of thousands of people for his insane belief. He was a bastard. I think you made the right choice."

Kaya only half-nodded in agreement.

Nash reached over and gave her a gentle hug. "You did the right thing. You're not a murderer. You're a hero."

She placed her hands on Nash's and squeezed. "But I'll have to live with that decision the rest of my life."

There was little Nash could say—so he didn't. He put his arm around her, and she rested her head on his shoulder, and they sat like that all the way to Flagstaff.

Nash and Kaya arrived at Northern Arizona University in the late afternoon and made their way to the Physics building, as instructed. They approached a young grad student who sat at a desk in the department's main office.

The student, who had long auburn hair in braids and wore a Native-American headband around her forehead, looked up when they approached. As expected, her eyes widened with astonishment. Nash knew that he and Kaya were a sight to see, both dirty and bedraggled. The student's eyes went straight to Nash's wounded hand, which he had wrapped in a paper towel.

"Shaving accident," he said, holding up his hand and giving her a lopsided grin. "We're supposed to meet Peter Somerton."

She looked at him skeptically. "Your name?"

"Jeremy Nash."

She frowned again, then said, "Yes, they're waiting for you in the nuclear physics lab. Go out this door and turn right. You'll see it on your left down the long hallway."

A few minutes later, they entered the immaculate lab and saw Somerton and another man sitting around several pieces of sophisticated monitoring equipment. The other man was small, bespectacled, and nervous looking.

When Somerton saw them, he said, "Jesus, where were you two? And why do you guys look like crap?"

"Gee, thanks," said Kaya.

Nash ran his fingers through his hair. "You don't want to know."

Somerton frowned and turned to the man next to him. "Let me introduce you to George Holbrook, Ph.D., head of the nuclear physics lab here. George is going to help us."

Everyone shook hands all around. Once done, Somerton crossed his arms over his chest and raised an eyebrow. "Now tell me what happened to the two of you."

Over the next five minutes, Nash and Kaya told the two men all that had happened.

"Fascinating," was all Somerton could say scratching his chin.

"You keep interesting friends, Dr. Somerton," said Holbrook trying to be pleasant.

Somerton got right to the point. "You found the missing piece?"

"Yes," said Nash. "Except we can't make heads or tails of the inscriptions." He took the fragment out of his pocket and presented it to Somerton, who took it carefully. "Granted, we've either been running for our lives, saving the Arizona flood basin, or too exhausted to put much thought into it."

"Don't sound so dramatic, old boy," said Somerton, grinning. He ran his fingers over the smooth stone reverently. "We'll figure this thing out one way or another. Speaking of which, I researched those micro-dots on the drive out here from Sedona—yes, I can drive and use my iPhone at the same time—and might have come up with something."

Nash sat on a stool at the corner of one the pristine lab tables. Admittedly, he wanted to lay his head on his arms and sleep forever, but he forced himself to focus on the professor's words. After all, his parents' killers were still out there somewhere. And Nash knew in his heart he was close.

Finally, some real answers.

"Go on, professor," he said.

"Well, several years ago, researchers from the Canadian National Research Council devised a way to use quantum dots—what they called tiny bits of semiconductor—to print invisible text onto surfaces, like documents. One of the council staff just so happened to be Northern Arizona University's very own Dr. Holbrook, who will take over from here."

The twitchy-looking man put on an air of professorship, and said, "The quantum dots the researchers used measured between three and six nanometers in diameter. The invisible text is kept secret because the intensity levels change depending on the color of the light source. For example, three single-color quantum dots can emit fluorescence corresponding to the code of two-seven-three when hit with four hundred and seventy nanometer light waves, but the code changes to three-five-three when hit with four hundred and fifty nanometer light waves, and six-nine-five when hit with three hundred and sixty nanometer light waves."

"The numbers two, seven, three and four hundred and seventy are on the invoice," Nash noted.

"Correct," said Somerton. "And thus, the correct code can be read only by those who know the key, which is the correct wavelength of light for each set of the three quantum dots contained in the micro-dots."

"And that correct wavelength is four hundred and seventy?" Kaya asked. "The number on the invoice?"

"Indeed it is," said Somerton proudly. "Four hundred and seventy nanometers or one billionth of a meter."

"So let's run the numbers," said Nash.

"Way ahead of you, old boy," said Somerton. "When I arrived here at the lab yesterday, I asked George to run the dots through his equipment." Somerton picked up a file sitting on the table next to him. He handed the file to Nash. "And here's what we found."

Nash opened it, with Kaya peering over his shoulder. The top sheet of paper was filled with techno-jargon and descriptions of a scientific project called KRATOS.

"I don't understand," said Nash. "My parents were not capable of this micro-dot technology—even if my mother was a physicist. Someone with even more sophisticated knowledge had to create this."

"You are correct, Mr. Nash," said a voice behind them.

Nash turned, and saw a robed man enter the room with a pretty young lady.

"Who are you?" asked Somerton.

And right on the heels of Somerton's question, Nash cried, "You!" He pointed at the robed man. Nash wasn't sure if anything could have surprised at this point, but seeing this prophetic specter sure as hell did. He jumped off the stool.

"You know this man?" asked Somerton.

"He's the man who's been stalking us since Roswell." Nash answered then turned his attention to the robed man. "How did you find me?"

To his surprise, the pretty woman answered. "I met your sister at the airport, Jeremy. She told us you would be here."

"Wait. What?" Nash's head was spinning. "Who are you?"

"I'm Agent Chandler with the FBI." She held up a shiny badge, which Nash inspected closely.

"How do you know my sister?"

"We were sorority sisters at college." Her face took on a somber tone. "Jeremy, I have some disturbing news for you."

Nash didn't know what to expect after the night he'd just had. "What news?"

Chandler described the encounter at the car rental place, Safford's attempt to run her down, and the subsequent accident. She saved the worst for last.

"Your sister is missing, Jeremy."

"Missing?"

"Yes."

"Missing how, exactly?"

"She was last seen with Stafford."

"Sweet Jesus." Nash ran his fingers through his hair and paced the small area before the lab tables. "This man who took my sister and ran you down, who is he?"

"He was my partner, although I had only recently been

assigned to him," Chandler replied. "We thought he was with the FBI. But he wasn't."

"You *thought* he was with the FBI?"

"We were conned."

"Then who the hell is he?"

The robed man broke in. "His name is Zack Safford. He was a mole working for the Project."

Nash's head was spinning. "The Project?"

"Yes, Project KRATOS. And that man who's been trying to kill you? His name is Addison Parker, leader of a Gladio team. They're hired assassins for KRATOS."

"But what's this all about? And how did you know my parents?"

"Through a Hopi shaman—David Alo."

"My grandfather!" Kaya gasped.

Nash stepped over to the older man. "I have no clue what's going on, but you seem to have a lot of answers. I suggest you start talking from the beginning."

With everyone now sitting around one of the lab tables, the robed man introduced himself as Jackson Wilcox, the uncle, amazingly, of the beautiful FBI agent.

Weirder and weirder, thought Nash. He fought his impatience. His sister was God knows where, but he suspected this man Wilcox —this eccentric weirdo—had the clues he needed to find his sister. For now, he reigned in his impatience, willing to hear the man out.

"I was involved in the initial planning of a scientific experiment called Project KRATOS," Wilcox was saying. "Which is the Greek word for *strength* or *power*."

So much for Nash's patience. "Look, we don't need a history lesson. I need to find my sister. Please, just get to the point."

Wilcox nodded. "Of course, son. But I do need to lay out a few things for you to understand what you're up against."

Nash felt as if he could crawl out of his skin. "Fine. Just hurry."

Wilcox nodded again. "KRATOS's purpose, I was told initially, was to compete with the Large Hadron Collider project initiated by the European Laboratory for Particle Physics based outside Geneva."

"CERN," Somerton noted.

"Correct."

"Why create another accelerator project?" asked Kaya. "What a waste of money."

"I can answer that," Holbrook said. "Science may be objective, but it's very competitive."

"Right," Wilcox replied. "We couldn't let the Europeans beat us to the Holy Grail of science, so to speak."

"In this case, finding the Higgs Boson," Holbrook remarked.

Nash was admittedly intrigued. "What's the Higgs Boson?"

"The Higgs Boson," Holbrook replied, "is the missing piece in the Standard Model of particle physics. If we could find the Higgs Boson, it would solidify the Standard Model. However, if the Higgs Boson cannot be found, or if something completely different is found, it could undermine the Standard Model and cause scientists to go back to the drawing board. Discovering the Higgs Boson will help scientists understand the fundamental laws of nature and describe the workings of the universe."

"It's sometimes refereed to as the *God Particle*," Wilcox added.

"The Seed of the Universe," Somerton noted.

"Correct," answered Wilcox. "And it wasn't until later, after I had been working for the Project for some time, that I discovered two troubling facts. First, the Project was being funded by a shadowy organization trying to bring about a New World Order."

Nash moaned. "Oh, sweet Jesus. Not another conspiracy theory."

"Not a theory, Mr. Nash," Wilcox replied pleasantly. "A fact. Enough of a fact that the Project is ripping the earth apart as we speak."

"Who is this shadow group?" asked Somerton.

"It's known only as The Committee. I don't have names, only that it involves people in high levels of society, the wealthy elite, international bankers, political leaders, and secret societies. In general, it involves a long-term master plan to create a one-world system. A global system with one ruling overseer."

"Why would they be involved in a scientific experiment like the Project?" asked Somerton.

"To control the energy source of the planet."

"Oil?" Kaya asked.

"No. The most powerful and non-expendable power in the universe—black holes."

"They're making black holes?" Kaya asked in astonishment.

"Yes. About one per second if they are successful—and using them to create an endless supply of energy."

"But how?" asked Kaya.

"According to Steven Hawking," Wilcox replied, "all black holes radiate thermal radiation proportional to their surface area and volume because of quantum tunneling. You see, black holes not only take but give. A very tiny black hole will radiate more energy than it sucks in. When it evaporates, it emits a furious burst of Hawking radiation. The smaller the hole the higher the temperature. In brief, a black hole can store a huge amount of energy in its rotation."

Nash knew his mouth was hanging open. This was a new theory, even for him.

Wilcox sat back and crossed his arms over his narrow chest. "And like an electric dynamo, a black hole spins and pumps energy out through cable-like magnetic field lines into the chaotic gas whipping around it, making the gas—already infernally hot from the sheer force of crushing gravity—even hotter."

"How do they contain these black holes?" asked Kaya. "Wouldn't they just fall through the earth, sucking us with them?"

Holbrook answered. "In theory you can contain them in an electromagnetic field. *In theory*."

"Correct," said Wilcox. "And that's what they were going to do. If the Project could continuously create micro-black holes, and contain them, they would be in control of an endless supply of energy and create a never-ending power source that they—and they alone—would control. The Committee knows, as we all do, that control of a vital energy source would give whoever has it leverage over the nations of the world."

"Like the OPEC cartel does now," Nash said.

"Right. But in this case, the results of Project KRATOS would give The Committee a monopoly on energy and thus a monopoly on political power."

"But something went amiss," Nash said.

"Yes. As you can see, their theories were wrong." Wilcox paused and looked them each in the eye. "And mine were correct." He next riffled through a briefcase he had set at his feet, pulling out a stack of newspapers. Nash noticed the headlines all spoke of the climatic and geological disasters that raged across the world. "I believe they're bleeding black holes."

"What does that mean?" asked Somerton.

"It means that not all are being contained," Wilcox replied.

"And these are the reasons for all these natural and geological disasters?" Nash almost snapped his fingers. It all made sense to his skeptic's mind. Much more sense than some ridiculous End Times prophecy.

"Yes," said Wilcox. "And such bleeding black holes would evaporate inside the earth."

Kaya jumped in. "But if they're *inside* the earth, how could they be causing chaos on the *outside*?"

"Unfortunately, if enough of them are not contained, they could negatively affect the electromagnetic field of the earth," answered Wilcox.

"Causing a pole shift?" asked Nash.

"Yes, it's possible."

"That explains a lot," said Somerton. He leveled his stare at Wilcox. "And you warned them of this?"

"Of course. I didn't seek to destroy our planet. Of course I warned them that this could happen. I told the Project leader Reuben Prescott the risk was too great. But he refused to listen. When I threatened to expose the plans of the Project, he tried to have me killed. I've been in hiding ever since."

"And my parents?" Nash asked Wilcox. "How are they con-nected with this—and you?"

"The Project is killing anyone who gets anywhere close to the truth, intentionally or by accident. Your parents got too close—inadvertently. I'm sorry."

"But how?" asked Nash. "How did they get close to...*this?*" He pointed to the printouts of the micro-dots.

"Your parents were about to release a socio-scientific paper that could pinpoint where the Hopi place of emergence was—the *sipapu*—and explain some of strange psychic incidents that have happened in the Northern Arizona region over the last twenty-odd years."

Somerton started nodding. He touched Nash's forearm. "Remember the partial abstract of the paper I spoke to you about? Your parents' paper."

Nash nodded absently and thought back to what Douglas had said at the conference mixer and the Blue Star Kachina dancers—and of their horrible deaths right before his young eyes.

Jesus, could there be something to this psychic bullshit?

Wilcox went on, "Your parents theorized that the *sipapu* and the source of these psychic incidents were somewhere in the vast cave network near the Grand Canyon."

"Cave network?" asked Nash.

"Hidden within the Grand Canyon are an estimated one thousand caves. Of those, three hundred and thirty-five have been recorded. Very few have been mapped or inventoried. Many of the caves are closed to visitation except for research purposes. My understanding, before I was hounded out of the Project, was that the Committee was going to build the accelerator somewhere underground in that vast cave network."

"How on earth can they get away with building this thing without drawing attention to themselves?" asked Nash.

"I don't know," Wilcox replied. "But I do know they were looking at private land in the area."

"But what about power?" Kaya added. "For something like the Project, they would need an immense and steady source of power. They just couldn't run a line, let's say, from the Four Corners Area without going unnoticed."

"Correct," Wilcox replied. "There was talk of using a nuclear reactor."

If his sister was alive, Nash had a very strong feeling they would find her at Project KRATOS. He said as much to the group.

Wilcox nodded gravely. "Quite possibly. Unfortunately, I don't know where the Project is housed, my friend. Your father worked with Kaya's grandfather to identify certain spots in the Canyon area where the *sipapu* might be. By means of an informant, the Project became aware of your parents' paper and decided to suppress it, obviously fearing the paper would accidentally expose the Project. But I was able to get my hands on a copy of the paper before it disappeared. And that's when I contacted your parents and warned them not to continue with their research."

Nash nodded. "My father would have never listened. He was a stubborn man."

"Unfortunately, you're correct. He didn't listen, true, but he did proceed with more caution. It was your father, after all, who came up with the notion to hide what they had found in the invoice and CD. I added the micro-dots, and we gave the invoice to Kaya's grandfather. When Prescott's thugs came to find out what Kaya's grandfather knew, he stayed mum, and a Mexican by the name of Garcia, an ugly brute with a scar running down from his right eyebrow to his cheek, with two henchmen beat him near to death. But Alo wouldn't say a word about the invoice."

"Garcia," Kaya hissed. "Bryan's assistant."

Nash could guess that Kaya had another score to settle. "What else do you know of my parent's death?" he asked.

"Last I heard they returned to the Canyon to get definitive proof for their paper, and I assume that's when they were killed. I never heard from them again, and that's when I fell off the grid and disappeared. But I knew the invoice would surface someday. That's why, when I heard of David Alo's death, I kept tabs on you, Mr. Nash." He paused a moment to reflect. "I believe your parents found the location of KRATOS and were killed before they could expose it. That's why I needed to find you and see if you were privy to your parents' clues." The man's eyes were almost pleading. "Tell me, Jeremy and Kaya. Did you two find the location of the *sipapu*... and thus Project KRATOS?"

Nash looked at Kaya. Together, they shook their head.

"No," said Nash. "We didn't."

Northern Arizona University
Flagstaff, Arizona

"I told you what I know," said Wilcox to Nash and Kaya. "So how about you tell me what you know?"

Nash and Kaya exchanged another look. Kaya nodded, and Nash decided to go ahead and trust this crazy-looking whack-job. After all, Alyson was missing, and Nash would have turned to anyone for help at this point.

Together Nash and Kaya explained what they knew about the clues, finishing with Nash saying, "Unfortunately, what we know doesn't point to a specific location, although we do have two clues left unsolved. The phrase, *Battleship belong to abandoned bunker in district*, and of course, the missing piece to the Hopi Stone that the codes on the invoice directed us to. Other than that, we're stuck."

Somerton had been studying the broken piece of the Hopi Stone while the group talked. "You know," he said, cutting in. "I think I might know what the symbols on this piece means. But to be sure I would need the main piece of the Stone—"

Kaya punched Nash on the shoulder. "Give him the rest of the stone, silly."

"Oops, right." He felt his face flush. "We recovered this from the Ecotopians."

He retrieved the bigger piece of stone and held it out to Somerton, who received it as carefully as if he were taking a newborn from Nash. Somerton held both pieces in his hand, awe in his bright eyes. "Fascinating," he whispered reverently.

"What do you see?" asked Nash impatiently.

"Yes, right. Look here."

On the table before him, Somerton carefully arranged the two pieces, now forming a perfectly intact stone. "On one side of the missing piece is an image of a man with a tail—kind of looks like a tadpole. Do you see that there? Good. Now, the little *y* on the main Hopi Stone matches the fingers of the man's right hand on this broken piece."

He pointed this out and then turned both stones over. On the reverse side of the missing piece were four wavy lines and a *V* above an oblong symbol around a man's reflection in water. "Do you see how the symbols now fit together?"

"Sure," said Nash impatiently. "But what the devil does it mean?"

"These are indictable of the Water Clan," said Somerton calmly—perhaps a little too calmly for Nash. "The tadpole here—or what some call *the lizard man*—is the Water Clan symbolism of the Anasazi tribe, the pre-Hopi of Arizona. And the wavy lines represent the four waves of migration around the world."

"The four races of people," said Nash.

"What's this Water Clan?" asked Wilcox. "And what does it have to do with the possible location of the Project?"

Exactly, thought Nash. *We need some answers. Enough with the archeology lesson.*

"Nash's parents were looking for the *sipapu*," Somerton said in his maddeningly calm delivery. "The story of the *sipapu* and the Hopi's emergence into the Fourth World does, in fact, point to the Grand Canyon. The *sipapu* and the Project's location could very well be one and the same."

"And if I remember my childhood stories," said Kaya. "The Sun Spirit destroyed the Third World in a great flood. Before the destruction, Spider Grandmother, leader of those who were the most obedient, placed the righteous into hollow reeds which were used as boats. When the people arrived on dry land, they saw nothing around them but more water. The Spider Woman then told the people to make more boats out of more reeds. Once done, they sailed east until they eventually arrived on the mountainous coasts of the Fourth World."

Somerton nodded eagerly. "Indeed, the stone here clearly symbolizes the Hopi tale of a water voyage from the West to the East. Now, in Kaya's childhood story, the Colorado River could represent the western ocean while the cliffs along the canyon could represent the Fourth World's rocky coasts."

"Fine," said Nash. "But how does any of this help me find my sister?"

"Maybe the second phrase on the invoice—the one you mentioned about battleships—can tell us," said Chandler, who had been listening with interest.

Nash recited the line: "Battleship belong to abandoned bunker in district." He shook his head. "I'm lost."

"Unfortunately, there are no battleships in the Grand Canyon," said Somerton. "Abandoned or otherwise."

"Not true," said Kaya, jumping out of her stool.

"What do you mean?" asked Somerton. "Wait! Of course, Battleship Rock!"

Kaya nodded. "It's in the center of the Canyon, a massive rock formation viewed from the South Rim." She grabbed Nash's arm and looked like she was about to kiss him but refrained. Nash, admittedly, could have used a kiss right about now. "Jeremy! I know what this clue means!"

"What?"

"Across from Battleship Rock is an old, abandoned uranium mine. The old Orphan Mine. The *abandoned bunker*. Get it?"

Nash felt his heart slam in his chest. Excitement and hope swept over him.

"Grandfather would speak of it often as an example of the white man raping the earth."

"And it would also explain where they would get the power to run the accelerator," Wilcox said. "If uranium is in that mine, it could be refined and used to run a nuclear power plant."

"Then it all fits," said Somerton. "The entrance to the Project and the *sipapu* is the abandoned mine. We can fly to the east rim and enter the canyon from there."

"Excuse me," interrupted Holbrook. "But if all this is correct—hell, if even a fraction is correct—don't you think we should contact the authorities?"

"And tell them what?" asked Somerton. "That there is a vast conspiracy to control the world and they're located deep in a mine in the Grand Canyon?"

Holbrook looked glum. It sounded crazy, and this was exactly the sort of conspiracy bullshit Nash would generally take great pleasure blowing out of the water. But now, with his sister missing, he was willing to try anything—and look anywhere.

"Then what's the plan?" asked Kaya.

Wilcox answered. "We need to stop the accelerator. If we can do that the formation of the black holes would cease and the climatic and geologic threats to the earth could be reversed. Unless—"

"Unless what?" asked Nash.

"Well, it's a one in a million possibility, but—"

Wilcox never got to finish his thought. At that moment, the entire building began to shake violently. Stools rattled, and the floor undulated, and Nash instantly grabbed Kaya and shoved her under one of the wide metal lab tables. Nash grabbed the befuddled Somerton and shoved the man under as well. Chandler had grabbed her uncle and followed suit on the other side of the table, and only when Holbrook was safely under did Nash dive in after.

The rumbling seemed to last an entire minute. Nash had been through earthquakes. But this was no earthquake. And when the shaking gave way to a mild undulation, Nash shot Kaya a confused look. Her face looked equally confused.

"What the hell was *that?*" asked Nash.

The FBI agent was already out and moving to the window. Nothing in the office had broken. The earthquake, if that's what it was, was more bark than bite, Nash realized.

293

"Have a look!" said Chandler excitedly at the window, pointing up.

Nash did so followed by Kaya. He wasn't fully prepared for what he saw framed in the massive window. The sky beyond had turned almost black with smoke. Nash followed the source and as he did so his lower jaw dropped.

Sweet Jesus.

The nearly 10,600-foot Mt. Humphrey, once an extinct volcano, was belching dark gray ash.

"My God!" cried Somerton from behind him. "Shit, that's the Snow Bowl. I go skiing there!"

"Is it erupting?" asked Kaya.

"No," said Nash. "We would have heard an explosion. Or felt it. The entire top of that mountain would be gone, as well."

In that moment, a nearby *wail* filled the air, screeching loudly.

"Emergency siren," shouted Chandler.

It sounded more like an air raid siren to Nash. Holbrook dashed to his desk and turned on an old radio. He played with the dial while Nash continued to watch the black columns of ash pour out from the volcano.

Holbrook settled on a dial and what came issuing out had them all moving at once. Northern Arizona cities and towns, including the Grand Canyon area, were being ordered to evacuate immediately.

Wilcox turned to Nash. "We are running out of time. If KRATOS continues to make mini-black holes—"

"Right," said Somerton. "We gotta go. We'll take my SUV."

"But how will we get downriver?" asked Wilcox.

"I have some friends who have boats on the Navajo reservation at the Little Colorado River," answered the eccentric professor. "I run the river with them into the Canyon now and then."

"Hold it!" Holbrook shouted. "What about the authorities?"

"You're welcome to stay here and convince them," Somerton replied. He looked at Nash and Chandler. "Now what about weapons? This is not going to a be tea party when we get there. How many do we have?"

"I have a forty caliber Smith and Wesson," Chandler replied, "and my uncle has a nine-millimeter Beretta with him."

"Good. I have an Army issue forty-five in my SUV," said Somerton. He looked over at Nash and Kaya who raised their empty hands.

"Wilcox, give your weapon to them," Somerton ordered.

Wilcox nodded and handed his pistol to Nash.

"I think Kaya should have it," said Nash. "She's the expert marksman here. Besides, I've had my fill of gunplay over the last few days to suit me."

"Whatever," said Somerton, who grinned, and actually seemed to be enjoying all of this. "Then we're all set. Let's go!"

Northern Arizona University

The group hurried down the hall only to see a tall buff figure round the far corner. Wilcox turned white as a sheet. "That's Parker," he said under his breath.

Just as the words left his mouth, Parker saw them, pulled a gun, and ran towards them.

"How they hell did he find us?" Nash said.

"Damn," Chandler cried. "Your sister told us at the airport that she was going to meet you at NAU. Safford knew that, and if he worked for the Project—"

Chandler was cut off by a bullet hitting the drywall behind her.

"Come," ordered Somerton. "This way." He quickly led them back towards the lab, locked the door behind them, and ran towards the back entrance past Holbrook who had a look of satisfaction on his face upon seeing them.

"Good," he said. "You agree with me about the authorities. I can...*Hey*! Where are you going?"

"Get the hell out of here!" Somerton shouted as he closed the exit door behind them.

Holbrook just stood there agape until he heard something loud smash against the lab door.

The group reached the parking lot and Somerton's SUV. It was a brute riding on very large off-road tires.

To Nash, it looked like a small house. "This is a SUV?"

"Yeah. Had it modified. It can take just about anything Mother Nature can throw at it."

Like a surreal blizzard, plumes of dark smoke and light-colored ash filled the air. Covering their mouths, the group dashed into Somerton's massive Hummer. Once inside, they each sucked in lungfuls of air. Somerton fired up the SUV, and within moments they were blasting out of the parking lot.

Somerton turned north when Nash said, "No. Go south. Go to the airport. I have my plane there. It's faster to the Canyon and we could avoid any traffic coming our way north of Flagg."

"Got it," Somerton replied. With windows up and the A/C running, they hit the streets—along with seemingly everyone else. Cars were everywhere. A cacophony of angry honks continuously pierced the air. With the swirling smoke, ash, and insane traffic, this was exactly how Nash pictured the end of the world.

"What do we do?" asked Kaya, voicing everyone's concerns, no doubt.

"There's a reason why I got this beast," quipped Somerton calmly. "We go overland."

And with that, the professor yanked the wheel hard to the right, pulled off the street, went over a curb, down a sidewalk, plowing over a pathetic tree sapling, burst through the wooden fence of someone's backyard, over a child's jungle gym as if it wasn't there at all, and then out into the surrounding woods.

"I just love the country," said Somerton, grinning at his terrified passengers.

Parker watched as they drove off. He cursed to himself, opened his Senao phone, and made a call.

"Where are they?"

"Heading south away from Flagg."

"South? They should be heading towards us?"

"No. They're headed for the airport. They may have a plane there."

"Inform your team. And I want you back here."

"I'll do my best. Mount Humphrey is about to blow."

"We know. That's of no concern to us. And your best better be good enough." Preston clicked off.

Parker knew what he had to do. "Follow me," he said to his partner. The man nodded.

The assassin removed his pistol from his shoulder holster, then opened his car door. He scanned the street; found the biggest SUV he could see—a Ford Expedition. He marched over to it, yanked open the driver's door, shoved the gun in the face of the terrified young man driving.

"Get out or die."

A few minutes later, Parker grinned at his partner as they followed the trail of destruction left behind by the Hummer.

Flagstaff, Arizona

The trip overland to the airport through back roads—and places where roads didn't exist at all—took a couple of hours. Occasionally Somerton reported seeing another SUV following them in the far distance, but they didn't have time to worry about that.

Gray volcanic ash clouded the afternoon into something closer to dusk. And as the fine dust covered the ground and windshield, swirling around the tires, hot red flames occasionally appeared from within Humphrey's Peak.

Jesus, it's going to blow, thought Nash.

The airport was surprisingly empty. In fact, it almost appeared abandoned.

No one in their right mind would fly in this shit, thought Nash. *So, what does that say about us?*

Like a madman—and Nash was beginning to think Somerton *was* a madman—they drove down the tarmac, dodging taxiing planes, to where Nash's Cirrus SR-20 was parked. They all exited, and Nash was shocked to see barely a scratch on the Hummer's front end. Kaya and Chandler proceeded to help Nash uncover the plane's protective canvas. Volcanic dust rippled off the heavy material as they pulled it off.

"Are you sure it's safe to fly this with the dust in the air?" asked Chandler.

"We'll find out," said Nash. "Everyone get in. It's gonna be a bit tight in the back so get chummy."

Nash sat at the controls, and Kaya took the co-pilot seat beside him. He turned over the engine, and it labored and coughed a few times. Nash worked the choke feeding the engine more and more fuel until it finally kicked over and started to hum.

"Good girl," he said, patting the dashboard.

Nash taxied the plane to the runway and rolled it to the very end. "We'll probably need all the runway we can get to takeoff in this air and with this load." He stood on the brakes and revved up the engine to the highest RPM he dared. When he felt the plane shudder and on the verge of coming apart, he stood off the brakes and hurtled the small plane down the runway.

He noticed Kaya crossing her fingers and closing her eyes. Crossed fingers were a good thing. Hell, they needed all the luck they could get.

The end of the runway came closer and closer. The small plane labored to lift off. Someone muttered a prayer behind him.

Prayers are good, too, he thought.

Finally, the wheels started to lift, and they were airborne. Nash looked over at Kaya. She was taking deep gulps of air.

"Piece of cake," he said, grinning.

Under darkening skies of volcanic dust, they flew over the town of Cameron and on towards the Little Colorado Gorge. A few dozen miles from the rim of the gorge, the plane began shuddering mysteriously.

"Is it the engine?" asked Chandler coolly behind him. Nash appreciated her calmness. "Clogging from the ash perhaps?"

Before Nash could answer, he saw small holes appear rapidly in the wing. Thirty caliber holes.

"I don't think so," said Nash, matching her cool. "Actually, I think someone's shooting at us."

Nash banked the plane and looked back over his shoulder. So did everyone else. Indeed, they were being followed by a small canard-shaped aircraft with a propeller in the rear.

"What the devil is that?" asked Kaya.

"Looks like a Long-EZ, home-built aircraft. The same kind that John Denver flew when he died."

"Jesus," cried Kaya. "I think it's gaining on us. How fast is that thing?"

"Fast."

"And us?"

"Not as fast."

"Shit."

"You can say that again," said Nash. "Hold on!"

Nash put the small plane into a steep dive towards the flat plain of scrub brush below. As he did so, with most everyone in his small plane screaming, bullets shot from a machine gun mounted under the front of the Long-EZ streamed past his side window.

Nash bobbed and weaved the SR-20 close to the ground, just skimming the scrub brush and twisted trees.

Their pursuer easily followed his maneuvers and continued to gain on them. Nash cursed. Someone might have vomited in the seat behind him, but he would worry about that later. For now, it was obvious the canard-designed plane was faster and nimbler than the SR-20.

More bullets rained down upon them, puncturing the plane in places it could ill-afford to be punctured.

"They're right behind us!" Somerton yelled. If Nash didn't know better, he detected more excitement than concern in the crazy professor's voice.

"I can't shake them," Nash stated more calmly than he felt.

He pulled up the controls and banked the plane hard to the right when a strong blast of wind hit the rear of the plane—*or was it shock wave?*

"*Holy Christ!*" yelled Wilcox. He was pointing out the window as Nash was banking the plane.

Nash got his answer. He looked to where the old man pointed. Humphrey's Peak, seen in the corner of the windshield about a hundred miles east, had erupted, which was putting it mildly. It had, in fact, completely blown its top. A rolling, menacing cloud of dust and debris was rushing at them as if the gates to hell itself had been thrown open.

"It's a pyroclastic flow!" Wilcox screamed. "Get up! Get altitude! *The flow hugs the ground!*"

"If I pull up, that'll put us right in that bastard's crosshairs," Nash said, gritting his teeth. "Now hold on!"

He pushed wheel forward and hurled the little plane towards the ground. From above, he saw that the Long-EZ immediately followed.

Come on you bastards. Come and get me.

Kaya screamed. In fact, she had been screaming for the past minute or so. Someone was praying hard behind him, and just as they reached the small canyon, Nash pulled the wheel hard into his chest. The plane stalled, and the SR-20 literally fell out of the sky deep into the gorge.

The high canyon walls raced quickly pass them as the SR-20 dropped like a rock. The Long-EZ tried to follow them down into the gorge, but it was too late for the little plane. Caught in mid-air by the superheated flow of pyroclastic cloud, it immediately flipped end over end, spinning and tumbling. Nash watched briefly as it slammed onto the side of a small mesa just below the rim of the gorge.

And as they plummeted, Nash fought for control of the stalled plane. The damn thing wasn't responding. "Pull on your controls, Kaya! Pull up on your wheel! Yes, like that! Good!"

Several terror-filled seconds passed as the two struggled with their controls until finally the Nash regained some control of the aircraft. But the ground was coming up fast. Too fast.

He shot a glance to his left and saw a sandy beach by the river. "Hold on, folks," he yelled. "This is gonna be rough!"

As the beach rapidly approached, Nash was just able to pull the nose of the aircraft up enough to keep the damn thing from tumbling ass over foot. The landing gears were pointless, and a few seconds later his little plane slammed hard into the sandy shore, skidding sideways in a hail of sand and rock and God knows what else. The starboard wing caught a tree stump, and the entire craft cart-wheeled—and flipped entirely over on its back.

When the plane finally came to rest, with a great wrenching of metal, Nash was certain that he was either dead or broken beyond repair.

And that's when he passed out.

Project KRATOS

Alfred Laveen was sweating uncontrollably in front of Prescott's desk—and it wasn't because of the humid temperature in the head man's office. Things were not going according to plan. In fact, things were nearly out-of-control.

Unfortunately, Prescott would hear none of it. "I don't care about any freakin' vibrations," he was saying.

"But, sir, the climatic and geologic incidents have increased exponentially over the last few days. We must scale back the accelerator."

"That's a negative," said Prescott. "There's no proof that the Project is responsible. But I'll make a deal with you. Once we have the engine, we can scale back the acceleration. End of problem."

"But it might take too long to—"

Prescott raised his hand. "Stop there. This project is to be delivered to The Chairman by tomorrow. Anything less will be unacceptable. Is this understood?"

Laveen nodded. "Yes, Mr. Prescott."

The little scientist turned and left. Prescott watched him silently, chewing absently on his inner cheek. He had felt the vibrations. Something *was* wrong. Very wrong. But he was damned if he was going to report failure to The Committee.

Better they all die—and the entire world with it—than to report failure to The Committee.

Little Colorado Canyon,
Grand Canyon

Nash was having a pleasant dream.

He was lying beside a lake with the sound of water lapping gently at his feet—his face bathed in a soothing warmth. Someone was calling his name from far away, but he didn't want to move from this pleasurable experience. The voice was followed by a nudge, and the nudge became more and more insistent, until finally someone grabbed his arms, and shook him hard.

"Jeremy! Damn it! Wake up!"

Nash opened his eyes and tried to focus on the voice. A figure emerged from his stupor. An upside-down figure. It was Kaya, and she was vigorously shaking him again.

"Okay, I'm up, I'm up." He tried to sit up, and as he did so, a thunderous pain exploded inside his head. "Oh, God," he moaned.

And then it all came rushing back to him. The plane crash, the mid-air dogfight, the volcano.

"Is everyone okay?" he asked.

"Somerton is dead," she said grimly, "but everyone else made it out alive."

Nash shook the last of the cobwebs from his head and realized what she had said. "Dead? Shit. And the others? Chandler? Wilcox?"

"They're okay. Just cuts and bruisers. We were lucky." She pointed down the beach. "They went down there. They saw a group of buildings. They think it's the place Somerton was taking us to. Now let's get you out of here."

Kaya released his seat belt, and Nash dropped a foot or two on his head.

"Ouch!" he cried out, whimpering.

"Sorry."

A few moments later, Kaya had Nash out of the badly damaged SR-20 and on his feet, explaining to him she wanted to make sure he had been okay before they attempted to move him, finishing with, "But you seemed to be enjoying your dream so much, that I figured you couldn't have been too hurt."

Slightly embarrassed, Nash turned and surveyed what was once his pride and joy. The wings of the SR-20 were crumpled, and the tail section was missing, no doubt somewhere downriver. Luckily, the cabin, though currently upside down and covered in mud, had stayed mostly intact.

Unfortunately, the same couldn't have been said for Somerton, who still lay inside the cabin, his neck broken. The man had apparently taken off his seat belt at some point in the flight. Without a seat belt, there was no way in hell he was going to survive such a horrendous crash.

Rest in peace, you crazy devil, thought Nash.

"Come on," urged Kaya pulling on his arm. "Let's catch up to the others."

"Wait!" Nash replied. He walked over to cabin and reached through a broken window near Somerton's body. Nash searched the dead man's pocket until he found what he was looking for. Somerton's Colt 45. "Okay. Now let's go."

Several minutes later they caught up with the others, who were examining a small group of buildings huddled together along the bank of the river. Nash had enough of guns. He handed it to Wilcox.

"Storage buildings," noted Chandler, as she approached one of them. "My guess is a river touring company uses them."

The federal agent reached them first and noticed the door to the closest building was unlocked. She pushed against the double doors, and the four of them entered the dark building. Wilcox found a light switch, and a moment later the building was lit from a bank of fluorescent lights above. They were in a warehouse of sorts, filled with rafting equipment. And sitting in the middle of the room on wheeled chocks were several thirty-five-foot motorized rafts made of sturdy rubberized fabric.

"Bingo," said Chandler. "We found our transportation."

Chandler grabbed a handful of life vests and tossed one to everyone. Once the life vests were on, the group hauled one of the rafts over its wheeled chocks out and towards the running river. At the beach, Chandler climbed into the motorman's seat in the rear.

The other three manhandled the raft into the river and quickly scrambled aboard. Almost immediately the Little Colorado River current grabbed them and soon the quartet was rushing downstream through the canyon in muddy water towards the much bigger Grand Canyon.

The heavy, muddy water reminded Nash of what his father would say of the Colorado River. *Too thin to plow. Too thick too drink.*

With the sky a hazy shade of gray, and the afternoon looking closer to late evening, the smoothly moving river suddenly turned anything but smooth.

"Hold on!" Chandler shouted over the growing roar of the river.

As ice cold spray drenched everyone on the raft, Chandler steered the raft straight into the rapids, doing a surprisingly good job of holding the tiny craft steady. Several bounces and a few tosses later, they cleared the rapids and continued down through the Little Colorado River.

"You should be a river running guide!" Kaya called loudly to Chandler.

"It's probably safer than being an FBI—"

"Holy shit!" cried Wilcox, pointing up.

Nash and the others snapped their heads up. Above them, the canyon walls on both sides were caving in, crumbling down towards them.

Another earthquake?

The massive, falling rocks pummeled the muddy churning river, sometimes just missing the little raft. Chandler did her best to steer clear of the missiles, but there was just too many of them. They rained down everywhere, causing the river to foam and heave, turning the water into a churning, frothing cauldron.

The tiny boat bucked up and down. It was all Nash could do to hang on for dear life. It took all his strength not to tumble over the rubber side.

Directly ahead, perhaps no more than twenty feet, a particularly massive boulder struck the river. The resulting mini tsunami threw the raft high into the air, and as it came down, Nash watched in horror as Kaya went over the edge.

He dove forward and caught her arm, just as the raft came crashing down. The jolt was too much for him to hang on with one hand.

The next moment, he found himself flipping out of the boat and into the cold currents.

Chandler watched as both Nash and Kaya tumbled out of the raft.

A quick glance behind her saw them both disappear beneath the turbulent surface. There was no going back for them. In fact, it was all she could do to keep herself from tumbling over the side. Her aging uncle was still hanging on, and she hoped they were through the worst of it, as the rocks were coming at them with less frequency.

But that was not to be.

Now deep within the Grand Canyon, the water level had risen considerably due to recent rains and the bizarre weather conditions. The river was swollen and angry, and the little raft was rapidly picking up speed.

Water crashed everywhere, booming like thunder. Water spray filled the air and obscured everything. At times, Chandler could barely see which direction they were facing. They were totally at the mercy of the roaring river. Worse yet, the raft was filling with water as the self-bailing system had long ago been overcome by the watery onslaught.

"Are we sinking?" she heard her uncle shout from somewhere.

"Just a matter of time," she shouted back.

And then, mercifully, she noticed that the raft was slowing down. The water that filled the raft had made it heavier and it began to lumber over the water.

The air cleared of icy spray, and she could finally see again. Within a few short minutes, the raft had slowed considerably, and Chandler could once again hear herself think.

As the raft entered Granite Gorge, the river widened and slowed giving Chandler the opportunity she needed to turn the raft around.

Wilcox gave her a weak smile, and she smiled back at her uncle as they made their way towards Battleship Rock looming unmistakably up from the clouded sky.

Neither of them spoke as they thought back to Nash and Kaya.

Grand Canyon,
Below Maricopa Point

Nash coughed up the last of the water in his lungs as he lay on the sandy beach. He looked over at Kaya who was lying on her side next to him.

When they had gone overboard, Nash's flailing hand had somehow snagged the Hopi woman. The next few minutes had been a nightmare as he struggled to keep both of their faces above the raging river, all the while praying the falling projectiles didn't drive them straight to the bottom of the river.

Miraculously, they had avoided the falling rocks. And even more miraculously, with Kaya in one arm, he had managed to maneuver them to the shore. Once he had dragged them out of the water, he spent the next few seconds coughing up the Colorado River.

It was then he saw that Kaya was not moving.

Oh, sweet Jesus. Please, no!

He rushed to her side and rolled her over onto her back. He pounded her hard between her shoulder blades and finally—finally—she started coughing, and as she did so, a great amount of clear vomit exploded from her mouth. She kept coughing, and Nash kept patting her back, relieved to be alive, but wondering how the others had fared.

It was then that a shadow crossed over him.

It was Garcia, and he was holding a semi-automatic rifle.

Garcia grinned, and the deep scar that ran along his jaw line seemed to grin, too. "I can see by the expression on your face, my friend, that you remember me."

Garcia wasn't alone. Two other men were with him, each armed the same. Garcia motioned to them, and the thugs hauled Nash and Kaya to their feet. Poor Kaya was barely coherent. Garcia ordered them searched. Kaya's pistol and Big Man's knife were removed.

Garcia stuck the pistol in his belt, but paused and studied the knife. "This looks familiar. What did you have to do to get that big Hopi to give it up?"

"Nothing," said Nash. "He left it in my friend's back."

Garcia laughed. "Aw, Big Man. He could always be counted on to do his worst."

"Well, the son-of-a-bitch is dead," spat Kaya.

"Aw, so the Hopi princess has found her fire. Good. I like fire." He walked over to Kaya and studied her maliciously, his scar virtually quivering. "I hope you'll be more talkative than your grandfather."

"You fucking bastard."

Garcia grinned again and snapped his gaze over to Nash. "And you. You're as persistent as your parents, Mr. Nash. So perhaps it's fitting that you will suffer the same fate."

Nash caught a flash of turquoise and silver on Garcia's wrist.

"*You* killed my parents," said Nash, pointing to Garcia's wrist.

The man smirked and looked at the piece of sliver and turquoise on his wrist. "Good guess, Mr. Nash. And, yes, your dying father asked me to hold this for him." He laughed and pushed up his sleeve, clearly showing Nash the silver and turquoise watch band. "Perhaps you recognize it."

Of course Nash recognized the watch. It had been his father's. The same watch he had promised to a young Jeremy years ago.

Garcia grinned again. "I bet you want to kill me, don't you? I bet you want to take this watch off my cold lifeless hand, don't you?"

Nash fought to control himself. "You bet right, asshole."

Garcia's smile turned into a snarl, and he thrust the barrel of his rifle into Nash's stomach.

Nash grunted and dropped to his knees.

"Introductions are over," Garcia barked. "Now, move!"

Nash was yanked to his feet again. And as he stood, he heard the unmistakable *whooshing* sound of a helicopter overhead. Within minutes a dark gray helicopter, the kind police use, landed on the sandy beach below the walls of the Little Colorado Canyon.

Battleship Rock
Grand Canyon

Chandler landed the raft at Pipe Creek in the shadow of Battleship Rock.

She and her uncle disembarked and walked through the muddy creek towards the base of Orphan Mine, which they could see in the distance. It was exactly as Kaya had described.

As they came closer, they could see a large hole at the base of the mine.

"That's the Glory Hole," Chandler stated. "Entrance to the mine."

A few minutes later, the two were standing at the edge of the open mine shaft that ran 1600-feet horizontally into the canyon wall. Above the entrance was a black pinwheel on a yellow background—the international warning sign for radiation hazard. To the right of the warning sign was a small metal placard that warned that radiation levels were high in the area with combined beta and gamma radiation exceeding 3.0 mR/hour. And next to the entrance was a small wooden structure. What appeared to be workman's quarters.

Chandler walked up to sign to get a better view. "I think you may be right, uncle. If those bastards are utilizing a nuke power plant down there, they have the uranium here to refine for the fuel. Are you sure it's safe to go in here?"

"Yes, as long as we keep moving." Wilcox suddenly ducked into the small wooden shack. Chandler heard her uncle rummaging about. When he reappeared at the doorway, his face slightly

smudged with dirt, he was grinning. He held up two large flashlights. "Bingo."

Twenty minutes later, after carefully picking their way over the loose stone, they made their way over the edge of the glory hole and through the horizontal mineshaft. They were careful not to cause any disruptions that might bring the rickety mine down on their heads.

At the end of the shaft, they saw what appeared to be an adit, or an entrance into an unfinished shaft. Chandler poked her flashlight into the dark hole.

"It looks like an entrance to a cave," she reported.

"Does it look safe?"

"Safe enough."

"Then let's go."

Chandler squatted down and slipped inside the shaft, with Wilcox following behind. Inside, the cave was damp and cool. Chandler led the way cautiously over the irregular floor, and a few moments later they found themselves in a limestone cavern complex filled with hundreds of stalactites and stalagmites. Beautiful at first, until the hundreds of shadows they caused appeared to be moving. Chandler shivered, gooseflesh rising on her arms.

Creepy as hell, she thought.

They made their way to the far end of the cavern, and the cave complex itself. They appeared to have hit a dead end. Chandler scanned the bleak stone walls around them.

"Nothing," she reported. "It's the end of the road."

"But this doesn't make sense," said Wilcox, scratching his chin. "All the clues pointed to this mine entrance as the—"

Wilcox never finished his thought.

At that moment, the floor of the cave buckled under their feet. They both braced themselves against a massive stalagmite. The floor shook briefly and then stopped as quickly as it began.

"Another earthquake," said Wilcox. "We need—"

Chandler raised her finger, cutting him off. "What's that sound?"

Wilcox cocked his head, listening. What had sounded like a small rumbling to Chandler was quickly growing into something much, much louder. Something thunderous. Something earth-shattering.

Chandler spun, her powerful light cutting through the inky darkness—landing on something moving, surging.

It was a wall of water, and it was coming directly at them.

The flood of water was upon them.

The raging water washed over them, slamming them hard against the far wall, and then sweeping them along. Their lights disappeared, extinguished by the raging waters, and Chandler found herself swept along in total darkness, separated from her uncle.

Somewhere above the roar, she heard him call her name.

Wilcox, with superhuman effort, was finally able to capture and hold onto an outcropping of rock. And as the freezing currents poured over him, he eventually pulled himself out of the water and onto the rock, where he sat shivering and catching his breath.

Where had the water come from?

Where had his niece gone?

He briefly buried his face in his hands and wept, certain the young woman he had raised by himself—after her parents had died tragically in a horrible house fire—had suffered an equally tragic death.

A few minutes later, he pulled himself together and, with a heavy heart, took in his surroundings. By no right should he be able to see where he was. And yet—

Light was emitting from something in the nearby wall. A

tunnel of some sort. No, a service passageway. There was something very familiar about the tunnel.

Could it be?

As he sat there shivering, he plumbed the depths his memory—going back well over twenty years...until it all came back to him.

He remembered the plans, plans he and his old team had worked diligently on. The plans for Project KRATOS.

They actually built it!

"Amazing," he breathed.

Remarkably, if the plans held true, he knew exactly where he was. This was a duct that would serve as an exhaust for a power plant.

Wilcox frowned, confused. The duct was clearly cool—not hot.

Worry about that later, he thought.

He carefully leaped off the slippery rock and landed loudly in the metal passageway. Dripping wet and knowing there was nothing he could do for his niece, he moved along the narrow passage, and within minutes he exited into a much longer tunnel.

And standing there on a pair of tracks was a service trolley.

Right where it should be.

Son of a bitch, he thought.

With no one around, Wilcox climbed into the cab, pressed the accelerator button to the floor, and was not surprised to see the electric motor came to life.

It all came back to him now.

He knew where he was going and what he had to do.

Several minutes later he stopped the service trolley in front of a small window. Inside, he saw the control room. He exited the trolley and made his way to an outside door.

Project KRATOS

Twenty minutes from the Little Colorado Canyon, Nash found himself flying low over what appeared to be an abandoned housing development. There were even street signs scattered through the development, marking future streets of the development.

They continued over the abandoned development until they reached what Nash assumed would have been the community clubhouse. The chopper landed outside of the building, and soon Nash and Kaya were led into the half-finished structure.

Perfect cover for a secret project, thought Nash, as he surveyed the abandoned-looking building.

Once inside, they were stewarded into a small room, where the door was closed firmly behind them. Garcia reached over and pulled a lever on the wall and immediately the floor blow Nash's feet began to drop beneath him.

Nash could not have been more surprised to discover himself in an elevator. To anyone observing the room, it would have appeared as just that...and empty room.

Kaya looked at him, raising her eyebrows. Nash shrugged. This was, after all, just another strange occurrence in a week of strange occurrences. In fact, Nash had almost come to expect the impossible.

They continued downward.

Many lighted levels swept passed them. Amazingly, Nash caught brief glimpses of people working in white lab coats on those levels. Eventually, the elevator stopped in front of a pair of white doors. The doors opened silently, and Nash was met by a rush of humid air which hit him in the face.

They were ordered out and led down a brightly lit corridor towards what looked like a small electric tram.

"Get in," Garcia barked.

With Nash and Kaya in the front and Garcia with the two henchmen in the rear, they took off down a long, semi-lit tunnel. Cool wind blasted their face.

"This is incredible," Kaya whispered to him.

"You would need a lot of electricity to power this place," Nash whispered back, wondering where the hell they were being taken. He went on. "I bet Wilcox was right. A nuke power plant of some sort."

Garcia overheard their conversation. "You're an inquisitive man, Nash, so I'll tell you how we did it," he said as if it was his doing. "We use a PBR—a Pebble Bed Reactor. Know what that is?"

Nash and Kaya shook their heads.

"It uses Uranium-235 molded into ceramic balls. The gas is circulated through the balls creating an efficient, low-maintenance, safe reactor with inexpensive, standardized fuel. And the Orphan mine offered plenty of Uranium-235, an isotope that could sustain fission chain reaction. And because the reactor is designed to handle high temperatures, it can cool by natural circulation. Okay, enough with the science lesson. We're here."

The tram pulled into a staging area, and they all disembarked. They were led through a large double metal door, and when Nash realized where they where, he couldn't help but be impressed.

They were in a cavernous enclosure. A deep, humming sound permeated the musky air, and the floor was vibrating slightly. In front of him were some semi-circular workstations with widescreen computers mounted on them. Above them were three ten-foot flat panel displays with graphic representations of different data displayed on them hanging from the ceiling. Behind a glass wall was something that looked like along circular tube that bent slightly to their left and right, and disappeared down a long tunnel.

"A particle accelerator," Nash said.

"Very good, Mr. Nash. Welcome to Project KRATOS," said a voice from behind him.

Nash turned to see an athletic looking man of medium height in his late fifties and dressed in the uniform of a successful CEO, walking down a flight of stairs.

"Let me introduce myself," he said pleasantly. "I'm Reuben Prescott. I'm in charge here."

Nash scowled at the man. "Then you're the piece of shit who ordered this other piece of shit to kill my parents."

Prescott raised one side of his lip. "Ah, yes. The Nash family has been a thorn in my side for a long time. Your parents' deaths were unfortunate, but necessary. Death is always an unpleasant business."

"You mean murder."

"Call it what you will, Mr. Nash. But in my world, it's business as usual."

Nash took in some air. How could anyone be so cold, so callous? He was dealing with animals, and there was no reasoning with animals. To calm himself down, he glanced around the mostly empty workstations.

"So where is everyone?"

"We're having some, ah, operational problems."

"Don't tell me," said Nash. "Something unexpected?"

"You wouldn't understand—"

"I know more than you think. You're bleeding black holes. Aren't you?"

Prescott spun on him. "And where did hear that?"

"From me," said a voice behind them.

They all turned and saw Wilcox holding a forty-five on them. The man was soaking wet.

"Well, well, the gang's all here," said Prescott, and if he was surprised to see Wilcox standing there, he didn't show it.

"I'm not that easy to kill, Prescott. Am I?"

"We shall see."

The old man raised the weapon and leveled it at Prescott. "Let them go or die."

Prescott nodded and rough hands released Nash, pushing him away. The same with Kaya. Wilcox waved them over, and Nash could see that the once crazy-looking man now seemed comfortably in control of a fairly volatile situation.

Either that or he really is crazy.

Wilcox kept his weapon on Prescott as he spoke again. "You screwed the pooch, Prescott. I told you what could happen. You wouldn't listen. But now we're all going to play nice-nice and you're going to shut this accelerator down." He glanced over at Garcia and the henchman next to him. "If you two want your boss to sign any more paychecks, I suggest you drop your guns. Nash, Kaya, get their weapons."

Nash retrieved one of the rifles, but as Kaya bent down for Garcia's, the scarred man turned on her before Wilcox could respond. He grabbed her and rotated her around in front of his body, using her as a human shield. He yanked Kaya's pistol from her belt.

"Party's over," he said, pointing the gun at Kaya's head.

"Good job, Garcia," said Prescott smoothly. "Drop your weapon, Wilcox, or the girl gets a much-deserved bullet to the head."

Wilcox reluctantly complied, setting the pistol down.

"Now, we'll—" started Prescott, but he was never able to finish his sentence.

Project KRATOS,
The Cave Complex

Gulping river water and struggling to keep her head above the churning surface, Chandler surged through the black unknown. Where she was, she had no clue—and where she would end up, she could fear the worst.

And scream.

She soon found herself tumbling down what appeared to be a narrow channel, a channel that mercifully slowed and eventually dumped her, free falling, into a small, roiling pool of filthy water. The pool appeared to be emptying under her feet into some kind of drain. And with the pressure of the rushing water subsiding, she was able to get her feet under her and swim away from the waterfall that was still emptying into this shallow pool.

The walls were covered with glowing green lichen which, remarkably, offered her some light. She surveyed her surroundings and what struck her first was the fetid smell. She appeared to be in a circular, man-made tank of some sort. A tank that stunk of excrement. It reminded her of a cesspool.

In fact, it was.

"Ah, hell," she moaned. Her voice echoed hollowly around her. "You have got to be kidding me."

The water at her feet was still circling a large drain, but now the pull on her was getting stronger. One slip and she could end up in the drain.

Flushed to death, she thought. *What a way to go.*

She pushed herself back against the smooth concrete wall,

found a metal handhold, and anchored herself against the force of the draining human waste matter. The odor was overpowering, and it finally got to her. She turned her head and retched violently.

Christ! I have to get out of here!

From this spot, she scanned the tank and saw that there were metal u-shaped handholds that went straight up from where she was standing. She reached for one, grabbed hold of the slimy metal, and began to climb.

She soon reached a manhole in the ceiling. She pushed on it with her shoulder, and it gave way to blessed clear air.

Project KRATOS

It was an explosion that silenced Prescott and rocked the control room.

The ground beneath Nash seemed to leap a foot or two in the air, and everything overhead—fluorescent lights, water pipes, and electrical conduit—immediately came crashing down, along with large chunks of the ceiling.

Nash leaped into motion. He grabbed Kaya and had just yanked her under one of the metal workstations when a metal lighting track and pieces of conduit smashed on top of the desk. Kaya screamed, and he held her close, and from that position, as the lights flickered crazily around them, he saw one of Prescott's henchmen take a massive I-beam straight across his head, killing him instantly. Kaya ducked her head into Nash's shoulder.

Nash watched a ten-foot flat screen monitor detach from ceiling and crash down on a man Nash assumed to be a project scientist. Dark blood oozed from under the screen and flowed toward them.

The ground, which had been shaking steadily, suddenly stopped. The scene before them was one of total destruction. Someone was moaning nearby. A few others lay dead. Electrical equipment, and God knew what else, lay in smoking heaps. A tremor or two followed, but nothing substantial.

"Where's Wilcox?" Kaya asked him.

Nash looked out from under the table and spotted the scientist across the cavernous room—alive. He had apparently taken cover under a heavy archway that led into another chamber. Even more important, he had retrieved his forty-five and presently had it pointed at Prescott.

Good man!

There was movement next to him, and Nash watched as Garcia pushed a massive piece of conduit off him and, holding a bleeding left arm, dashed out of the control room.

"The bastard's not getting away," said Kaya, and she scrambled out from around Nash. The Hopi woman scanned the destroyed room wildly and found what she was looking for—an Uzi, which she pried from the curled fingers of a dead henchman.

"Wait for me," said Nash.

"Leave him be," said Wilcox, now walking toward them, picking his way over the debris. He made Prescott follow in front of him. "We have to shut down the accelerator."

"The bastard as good as killed my grand—"

"I think the fate of the world is more important than a grudge match, my fiery friend," said Wilcox calmly. He turned to Prescott. "Now, let's turn off your little machine."

"I can't," smirked Prescott. He pointed to the destruction around him, in particular one of the workstations next to him. "That was the control panel. It's gone. All gone. It's useless now. The accelerator can't be shut down."

Wilcox looked at Nash. "Actually, there is a way. There's a substation in one of the monitor caverns...I think, near the containment vessel. We could shut down the accelerator there."

"I'll take care of it," said Nash. "Which way?"

Wilcox gave him directions, and Nash was about to set off when Kaya grabbed his arm. "I'm going with you."

"I need you here with me, Kaya," said Wilcox.

Nash nodded to Kaya. "It's okay. Stay with him. I can do this alone. And don't worry. Garcia won't get away."

And as Nash was about to turn away, he caught sight of Prescott. In particular, Prescott's odd smile.

He knows something, thought Nash, and then turned and quickly dashed off.

Project KRATOS,
Containment Vessel

Nash hurried down the long tunnel that contained the accelerator—the very accelerator that was causing the mini-black holes.

The very accelerator that was causing the world-wide catastrophes.

The tunnel was filled with a strange humming sound, and Nash suddenly had a terrifying vision of himself being sucked into a mini-black hole.

He ran a little faster.

The tunnel was quite cold due to the thousand or so superconducting magnets surrounding the accelerator tube, which kept the operating temperature of the accelerator at -271 degrees centigrade. Luckily, the monitor cavern with the substation was only several minutes down the tunnel.

Still, by the time he reached the end of the tunnel, Nash was breathing hard. The tunnel itself led straight into the monitor cavern, and following the instructions Wilcox gave him, Nash looked for the monitor display containing the accelerator status. He soon found it next to a small screen that had a digital counter on it. Under the display was a small plastic label that read **Black Hole Count vs Energy Output**, and it was ticking off numbers at a furious rate.

That can't be good, thought Nash. He suddenly realized the fate of the world could very well be in the hands of a man who was not particularly technically inclined.

Off to his right and several yards down from him, was the

Containment Vessel Room. The hair on the back of his head and arms, he realized, were standing on end from static electricity coming from the room. There was also a strange bluish glow emanating from two twelve-inch windows set in a door.

"The cradle of the universe—*the God Particles*," he said to himself, quoting Wilcox. He marveled at the bluish light for awhile, and then reminded himself to get back to the task at hand.

"You're saving the world, remember?" he mumbled.

Nash found the lever that Wilcox told him of above the accelerator status screen and slowly—slowly—pulled in down towards him.

Immediately, the loud humming in the tunnel ratcheted down and started its decline. *Job done. World saved. What's next?*

He had just started back towards the control room when his curiosity got the better of him.

"Why not just take a peep at the God Particles?" he said aloud to the empty room.

A few cautious steps later, he found himself outside the metal door to the containment vessel.

Here, Nash hesitated a moment and thought hard about what he was doing. Suddenly, standing in the bluish glow, this didn't seem like such a good idea. And after some serious internal dialogue, he finally went ahead and reached for the rectangular door handle and clicked the door open.

He stepped into the room slowly. Immediately he saw a Plexiglas box several feet from him. Inside was a clear, three-foot high cylindrical container with silver wires crisscrossing around it and deep inside it. The clear cylinder was attached to a metal frame surrounded by what appeared to be solar collection panels. Surrounding those were cryogenic cylinders that pumped sub-zero temperature gas into the Plexiglas box.

Incredible!

Nash stood there briefly in awe of the magnificent display of light, which pulsed with electrometric energy threads that erupted every few micro-seconds.

Beautiful! he thought again, and then added, *Now get moving. Sight-seeing is over.*

As he turned to exit the room, Nash stopped short. There was a man standing in the doorway, holding a pistol loosely in front of him, grinning. It was the same man Nash had seen in Sedona, the same bastard who had leveled that shopping center and killed God knows how many people in the process. The man known as Parker. The Project's hired killer.

I'm dead, thought Nash.

Parker stepped casually into the room. The man was smaller than Nash remembered, but he was clearly powerfully built. "You've cost me a lot in my reputation and resources, Mr. Nash." Parker spoke almost conversationally. That he was about to kill a man, obviously concerned him little. Mostly, Parker seemed just as intrigued as Nash had been by the beautiful displays of light. Unlike Nash, he didn't allow the lights to distract him for very long. "It's time to settle up, Nash. Are you ready to die?"

"I wouldn't fire a weapon in here if I were you," said Nash, making shit up as he went. "A spark in here would cause an immediate chain reaction. By shooting me, you are effectively blowing yourself up."

That got the bastard thinking. "You might have a point there, Nash. I thank you kindly for your concern for my welfare. It's a shame I can't reciprocate that. Now get the hell out of this room."

"So that you can shoot me? Sure, sounds like a great idea, you dumb fuck. Actually, I'm pretty content right here."

Parker ran a hand over his rather handsome face. "I'll shoot you here and take my chances."

"Go ahead, shithead. I'd love nothing more than to know that I died taking your pathetic ass out with me."

Nash was bluffing. He had nothing. He had no clue how the

reactor would respond to gunfire. For all he knew, the Plexiglass case—or whatever it was that surrounded the God Particles—was bullet proof. But Parker clearly didn't know that. Parker was just a thug—perhaps a well-paid and highly skilled thug—but a thug none-the-less.

And Nash was counting on the man's ignorance, and common sense, to keep him alive.

Great, he thought.

"New plan," said Parker suddenly, holstering his pistol under his shoulder. "I'm going to beat the shit out of you and then drag you out."

Nash had counted on that. If he was going to go down, he wanted to go down in a fight. Parker cracked his neck, rolling his squarish head on his massive shoulders, and then charged Nash.

Nash, no stranger to fights, knew he was in for the fight of his life. Parker didn't disappoint. The man was powerful and stacked with muscle. And being shorter than Nash, he adeptly used his leverage.

In a blink of his eye, Nash found himself picked up off the ground and briefly airborne. A moment later, the son-of-bitch was driving Nash hard into the ground, landing on top him. The air burst from Nash's lungs. Above him the God Particle machine hummed and vibrated and spat its eye-popping supercharged energy.

Parker, hovering above, proceeded to level punch after punch. Some landing squarely, rocking Nash, but most missing. Still, the ones that landed were doing a job on Nash, and he knew it was just a matter of time until this brute beat him into a bloody pulp.

Nash, who had seen his fair share of Mixed Martial Arts fights, knew that he had to cover his face. Once done, he had to find his feet, no matter what. On his feet, Nash knew he could take this bastard.

First things first.

Still absorbing blow after blow, Nash freed one of his arms, and swung his arm and leg as hard as he could to one side. Parker rained down even more blows, but Nash, amazingly, seemed impervious to them.

It was fight or die.

Once on his side and using his other arm to protect the side of his face and ward off the majority of the blows, Nash began positioning his feet under himself. First up on his knees, and then on the balls of his feet.

Now the bastard was hanging on to Nash, or risk falling. And then Nash burst forward, running, and finally broke free.

Nash stopped and turned and was not surprised to see Parker directly behind him, ready for another take down. As Nash continued to turn, he swung a punch as hard as he could, driving his fist down into the side of the smaller man's face. It was a hell of a punch. Parker dropped to a knee, and Nash continued throwing punches as hard as he could.

The sound of bone hitting bone echoed in the small chamber. Blood sprayed from open wounds on the Parker's face.

And just as Nash was about to level another punch from his own broken and damaged hands. Parker lifted his face and pulled his pistol out of his shoulder holster. The killer grinned through the blood dripping down his face and said, "I guess we both go down in flames, mate."

He fired the gun, but his aim was wobbly at best. Nash ducked and jumped out of the way as the bullet went errant— but not entirely so. Glass shattered above Parker's head, and as Nash rolled away, he heard the killer scream. Nash turned in time to see a stream of cryogenic fluid raining down over the man's contorted face.

Nash scrambled across the room. Back through the door and slammed it shut behind him. Gasping, he turned and looked through one of the long windows on the door into the containment vessel room. What he saw both horrified and fascinated him. Parker was literally evaporating before Nash's eyes. The killer's body was now being pulled apart in a process called *spaghettification*, where an object near a black hole is stretched lengthwise and compressed widthwise.

It was not a pretty sight.

Even through the heavy metal door, Nash could hear Parker's screams as he was torn apart by the micro-black holes.

As Nash watched what had once been a human being pulled and stretched as surely as if he had been standing in front of a funhouse mirror, a bluish sparkling haze of micro-black holes engulfed the killer, and as it did so, Parker began evaporating slowly—and obviously painfully—piece by bloody piece.

Nash pulled himself away from the door and headed back to the control room.

Project KRATOS
Control Room

When Nash returned to the control room, Kaya gasped. "Oh my God, Jeremy! What happened?"

Nash explained the struggle with Parker and its bizarre aftermath.

Kaya covered her mouth as he spoke, but Wilcox looked concerned.

"You said the containment vessel room was damaged?" he asked.

"Nash nodded. "And the Black Hole Count vs Energy Output was off the charts."

"That explains the energy spike we just saw on the overhead monitors," he said, then stepped over to Prescott. Wilcox held his pistol loosely at his side. Too loosely for Nash's comfort. Wilcox spoke to Prescott. "And energy spikes can be fatal. Where can I re-run that spike and see its effect?"

Prescott shrugged. "At Workstation Two, if the computers there are still working."

Wilcox moved to the workstation and called up what he called a reporting routine. "It's encoded," he reported. "What's the password, Prescott?"

"Why would I have the password?"

Wilcox surprised the hell out of Nash by walking in front of Prescott and casually shooting the man in his right thigh. Prescott seemed equally surprised, just before he collapsed in pain, screaming, blood running through his fingers.

Kaya gasped.

"Holy shit," said Nash.

The gun never wavered in Wilcox's hands as he stood over the writhing Prescott. "Would you like me to shoot your other leg?"

"You crazy son-of-a-bitch."

"I think we're all crazy in here," said Wilcox calmly. He pointed the gun at Prescott's other leg. "Care to give me the password?"

"It's four-seven-alpha-zero-fox-lima-five."

Wilcox motioned for Nash to type in the password at the console. Nash jumped into motion, doing as he was told. The last thing he wanted to do was piss-off a crazy guy with the gun. When Nash was done typing, a master reporting routine immediately appeared on the screen.

"Find the containment vessel activity history," Wilcox asked, still standing over Prescott.

Nash nodded, scrolling through the different reports, and found what Wilcox needed.

"Good. Please read it to me, Jeremy."

Nash frowned.

"Read me the report. What's the problem?"

Nash felt that a specter of a conspiracy theory had suddenly come to life. "There's dozens and dozens of documents and reports from someone," he hesitated a moment not believing what he saw, "called the Chairman of the Committee." He looked incredulously at Wilcox who smiled and nodded. Wilcox looked like the cat that swallowed the proverbial canary.

Wilcox tuned on Prescott. "Is this what you're hiding? I think the authorities would love to read these."

"Not gonna happen," said a voice from behind them.

Nash turned to see a stocky, middle-aged man with thinning red hair standing in the control room doorway.

"Who the hell are you?" Wilcox demanded.

"The name's Safford." He pointed a pistol at them. "Now drop your weapons."

Jesus, they just keep coming out of the woodwork, thought Nash.

Wilcox held his pistol steady on Prescott. "I don't think so."

Safford, Nash realized, was holding something just out of view. Something that appeared to be struggling. "Tit for tat," said the man, and yanked Alyson Nash from behind the doorway.

"Alyson!"

"Jeremy!"

"Very touching," said Safford, and he stood behind Alyson, holding her tightly around the neck and shoulders. He pointed the pistol at her head.

Alyson was a mess, dirty, and her clothing had burn marks on them. "Jeremy..." she whimpered.

Nash started towards her when Safford turned to him. "Far enough, Mr. Nash." Next, he looked at Kaya and Wilcox. "Let's try this again. Drop your guns. Now!"

Nash looked at Wilcox and Kaya, "Drop them. Please?"

Kaya and Wilcox looked at each other, and then set their weapons down.

Prescott cackled like something wicked. He jumped up to one foot and leaned on a workstation. There was a pool of blood where he had been lying. "Excellent. Now shoot them. Shoot them!"

Safford shook his head. "First things first, Mr. Prescott."

"What the fuck are you talking about?" screeched Prescott. "Kill them, now! That's an order."

"Sorry, but I have orders from The Chairman," replied Safford. "Orders I must execute first."

"What orders? What the hell is going on?"

Safford smiled, and said, "We call it Plan B." He pointed his Glock at Prescott and fired two bullets into the man's chest, directly over his heart.

Prescott looked down, wide-eyed, utterly confused, and then collapsed, dead.

Safford next looked directly at Nash. "And The Chairman

has something for you too, Mr. Nash." He took a bead on Nash with his pistol—

And that's when his sister went ape-shit crazy on her captor. Alyson threw himself at the man, clawing at his face and eyes and throat, screeching like a banshee.

Safford, with a Herculean effort, threw her off him. Alyson skidded on her ass across the polished floor, and Safford, his face bleeding from numerous deep gouges, had just raised his weapon to Nash again when a voice spoke behind him.

"Drop it, asshole."

A woman was standing behind Safford. A woman who was nearly unrecognizable. From what Nash could tell, the woman appeared covered in shit.

But Safford was in the process of doing something very stupid. He didn't drop his gun. Instead, he was swinging around and would have fired at the ooze-covered woman if she hadn't fired first.

Chandler calmly put a half dozen bullets into the man, including a few in his throat and head. Safford dropped dead.

Wilcox dashed over to his niece as Nash ran to his sister. She threw herself in his arms and cried briefly. The relief he felt nearly made him weep as well. This was the second time his sister had been kidnapped.

"No more kidnappings for you," he said, patting her back. "My heart can't handle it."

She nodded and cried some more. And at that moment another, low rumble vibrated through the control room. The rumbling continued. Indeed, it seemed to be growing in intensity.

"What's happening?" asked Kaya. "Jeremy shut down the accelerator."

"It's not the accelerator," said Wilcox. He walked to a computer terminal and read the containment vessel activity history. When he looked at the group, the color had drained from his face.

"What's wrong?" asked Nash.

"God. I hope..." was all he said as he furiously typed a set of commands into the computer.

He looked up and whispered almost in horror. "*Quark bomb.*"

"What are you talking about?" asked Nash. "What the hell's a quark bomb?"

Wilcox pointed to a simulation.

"What's that?" asked Nash.

"What the computer is projecting," Wilcox said.

"How accurate is it?"

"Nearly one hundred percent."

"Go on."

Nash saw a bright red ball of energy which was growing steadily larger beneath a computer simulation of the Project.

"What you're seeing here is a transformation of mass—"

"In English, Uncle," said Chandler.

"The Project's accelerator is designed to accelerate protons and collide them to create new particles by reaching a high state of energy never reached before in a collider. In such a scenario, not only can mini-black holes be formed but also something called *stangelets.*"

"*Strangelets?*" asked Kaya.

"They're particles that have unknown and possibly very dangerous properties. You see, with the collision of the protons, the quarks inside can be set free. Additionally, the gluon energy that makes up a great deal of the proton energy could accelerate these quarks and cause a chain reaction in which neighboring protons and other atoms would disintegrate."

He paused moment. Deep concern on his face. "With the collider running wild due to the earthquake and the damaged containment vessel...we get a quark bomb."

Nash remarked. "That doesn't sound good."

"Trust me, it's not. The process would even use the collider itself as material for the quark bomb. Free quarks releasing even more free quarks. A chain reaction."

"And this is what the simulation is projecting?" asked Nash.

"Appears to be, yes."

They continued to watch the simulation as the red ball of energy grew larger and larger, and soon, what appeared to be a barrier of some sort, surrounded the expanding ball of hot energy.

"What's that?" asked Nash.

"The chain reaction will cause an enormous amount of heat melting all the material around it. This melted matter will pose a barrier to the quarks—like you see there on the simulation. The barrier slows the quarks down and mixes with normal matter and the matter transformation would cease."

"Then that's good news," Chandler remarked.

"No. Not exactly. The reaction of the collider will cause an ultra-condensed quark object out of the material located in a one-hundred-meter radius around the center of the vessel."

"And then what?" asked Chandler.

"And that!" Wilcox said pointing to the computer simulation.

The barrier collapsed and a stream of hot liquid drained out of the empty hole created by the collapse. It was now sucking everything above ground down into the earth.

"*Good God!*" Nash exclaimed. "Are you saying that's going to happen?"

"Not me. The computer simulation."

"I don't understand—" said Alyson.

"When the barrier collapses, a gravity wave will radiate out from the collider, and a quark bomb will be created. And due to gravity and its enormous weight, it will fall towards the center of the earth—and bring with it anything around it within twenty square miles."

"Including us?" asked Kaya.

"Especially us," said Wilcox.

"So, what do we do?" asked Alyson.

"We get the hell out of here," said Nash. "*Fast!*"

Project KRATOS

Nash and Kaya led the others to the electric tram they had come in on. Nash pushed a few buttons and got the thing working, and soon the group arrived at the elevator that would deliver them above ground.

As the vibrations grew steadily worse, Chandler, Alyson, and Wilcox nervously entered the cramped elevator first. Nash, who had waited for Kaya to go back to the tram to retrieve her Uzi, looked up just as a big chunk of ceiling broke free.

"Oh, shit!"

As Kaya approached, he dove backward, grabbing her and pulling him with her—just as a massive chunk of cement dropped down behind them. The floor continued to shake, and more debris rained down around them. Pieces of conduit, metal piping, and rock all broke free and fell from the ceiling. Nash and Kaya continued to scramble deeper and deeper into the hallway, until they finally found safety under a massive supporting arch.

They waited out from whatever the hell the physics experiment gone wrong, holding onto each other, and Nash wondered how the elevator was holding up. When the shaking quieted down to a fitful tremble, he heard his sister screaming his name from beyond the pile of debris, which now completely blocked access to the elevator.

"Wait here," Nash told Kaya. He scrambled over the debris, and when he got as close to the elevator as he could, he shouted. "We're blocked. Is your elevator still working?"

Alyson waited, and when she answered there was pure panic in her voice. "Yes, but we can't go on without you."

"You guys go on," said Nash. "We'll find another way—"

Wilcox jumped in. "Jeremy. Go back to the control room and head towards the monitor room you were in before. To your left you will see a hallway. It should lead to a large service lift. Take that out if you can."

"Will do," Nash replied. "You guys go on. There's a good chance you'll see a helicopter up above. The one we came in on. Convince the pilot to save his and your skin."

"We'll wait for you!" Alyson cried, as the elevator doors closed, and he heard it rumble away.

Project KRATOS,
Above ground

Chandler, Wilcox and Kaya emerged from the elevator and scanned the Clubhouse. The building was abandoned. Outside were three helicopters. Two were just lifting off while another seemed to be sitting there, idling.

"Looks like the pilot is waiting for someone," Alyson said.

"Well, he may not know it," Chandler replied, "but he's waiting for *us*." She turned to Alyson. "Stay here out of sight with my uncle."

With that she slipped over to the helicopter.

The young pilot, no more than thirty, looked down at her through the massive windshield and frowned.

When she arrived at the chopper's cargo door, the pilot leaned back and asked, "Who are you? Where's Mr. Prescott?"

"He won't be joining us." She reached behind her and removed her pistol from her belt. She pointed the weapon at the pilot's head. "Now, hand me your gun."

The pilot studied her briefly, and then nodded. He carefully removed the pistol from his shoulder holster and handed it to her. Chandler waved Alyson and her uncle over.

"Now what?" asked the pilot.

"Now we wait," Alyson said in a determined voice. "We wait for my brother."

Project KRATOS

Once past the control room, Nash and Kaya found the service lift. Nash examined it.

"Do you think it's safe?" asked Kaya.

"At this point, we don't have much choice, do we?"

They entered the service lift, and Nash, with a bad feeling about this elevator, reached up to pull down the chain link safety gate. It went down just a few feet and stopped.

He tried again. "Shit. It's stuck."

He yanked it again, and this time the heavy gate broke free in his hand and tumbled to his feet in a heap.

"You have got to be kidding me," said Nash. He tossed the broken handle aside, where it clattered into a far corner. "Fine. We'll do without it." Inside, he examined the lift controls, found the proper button, and pushed it. Immediately, the lift began to rise. "Stand back from the edge of the open lift, Kaya. This could get bumpy."

She nodded and stood next to him as the lift started to rise.

Then Nash heard the sound of running feet echoing along the corridor just outside the rising elevator. Kaya heard it, too, and had just swung her Uzi around when a man leaped into the open lift.

It was Garcia. He grabbed the Uzi from the startled Kaya, threw her hard into the far corner, where she crumpled in a heap. The weapon itself clattered across the lift's floor where it tumbled over the edge into the black void beyond.

Garcia faced Nash. "Mind if I tag along?" asked the scarred

Latino, grinning. He casually reached behind him and removed Big Man's knife from his waistband. He tossed it from one hand to another. "Remember this?"

Garcia stepped forward, holding the knife out before him like a man who was used to knife fights. Nash had never been in a knife fight in his life.

The lift suddenly shuddered. Garcia looked away nervously, and Nash used that opportunity to pounce.

Nash's first order of business was to work the knife free. He grabbed Garcia's wrist just as the man brought the knife up. But Nash was there first, and he succeeded in wrapping both his hands around the man's thick wrist. Nash's momentum drove both into the side wall of the lift. Nash pinned the man's hand against the wall, and repeatedly slammed it over and over even while Garcia used his free hand to hammer punch after punch into the side of Nash's face.

Something had to give here, and it was the knife.

It dropped free, and now both men were falling, clawing at each other across the cold metal floor of the lift. The man fought dirty. His fingers and nails repeatedly reached for Nash's eyes. Nash, who had found himself on top, drove an elbow hard into the man nose, breaking it.

With superhuman strength, Garcia grabbed Nash's collar and turned his hip, and despite his superior position, Nash found himself rolling towards the open edge of the lift.

Nash scrambled and clawed but the man was using his feet to gain leverage off the far wall. Nash found himself inexorably forced to the edge of the lift. A second later, his head had slipped out into open space.

Cold air rushed over him. His shoulders were now forced over the ledge. Nash was losing all leverage.

Through the blood that poured from his broken nose, Garcia grinned wickedly and said, "Now join your parents."

"I don't think so," came a voice from behind.

Kaya was standing over him. She had the broken gate handle in her hand. And before Garcia could do anything, she swung the heavy handle as hard as she could catching the him along the side of the head.

Garcia released his grip, which gave Nash all the chance he needed. He kneed Garcia in the groin and heaved. The Latino killer tumbled over him and out over the ledge. But he wasn't gone yet. A scarred and bloody hand still held on to the metal ledge.

"Help me, please!"

Nash grabbed his dangling arm and pulled on it.

"What are you doing, Jeremy?" screeched Kaya.

Nash quickly removed his father's watch band from Garcia's wrist. "I'll take this. To borrow a phrase, go deeper into hell, you son of a bitch."

Nash released the man's hand, and he heard Garcia's echoing cries fade rapidly as he plummeted down into the elevator shaft until the cries abruptly stopped.

Project KRATOS,
Above ground

Wilcox was getting worried.

The earth was shaking beneath their feet, and he knew that at any moment the gravity wave would initiate, and the land below them would be literally sucked into the earth.

"We can't wait any longer," he said anxiously.

"Please! We can't leave without my brother," Alyson demanded. "Five more minutes."

"But the computer projection—"

"Screw the projection. He would wait for you!"

"Look," shouted Chandler, pointing towards the Clubhouse.

Alyson snapped her head around. Running from around the back of the building was Nash and Kaya. Alyson screamed with joy. She waved to them, jumping. "Jeremy! Kaya! Over here!"

Her brother waved back and took Kaya's hand, and together they made a mad dash to the helicopter.

Nash had just reached the open hatch when the ground beneath gave a large jolt. But this vibration was unlike any of the shaking they had felt earlier. It seemed to be coming from deep within the earth. Indeed, the ground beneath him seemed to be shifting, falling away.

"The gravity wave!" shouted Wilcox.

Nash and Kaya threw themselves through the open side hatch, and Chandler pointed the pistol at the pilot. "Get this bird in the air! Now!"

The pilot complied. The rotors came to life as the helicopter itself shifted and buckled. Nash looked out the side hatch and was utterly shocked by what he saw. The ground was pouring downward as if into a massive drain.

Or like a giant hourglass.

The rotors strained to rise against the strong force pulling the chopper downward.

"*Go, go, go!*"

"I'm trying!" cried the pilot. "It won't lift!"

The pilot struggled against the invisible force, but instead of the chopper rising, it sank into a growing chasm below them.

"*Christ!*" Nash yelled.

The chopper leaped wildly into the air, spinning in circles, nearly out of control. The pilot fought the cyclic control stick. Nash held on to anything he could find, and so did everyone else. Beneath them the ground continued dropping away. A massive chasm was forming below them. The chopper dipped and spun, but finally the pilot got it under control.

Newly formed chasm walls rose up around them, but the chopper quickly gained altitude, its rotors straining hard, and soon they had cleared these strange vertical valley walls. A few moments later, they were clear.

Nash looked down at a sight that was both mesmerizing and horrifying.

A hollow of sunken earth miles in diameter had disappeared into what appeared to be a vast, empty void.

They flew silently on for many minutes until Wilcox spoke up. "We need to land and make a report."

Chandler said to the pilot, "Fly south to Flagstaff. The EPA has an office there. They also have a helipad."

The pilot nodded.

As they flew, Kaya put her arm around Nash's shoulder, and

345

said, "We need to return the Hopi Stone and the missing piece to the Fire Clan."

Nash nodded. Then an idea occurred to him. "So, does this make *me* the true Pahana? I mean, I found the missing piece, and I'm mostly white. What do you think?"

Kaya laughed. "Perhaps. Let's see what Kikmongwi has to say."

Wilcox jumped in. "May I accompany you to the Fire Clan?"

"I'd like to come, too," said Chandler.

Nash looked at Kaya. "What do you say? A Hopi pilgrimage?"

Kaya smiled. "So be it."

Hotevilla, Arizona

The next day in Hotevilla, after spending the evening answering numerous questions from every government official on the books—with the promise that many more interviews were still to come—the group found themselves sitting in Grandfather Martin Kikmongwi's small home.

Nash had just presented the complete Hopi stone to the aged holy man, and now he returned to his seat next to Kaya and his sister. Nash noticed that both women seemed to be holding their breaths, waiting for Grandfather's response.

When his response came, Nash could not have been more disappointed.

"I am sorry, my white brother, but this is not the missing piece that the Pahana would bring when he returns. This missing piece has been created by another, perhaps by your father to help you find the white man's project."

"So, I guess you're not the Pahana," Alyson whispered next to him. "Probably a good thing, since your ego is already big enough."

Nash elbowed her.

After sipping tea and visiting with the elder Hopi, the group soon left and found themselves in Nash's rental.

"Well, that's that," Nash said. "The Hopi's are still waiting for their Pahana." He turned to Wilcox. "But I do have one question. This *quark* object. Where is it now, and what will happen because of it?"

"It probably arrived at the center of the earth. What will

happen to it? I don't know for certain. It could just sit there in the center of the earth, dormant or..."

"Or what?" asked Nash.

"Or it could attract more and more quarks, turn all matter into quarks, and sometime thereafter," he paused to reflect, "a new bluish star—a Quark Star—will appear in our solar system that will flare briefly for a while then fade away into oblivion."

"The Blue Star Kachina," Nash whispered.

"...to usher in the next world," Kaya finished.

Somewhere Over the North Pacific

The Chairman gazed out the widow of his Mach 1 plus Aerion private jet as it approached the frozen tundra off in the distance.

Momentarily distracted by the barren beauty before him, he returned to reading the report of Project KRATOS and its aftermath under the cold halogen light of his private cabin that glinted off the titanium metal of his prosthetic hands.

And he was not happy.

He made a mental note of this Jeremy Nash for the future and realized he might be able to kill two irritating birds with one stone.

Yes. That could be possible.

Epilogue

P*oor, crazy bastard.*

Jeremy Nash was flushed by applause and adrenalin. After his much-publicized lecture at Germany's famed Des Liein Skeptics Club in Humboldt University, he decided to take a walk through Berlin to the Brandenburg Gate before returning to his hotel.

His thoughts, predictably, were on Alfred Tillman, the Jewish scholar and professor.

Or, as Nash had previously preferred to categorize him, "the nut job."

Immediately, he regretted his choice of words. After all, Nash had just been informed by one of his colleagues that Tillman, a man who had been hounding Nash for years about various Nazi conspiracies, had been found murdered just that evening.

What did you get yourself into old man, you crazy son of a bitch?

It had stopped raining and Nash could see a hint of the moon behind the retreating clouds as the celestial body cast an eerie silver glow on the wet streets.

As an expert debunker and bestselling author of conspiracy theories, myths, and legends, Nash had often been confronted with kooks before. It came with the territory, and his adult life contained a never ending supply of those who aggressively confronted Nash on his skeptical inquiries into those shady untruths waiting to be exposed.

But this Tillman character took the cake. As a well-known crypto-historian, the man's delusions of German conspiracies to push forward the master race—dating back to World War II—bordered on the paranoid.

He should have been committed.

Nash paused, lifted his face to the cool wind, and hoped the insane professor was finally at peace.

He also, briefly, wondered who had killed him.

He turned back at the Brandenburg Gate, back to where he was staying.

Later, deep in thought, he almost missed the entrance to his glitzy hotel. Too flashy for him, but the Skeptic Club had paid his way, and who was Nash to say no to complimentary champagne and fresh berries in his hotel refrigerator?

Nash stepped into the brightly lit foyer. It was late, and the lobby was mostly empty. Nash had traveled alone and planned to spend the next day perusing the various sights and sounds of Berlin before heading back to his home in Roswell, New Mexico. Roswell—an ironic home base for one of the world's foremost skeptics. Nash liked the juxtaposition. He thought of himself as bringing balance to an otherwise delusional town.

He was seriously looking forward to settling in with his laptop, finally getting around to working on his latest book, *A Taste of the Apocalypse*, and uncorking that free bottle of champagne. Which was why, when a rotund, red-faced man hurried up to him, Nash inwardly groaned.

The man thrust a police badge in Nash's face. "Herr Nash?" he asked in English with a heavy German accent. "Jeremy Nash?"

Nash noticed two other figures approaching—two other imposing figures. Nash frowned. "I'm Jeremy Nash. What can I do for you, officer?"

"Herr Nash, you are under arrest."

A Message
From the Author

I relished writing this book! If you enjoyed this second volume in the *Chronicles of Jeremy Nash*, would you consider doing two things?

First, sign up for my newsletter at www.frankfiore.com, and I'll be sure you're the first to get news on future installments in the series, in addition to info about my other titles.

Second—and this is a big request—if you liked this story, would you consider leaving a review wherever you bought this book, or on your favorite social media platform? I want as many readers as possible to discover this story, and your voice can help do that. Leave a review and tell a friend! Word-of-mouth is still the best way to introduce this story to other readers.

Lastly, *Thank you!*

Thank you, dear reader, for giving your time to read this book. It means a lot that you trusted me as the author to entertain, and hopefully excite, you with this story. Stories need an audience, and I appreciate you being my audience for just a little while. Thank you.

There are, of course, plenty of crypto-historical events, locations, and artifacts yet to be discover, examined, and explored; and lots of questions about the lives and predicaments of our main characters that need answers.

And so, dear readers, just for you, here's—

—a sneak peek at—

Black Sun

Chronicles of Jeremy Nash
Book 3

Prologue

*T*ime is running out, shuddered Professor Alfred Tillman as he nervously made his way through the damp night towards his flat in Kreuzberg.

Kreuzberg, near the old American Checkpoint Charlie crossing point into East Berlin, was a neighborhood suspended between two worlds. A ghetto slum for immigrants, it also served as a criminal haven for drug dealers. Tillman knew the neighborhood wasn't safe during the best of times, let alone the dark of night.

He picked up his pace.

Shortly, he rounded a corner and found himself on an even bleaker street. Trash cans everywhere. Open sewage in the streets. Tillman wrinkled his nose and ducked into a dilapidated four-story apartment building. He paused at the name registry, found the one he was looking for, and rang the bell.

"Who is this?" asked a suspicious voice on the other end of the intercom.

"Alfred Tillman. I need to speak with you. It's important."

The voice turned affable. "Oh, yes, professor. Please come up."

The door buzzed open. Tillman was just stepping through the entrance when he heard the sounds of footsteps on the sidewalk. A man was turning the corner outside, walking casually toward him, smoking a cigarette.

Tillman quickly and silently closed the door behind him.

About the Author

Frank F. Fiore is a five-star rated author of novels in multiple genres including Contemporary Fiction, Tecno-Thrillers, Action/Adventures, Sci-Fi, Historical Fiction, and Westerns. He lives in Arizona with his fetching wife, Lynne.

Connect with Frank online at:

www.frankfiore.com

Also Available From

WordCrafts Press

The 5 Manners of Death
Darden North

House of Madness
Sara Harris

The Five Barred Gate
Jeff S. Bray

The Edurants
KL Palmer

The Restless Earth
Alan Cockrell

www.wordcrafts.net